Ragnarok

RAGNAROK

A novel

D. G. COMPTON AND JOHN GRIBBIN

LONDON
VICTOR GOLLANCZ LTD
1991

First published in Great Britain 1991
by Victor Gollancz Ltd,
14 Henrietta Street, London WC2E 8QJ

A catalogue record for this book is available
from the British Library

ISBN 0 575 05110 8

Typeset at The Spartan Press Ltd, Lymington, Hants
and printed in Great Britain by
St Edmundsbury Press Ltd, Bury St Edmunds, Suffolk

PROLOGUE

The square metal rungs of the ladder were wet. The young woman went down them carefully, holding fast to the slippery handrail. The whole ship was beaded with moisture; last night's heavy fog had lifted, but only to the masthead, giving perhaps half a mile's visibility and leaving the air unseasonably cold and damp, even for Iceland. The first week in August, and already summer seemed to be over.

A rugged wooden workboat, painted black, was tied up alongside the research vessel. She stepped down into it. The woman was wearing an insulated wet suit, bright blue neoprene foam, and her long blonde hair was scragged back in an untidy pony-tail. Face mask, oxygen cylinders, insulated gloves and flippers were already on the centre thwart. She sidled past them, went back to the engine, started it, and checked the rudder lines to the wheel amidships. The man up on the research vessel's deck threw down the stern rope to her. She caught it neatly, stowed it and went forward. Engine fumes gathered in the still air, the exhaust pipe bubbling as the motorboat rocked on the slight swell coming in from the Atlantic.

She cast off forward, moved back to the helm, and swung the boat away from the ship's side. Ahead of her, the yellow minisub was already diving. She turned and waved to the man up on the deck. Black-bearded, massive in stained blue overalls, he gave her a thumbs-up in return, and shouted something she couldn't hear. When she looked forward again, the submarine had disappeared, leaving only a swirling pattern of eddies.

Anxiously, she scanned the beach and the surrounding cliff tops. Nothing moved. Above, the sky was opaque, grey and lowering. Ideal for their purpose. The boat reached the submarine's diving station, but she continued past it, maintaining the same steady speed and course. Her face, as she stared purposefully ahead, was emphatic rather than beautiful – a high forehead, deepset blue eyes above a generous mouth, good skin and marvellous teeth. American vividness, undimmed by the years spent in Britain.

Although the boat was equipped for diving, she hoped she wouldn't have to. Icelandic waters were bitterly cold, even in summer. Her job in Helgavik that morning was to provide a marker, to locate the black-hulled boat at a point some five hundred metres from the cliffs to the east, and a similar distance from the shingle beach to the north, and anchor there. Directly beneath her, the two men in the tiny submarine would lay the first of the paired cylindrical units carried in the sub's twin cargo pods.

She didn't envy them. The submarine was built for deep-sea scientific research. Electrically powered, its hull was a flattened dish in the centre of which its two-man crew lay prone, side by side, navigating through armoured-glass observation ports. The heated and pressurised work space was designed to fit two human bodies, and not much else. Even though she didn't suffer from claustrophobia, and had often crewed the submarine in warmer waters, she had never grown used to the close confinement, the sweating metal, the eerie sense of isolation. And she particularly didn't envy her friends their task today – the risks involved, and the terrible weight of their responsibility.

She slowed the motorboat. Looking over the side, she could clearly see the flickering yellow shape of the submarine in the shallow water, slipping gently astern beneath her. She was reminded of how visible it would be from a coastguard helicopter, and instinctively glanced up at the sky again. Their cover story was excellent – but still . . . The overcast was still total. But it was thinning, with the sun's pale disc occasionally showing above the cliffs on the eastern side of the bay.

Not helicopter weather – yet. Not for another hour at least. Time enough. Nor, beside this isolated fjord, would there be shore observers. To the north the cove was bounded by a long, flat beach, at one end of which stood a small, stone rescue hut. Behind this beach a deep valley, once a glacier bed, covered now with low, scrubby bushes and ragged patches of arctic grass, wound up to higher ground. Elsewhere the cove was surrounded by black lava cliffs, veined with red, a nesting place for seabirds. Above, the land was barren. The nearest village, Hellnar, lay three miles away, along the coast to the west.

The young American woman stopped the boat's engine, checking her position as she drifted on. Except for the cries of the seabirds, the cove was silent. She went forward, unshipped the anchor, waited a moment, then swung it overboard. Its line snaked after it, down through the ice-clear water. The bottom here had shelved to less than five fathoms. Behind her, in the centre of Helgavik cove and to the west, the water was deep; the chart showed eighteen fathoms at low tide. The research vessel was moored close under the far cliffs, sheltered by the headland from the gales they must expect during their stay here. Even in summer, the North Atlantic was seldom calm for more than a week or so.

She waited, trying to relax. The submarine, moving cautiously in such shallow water, would take time to find her. But it was the accessibility of these shallows, and the cove's critical relationship to the fault lines of the Reykjanes Ridge, that had made them choose Helgavik. The Earth's crust here on the seabed was very thin, and subject to continual spreading. Eruptions were frequent. Entire new islands, black and angry, sometimes rose hissing from the water.

She shifted her position, looking down again into the water. She could see the bottom, could imagine the tearing pressure of the molten magma close beneath it. How easily the crust might fracture, releasing the red-hot magma in lava flows that would seethe and bubble across the ocean floor, heating the water instantly to boiling point and beyond, engulfing her in a violent, lethal turmoil of superheated steam and sulphurous gases . . .

But not today. Today, the lava reservoir was contained. She stiffened: the submarine was under her now, settling on the bottom. She could see it clearly, the spare brown weed parting around it, the small puffs of lava dust it raised as it grounded. And – she could picture it almost as clearly, in her mind's eye – when it lifted again, it would lurch slightly to the left, asymmetrically lightened by the release of the contents of its starboard cargo pod. With the thought, she scanned the silent cove and the sky yet again.

Now, at last, there was movement on the cliffs to the west. It was almost a relief to see it.

A well trodden track led down from the ridge. Two orange-jacketed figures had emerged from the mist and were briskly making their way down it. She reached for her binoculars. A bearded man and a lean, high cheekboned woman, both in green walking breeches and orange anoraks, wearing tall, aluminium-framed backpacks. Hikers, clearly. This was, after all, the tourist season. She followed their progress with the glasses. The man saw her, and waved. She waved back. They *must* be hikers. It was too soon for anything else. The opposition knew nothing. *Could* know nothing – yet.

The couple reached the beach and paused there, shading their eyes as they stared out across the water. She waved again. Cheerfully. She was grateful that the distance was too great for conversation. Glancing down over the side again, she saw that the yellow submarine had gone.

If all was going according to plan, it had left behind it on the seabed a thick metal cylinder, also painted yellow, which contained a side-scan sonar unit, the transmitting component of an electronic system for analysing underwater geological formations. This was their cover – a research technique which utilised a beam of ultrasound, travelling laterally through the material of the seabed to be received by a second component, where it provided information about the rock strata through which it had passed.

The submarine would now be positioning, a precise distance away, the cylinder disguised as this second, receiving component. Outwardly, it was in every respect identical to the real thing.

She leaned on the boat's gunwale and folded her arms. Perhaps, to the watchers on the beach, she was fishing. She imagined the scene from their point of view: a moored motorboat with one idle occupant, the unbroken water of the cove, and in the background the shabby, rust-streaked research vessel at anchor. Not, she hoped, an intriguing prospect.

The two hikers conferred. The woman pointed to the rescue hut; the man shook his head. They turned and walked along the beach, stopping now and then to look back. The young woman in the boat didn't move. Suddenly, she feared them. They were unknown, and the unknown was dangerous.

Dramatically, the water heaved upward between her and them. The submarine surfaced. She watched, horrified, as it emerged gently into view, a hundred metres or so to port. Water streamed from its flanks as it lay motionless, an upturned, dazzling yellow pie-plate, listing steeply, its starboard rim angled up out of the water. The central hatch, opened from within, fell back with a clang that echoed from the cliffs. A man's head appeared, his face turned towards her. Beyond him, on the beach, the two hikers had stopped in their tracks, transfixed.

Before the man could speak, she knew what he was going to tell her. The sub's angle allowed of only one explanation. She was already reaching for the oxygen cylinders on their harness as his words came across the water.

'The bloody thing won't release,' he shouted. 'The pin must've jammed. You'll just have to come down with us and free it. I told you the thing was too heavy. Christ, what a mess . . .'

Quickly, she pulled the cylinder harness up between her legs and snapped the buckle; a weighted belt went over it, around her waist. He was over-reacting. Of course he was. She rinsed her face mask over the side and put it on, high on her forehead. She reached up for the air hose, wriggling the mouthpiece into position under her lips, and tested the flow. She fixed the nose-clip, and pulled the mask down over her eyes. Hell, she'd have over-reacted herself in his position, on the seabed, struggling with the release mechanism, knowing the delicate and lethal nature of the cargo he was trying to get rid of.

Slipping on her insulated gloves, watchers on the shore forgotten, she backed up to the boat's side and launched herself over it, down into the merciless arctic water.

I

Day One   AUGUST 4. WEDNESDAY.

Professor Graham had been up since before dawn, sitting on the beach in front of his house, on a massive rib of sun-bleached driftwood. He sat at his ease, cultivating stillness, legs crossed. One bare foot was planted firmly in the dry sand; the other leg, equally motionless, was crossed over this anchor. Only his hands, which he kept in his lap, anxiously picked and fussed at one another whenever he forgot to check them.

He was waiting for his daughter Colly to telephone from the research vessel.

A tall, big-boned old man, he wore shabby white canvas slacks, belted high and showing improbable amounts of blue-veined shin, with a heavy, shapeless, oatmeal-coloured sweater. His face was tanned and firmly fleshed, still handsome, with clear, bright brown eyes deepset beneath a high, wide forehead. His beard, grizzled and cut short, was barely more than stubble; his silver-grey hair so fine and frail that it stirred even now, in the almost imperceptible breeze coming in off the ocean. He waited on the beach, carefully relaxed, turning his face up to the pale warmth of the newly risen sun.

He liked Maine summers: they spared him the heat and humidity of places further south, around Boston or New York. He was in excellent health, lean, his back straight; but he still appreciated the huge, cloudless skies, the gentle, undemanding radiance of the season. Summers in Maine were good for an old man's bones.

The tide was low that morning, surf rolling in distantly along the wide, two-mile sweep of the glass-bright sand. Behind him a pair of bluejays darted noisily through the pine trees growing in the dune grass along the shore. The big rambling houses among the trees were mostly summer homes for wealthy New York and Philadelphia families, plus a growing contingent down from Canada.

Robert Graham hadn't slept well. Now, although he waited with a show of patience, gazing quietly out to sea, into the eye of the rising sun, his thoughts were straining far beyond the horizon, two thousand miles and more, to a cove on the bleak Icelandic coastline. The ship must be there by now. He could picture her vividly, anchored within the curve of the high, black lava cliffs. He pictured the minisub, stealing down through the dark water, following the fault lines . . . In the house behind him the parlour clock chimed briefly. Six thirty. Colly should have called by now. He plucked nervously at the frayed hem of his sweater. Something had gone wrong.

He'd bought the house for his retirement, then never retired. It was old, from the nineteenth century, and big – built to no particular style or plan. Wooden, like most Maine houses, grey weathered shingles under a grey-green roof, with a turret at one corner to view the islands, a Dutch gable somewhere else, Edwardian fretwork here and there, and a wide screened porch along the front. A big house. Far too big for one old man on his own. But he preferred dust and the occasional cobweb to a live-in housekeeper. Now that his wife was dead he chose to manage on his own – up here on the coast, and also in his apartment down near the Bell Laboratories in New Jersey.

He stilled his twitching hands. Anything could have happened. Something trivial. It was much too early to start worrying. He told himself not to fuss.

His daughter's call came through twenty minutes later, via the High Seas Operator on the ship-to-shore link. The time was six fifty: ten fifty in Iceland. When the big extension bell rang on the side of the house, Professor Graham got stiffly to his feet. He knew Colly would wait for him, but he still ran, back up the beach, across the porch and into the sun parlour. He stumbled on the last two steps, caught frantically at the doorpost, saved himself. He snatched up the telephone.

'Colly?' His voice was anxious, his breathing laboured.

The receiver gave out explosive crackles. Then: 'Fard? Father? Is that you? Sorry I'm so late, Fard. There was a hell of a wait for the connection.'

'Colly? My dear, it doesn't matter. So good to hear your voice.'

'And now the line's terrible. Fard? It is you?'

'It's fine my end.' Raising his voice. 'I can hear you perfectly.'

'What? How are you, Fard? You sound kind of breathless.'

'I was down on the beach.' He checked, thinking how crazy he'd been. What if he'd fallen and broken something, a leg or a hip or something, what then? The whole operation in ruins. He winced. 'How are things up there, Colly?'

'Fine. Fine . . . It's been foggy, but it's clearing now. We came in around dawn, dropped anchor just where we'd planned. Great place. Flynn's a wizard.'

'I always knew it.'

'You're *sure* you're all right?'

'I ran, that's all.'

'Wouldn't you just know it?' She laughed. 'We've checked in again with the coastguards. They'll be round to fix our permits, but not until the fog lifts down their way, too.'

It was small talk. Trivial. Simply filling in. But everything about her interested him. Everything about the ship. 'It's good to hear your voice, child.'

'Me too.' She paused. Her voice changed. 'Werner's been down in the sub. Werner and Kass. No problems.' She cleared her throat. 'No problems at all. Went like a dream. We're in business.'

They were in business. The pre-arranged phrase. *They were in business* . . . He put off believing the words. He had to wait. What she had told him was so momentous.

He asked her, unnecessarily, 'Really no problems?'

'Well, a release pin stuck. But we soon fixed it. Otherwise, fine.'

The pins had always been a bother. 'You're sure? You really mean that?'

'You have to trust us, Fard. Everything's fine. I really mean it.'

He didn't answer. He'd run out of questions; run out of excuses not to believe. She spoke again, but he wasn't listening. His hand was shaking so much that he could scarcely hold the receiver to his ear. Everything was fine. The two units were in position on the seabed, and the countdown to Ragnarok had begun. *They were in business.* The next move, dear God, was up to him.

He grasped the telephone receiver firmly in both hands, fighting sudden blind terror. He wasn't up to it. He'd fail. He was too old . . . Outside on the beach, the sun shone, warm and golden, and the surf came rolling in. He gazed at it, unseeing. A small dark cloud passed across the sun. As the scene dimmed, then lightened, his own mood lifted again with the return of the sun. It had just been a momentary nervousness. Nothing important.

He and Colly said little more. There was little more to be said. He sent the four of them his love. She told him to take care, and he promised that he would. She rang off. There was no point in prolonging the conversation; the line was terrible, anyway.

He leaned against the faded pine panelling in the sun parlour, trying to drum up the courage he'd believed would sustain him. Ragnarok. The end of the world. Ragnarok, the time of destruction . . . He closed his eyes, but couldn't escape it. The poet's vision came to him. He saw the ocean rise, engulfing villages and fields and forests. He saw volcanoes pour forth fire as the long winter of ice and snow gripped the bones of men. The sun at noon grew dark, the moon was lost in blackness, even the brightest stars faded from the sky. Ice-clouds and fire did battle until the flames reached up to heaven, and earth sank into the ocean, black and smouldering. Now there was naught but darkness and silence unbroken. The end had come – *Ragnarok* . . .

He shuddered deeply. *Save us from that, dear Lord*, he prayed, to whatever God might be listening.

Eventually, he found the necessary strength: or if not the strength, the ability to accept. The decisions had been taken long before. It was impossible to go back on them. He didn't want to. Suddenly, he straightened his back, stood away from the wall, and phoned for a cab to take him to the airport.

While he waited, he changed into his smartest lightweight city clothes. They made him feel a different, braver person. His suitcase was already packed, so to fill in the time that still remained until the cab got there he walked down the beach to his neighbours' house. The Grahams had had a key to the Abernatheys' place for years. The Abernatheys never came to the beach in August – they said the tennis club got too crowded – so either Ruth or Robert had always kept an eye on things. Now his wife was dead. Ruth had been dead for more than a year, and he still grieved. If Ruth had not been dead, he wouldn't have teamed up with Colly in this enterprise, and wouldn't be flying down to New York today.

The Abernatheys' downstairs telephone lived in a dark little lobby off what Chuck Abernathy called his 'den'. Robert didn't much like Chuck, and he doubted if Chuck much liked him, but they'd always been neighbourly. He let himself into the empty house and checked the small Zenith computer he'd already set up in Chuck's den, and the modem that connected it, via the telephone, with the international network. As a physicist, communications technology was second nature to him now. His daughter could call at any time, and leave her news safe in the memory of the Zenith: he could do the same, from wherever he was. And either of them could read the messages stored in the computer's memory. But there were no outgoing calls from the Abernatheys' house, nothing that could be traced back to this point. Usually, gadgets like this delighted him. An electronic dead-letter drop, the spy stories would call it. But today, the fun had gone. He checked everything was in order, and locked the house up securely once more.

Robert walked back along the beach to his own house very slowly. He could see the taxi waiting now, where the dirt road ran into the sand, and he waved to the driver. But he didn't hurry. He was saying goodbye. There was a lot of his life, and Ruth's, wrapped up in this mile or so of sand dunes and rocks and sea and sky. He knew he'd never see any of it again, and it wasn't easy, as he grew older, letting things go.

The cab driver carried his case out, grunting at the weight – on the sandy path the rollers built into its bottom edge were useless – and heaved it into the car's trunk. Since this was Maine rather than one of the big cities, Robert sat beside him on the wide front seat, his briefcase between his legs. The driver was friendly. He asked the professor where he was from. He said he liked the accent – that he had a son in England himself, in Oxfordshire, a medical orderly in the USAF, and two grandchildren there. The professor told him he had a daughter, not yet married, and not in England. He found it hard to be frank and companionable. Already a chasm had opened between himself and what he now thought of as the real world.

He tried to find a word for himself. Only *terrorist* would do. It seemed at first ridiculous, melodramatic. He didn't have the terrorist's arrogance, or his exultation. He shared their amateurism, certainly, and perhaps their anger – but an intellectualised sort of anger that most terrorists, surely, would hardly recognise. Apart from that he was merely determined, optimistic, and secretly very afraid that someone might cause him physical pain.

Nevertheless, his weapons were undeniably those of the terrorist. The ultimatum, the deadline, the explosive device, the threats of death and destruction. He was, *tout court*, a terrorist.

The taxi got Professor Graham to Portland airport a few minutes after the Delta businessman's flight to New York had left. It didn't worry him. He caught the next, an hour later, and was still at La Guardia by mid-morning. From there he took a taxi to the United Nations building on the East River, at the corner of East 42nd Street and First Avenue. There was a hold-up on the Triboro Bridge, a minor collision blocking the westbound traffic lane, and the twelve-mile journey took almost as long as the flight down from Maine.

Once at the UN, Robert asked his driver to wait. He was an old enough New York hand not to leave his suitcase in the back. Troublesome though this was, the case was in fact well worth driving off with. It contained three thousand dollars in cash, one very expensive and sophisticated portable computer and other electronic equipment, as well as the usual clothes and personal effects – plus a shabby homburg hat and a blue double-breasted suit, now shiny in places and slightly too big for the professor, which his wife would have liked him to throw away at least ten years earlier. And it all belonged to a criminal, a *terrorist*, a man with no possibility of legal redress.

The city was stifling. He stood on the pavement by the cab for a moment, leaning on its roof gutter, gasping for breath. A thin yellow haze hung over Manhattan, mitigating none of the sun's heat; intensifying it rather, battering it to and fro between the buildings. There was brightness, but there were no shadows. The hundred and forty-nine flags of the member nations drooped limply down their staffs along the front of the UN Plaza. A yellow school bus, lights flashing, was unloading children too enervated to do more than wait in a docile group until their teachers had counted them. Back in Maine, scarcely heeded news reports had warned over the past week of drought worse than '88, with temperatures set to reach a new record high for the whole year. Here, it was easy to believe them.

At the onset of his wife's final illness Professor Graham had given up his campaigning work for SANE – Scientists Against Nuclear Extinction: work that had gained him a Nobel Peace Prize some six years before. Since then, he had not thought to renew his UN pass, so he was obliged to go in by the same door as the tourists. One trust fewer, he told himself, for him to betray.

As he approached the barrier he paused, gratefully rested the suitcase by his foot, opened his briefcase and took out two thin, sealed blue plastic folders, which he tucked under his arm. Then he struggled on. Just past the barrier, a guard in a booth relieved him of both his pieces of luggage, giving him a numbered plastic disc instead. He slowly crossed the hexagonal stones of the plaza and entered the public lobby to the General Assembly Building.

The air conditioning chilled him instantly, drying the sweat on his forehead. Beneath the famous Foucault pendulum he joined the queue passing through the metal detector. The need for such precautions was sad, he thought, in a place like this, dedicated to peace and conciliation. Then he frowned, realising the irony of his own purpose there.

The huge silver ball swung silently on its wire, not so much to demonstrate the earth's rotation, perhaps, as to suggest its tranquil continuance.

Once through the scanner, he went straight to the central public information desk and begged the use of one of their internal phones. Pressing the receiver close to his ear, he punched in the private four-digit number for the Secretary-General's office, up on the thirty-eighth floor of the Secretariat Building. He found the contained sibilance of the crowded concourse intrusive, making it difficult for him to hear.

A woman answered. He recognised her voice: Donna MacIntyre, a motherly person, the Secretary-General's private assistant.

'Bob Graham here, Donna. Is Georg around anywhere?'

'Professor Graham!' She sounded genuinely pleased. 'What a surprise. We haven't had sight nor sound of you in ages.'

'A year or so. I've not been doing much. My wife died, you know.'

'I heard. I was truly sorry. We all were.'

'That's kind of you, Donna. Is Georg available?'

'The Secretary-General's engaged. Can he call you back?'

Robert had hoped as much. Even as betrayals went, that of their long and close friendship would have been particularly difficult, face-to-face. The betrayal of the Peace Prize he could live with, even justify. But to use an old and wise friend, to cheat him and lie to him and use him, was ugly, no matter what. This way, at least it could be done through an intermediary.

'I'm afraid not, Donna. I'm downstairs, at the public information desk. And I have something for him. It's very important.'

She hesitated. 'He's with an ambassador, Professor. I really don't think I can disturb − '

'No. No, of course not. May I see his Chef du Cabinet, then?'

'It really is important? Hold on, then, Professor. I'll see if I can fix it.'

He held. He was amused, as always, that Georg's right-hand man should be known as his *Chef du Cabinet*. Possibly the title had been chosen to suggest Gallic urbanity − was not French, for all its Cartesian exactitudes, still the true language of diplomacy?

Donna fixed it. He'd known she would. It was precisely this ability to reach important people, the leverage of his many years in the peace movement, that made the operation possible. Powerful men knew him. If not on Bill and Harry terms, then they knew *of* him. Bob Graham, the Peace Prize man − and hadn't he won the Nobel for Physics, too, some time back? Something to do with lasers? Prizes made a difference, as did creating a public nuisance for a very long time. He'd been a professional peacemaker, and powerful men listened to professional peacemakers. They might do so only for the look of the thing; but, although that was a pity, it was better than not listening at all.

These, then, were the privileges he was principally betraying: the goodwill, the trust, the respect, the honour.

He waited with these bleak thoughts by the information desk, until a security guard came to take him up. Once out of the public lobby he was frisked with embarrassing thoroughness − clearly the guard had little faith in electronic metal detectors − then they went up together in the lift to the thirty-eighth floor, and through a hushed reception area to the office of the Chef du Cabinet.

Robert had seen the Secretary-General's 'Chef' before, distantly, at various receptions, but they had never been introduced. He found the man ill-judged, disappointingly brash. He shook Robert's hand over-vigorously, clapped his shoulder, called him Bob, and jovially suggested that he call him Henry.

'Sit down, Bob. Relax . . . Donna tells me you've something for the boss. Maybe we can help you. Just say the word. We'll sure as hell try.'

His manner provided a distraction – almost – from the moment's fearsome significance. He was gesturing Professor Graham to a chair. His office, like that of the Secretary-General, looked out across the East River. It was an impressive panorama, but Robert turned the low, black leather chair away from the view, settling with his back to the window. He must focus his attention, his whole being, on the single, terrifying purpose of his visit. As a result of this meeting, for better or worse, the course of world events would be changed. The months of planning were at an end. Now, suddenly, was the moment when theory became practice, when the full burden of responsibility was understood, weighed, and accepted.

Tiredly, Robert straightened the two blue folders on his knee. He hesitated, cleared his throat.

'What I have is not actually for the Secretary-General himself,' he said, gaining confidence as he went on. 'I was hoping to use him as a go-between. The fact is, I need to reach a couple of UN ambassadors. The American, and the Soviet.'

Henry whistled softly. 'Donna said it was important. And I guess you don't fly much higher than that. Now tell me, Bob – what's the story?'

He shook his head. 'You'll just have to trust me on that. If I can't reach the ambassadors themselves, I need someone pretty high in their delegations. The scientific advisers would be good. *Especially* the scientific advisers.'

'Reach them, Bob?' Henry leaned forward. 'You mean, talk to them, personally?'

'No, no. Not at all. I'm explaining badly.' He held out the sealed folders. 'It's just these. I need these to reach the top men – as near the top as you can. And in such a way that they won't sit with some girl in the typing pool until a week come Labor Day. They must see the contents today.'

'Internal mail? Express delivery? That sort of thing's no problem.' Henry was clearly relieved. Immediate personal access to heads of delegations was not a favour to be granted lightly, even to professional peacemakers. 'No sweat, old buddy. We run the best express delivery service in the world.' He took the folders, eyed them curiously. 'More fact sheets from SANE, I guess. It's a great job you guys are doing – I didn't know you were still with them. But it fair breaks my heart, listening to all the fucking double-talk coming out of Geneva, and – '

'No.' Robert interrupted firmly. '*Not* SANE. Nothing to do with SANE. Not this time.' Any hint of that sort of connection, and he feared that the folders would be trashed, unopened. 'More important.'

He caught Henry's raised eyebrow, imagined the thought going through his mind – more important than nuclear war? – and backed off a little. No point in overselling at this stage and getting labelled a crank.

'It's – something of my own. Some research I've been doing. I'm over with Bell, you know; in New Jersey.' He paused, to let the implications sink in. If anyone wanted credentials, Bell labs couldn't be beaten, with their laser work being turned into Star Wars weaponry over at Livermore. 'It's something I want the ambassadors to know about. Something to help focus their minds.'

Henry laughed, expansively. 'Never any harm in that.' He held the folders up to the light. 'Nothing classified, I hope? Nothing Ma Bell and Uncle Sam wouldn't be too pleased to know you're spreading around?'

Robert gave him a straight old-fashioned look. Henry laughed again, having the grace to be embarrassed.

'I know, I know . . . and your real name's Rosenberg.' Hastily he checked the destination labels on the folders, clipped on his own compliments slips, scribbled a personal note on each, then put them in his out-tray. 'There you are. No sweat.'

Professor Graham leaned forward. 'I'm afraid I'm going to have to be rather particular about this. D'you mind if I ask Donna to lay on a special messenger? I'm hoping to get this stuff delivered within the next hour or so – if that's at all possible?'

Henry eyed him thoughtfully. Robert could see the situation assessment going on behind his shining, unlined forehead. Some old guy wanting favours. Dapper enough, and up together, but old, and picky. Probably not worth the fuss he was making. But not just any old guy. Some old *quite famous* guy, and a long-time friend of the boss . . . His decision took less than three seconds.

'Tell you what I'll do, Bob. Why don't I just take them round myself? It's lunch time, near enough . . . then maybe you and I could go out for a bite' – he reached for a large desk diary, checked in it – 'No, I guess not. Have to take a rain check on that. My girl's got me lunching with a PPS from some trade mission.'

Robert was relieved. Lunch would have been hard to refuse, but an appalling strain. They both stood, Henry with the folders in his hand. With a conscious effort, the professor dragged his eyes away from them. There was nothing more he could do. They were on their own now.

'That's very kind of you,' he said.

'Not a word. My pleasure, Bob. And the Secretary-General's sure as hell going to be sore that he missed you.'

They walked into the reception area. 'Apropos of that,' Robert said lightly, 'would you leave a note for him to expect a call from me around four thirty? If he can't make it, fine: I'll leave a message.'

But he had no doubt that Georg *would* make it – and that there would be a few additional listeners on the line. By four thirty the folders would have risen to a reasonably high diplomatic altitude. High enough, he felt sure, for word to have got back to the Secretary-General – and to get him a hearing, if nothing else as yet.

They parted by the lift. There was little chance that Henry really would deliver the documents himself, but Robert wasn't worried. He'd see that they got priority attention, which was all that was needed. Access to the centres of power. Next stop the President of the USA and the First Secretary of the USSR. Robert felt a little ashamed, as if he were suffering from delusions of grandeur. And yet, anything less than those two leaders of the superpowers and he was wasting his time.

In the booth by the entrance to the plaza he exchanged the plastic disc for his briefcase, and what the attendant insisted on calling his *valise*, and sidled through the barrier. The guard there let him out into the street. His taxi was waiting, and he climbed in, lugging his suitcase after him on its rollers. 'Grand Central Station,' he said through the armoured partition. The car pulled out from the kerb and merged with the traffic. He sat back on the slashed plastic seat and mopped his face. He'd got in, and now he'd got out again. He'd been allowed to make good his escape. Professor Graham, that harmless old white-haired guy in the natty Saks seersucker suit. Professor Graham, that bastard terrorist who delivered that load of shit he calls an ultimatum.

And now he was going the four blocks to Grand Central Station. There were two reasons. First, the station had one of the few easily accessible men's public washrooms that he knew of in Manhattan. And to go to Grand Central Station was to suggest the intention of leaving New York. Which, when his taxi driver was inevitably traced and questioned, would be no bad impression to have created.

The driver put him down outside the station, suitcase beside him, and he paid the fare, then turned and fought his way in through the swing doors. The suitcase's rollers helped, but the swing doors weren't easy. The various flights of stairs were worse – those down to the washroom the most taxing of all. It was curious, he thought, how often people in public places were expected to piss underground. He needed that relief, certainly; but also he needed to change his clothes and shave off his beard.

He located an empty cubicle, used the toilet, changed into the old blue suit, knocked out the dents in the homburg, put away the seersucker, flushed the toilet. At a wash basin on the wall opposite the cubicles he took razor and soap from his briefcase and shaved. It took time, and was painful, and he didn't do a very good job. But it didn't matter. In fact, it was all to the good. Old men in shapeless blue suits under battered homburgs might very well carry a bit of stubble. And it might help to mask the bleached look of his unsunburned chin.

Men came and went, but none studied him closely. Most looked pointedly the other way, knowing that old guys who shave in public washrooms are likely to demand a dollar for a cup of coffee.

He looked in the mirror. His beard had never been much, and the change wasn't dramatic. But he and Colly had discussed this, and had decided their best hope was the anonymity of the city streets. Old people didn't really signify; they merged with the graffiti and the uncollected garbage sacks. Anyway, no practical level of disguise would survive a searching, face to face confrontation. So they decided on differences of style rather than detail. Professor Robert Graham entered the washroom; a close cousin, Richard Goldstein, older and poorer, left it.

The false name was to muddy the trail for the men who would inevitably come hunting him. Richard Goldstein, to match the initials on his case: Richard because it wasn't Robert, and Goldstein because he thought it better not to advertise his Britishness. A slight central-European accent would be more likely to fool New Yorkers than his American which, even after so many years, was still terrible. He didn't intend to speak much, anyway.

His next taxi driver found him a hotel. Cheap and clean, he asked for, and the driver took him down on the west side, past the topless bars and porno shops, to a place on the edge of the garment district. He knew it was the garment district because there were men in the street pushing clothes trolleys, or drinking out of bottles in brown paper bags.

The Hotel Paramount, one door and a window wide, six floors high, between a dry cleaner's and a boarded-up camera shop. Not what he'd have called cheap, and not what he'd have called clean, either. But it was an improvement on the dives he'd seen on the way there, offering Day Rate Specials.

There was a young black man on the desk. His name was Woolston, Robert learned on the way up to his room. Christian name or surname, the desk clerk didn't say; and Robert, his accent still an embarrassment to himself, didn't ask.

Woolston uncomplainingly carried up his suitcase, dumped it on the narrow, unmusical bed. The room being on the fourth floor, with no lift, showing it for Robert's approval was only a formality: he didn't have the energy to look any further. He tipped Woolston generously. The black man accepted his dollars, but lingered companionably, scratching his chest through his grimy singlet.

'You did a good thing, Mr Goldsteen, taking a room at the back. The front gets all the sun.' He ambled across to the window, switched on the air conditioner, sniffed the air being drawn in, and smiled as only a friendly coloured man can. 'No trash cans neither. You lucked out. I tell you, day like this they stink real bad, Mr Goldsteen, lower down.'

He had booked in as Gold*stein*, and wondered if he should correct his new friend. At his age, he decided, a real Mr Goldstein would have become inured.

Woolston jerked a curved brown thumb. 'Phone's down in the lobby, if you need it. Coke machine too.'

'Thank you, yes. I saw them.'

'Bathroom's down one. I'd take my shower late if I was you, Mr Goldsteen. That old furnace is fair dying on its legs.'

Professor Graham knew the feeling. He had a phone call to make later in the day – but from somewhere other than the pay phone down in the hotel lobby.

'Nice television, Mr Goldsteen.' Woolston leaned down and turned it on. Gales of studio laughter and a black-and-white game show that revolved disturbingly up the screen. He turned it off. 'Just needs fixin'. We got a lot like that. Serviceman could fix it no time at all.'

The professor didn't argue. He had no interest in TV. He was tired, and he wanted Woolston out. He stood quietly by the open door until the black man took the hint. A new friend for whom, that afternoon, he had no room. He closed the door, slipped off his shoes, and lay down on the bed, intending to rest his legs for a few minutes before he unpacked.

He closed his eyes. The air conditioner rattled and dripped. He fell asleep.

2

Early that same afternoon, many time zones to the east, in Rome, on another very similar bed, in another very similar hotel room, another man, not at all similar, was lying. Alessandro Scotti was naked, and he was not alone.

He sighed. The woman talked too much, wanted too much. But that was her nature. Women's demands were insatiable, but they had their uses. He closed his ears to her cajoling. If he hadn't satisfied her, so much the better.

He ran the index finger of his right hand lightly up the firm, unpuckered slope of her belly, making her squirm and catch at his wrist, trying to guide his hand down between her legs. He resisted, stopping her protests with his mouth on hers. She moved in response, sliding her leg over his, but he pulled away.

'Not now. I have work to do.'

'Bastard.'

He reached for his wristwatch from the bedside table, glanced at the dial as he strapped it on.

'I've been here for nearly two hours. In three more, perhaps less, I'll be back. You think you can wait that long?'

She smiled, looking down past the thick black hair on his chest and stomach. 'Obviously *you* can.'

He swung his legs down on to the floor and stood. Such taunts didn't worry him – his true pride lay in his profession, not in his balls. And he knew she'd be waiting – they always were.

He got dressed, quickly but carefully. His shirt was dazzlingly white, with a narrow dark blue tie, complementing the expensively tailored suit and hand-stitched pointed shoes. Glancing in the mirror, he caught her eye. She had curled up sideways on the bed and was watching him speculatively. He ignored her, brushed his hair attentively forward and sideways, covering much of the thin white scar that traced a line from his left temple down past the eye socket, almost to the tip of his left earlobe. A further inch, and major blood vessels in the neck would have been severed. But it was an old wound, ancient history, and no man with a knife would ever get that close again.

From the chipped washstand by the window he picked up his own knife, a long slim blade in a soft leather sheath, and half withdrew it, twisting the steel so that it caught the light. Women liked to see such things. Then he slid it back and, bending swiftly, fastened the sheath to his right calf, beneath the immaculate trousers.

All that now remained on the washstand was a small crocodile-skin handbag, large enough to carry perhaps some money, a cigarette lighter, wallet, car keys. The sort of accessory no smart Italian male, with an eye for the cut of his suit (as well as for the pickpockets on every Rome street), would be without. This bag, however, contained none of the usual items. Still apparently ignoring the woman on the bed, he opened the flap and took out a small automatic pistol, made bulky by a short thick silencer. Snapping the magazine out of the butt, he checked that it was fully loaded, testing the spring. Then he returned the magazine to the gun, and the gun to the bag.

With a last glance in the mirror and a tiny straightening of his tie, he went to the door. The woman stretched luxuriously, her hands gripping the edge of the bedhead. She smiled again, lazily.

'Don't be long,' she said. 'And tell me all about it.' She knew he never would.

He blew her a kiss. 'I'll get the desk to send up some cognac. Make you feel at home. OK?'

He went out quickly, and down the stairs. She was beginning to get on his nerves. Gabby, demanding; she was also becoming something of a lush. It was time for a change. She could consider the cognac his going-away present. No woman had been a real part of his life since... He touched his scar absently, an unconscious gesture, as if pushing back a stray wisp of hair. No point in remembering that. Women still had a place in his life. A man's body had needs that should be satisfied if it was to function properly. Food, exercise, and sex. All were important, but none was more important than the others. A fourth need, love, he admitted but chose not to think about. His body and mind worked well without it. And his soul? That was priests' business. Maybe he'd look one up one day.

The street was hot and dusty. Nobody stayed in Rome in August unless they had business there. Only the eternal tourists crowded the streets, looking for new ways to be parted from their money. Siesta time wouldn't be over for another half-hour or so, yet already they were cluttering the pavements, shrieking, stinking of cheap deodorant, sucking green ice creams and asking the way to the Via Condiotti, or the hideous Trevi fountain.

In spite of the heat he chose to walk, not seeming to hurry yet slipping smoothly through the gaudy crowds. Past the Barberini Palace and the planetarium, across the Piazza della Republica and down through the furnace heat of the bus depot. Outside the main railway station, the wide concrete had been baked by the unobstructed rays of the sun until it now threatened to burn the shoes off any pedestrian foolish enough to linger. At the side of the railway station a line of airport buses stood, unattended as usual. Two English students were loudly explaining in French to an oriental-looking girl with a rucksack that bus tickets had to be purchased *before* boarding the bus, and an Italian family, all talking at once and surrounded by suitcases, were arguing explosively with a porter, who responded with eloquently offensive shrugs.

The telephone was just inside the main post office, the only post office in Rome open after two p.m. He slid his phone card into the slot and punched out a number. A man answered at the first ring.

'Globewide Travel.'

'Scotti.'

'Excellent. Your client arrived on schedule. The airport bus should be with you in fifteen minutes.'

'Is he expecting me?'

'I would say not.'

'A pleasant surprise, then.'

'Undoubtedly.'

The connection was broken: Alessandro hung up. Fifteen minutes to wait. He went out to the newspaper kiosk and bought

that morning's *Stampa*, also a broad fibre-tipped pen. Among the
rubbish fallen from a nearby overflowing bin was a flat white carton
from the pizza stall in the station. Stripping off the greasy sides, he
wrote on the bottom in large black letters: FARUQ HASSAN.
Then he joined the untidy mass of people waiting in the shade by the
bus terminus. From time to time he turned a page of the paper, as if
reading it; but covertly his gaze was assessing the crowd around
him. It was just possible that the police might have an interest in
Mr Hassan. It was also not beyond Il Signore to put in a second
man, just to keep an eye on him. Il Signore di Genova – the
gentleman from Genoa – was not the most trusting of employers.

The bus came in. His companions surged forward, were beaten
back as the bus doors opened and passengers fought to get off.
Alessandro hung back, watching for other watchers. None was
visible. He shrugged, quickly folded the newspaper, and left it on
the ledge of the doorway where he had been standing.

His client was easily identifiable, even among the small crowd of
his fellow Arabs. Naturally, having flown in together from North
Africa, several of them had ended up on the same bus. But Hassan
had clearly made no attempt to disguise his appearance. A brave
man – or a very foolish one. Alessandro didn't need to check him
against the photograph *Il Signore* had supplied. The likeness was
unmistakable.

Alessandro eased forward through the crowd, holding the
cardboard nameplate at shoulder height.

'Mr Hassan?' He spoke in French, Hassan's second language.
The Arab's head jerked round, eyes wide. 'Mr Faruq Hassan?'

His tone was polite but not servile, the nameplate a guarantee of
official respectability. The Arab held his small travelling bag close
against his chest, still wary.

'Perhaps you were not expecting me? I have been sent to look
after you. To take you safely to your hotel. I have a car waiting – it
has all been arranged by our mutual acquaintance.'

He leaned forward, eased the bag gently from Hassan's hand.
Before the Arab could protest, he was being guided, a tactful hand
on his elbow, through the crowds to the other side of the station.

'Wait.' Hassan stopped abruptly. 'You know my name, I do not
know yours. I told nobody I was coming to Rome. How – '

'Forgive me. Alessandro Scotti, at your service.' His outstretched hand was ignored. He went on smoothly, 'Our friend knows most things, if not quite everything. You must be aware of that. You could not think that he would not know of your sudden departure from Tripoli? Naturally he does not want you to feel alone and unappreciated, here in Rome. I assure you, Il Signore takes good care of all his friends.'

The Arab stared at him, still unconvinced.

'You must not be afraid, sir. Had Il Signore wanted you dead I could have shot you easily, as you got off the bus. Come now . . .'

They moved off together, Hassan looking anxiously back over his shoulder. Behind the station, in the Via Marsala, the usual clutter of double-parked cars ignored the no waiting signs and were in turn ignored by the overworked police. A dark-skinned urchin in tattered cut-down jeans, perhaps ten years old, was lounging on the bonnet of Alessandro's small yellow Fiat. He jumped down at their approach and opened the door with a flourish. Rewarded with several crumpled banknotes, he ran away down the line of cars to where another was just being parked, and addressed his streetwise patter to the occupant as she emerged.

Alessandro laughed softly. 'Nobody can be trusted in Rome these days,' he told his companion. 'Leave your car unattended for five minutes, and somebody will surely steal the wheels, or the radio.' He handed Hassan into the car, walked around to the driver's side, and got in himself. 'Luckily for you and me, though, these kids are well-organised. Like prostitutes, they have their beats. And for a few hundred lire, one can always be found to stand guard.'

He eased the car out into the flow of traffic, steered with his knees while he lit himself a cigarette, offered one to his passenger, was refused. He stabbed the accelerator, changing lanes to an operatic chorus of angry car horns.

'Of course,' he went on, 'we all know that it is this same kid who, if he does not get paid, will steal the radio himself – and probably kick in the radiator grille as well. Life is like that. We have to play by the rules, don't we?'

Hassan was relaxing. 'Rules, yes. I'm glad to hear you say that. Supply and demand – these are rules that even Il Signore di Genova must play by.'

Alessandro made no comment. They were already in the Via Nazionale, heading downhill fast. He swung out, blasting his horn, to overtake a dawdling Peugeot with British numberplates. They passed at speed under a flashing red light.

Hassan looked back uneasily. 'Where are you taking me?'

'To your hotel. You will like it, I'm sure. The food is excellent. It is a hotel sometimes favoured by the Prime Minister himself, so it has its own permanent guard of carabinieri. I tell you, it's the safest hotel in the city.'

'Listen. I don't like being organised. I'm not here for a good time. I do not want a good time. I'm here to see ... our mutual acquaintance ... Il Signore. It's a matter of business. You would not know – I've been doing some important work for him.'

'Somebody will come to the hotel. You can talk then. Be patient. Look – we're nearly there.'

They found a space in a quiet side alley just off the Piazza Navona, bumping the car parked behind them far enough along to let them in. Before locking the Fiat Alessandro leaned in and, with a wry smile, removed the radio from its slot in the dashboard. He tucked it under one arm, together with his crocodile handbag, and picked up Hassan's case. He knew the value of that case. The Arab might be scared shitless, but he'd be hoping for the best, and he certainly wouldn't want to make a break in a strange city without any of his possessions.

Alessandro led the way down the alley. 'I'll only stay for a few minutes – just long enough to see you settled in. As I said, if you want to talk business you need someone else. They'll be in touch. This way, please.'

The hotel really did have a carabinieri guard. One, lounging in a van at the side of the building, was smoking a thin black cigar. The other, propped casually against the hotel wall in the shade of a tall plane tree, was discussing last night's football match with the doorman. Alessandro led his companion to the marble-topped reception desk.

'Mr Faruq Hassan. You have a booking for him, I believe?'

'Yes, sir. Sign here, please ... Your passport, Mr Hassan? It will be returned later. Room twenty-three. I hope you enjoy your stay in Rome.'

An elderly porter took them up to the room, though Alessandro carried the case still, and they could easily have found the way for themselves. The porter opened the door, showed them in, and drew their attention to the operating instructions for the huge colour TV, for which Alessandro paid the old man five hundred lire.

He put the case on the mahogany luggage rack, and the radio on the chest by the door, ready for when he left. Hassan had already crossed to the little refrigerator and was unlocking the minibar.

'I need a drink.'

'I thought Muslims didn't indulge? But I expect that's a habit you picked up in America.'

Hassan looked up, surprised.

Alessandro spread his hands. 'No, Il Signore doesn't tell me everything – just enough to do my job. You are a technician, a valuable man. You studied in America and you've been doing important work for certain people in North Africa. And now you have come here to . . . talk business.'

Hassan uncapped a miniature bottle of brandy, poured it into a glass, and added ice. 'All I want is a proper reward. The work I've been doing is highly skilled, and not without danger.'

'I'm not a businessman, Mr Hassan. But Il Signore tells me you've already been paid.'

'A pittance.' He tipped back his glass. 'I was a fool. I didn't realise how valuable my skills were. They cheated me.'

'But a bargain is a bargain, Mr Hassan. Surely, in any business, a bargain is a bargain?'

He opened his crocodile-skin handbag, and carefully took out the silenced automatic.

Hassan stepped back. 'You can't do anything to me. I have powerful friends. The Dreamer himself advised me to come here.'

'The Dreamer likes to have his little joke. He also likes others to do his dirty work for him. How, Mr Hassan, do you think we learned that you were on your way to Rome?'

'I don't believe you!'

'Far better for you to have disbelieved me earlier.' He raised the gun. 'But, now that it is too late, Mr Hassan, a word of wisdom. The Dreamer has no friends. Anybody who thinks otherwise is fatally mistaken.'

'No . . .'

'*Fatally* mistaken.'

He shot the Arab. A single shot, through the centre of his forehead, the silenced gun making no more noise than a popping champagne cork. The low velocity bullet, messily exiting the back of Hassan's skull, barely chipped the wall behind him. Eyes and mouth still open, the dead man crumpled at the knees, then pitched forward, face down, on the bed. The brandy glass fell, scattering ice across the carpet.

Alessandro stood for a few seconds quite still, listening. Then he carefully put the gun back in its bag. Stepping over the dead man's legs, he pulled a blue handkerchief from the right-hand pocket of his jacket and, leaning down, used it to pick up the misshapen piece of lead that lay neatly in the chip in the wall, returning it, inside the handkerchief, to his pocket. Back on the other side of the body, he reached for the car radio, then half rolled Hassan's remains to one side, meticulously avoiding the small spread of blood. With one hand supporting the body on its side, he laid the radio carefully beside it, up under the dead man's chin, then allowed the corpse to fall back, half covering the radio. He stepped back, observing the set-up and nodding thoughtfully. Finally, he leaned forward and turned the unobscured knob of the radio. It clicked like the ratchet on a kitchen timer. Satisfied with his handiwork, Alessandro slipped quietly from the room, shutting the door behind him and hanging the *Do Not Disturb* sign on the handle.

Outside the hotel, he ignored the small yellow Fiat, hired that morning from the airport with a false driving licence in the name of Faruq Hassan, and walked briskly down the length of the Piazza, past the artists setting up their canvases for the evening tourist trade, past the fountains, and down to a small ice cream parlour. Ordering a black cherry sorbet, he sat down at a table and waited. The day was as hot as ever. The towering stucco housefronts trapped the heat. Countless caged canaries on countless tiny balconies fluttered and sang in their cages.

Twelve minutes later a rumble from the far end of the square, and a flurry of excited people running from the direction of the hotel he had so recently left, told him, even before the wailing sirens, that his day's work was complete. Il Signore had requested special treatment for Faruq Hassan. Of course Alessandro could have shot him as he left the bus. But that would have meant a police inquiry. Inconvenient connections might have been made.

On the other hand, few questions inconvenient to Il Signore would be asked about some Arab who arrived from Libya, checked in at a hotel known to be frequented by the Prime Minister, and then had the ill fortune to blow himself up while setting a bomb. Naturally none of the known terrorist organisations would admit that one of their agents could be so clumsy. A few paragraphs in the paper, yet another inquiry into police inefficiency, and the incident would be forgotten. Il Signore would be delighted. An artistic piece of work. It would confirm Alessandro's already excellent reputation.

He pushed back the empty sorbet bowl and got to his feet. The day had turned out well. Just one more time, perhaps, he would go back to the woman waiting in the hotel room. He'd take her out. Maybe they'd make a night of it.

While Alessandro was planning his night on the town, it was still afternoon in Reykjavik. In the tall brick building on Langavegur that was Broadcasting House, television reporter Pétur Einarsson had been hanging around with Finnur for nearly two hours. The fog outside the newsroom window looked as if it was there to stay.

Finnur Sigvaldson was Pétur's cameraman, a serious-minded technician. Thickset, with broad, almost Eskimo features, he was as reserved as Pétur was gregarious. By rights they should have made a terrible team. But somehow they didn't – mainly, outsiders surmised, because Finnur provided a kindly, neutral shoulder for the girls Pétur was keeping on hold to weep on.

That Wednesday morning, the newsman had got in at ten. Finnur, typically, had been in the cutting room since eight thirty. The producer for that evening's Holy Hour – the nightly news slot all Iceland was enslaved to – had asked for just seventy seconds, including lead-in, out of their previous day's lengthy interview with the building contractor, and Finnur had already found them. Pétur viewed the footage and, as always, approved. It was bloody dull, but the whole damned interview was bloody dull. The new city car park was a bloody dull subject. He'd checked with Research for additional background. They didn't have any. He'd passed the tape on and forgotten about it.

The fog outside looked as thick as ever. He checked with the coastguards in case they knew something he didn't. They didn't – clearing down south, but not here, not yet. He pounded a free cup of coffee out of the machine and morosely settled down to wait. Finnur was sterilising his tape heads, or whatever stupid thing it was cameramen did.

There was a British research ship anchored in Helgavik, a cove a few kilometres to the east of Anarstapi on the Thórsnes peninsula. The ship had arrived in Iceland two days earlier, clearing customs and immigration in Akranes, but had then left for Helgavik without completing the documentation from the Icelandic Research Council. The coastguards had agreed to handle this chore. They'd be flying the hundred-odd kilometres up across the Faxaflói as soon as the weather permitted, and Pétur had organised a lift for himself and Finnur in their helicopter. He'd also used the ship to shore to obtain permission for an interview and some filming from the research team's leader – curiously enough, a woman. The British visit had been in the pipeline for weeks, and was clearly newsworthy; the fact that the expedition was headed by a woman made it more so. And the ship had an Icelandic name, *Fimbulvetr*. It was there on some privately-funded seabed survey, looking for rare earth minerals where the volcanic crust was thinnest. And good luck to them, he thought. There hadn't been an eruption around Helgavik in decades, but that meant nothing.

He'd talked to the National Research Council just down the road, but it had largely been a waste of time. The minister was predictably keeping a low profile: the environmental/political implications of any find of rich deposits along the Thórsnes peninsula could be discussed only when, and if, such deposits were proved. Bloody politicians.

Pétur was intrigued, though, by the name of the British ship. As any eight-year-old Icelander knew, the Fimbulvetr was the long winter described in the ancient poem Voluspá, the three long years of winter that would follow Ragnarok, at the end of the world. It seemed a crazy name for a commercial research vessel, presumably supposed to be working for a bigger and better future.

Still, the British were a crazy lot. After his Oslo degree he'd spent three years in London taking Media Studies at University College, and their dirty, noisy city fascinated him. He'd had a good time: fine concerts, fine theatres, fine women. But he'd never made them out. So incredibly disorganised. The older ones even had a name for it – muddling through. They claimed respect for their past, but often as not they got it wrong. Probably this *Fimbulvetr* was part of the same cheerful mess, some misguided scientist's idea for making a good impression on the natives.

The coastguard captain called back an hour later. The easterly wind was thinning the fog, and if Einarsson wanted a lift he'd better get himself over to the airstrip pronto. Caught on the hop, expecting to be told it would be no go for the day, Pétur scrambled himself and Finnur over to the airstrip. The Aérospatiale helicopter, with them, the coastguard captain and his pilot inside, then sat on the tarmac for another thirty minutes while the easterly blew and the fog clung on by its toenails.

Eventually they left. The flight across the bay was rough and uninspiring, a journey between grey skies and greyer sea, the snow-capped cone of Snaefellsjökull hidden by low cloud. Until suddenly, just as they were approaching Búdhir, the sun broke through and the coastline ahead was green, a brilliant scarf of summer vegetation against the dusty colour of the cliffs behind. The sun shone and Pétur's sour mood passed. He leaned forward eagerly. The helicopter dipped, flew over Búdhir's wooden church and cluster of bright little houses, then on westwards, along the coast.

It was the pilot who first spotted the British ship. Helgavik was a large cove, nearly landlocked. Once there had been a fishing station, three hundred fishermen, fifty boats. Now there was only a rescue hut on the pebble beach. The *Fimbulvetr* lay well inside the cove, close under the steep lava cliffs to the west.

Beside Pétur, the coastguard captain grunted. 'If the British master got in there in last night's fog he knows his business, all right.'

The ship was sturdy, perhaps thirty-five metres in length, her hull painted a shabby orange, her superstructure principally white. The wide enclosed bridge, with radar scanner and RDF equipment, lay well forward, an open upper deck behind it. Tall, tapering engine exhaust funnels, painted blue, stood at each of the rear corners of the after working deck which was cluttered with winches, and there was a gantry at the squared-off stern for lifting heavy equipment. This gantry was swung out over the water, a bright yellow minisub hanging from it.

As the helicopter approached, a young woman in jeans and green anorak came out on to the starboard wing of the bridge and stared up, shading her eyes. She was joined immediately by a massive, black-bearded man wearing blue dungarees. Finnur was filming the ship as the helicopter pilot put down on the water a couple of hundred metres away and cut the engine. *Fimbulvetr* was clearly a working vessel, not new or recently refitted, but looking well found and capable. Advisedly so, since the Icelandic coast, even in summer, was no place for amateurs. Pétur was unsurprised. The British might be crazy, but they were a seafaring people.

He turned his attention to the woman. She was shouting down to someone on the starboard davit, stopping them from lowering the ship's boat. The coastguard helicopter carried its own inflatable dinghy, which was already being put in the water. From the research applications he'd seen at the Council office, Pétur already knew the woman's name, the subject of her doctorate, her Oxford college, that she headed this project and that she had an American passport. Until now, however, he had not realised how young she was.

Finnur and the coastguard captain were down in the dinghy. He lowered himself after them, tape recorder slung over his shoulder. The outboard started, kicking them the short distance to the ship's ladder in a shower of spray, The water in the cove was dead calm, mirroring exactly the red and black lava of the cliffs, and the fringe of arctic grass clinging to their rim. The reflection scattered as the dinghy's wake spread.

The woman, Dr Colly Graham, was waiting for them on the after deck. The man beside her, who had been at the davit, was lean and muscular, perhaps ten years her senior, with a bluish cleanshaven jaw and high Slavic cheekbones. Dr Graham herself had a very American face, wide open and smiling, marvellous teeth, long straight fair hair tied carelessly back in a ponytail with what looked like an elastic band. But she and her companion radiated a tension that belied their easy greeting. The black-bearded man was still up on the bridge wing, leaning on the rail, watching them.

The coastguard captain introduced himself, then his two friends from Icelandic television. They shook hands. Her companion was Dr Dietrich, the team's mineralogist. Finnur asked if he could film around the ship, and she told him to be their guest.

'If you meet another guy that'll be Kass – Kassim Latif. He's our laboratory assistant. And a wiz in the minisub.'

There were the research licence formalities to be dealt with. The coastguard went up to the bridge with her to confer with the ship's master. Pétur wandered aft, looked at the tiny submarine hanging from the gantry. It was a dishlike, two-man craft, with grapples and scoops for collecting samples. Manning it had to be one of the most cramped, uncomfortable, nightmarish jobs Pétur could imagine. He enjoyed skindiving himself, but that was liberating, a very special sort of freedom. To be shut up in that tin contraption would be like being trapped, lying in your own coffin.

He lit a cigarette, turned back towards the bridge. Finnur was up the rungs on one of the exhaust stacks, getting overall shots of the ship, her courtesy Icelandic flag and the British ensign on the starboard yard-arm. Otherwise the deck was deserted. Pétur frowned. Doctors Graham and Dietrich, this Kassim Latif and the bearded ship's master – on a vessel this size there had to be other crew members.

He climbed to the upper deck, came to the deckhouse there, looked in through an armoured glass window. Some sort of small laboratory. A stainless steel sink, a long aluminium-topped work-bench with drainage ducts down across the floor, racks above it and carousels for storing samples. Or perhaps spinning them. He'd no idea. It all looked very clean and unused. So far, of course, it would be. But not a soul in it.

He listened. Everything seemed to be shut down, except for a small diesel engine thumping somewhere. The loudest sound was that of the birds, probably guillemots, nesting on the cliffs. And then a thud behind him as Finnur jumped down on to the deck.

Pétur took out his interview notes, scanned them, finished his cigarette and tossed the butt into the water. In front of him a teak stairway led up to the bridge. The door at its head opened.

'If you're the television man, and you have to be, then come you on up. We've been tested in vain for syph and communistic affiliations, so now it's snort time. Come you on up, I say. And your happy-snapper friend, wherever he may be.'

The ship's master was even broader than he'd seemed from a distance: his dungarees filled the doorway. Pétur climbed the stairs. A large hand was offered.

'Captain Flynn. And you'll be Thorleifur Thorleifursson, or some such polysyllabic wonder.'

Before Pétur could take the hand it was pushed aside, as Dr Graham somehow eased herself into the opening.

'Please forgive us, Mr Einarsson. Flynn's jokes are terrible, but he's a great captain.' They made room, and Pétur entered the wheelhouse. 'The name *was* Einarsson, wasn't it?'

'Pétur, please – we Icelanders always use given names.'

'Great. Then I'm Colly. My mother's idea, that. The Colleys of upper New York state were her grandparents, and fine godfearing people . . .' She laughed, anxiously, her eyes strangely bright and restless. 'And Dr Dietrich here is Werner. And I don't know why, but Flynn's just Flynn.'

The hand was offered again, and Pétur took it. The bearded man peered closely into his face. 'Peter, is it? No hard feelings, Peter. But there's a finer rhythm to the other. Like chronic cardio-sclerotic. Wasn't it Yeats himself who said he'd rather be chronic cardio-sclerotic than Lord of Upper Egypt? And him dying of the thing itself, poor man.'

Pétur looked around the bridge. The coastguard captain was at one of the chart tables, a glass already in his hand. He caught Pétur's eye and shrugged discreetly. There was a performance going on here, but whether it was Flynn's alone Pétur couldn't be sure. He was saved by Finnur's arrival from the deck below.

Introductions this time were brief. Finnur lowered the camera from his shoulder and rested it on the engine control column. 'You have a good ship,' he said stiffly.

'I'm glad you think so. We do, too.' Dr Graham went across to the chart table where bottles and glasses were laid out. 'She got us here and she'll get us home again. And now, as Flynn says, it's snort time. Pétur, Finnur – gin, whisky, vodka?'

They both had empty stomachs. Pétur held his whisky glass warily, scarcely sipping it. Finnur, who was reputed to film even better cross-eyed than sober, was less cautious. They talked, like tourists, of the weather, of Iceland's short summer and the recent run of storms, of how all Icelanders seemed to speak such good English, and of the best places to buy Icelandic knitwear.

The coastguard emptied his third glass and carefully did up the top button of his uniform jacket. 'Pétur has an interview to film. I'll leave him to it. If I could see the ship, perhaps?'

'Why not?' Colly Graham took his glass. 'Werner'll take you. Flynn can go along too, if you like.'

Finnur cleared his throat, muttered something about the captain staying.

The woman laughed. 'I see what you mean. Never does any harm to have an old sea dog in the background.' She waited until Dr Dietrich had led the coastguard away, then untied her hair and let it fall easily about her face. 'Now – where do you want me?'

Pétur leaned against the wheel and took out his notebook. 'A little information first, please. So that we both know what we'll be talking about.'

He went through the basic facts with her, the nature of the project, its purpose, the team's backers.

'My father and me, more or less. He's put together some US funding, too.'

'Your father?'

'Professor Bob Graham. The Peace Prize man.'

Pétur winced. 'I'm sorry. I should have made the connection.'

'Yeah.' She eyed him frankly. 'I guess you should. With the US Air Force base you've got here, you people have never been exactly neutral. How long would you have lasted, had the missiles ever really started flying? Say six minutes?'

So she was on her father's side. It was to be expected. He smiled ingenuously. 'I agree with you. But none of this on camera, please. It has its place, of course, but not in our little piece.' He changed the subject. 'These rare earth minerals – what exactly are they?'

'We really need Werner for that. But I can give you an example. There's a silicate used in the intense white glaze they put on satellites. Nothing else will do, and it's found in tiny quantities, mostly on the west coast of Africa. We think you may have it here. The conditions are right. And it'd be a bonanza if you did.'

'Good. We'll keep that in. And how long are you planning to stay?'

'Oh, seven, eight weeks. Till the weather breaks.'

'Here? Here in Helgavik?' He'd created the opening he wanted. 'I only ask because there seem to be so few of you for sailing in such dangerous waters.'

'The four of us didn't bring the ship here from England!' Her laughter was unforced. 'We *can* work the ship, but we'd rather not. We just worked her round the coast from Akranes – left our proper crew there a couple of days ago when we cleared customs. We had six men on the voyage up from Liverpool, but we don't need them again until we go back. You can always hire sailors. Meanwhile, we share the housekeeping – cooking and so on – and Flynn tells us which buttons to press when we chug back to Akranes.'

'You feel safe here, with so few of you?'

'Well, it's not ideal. But crews cost money, Pétur. You must realise we're doing all this on a very low budget. We're safe enough until the end of September. Flynn says it's a good anchorage – good shelter, the bottom holds well. So the answer to your question is yes, we're staying out here. There's plenty to be done – detail charting, and so on.'

'I saw the submarine. You've been down already?'

'Not me personally, though I have been known to con her. Kass and Werner took a ride this morning. The water's clear as crystal, which is a help. We do have lights, though, if things get murky.' She paused, weighing him up for a moment with her stare. 'We call the sub "Beatle", by the way – for obvious reasons. I guess even Iceland didn't escape them.'

'They never made it here in person, but the songs did – over the government's collective dead body.' He laughed, professionally wrinkling his eyes. 'They distracted our young people, you see, from the proper study of Voluspá . . . and that reminds me. The name of your ship, *Fimbulvetr* – a frightening name for anyone who knows the sagas. How did you come to choose it?'

She tilted her head, pushing her hair back out of her eyes with a square, well-scrubbed hand. 'Ragnarok, you mean? The end of the world?' He nodded. 'But that's only half the story. You must know that. In Voluspá, what comes *after* the long winter and the final terrible battle? What *follows* the Fimbulvetr? The renewal of life, remember? The earth rises green and fertile again, and the sons of the gods remember the past only as an evil dream. It's a story of hope, really, of renewal. Of something beyond eternal winter.'

He liked that. And her enthusiasm, clearly genuine, would come across well on video.

'Hope through these rare earth minerals?'

'That's part of it. Those and other necessary changes – the world's in such a mess, it can only get better. We want to do our bit to help – but you don't want me to talk politics, I know.'

'Not at all.' He was impressed; she'd done her homework on the sagas, and she was sincere. People always liked that, even if they didn't agree with the message. At least this wasn't some crass commercial outfit intending to exploit the naive Icelanders. 'It sounds very good. You can say all that again, on camera, just as you told me. Then you'll be Iceland's favourite lady.'

She tossed her head, pleased. Then her expression changed. 'But we don't want to be *too* popular. We have to work. We can do without crowds of sightseers.'

'You might get a few over from Ólafsvík, maybe.' He shrugged. 'No more than that. This cove isn't exactly on the main road. There may be hikers passing through, but they won't bother you.'

He closed his notebook. While they were talking, Finnur had been setting up, shooting establishing scenes – the bridge interior, the after deck with the yellow submarine hanging from its gantry, the Captain leaning on the rail and looking like an old sea dog. Now Pétur and Colly joined him and Flynn out on the bridge wing.

Amazingly, the sun was still shining. Dr Graham leaned on the rail beside Flynn, sunlight striking across her face, heightening its strong bone structure. Her eyes were very blue. She wore no makeup, and her tan was pale in the creases at the corners of her mouth and eyes. She was a beautiful woman. And there was something more – she was not afraid of her beauty.

He switched on his recorder, checked the levels, nodded at Finnur. He did his lead-in straight to camera, then turned to Dr Graham. It was a good interview. Everything went well. She spoke easily, chatting just as they had done before. He led her along the planned path, she followed.

Then he sprang the surprise question, a trick he always tried with confident subjects. Otherwise the thing might come out looking too pat.

'Tell me, Colly – tell me about being a woman, and in charge of this operation. In charge of men like Captain Flynn here. Are there ever any problems?'

She glanced at Flynn, then looked sideways at Pétur. 'Flynn? In charge of Flynn? Nobody's in charge of Flynn. I reckon nobody's been in charge of Flynn since he quit his stroller.'

She was turning his question. He persisted. 'But you're at the head of the team, the only woman on board. Are there never any problems?'

She gave him a long, cold stare. 'Has anyone tried to rape me, you mean? The old gang bang? If that's what you're getting at, the answer's still no. This is a busy ship, Mr Einarsson. I guess we're just too fucking tired to fuck.'

There was a long pause. Pétur, for once, was speechless. He had seldom seen anyone so angry. Finnur, hissing delightedly through his teeth, left the camera running. Flynn stared straight out to sea, suppressing a rumble that might have been laughter, or an incipient volcanic eruption.

Suddenly, the woman relented. Her expression relaxed.

'Problems? Of course there are problems. Authority always brings problems. But not because I'm a woman. I really do believe we've grown out of that.' She smiled at him wickedly. 'Besides, that's surely a question better addressed to your prime minister. She has much more experience of being in authority over men than I have.'

And there, at last, was a cue. The earlier response could be cut – although Pétur already anticipated that it would surface again in the Christmas collection of memorable moments, for private screening at the office party.

He cleared his throat. 'Speaking of the Prime Minister, Colly, or rather the government as a whole, what exactly is their attitude to the work you are doing here?'

'They've been most helpful. Cautious – they don't want heavy industry moving in here and destroying the environment. But I can understand that. I'm a member of Greenpeace myself. Among other things.'

It would not, he thought, be a good moment to mention that some Icelanders were not too happy about Greenpeace's campaign to save the whales. He let it pass. He thanked her, and the interview was at an end.

Just then Werner Dietrich appeared on the deck below them with the coastguard captain and a slight, close-bearded young Asian wearing an untidy turban. This must be the laboratory assistant, Kassim Latif. He sidled away after being introduced, keeping himself very much in the background.

The coastguard was anxious to be off. When they reached the ship's ladder Pétur paused and nudged Finnur, who dipped into his rucksack, producing a large black-glass bottle. Pétur presented it to Dr Graham.

'With the compliments of Icelandic Television. It's our national drink – Brennivin. Drink it ice-cold, and treat it with caution. Some call it the Black Death. It'll clear blocked drains, if nothing else.'

It was the standard company presentation to visiting foreigners, and the standard company joke. He looked around the little group. 'You've got quite a United Nations here – American, Irish, German, Indian, and all under the British Flag . . . Is that intentional? A demonstration of international friendship and co-operation, perhaps?'

'Not really, it's just the way things worked out.' She smiled. 'But you can say so if you like. After all, we *do* come from different countries, and we *are* all friends. But my father's only a naturalised American – he's still so British you wouldn't believe. And Werner's British too, by the way. He was an East German once, back in the days before reunification, but now he's British.'

Pétur waited. There was a story there, for certain. Any one-time East German who was now British must surely have a story to tell. But Dr Graham outwaited him. She'd said all she was going to say on that subject.

He didn't press the matter. They were here for weeks. There'd be another time.

'You've all been very helpful. Thanks again. If you've a TV on board, you can catch the show at eight. And I'll see you get a transcript. I may come to see you again, if you'll let me. Home news isn't easy to find on this little island, so if we get a good response – and I'm sure we will – there'll be a chance for a follow-up.'

'Of course. Any time. You know where to find us.'

He followed the others down into the dinghy. They returned to the waiting helicopter, where the pilot put away the book he was reading and gave them a hand up on to the starboard float and into the cabin, then stowed the dinghy.

The coastguard was checking his safety straps. 'A charming woman,' he said. 'And that German knows what he's talking about. Very impressive. The Indian too. They have a huge chart of the cove in their plotting room. It's marked out in squares, with spot depths already entered. And the volcanic fault lines. I never thought there'd be so many.'

Pétur was organising his notes. A charming woman indeed. And his instinct told him she was up to something. They all were. There was real excitement on the ship. A silicate for painting satellites? It had to be something more than that. He made a note to look up rare earth minerals and to make time for a second visit, very soon. It wasn't oil, or gold. Too obvious – and surveyed for before. Uranium? Was uranium a rare earth mineral?

The engine's deafening chatter prevented any further conversation. As they took off, he looked down at the ship. A very charming woman. If he drove over one evening they could have dinner in Olafsvik. She wasn't one to mind the stiff walk up to the road. Dinner, and a chat about rare earth minerals. Two birds with one stone.

Back on the *Fimbulvetr*, Colly Graham was watching the helicopter as it flew out across the bay and disappeared behind the sheltering curve of lava cliffs.

Werner put his arm gently round her waist. 'That reporter will be back.'

She leaned back against him, suddenly exhausted. She hadn't realised how much her act was taking out of her. Such a show of openness and so many lies. 'I'm afraid he will. But only for his score. He's not dangerous.'

'His score?'

'The list he keeps in a little black book somewhere. Women he's slept with – rated from one to ten.' She twisted her head round to look up at Werner. 'Tall and blond and very full of himself. Didn't you spot it? I did – that's why I gave him the teeth and hair treatment. High voltage stuff.'

Werner kissed her forehead. 'I knew you were up to something, Colly.'

'Oh, Christ . . .' She closed her eyes, frowning and shaking her head. How cheap it sounded. Cheap, cheap, cheap . . . Still, she hadn't let the chauvinist get away with the entire sexist bit. She'd stood up to him just once. And besides, they might need him later. An outlet for information.

She eased herself away from Werner, turned to Kass. 'And how did it go with the nice little coastguard? He was real. A guy you could get on with. I liked him.'

Kass was still staring up at the cliffs. 'We showed him everything he wanted.' The lilting accent always became more pronounced when Kass was under stress. 'Werner is blinding him with science, and yours truly is letting him poke inside a core sampler. But I am thinking, he's not a foolish man, and he was very interested in our chart. But he isn't suspecting anything.'

Flynn leaned between them. 'Sure, how could the poor man? Aren't we all just as innocent as the day is long? Saving the godless carryings-on between our two leading scientists, and herself so fine and righteous to the TV feller, as innocent as –'

'Judas Priest, Flynn – give the stage Irishman a rest, can't you? They've gone, and I've just about had it up to . . .' She checked herself. His grin was still in place, but the eyes above his beard were unamused. 'Sorry, Flynn. It's not you I'm angry with really. It's them.' The sweep of her arm took in the deserted cliffs around them, and the whole world beyond. 'I'm just on edge.'

Werner, ever tactful, murmured, 'Aren't we all?'

Flynn hadn't moved. Colly laughed, nervously, then discovered the bottle she was still holding. 'Here, Flynn.' She mimicked the reporter's meticulous Scandinavian vowels exactly: 'With the compliments of Icelandic Television.' Now she held out the bottle. 'We love you, Flynn. We love you just the way you are. OK?'

He took the Brennivin. 'OK, Chief. OK.'

There was an awkward pause, broken by a sudden flurry of screeching seabirds on the cliffs above. Werner shifted his feet, then glanced at his watch. 'Four o'clock,' he said thoughtfully. 'That's one o'clock in New York. Too soon for any real progress, I suppose?'

It was much too soon, and he knew it. But he had redirected their attention.

Colly took the cue. 'Poor old Fard. He'll just about be through at the UN, I guess. So what'll he do now? It's going to be a long day for him. And lonely. At least we've got each other to bitch at.'

Greyness seemed to have descended over her companions. She struck a pose, making the effort to lift them out of it.

'How *about* that, folks? One o'clock in the dear old US of A. And that, my friends, is soap time on TV. Leading off, today and every day, with *All My Children*. How *can* you bear to miss it?'

3

In the Paramount hotel, Robert Graham, now to be known as Richard Goldstein, slept for less than an hour. Roused by the distant whoop of a passing squad car, he sat up on the bed, looked at his watch, relaxed. Nearly three hours remained until his promised telephone call to Georg at the UN. He lay back carefully, unknotting the cramps that had gathered in his back and shoulders, clasped his hands behind his head, and for the first time examined his surroundings.

The room was horrible. The bed was a noisy wreck – he could only marvel at the energy that must have gone into wrecking it. There was one hideous, plastic-seated upright chair, and no proper table for him to work at, only a cigarette-burned dresser in walnut veneer, with nowhere for him to put his legs. The fan in the air conditioner was about to fall apart, he already knew the TV didn't work, and there were distinct bug squash-marks under the colourwash on the walls.

All in all, it was ideal. Anybody who knew meticulous Professor Graham at all well would probably reckon that a room like this was the last place he'd be found.

He felt like a character out of a Raymond Chandler story. Hotels like this were clearly timeless. All the room really lacked was a red neon sign flashing outside the window.

He got up stiffly, pushed back the grey net curtain, and looked out. An iron fire escape, and beyond it a blank, black brick wall, maybe twenty feet away. Too close. He smiled to himself. No, just right. The whole hotel was perfect. It asked no questions, and if others asked them it would certainly give unhelpful answers. He went out of the room and down to the toilet on the floor below. Unsurprisingly, it reeked of Lysol.

On his return, Robert unpacked his PC and set it up. Scarcely bigger than a glossy magazine, it opened to provide a full typewriter keyboard and a flat screen twenty text lines deep. You could get smaller computers, but this was the minimum practicable for anyone who planned to do some serious writing. As a word processor, it would operate on its internal battery for three hours between charges, or it could be plugged directly into the mains, recharging the battery while in use. It also had connections to enable it to talk to other computers – and the whole thing would slip easily inside his briefcase.

They had planned for him to write a daily log. If their ultimatum failed, and the countdown ended in disaster, the world had to know why it had happened. They wanted a true record of events to be available, something to counter the official lies that would inevitably be published; something to help future generations to understand, avoid making the same mistakes again.

The room's only wardrobe space was behind a curtain on a batten across one corner. He hung his clothes there, then hesitated, the thick bundle of banknotes in his hand, looking for a hiding place. He taped the bundle, in the end, to the back of one of the middle drawers of the dresser. A waste of time, probably, but he felt better for having made the effort, no matter how feeble.

He checked his watch again. He was hungry. He also wanted, for his own peace of mind, to confirm the post office box Colly had set up for him a couple of weeks before, while passing through New York for the last time, on her way back to England and *Fimbulvetr*. They needed somewhere for him to send the PC's floppy disks to each day, after he'd written up his log. When he was taken – and none of them had any doubt that eventually he *would* be taken – it was important that his record should be safe. And there were messages, left in Oxford, that would go out automatically to alert Colly's friends in the environmental movement to collect and read the disks.

He still felt tired, and his shoulders still ached. He made his way slowly down the stairs and out into the airless street. There was a deli right across the way, which offered him hot pastrami on rye for two-sixty, and an off-peak discount for senior citizens. The old man liked that. It went with his suit. He might get noticed if he spent like a man with three thousand dollars, cash, at his disposal. Besides, the money was strictly for emergencies. Banks were out of the question, and nothing rang alarm bells faster than using a black-listed credit card.

The sandwich, and a mug of excellent coffee, restored him. Walking more upright now, he went in search of a subway station. Times Square turned out to be closer than he'd thought. The hotel looked better and better. For a man needing to take a daily subway ride, the location was ideal.

He took a train to East Fifty-sixth, to the post office just a block from the subway station. The street was stifling, and it wasn't much better in the dark and dusty lobby, with its wall of little glass-doored boxes. In his pocket was the combination number his daughter had sent him. The box was in his mother's name, Lily King, for no other reason than that Colly had been thinking of the old lady when she filled out the form.

Robert opened the box, took out the junk mail and the card he'd sent himself three days before, just to make sure the system worked. On the back he'd written: *When you read this you'll be dead.* In effect, they were all dead now, he and the four up in Iceland. It had seemed witty at the time. Now, it made him weep. He tore the card up and flung the pieces in a bin. The system worked.

After the post office, he hurried back towards the subway: it was nearly four thirty. The pay phone he had chosen was only a short ride away, down in the Battery, right at the end of Manhattan Island, in a dusty little communal garden on the waterfront, close to where the ferry trips started out for the Statue of Liberty. From where he stood to dial he could see the statue.

No symbolism was intended. He'd visited the park before. He liked it.

Donna MacIntyre recognised his voice and put him through immediately. No chat this time, presumably on the Secretary-General's instructions. But Robert had known her a long time – he wished she could have been told the truth. She might even have been on their side.

'Bob? Where the hell are you?'

'I don't believe you expect me to answer that.'

'I don't know what to expect. I certainly never expected to be talking to you like this.'

'Are you alone?'

'No. At this moment I have the United States' Assistant Ambassador to the UN with me.'

'Good. They're taking me seriously, then.'

'For God's sake, Bob, of course they're taking you seriously! Whatever kind of crazy stunt this is. Nothing from the Soviets, yet, but the lines are hot with external traffic.'

'Not a stunt, Georg. We're serious. We – '

'Bob – listen. I'm handing you over to the Assistant Ambassador.'

'NO!' He raised his voice. 'I *won't* speak to him. I will not . . .' he pounded the coin box with his bony fist. 'Georg? Are you still there? I won't speak to him. Any voice except yours and I ring off.'

'OK, OK.' It was still Georg. 'Calm it, Bob. OK?' There was a rustling at the other end of the line. 'Now listen to me, Bob. Just *listen.* Obviously you believe you've thought this thing through. But – '

'No buts. I can only talk to *you*, Georg. You have to understand that. It's in the ultimatum, and I mean it. I'll be calling every day, and I'll only talk to you. Otherwise I'll get bogged down. You know politicians, Georg. But we trust each other.'

'We used to. Bob, what you're asking these guys can't be done. Not in two weeks. It's just not on.'

'Two days will be enough, once they see there's no alternative.' He eyed his watch. He'd been talking for too long already.

'Bob, do you realise just what it is you people are threatening?'

'Nothing as bad as the nuclear threat that's been hanging over us for fifty years.'

'Does that make it right? Think, Bob. Does it?'

He closed his eyes. Oh yes, he'd thought about it. And some time, not now, but some time, he'd try to explain to Georg that unclouded righteousness was a luxury a man might have to do without. His position, professionally and politically, was unique. Other men might do nothing, and say it was the right thing, because it was their only option. His choices were not so simple.

'Another minute, Georg. No more. This call is just to tell you we're serious. We mean what we say.'

'Right now, Bob, I'm looking at the list of your people up there in Iceland. My God, your own *daughter*. Call this off, for all our sakes, before it gets out of hand.'

'I'll ring again tomorrow, at the same time. And by then I expect definite word from both heads of state.'

'Jesus – they can *say* anything. You know that.'

'I mean instructions, actually sent. Cables you personally have read. Publicity. I want to read it in the paper, see it on TV. And I need you, Georg. You're my honest broker. You won't cheat me.'

'And if I refuse?'

'You can't.' There was a long pause. 'You can't, because you know I'm right. You know it'll work. Deep down, you're on my side, Georg. You can't refuse.'

A weary sigh came over the line. 'What if one of them meets your terms and the other won't?'

The second hand on Robert's watch seemed to be racing round. 'Then I ring again the next day. And the day after. And the day after that. Until either they *both* agree or – it's in the ultimatum. If they're obstinate enough.'

'I can't guarantee – '

'Two weeks, Georg. That's all they've got. We both know it can be done in less than that.'

He rang off. There was no point in goodbyes. The message had been delivered.

They'd had many fine evenings, he and Ruth, in Georg's house out on Long Island. The two men were of one mind. Although now a career diplomat, once Georg had been a practising doctor, a pacifist who had volunteered to work with the Red Cross in West Africa. Once a formal Christian, over the years his faith had simplified. Like Robert, he now found it sufficient to believe in the perfectibility of mankind.

That was why Robert dared to turn to Georg now. He knew only too well what he was doing. He was presuming on Georg's friendship, exploiting his loyalty, and relying on his virtue. Georg *was* an honest broker.

He left the little phone booth and sat on a bench in the garden. Nothing grew there, in August, save privet and dry bleached weeds and moulting pigeons. He should have left the place at once, in case agents were already on the way to the phone there; but he was tired. He needed the rest. That morning he'd been on a beach in Maine, looking out across Casco Bay. Now his view was New York Harbour. And in the hours between, for better or worse, mankind's destiny had been inexorably altered.

With the departure of the helicopter, Colly had gone down to the *Fimbulvetr*'s wardroom. She was there with the others now, looking over the housekeeping inventory, making sure that the ship's supplies would last, if it came to that, for the full fourteen days of the Ragnarok countdown. Before going ashore in Akranes for his return to Britain, the *Fimbulvetr*'s steward on the voyage up from Liverpool had presented her with what seemed a comprehensive inventory. Now Colly read it aloud, asking occasional questions; Werner was there to make sure that Flynn gave her serious answers.

Werner Dietrich was solemn, bordering on over-earnestness. He had all the obsessive thoroughness of the German stereotype, but curiously little of its sentimentality. He was humourless; but he was also loving. Physically, he was of medium height, lean, his features haggard and darkly interesting. And he loved Colly Graham with total, selfless, devotion.

His obsessive nature had shown itself early. Born in Magdeburg in 1950, of working class parents, simple and direct, who had dealt with his boyhood tantrums simply and directly, he had grown up with a healthy recognition of life's limitations. Nevertheless, he decided while still in high school that the particular limitations of life in the German Democratic Republic were unacceptable, and he conceived then his most enduring obsession: to escape to the capitalist west.

He lived with his parents, Otto and Bessi, and an older sister, Ilse, in a suburban workers' residential block: his father worked in the local brewery. Their lives were drab, but Werner was not so naive as to imagine that the lives of brewery workers in Munich or Birmingham were very much less drab. It wasn't capitalist prosperity that obsessed him, but capitalist freedom. The *idea* of freedom. Freedom as an efficient way of running things. Such an idea, in a country clearly neither free nor efficient, was both attractive and agreeably logical.

Werner was scientifically inclined, and an above average student. Thinking already of a marketable skill for his future life in the west, he studied nuclear physics. After three years at the modern technical college in his own city he went on to the prestigious university in Halle, and soon after enrolling there requested a change to the mineralogy department. He was by then making serious plans for defection – probably while a member of the GDR delegation to some international scientific congress – and he had learned that nuclear physicists had by far the greatest difficulty getting visas for travel to such meetings.

But the change in scientific direction also involved his developing conscience. What had begun, while he was still in Magdeburg, as a vague fear of being asked some day to work on weapons research against his own country, had developed by now into a passionate hatred towards weapons research of any kind. In economic terms he was prepared to believe his government's official line; that the west's industrial machine depended entirely on war, or the threat of war. But he was uninterested in politics, and the armaments industry worldwide repelled him. The defection he planned was a personal, not a political, gesture.

To his course adviser, he justified his change of direction by emphasising his preference for fieldwork, for the practical over the largely theoretical. His academic record was sound, but not so outstanding as to suggest any possibility of a major contribution in nuclear physics, so the authorities agreed. He joined the mineralogy department, and graduated in 1974.

He made sure, all the while, that his life was politically unexceptionable. At school when his country sent troops into neighbouring Czechoslovakia in 1968, and later exempted from full-time military service by his university studies, he performed adequately in all the part-time army duties expected of him. He was attentive to his parents, and spent a part of most summer holidays with his sister and her husband. There was the required political activity, of course, nothing to be remarked on, for or against. There were women, but none were very serious. He worked hard and well, gained a junior teaching post at Halle, conducted useful research connected with the GDR's lignite mining industry, and in 1978 was awarded his doctorate.

His determination to defect never faltered. When capitalist post-urings might have dented it, the day-to-day realities of his own country ensured that he stuck to his aim. And in 1979, Dr Werner Dietrich obtained an exit visa to West Germany to attend a research conference at Heidelberg University. Once in Heidelberg he presented himself immediately, together with his considerable savings already converted into Deutschmarks on the black market, at the central police station by the Rathaus. He became a political refugee.

Three months of uncertainty followed. Uncomfortable lodgings, interminable interviews. Finally, he was granted a West German passport, and flew out to New York the next day. His English was scarcely adequate and, primed by TV, he knew his social attitudes to be uncomfortably puritanical by the standards of the society he was entering, but the sheer size and exuberance of the USA beckoned him – as did its distance from Europe, symbolising the break with his past.

In a few days, he knew he had made a mistake. America's un-ashamed consumerism shocked him even more deeply than he had imagined. He saw the USA as a country that recognised human greed as its greatest natural asset. It was the richest nation in the world, and it had grown rich by choosing ambition – usually simply another word for greed – as its prime virtue. Its institutions claimed to control this greed and direct it for the common good, but the control, if there had ever been any, had clearly broken down. At every level, greed ruled. Greed and its child, corruption.

At the same time, America's fervent brand of religiosity preached a disturbingly human-centred view of the world, with mankind in God's image, given dominion over the land and all the birds and beasts that dwelt in it. Dominion, he learned, meant the right to take, to enslave, to plunder. *This land*, a popular song told Americans, *is made for you and me.*

And freedom? The principal freedom he saw in action was the freedom to exploit, use up, discard. The waste, of people as well as materials, appalled his frugal soul. It worked as a way of running things only because the country itself was immensely wealthy: rich in climate, in resources, and in the talents that had flowed into it. They flowed in attracted by its riches, and so it grew richer – while other parts of the world got poorer, and nobody, it seemed, gave a thought to the needy.

He was shattered. An appeal to the very worst in human nature. Was that all western freedom really added up to?

Werner's pious outrage came partly from simple culture shock. Another country's sins are always more heinous than one's own. Also, his communist background caused him to oversimplify. If he had stayed longer, he might have discovered the narrowness of his vision. But if he was unimpressed with the USA, the USA was equally unimpressed with him. Neither universities, nor government, nor commercial institutions needed him. After only six weeks, he flew back across the Atlantic.

Intending to settle in West Germany, where at least he would have no language difficulties, he stopped off in London simply to revel in the freedom to travel. For as long as his money lasted, which wouldn't be much longer, the whole non-communist world was open to him. *There* was a freedom beyond reproach.

But he went no further than Britain. Its old, dirty, cramped cities were close to what he was accustomed to. Its shabbiness appealed to him: its intellectual confusions also, for he too was confused. It managed somehow to accept the profit motive while retaining a bone-deep distaste for the successful businessman. Divided and resentful, its poor still claimed to be proud of their poverty, while its rich still apologised for their wealth. Although many of the features that struck a chord with Werner in 1979 were to change during the Thatcher years of the 1980s, he was hooked by that first glimpse of a nonsensical, inefficient, but free culture. In Britain, for the first time Werner *felt* free. It was not a thing lightly said. He was free to read, speak, listen, learn. He was also free to reject. And for him, from Magdeburg, that was the strangest and most precious freedom of all.

He got a teaching job at an understaffed, overcrowded technical college in Birmingham. And he became, five years later, a British citizen. He was still concerned about his family. He wrote, suggesting that they join him; but his sister now had children in school and his father was close to retiring age. Their lives suited them. And after reunification, of course, there'd been no reason at all for them to leave.

He was in Oxford by then, seeing out the end of the eighties, working with Dr Colly Graham and living in a flat in the same ugly Victorian north Oxford house where she lived. It had a diamond pattern of glazed yellow bricks across its front, and a patch of muddy garden filled with dustbins and bicycles. Their flats were on the same floor, across a landing two flights up, hers facing the road and his a row of lock-up garages.

It was nearly a year before they became lovers – he was ten years older than she – but she had been aware of his obsession from the first moment he had seen her, sitting in the rain with one of her students on the low wall outside the Earth Sciences block on Parks Road. They hadn't been aware of the soft drizzle, she and the girl she was with, and he'd been very German and formal, bowing damply, introducing himself as her new colleague. She'd been very American and laid back, and he'd taken them in out of the rain to drink terrible coffee in the cafeteria. And he'd been in love with her ever since.

He watched her now, in the wardroom of the *Fimbulvetr*, studying the cold-room inventory with Kassim, doing calculations on a scrap of paper. Her attitude to him, he knew, was less serious, less involved; he accepted that as the way things had to be. But in the countdown to Ragnarok they were powerfully united. They were there together in Helgavik. His convictions were her convictions. His determination was her determination. And he would die afterwards, just as she would.

Colly frowned, returning the inventory to a clipboard that already held the galley provisions list, details of the alcohol held in the bonded store, and the general housekeeping goods kept in the forward locker area.

'Two weeks,' she muttered. 'That's four people for fourteen days – fifty-six breakfasts, lunches and dinners . . . Hell, I don't know.' She looked up. 'It's easy to see I've never done this before. Down in the Red Sea we had a cook, and – '

She broke off as Flynn reached for the black bottle of Brennivin. 'Did you say four people? Sure, it's only three people and a vegetarian. You can send Kass out to chew grass if things get tough.'

The Indian flung down his pen. 'I know you all find it jolly fun, taking the piss out of my religion.' The banter bored Werner. It was friendly enough, but he'd never found it funny. 'A fat lot of good will it do you. You can see how fit I am on beans and rice. Superfit. Are you superfit, on tripes and liver?'

Flynn uncorked the bottle and poured. 'Beans and rice? Load of bloody fartmakers.' He drank, shuddered, and drank again. He was seldom the worse for wear; but often pretended to be, Werner had realised, for the latitude it gave him. But this had gone far enough.

'I must remind you all,' Werner pointed out, 'that if we do need anything from Hellnar, now is the time to get it. The village is five kilometres away, at least, and the shops will close soon. And tomorrow it will be too late.'

By dawn the following day, midnight in New York, they had to assume that the opposition (the blanket term they used for agents of either superpower) would be arriving in Iceland, if not already deployed there. From then on, abductions, sudden death, 'accidents' of all kinds would be easy to arrange. After daybreak, none of them would go ashore. Until the countdown ended, *Fimbulvetr* must be self-supporting, self-reliant.

Flynn reached across and patted Werner's arm. 'Don't fret yourself, Adolf. The list's fine. Indeed, we'll be hard-pressed to get through the half of it.' He considered. 'Which is not to say that you and Colly shouldn't do the trip anyway. Make a good impression on the locals. Take the ATV and ride in to Hellnar. Spend money, Laugh. Crack a few jokes. Make like the nice guys we know you are.'

'Flynn's right.' Colly stood up. 'We can always do with fresh milk, and bread. And it'll give us a chance to talk to the villagers about our research. Otherwise they'll only invent their own stories about the mysterious British ship nobody ever leaves. We don't want them getting too curious.'

'Make the work sound boring,' Flynn added. 'All underwater. Nothing to see – not worth trekking out here for.'

'Hell, it *will* be boring.' She shrugged. 'If we ever actually do anything.'

Werner felt the determined lightness at the table. That afternoon, Kassim excepted, they were all behaving as if nothing really mattered. Well, the two weeks had scarcely begun.

The journey to Hellnar was agreed. Kassim lowered the threewheeler All Terrain Vehicle from the Munro davit into – or rather, on to – the motorboat. It sat across the boat on a wooden platform, sticking out on either side; taking the ATV ashore was strictly a fair-weather job. It was past five o'clock, but the sun was still high overhead. Colly and Werner went in the boat with the muscular Flynn to help get the ATV with its fat, studded tyres ashore on the pebbled lava beach. Then Flynn took the boat back to the ship, and Colly and Werner set off on the Honda, along a narrow, rocky glacier bed leading up the side of the valley to the road. It was a steady climb; more than a kilometre.

The road wound along the clifftop between low grass verges. Scattered across the high barren landscape to their right were lava beds dotted with vivid yellow lichen, rocky outcrops, and stark lines of crooked telegraph posts leading away into the empty distance. The western peninsulas of Iceland, continually battered by Atlantic gales, were the bleakest areas of a bleak island. Nothing grew on the high land there save arctic grass and the most tenacious of mosses and lichens. The ground was shaly, mostly solidified volcanic lava and broken ash. And very old, dulled by the centuries to a uniform grey.

In many places the road had been recently repaired – an annual labour, Werner saw, judging from the signs everywhere of violent erosion, with deep gullies spreading like veins across the land. But the tarmac surface itself was good, and the red ATV buzzed along it briskly, the wind cool in their faces. To their left the land dropped steeply and the bay was spread out below them, shimmering in the afternoon sunlight, cliffs like fortresses closing around it. Ahead of them, a lighthouse and two monstrous lava blocks. And, far away on the horizon to the right, a misty line of snow-capped peaks.

They passed a small flock of sheep, anxiously grazing the scrubby verge, which scattered at the approach of the noisy vehicle. Then a lane led off to the left, down to Hellnar. They entered a sheltered valley, shrubs and little walled pastures, and a sudden profusion of wild flowers. Hellnar itself was a quiet village round a good fishing harbour. The steep-roofed houses were bright, in the Icelandic fashion, their corrugated iron walls painted in clear reds and greens and blues. Huge piles of nets lay on the jetty, and racks of fish hung drying along the rocks beyond.

Werner stopped at the wide quayside. Their red ATV attracted a lot of attention. Soon, while Colly did the shopping, he was giving the children rides out to the end of the jetty and back, while their elders stood watching, and clapped and laughed. Even the littlest children seemed to have some English – and besides, the language of shiny red paint and chromium handlebars and noisy engines is universal. Werner got on well with children; also, this was the best way he knew of encouraging the people of Hellnar to think kindly of the *Fimbulvetr*'s crew.

Colly returned, carrying cartons of milk and other packages. She stowed them in the Honda's panniers and climbed back on to the pillion seat. Shadows were lengthening across the village. The children stood in a close circle as Werner started the engine, waved, then kicked down the gear lever, and a path opened through the crowd.

Suddenly Colly was pounding on his shoulder. He rode the clutch, his gaze following her raised arm. In the mouth of the harbour a small, rugged fishing trawler was edging slowly into view around the cliffs opposite the jetty.

At first sight she seemed an ordinary working boat, her decks cluttered with nets, sides rust-streaked from the trawl warps. But she carried an intricate array of telecommunications antennae aloft; and a Soviet flag hung from her yard-arm, limp in the still evening air.

Werner eased back the Honda's engine to a murmur, turned to Colly. 'Because of us? So soon? How long can it be since your father delivered the ultimatum?'

Colly shook her head. 'No. It's just not on. Well – maybe . . . if they already had a ship in the area.' She eased her crash helmet. 'Even so . . . No, it's just coincidence. I mean, there must be dozens of Russian ships in these waters.'

The villagers were quiet now, watching as the Russian vessel slowed, coming neatly alongside a local trawler already moored in the pool. An exchange of hails came faintly across the water, then conversation and friendly laughter. The local crew caught ropes and made the Russian fast.

Werner gunned the Honda. Some coincidences were more than he could accept. He felt they were in terrible danger. He spun the ATV's rear wheels as they took off, raising shouts of encouragement from the children, and rode away up the narrow street. Behind them, some of the children waved until they were out of sight. But most were already running off to the jetty to inspect the new arrival.

'I guess we're well out of that,' Colly, leaning close against his back, shouted against the racket of the engine. 'No point in taking chances.'

He didn't answer. They rode up the valley, sunlight golden on the hay already cut in some of the tiny meadows.

'Our last time ashore,' Colly yelled. 'I'm glad we came. Are you?'

She was saying that they might never see fields, or friendly, ordinary people, again. He took one hand from the controls and gently touched the arm that was round his waist. Her hand found his and gripped it. They both believed in the success of the *Fimbulvetr*'s mission. Beyond that it was not useful to think. The Russians, it seemed, were already gathering. The Americans, with their airbase on the island, would not be far behind.

The day was ending. In Rome it was five to midnight. At a stained, baize-topped table in the upstairs room of a café on a cobbled alleyway close to the Vatican walls, Alessandro Scotti quietly slipped the single card he had drawn, a king, in beside the two kings he already held. His other two cards were rubbish. Mario, sitting opposite him, had also drawn one card only. Opening, he now pushed out fifty thousand. The next two players folded. Mario had a way of filling straights you wouldn't believe. Alessandro sighed. This could be expensive.

He'd been back to the hotel. The woman had gone, taking her cognac with her. Anger had quickly changed to relief. There were better, less strenuous pleasures for a hot August night. And hadn't he already decided that he was finished with her? Now he met Mario's fifty and doubled it. He owed his three kings at least that much. And he had a feeling that *Il Signore* would soon have another termination for him. He hoped so – they were well paid. And besides, he enjoyed the challenge. He was a man of ideas, and he never repeated himself. A radio this time, a vacuum flask next. Or perhaps a camera. With a little ingenuity, many different containers were adaptable to his needs.

Mario raised him again. Alessandro whistled softly, tunelessly through his teeth. A bluff, he decided, and reached for his wallet . . .

*

In Iceland, it was almost eleven. Well wrapped against the gathering night, Colly Graham was circling the *Fimbulvetr*'s deck. She had taken the first watch of the evening, up to midnight, glad to avoid the Icelandic TV news down in the wardroom. Her voice coming from a tape recorder was bad enough – West Coast sincere, even after so many years in Britain – but her over-ripe performance that afternoon would be a real pain to watch.

As soon as it was over, Werner had been up to report. Very sympathetic, he'd said; she'd come across well. But then, she thought, *he would*. No – that wasn't really fair. It was just that sometimes, these days, his unswerving devotion really bugged her.

The interview had been shown in English, unsubtitled. Although the English language service provided by the US NATO base at Keflavik was not available in the country at large – successive Icelandic governments had argued that it was not in their nation's cultural interest – English was generally understood.

Colly leaned on the rail, listening in the darkness to the faint rustle of waves out on the rocks at the entrance to the cove. She was tired. The six-hour rota of watches would be hard on all of them, but was unavoidable. They did not expect a sudden frontal armed attack, not if the opposition were taking the ultimatum at face value; but to be overpowered by stealth was always a possibility. Or so the opposition might believe.

The air was very still, the sky clear. Shortly the moon would rise. She pictured the Russian trawler in Hellnar harbour. Were Soviet agents already on their way across the cliff tops? Waiting. Waiting was all their great adventure now came down to. Two frantic years of preparation, and now they simply had to watch and wait. While, God willing, the world's two most powerful men, in the discreet privacy of their inner councils, were pressured into allowing their age-old pride and fear and greed to be replaced by a different pride, a different fear, and something other than selfishness . . .

In New York the time was now seven o'clock. Robert Graham, returned from a greasy-spoon supper in the deli across the street from the Hotel Paramount, was up in his room, seated at the keyboard of his word processor. He stared at the blank screen, cracked his stiff knuckles, wondered how to begin. The log had been planned as a historical document: a relic, once they were all dead, that would somehow set the record straight. He perceived it now, however, as a more personal matter: a conversation between himself, one old man, and the future.

A rather one-sided conversation, but still . . . He straightened his back, took a deep breath, and started tapping at the keys.

Life on Earth, *he wrote*, survives, and always has survived, on a perilous edge between fire and ice. The black, limitless cold of space mitigates, and at the same time is held narrowly at bay by, the heat of the sun above and the furnaces beneath our feet. Norse people, because of their unique geographical position, have understood this truth for centuries. The balance can be easily upset. Small changes can wreak widespread havoc.

In Norse mythology, a mighty ash tree stands at the eternal centre of creation, and beneath the vast span of its branches lie many worlds: of gods and dwarfs and giants, of the living and the dead. The world of humanity was fashioned by the gods, long ago, from the body of an ice giant, whose name was Ymir. From Ymir's skull the gods made – '

Robert broke off. There was a sound at his door, not so much a knock, more a confused scratching. And then the desk clerk's voice.

'Mr Goldsteen? It's me, Mr Goldsteen. Woolston. I got this TV for you, Mr Goldsteen.'

Robert sighed. Just then he had no interest in TV. He got stiffly to his feet. 'Coming . . .'

He cleared the screen, saving his words to disk, went to the door, opened it. Woolston was staggering under the weight of a huge TV set on tapered black metal legs.

'Room down a floor, Mr Goldsteen. Guy checked out just a while back, so I thought . . .' He tailed off, his gaze straying past Robert, to the portable PC. His eyes widened. 'You some kind of computer hacker, Mr Goldsteen?'

'Not really. I'm working on a text book, that's all.' Robert had his story ready, the dullest he'd been able to think of. 'A Latin primer. I'm a retired schoolteacher, you see.'

He stood to one side, letting Woolston in with the TV set. It never even got connected. Woolston was drawn, like a bear to honey, by the word processor. Anything to do with it, even writing a Latin text book, fascinated him. 'How much does something like this cost, Mr Goldsteen?'

He was ready for that one. 'I don't really know. My publishers lent it to me. Just for a couple of weeks, while I'm here in New York. I didn't actually write the book, you see – I'm just revising it for them. This way I can work on my own, without cluttering up their office.'

Woolston was scarcely listening. Publishing didn't interest him, but computers clearly did. Robert was obliged to conjugate an irregular verb or two on the screen – *claudo, claudere, clausi, clausum; cado, cadere, cecidi, casum* – then show him how to move the words around on the page. He learned fast. His curved brown fingers were quick and neat on the keys. Soon he had edged on to Robert's chair and was transposing paragraphs unaided, using the spelling checker. He kept at it, grinning happily, working to Robert's dictation, fingers flying until a voice bellowed up the stairs for service. He left reluctantly.

'We must do this again,' Robert told him, fired with a desire to help. The man was wasted on the desk of a dump like the Paramount. Designers talked about some computers being user friendly; well, some people were just naturally computer friendly.

Robert closed the door behind Woolston and returned to the keyboard. It was after eight now, and he was fading fast. He junked the material Woolston had been playing with, recalled his own file, and continued.

. . . From Ymir's skull the gods made the dome of the sky, from his blood the rivers and oceans, from his flesh the earth, and from his bones the mountains. Man and woman the gods made from two trees that stood upon the seashore. Time, also, they created, making Night and Day to ride across the sky in swift, relentless chariots, their paths lighted by two beautiful children, a boy called Moon and a girl called Sun.

But Moon and Sun are eternally threatened, for a pack of ravening wolves pursues them. And on the day when the terrible leader of the wolves catches up with the girl called Sun, and devours her, on that day the old world of humankind must end. For this is the time of Ragnarok, the time of destruction. It is the time of licentiousness, of fear and hatred between all men, of wars and sinfulness. And then, with the devouring of the sun, the world is plunged into bitter cold and darkness. Volcanoes pour forth fire and smoke. Fimbulvetr, the long winter of ice and snow, grips the bones of men.

But Ragnarok is not the end –

Robert hesitated. He couldn't go on. He closed his eyes, resting his head in his hands. There lay the difference. Ragnarok is not the end . . . there lay the tragic difference between the long winter of Ragnarok and the nuclear winter that would follow World War Three; or between Ragnarok and the total destruction of the planetary environment by man – as certain, unless dramatic changes were made soon, and hardly less swift, on a geological timescale, than nuclear destruction. He sighed. This week, this month, this year, the nuclear holocaust was an unfashionable thought. Germs, too, were out, since the Middle East had calmed down and gone back to what it did best, getting obscenely rich on the West's incontinent greed for oil. Modest arms reductions were trumpeted, while all the thousands of megadeath weapons – nuclear, binary, bacteriological – that came newly into service each year were conveniently forgotten. Superpowers tacitly acknowledged each other's spheres of influence, with US troops seemingly a permanent feature in Latin America, the *quid pro quo* for turning a blind eye to the strife in eastern Europe following the Gorbachev spring.

While all this scarcely rated a mention in the news media, environmental concern was allegedly at the forefront of public consciousness. Deforestation, desertification, the ozone layer, the greenhouse effect, and rising sea levels were the new watchwords, while in many developed countries ecologically aware Green politicians gathered enough votes to frighten the old, conservative governments, but not enough to win power. While inhabitants of the Third World became hungry enough to begin rioting in the streets, and their governments spent over £28 billion each year on importing arms, many intended for use against their own hungry people. Not to mention the £3 million a day that had been spent on the Gulf War by the British government alone.

At the same time, well-meaning efforts to bring aid to the worst affected regions made the news on TV, but were in reality themselves no more than stopgap measures; relief workers saw how insignificant their efforts were, and bitterly commented that the sum of money needed per year to provide adequate food, water, education, health and housing for everyone in the world was roughly equivalent to the amount spent worldwide on arms every *two weeks*.

Much of that expenditure, Robert knew only too well, now went into space 'defences'. Smiling leaders signed flashy reduction treaties to get rid of obsolete weaponry, then went home to apportion more funds than ever to their high-tech war machines. Robert forgot none of this. He shared, passionately, Einstein's belief that peace could never be built upon preparations for war. It was a nonsense. The material cost alone, crudely scorning far more genuine human needs, was bitterly destructive, responsible for more misery since 1945 than both World Wars put together. And still it had not removed the spectre of World War Three. After that, after the nuclear winter, there would be only an outraged wilderness, poisoned for millennia to come.

But after Ragnarok? After the cleansing long winter promised by the Icelandic myth makers? Why, *then* the earth would be renewed. Multitudes would perish, but within the tree of creation a man and a woman sheltered, ready to come forth to people a land greener and more fertile than ever before. The ice, eventually, retreats; and the earth sings again, and dances.

It need not happen. He still hoped it would not happen. But if it must happen, it was the least evil of the three options. An opportunity to start again . . .

4

Day Two AUGUST 5. THURSDAY.

Robert Graham woke late. It had been his first night in downtown New York for many years, and the city noises hadn't made sleeping easy at first. Every fire truck and police car and garbage disposal unit in Manhattan had gone by under his window, it seemed, and the wrecked bed hadn't helped. By the time he did get to sleep, he was so tired that little short of an earthquake could have roused him early.

The replacement TV set worked well. It brought in the usual morning parade of murders, diet book authors, and tax cut speculations. Also, by way of an aside, news of the recall to Moscow of a senior Soviet negotiator at the Geneva talks. It was no big deal, admittedly; but it just might be a straw in the wind that Robert had set blowing through the corridors of power.

Before going to bed he'd managed to plough on with the log for another hour or so, outlining the logic behind his team's plan. Now he put the floppy disk (actually a hard plastic square) into an envelope, addressed it to Lily King at her Post Office box number, and sealed it ready for mailing later.

His next task was to compose his first day's message for his daughter, tap it into the word processor, and convert it into a few seconds of electronic screeching on the cassette tape of what looked like, at first sight, an ordinary pocket dictaphone. There was the gist of his conversation with Georg to go on to it, a comic description of the Hotel Paramount (but no clues to its location) and not much else. Colly worried for him: she would be very watchful. He hoped he'd got it right. The conversation with Georg to show he wasn't too cheerful; the hotel to show he wasn't too solemn.

He took the 'dictaphone' and its telephone interface – two rubber cups that fitted neatly over the ear- and mouthpieces of a standard telephone – downstairs to the booth at the back of the lobby, breaking his journey to shave in the bathroom. It felt odd, shaving; like really being someone else, Richard Goldstein.

The phone booth shared the back of the narrow entrance lobby with a dented soda machine. He hooked up the interface and started the tape rolling. With a series of whistles and beeps, the machine 'dialled' its own way into the telephone network, and made the connection to the Abernatheys' place up in Maine. His brief electronic message was transmitted into the computer waiting up there, then the tape switched to record and absorbed the meaningless blur of noise that was Colly's message to him, ready to be decoded by the Zenith upstairs.

It was simple – far simpler than trying to contact the High Seas Operator via a New York pay phone, then leaving a message for the RRS *Fimbulvetr*, when and if it happened to call in. A message, moreover, that had to be comprehensive, innocent-sounding, tender, and also very short. With the further probability that the opposition would be watching out for just such a message, and would begin tracking him down as soon as he mentioned the ship's name. The chances that the authorities would think to monitor the Abernatheys' line were virtually nil.

The exchange took less than a minute. Woolston was at the reception desk, not busy: there seemed to be few guests at the Hotel Paramount. He beckoned Robert over. Robert joined him, leaned on the desk. For both of them, it was going to be a long day.

'That's a neat gadget you've got there, Mr Goldsteen.'

'It's a computer interface.' Robert showed it to him. 'I phone in text to my publisher. Another computer there answers me.'

'That doesn't sound too friendly.'

'It's not. Time was when you took the typescript round in person, and got to take coffee with a nice dumb secretary.'

Woolston handed the interface back. 'Things are tough all over, Mr Goldsteen.'

There was a pause. Robert's powers of invention had run out.

'I swear you ain't had no breakfast, Mr Goldsteen.'

'I seldom do. My doctor tells me I must watch my figure.'

'Well, I ain't as pretty as no dumb secretary, but a cup of coffee won't give you no fat attack.'

He lifted the desk flap so that Robert could see a small electric hotplate on the floor behind it, connected to a wall socket by a length of frayed cable, and supporting a stained enamel percolator.

Robert hesitated. A little central-European reserve seemed in order. 'That is very kind of you,' he said. 'But I do not think I – '

Woolston banged the bell on his desk several times, loudly, then held up one finger for Robert's further attention.

'A nice young black guy like me, Mr Goldsteen, might get to feel a might teed-off if a nice old white guy like you didn't care to drink a cup of coffee with him.'

Which was undeniably true. Robert faced the difficulty, held up one of his own fingers alongside Woolston's.

'More grey,' he suggested.

'Say again?'

'Grey. Mottled grey, not white. Mottled grey all over.' He opened a couple of shirt buttons, demonstrating. 'See what I mean?'

Woolston laughed, pleased at that, and brought out two mugs, respectively lettered Frank and Harry. He gave Robert coffee the way he took it himself, straight from the pot, nothing added. They sipped appreciatively, in friendly silence, staring out through the glass hotel door. Two men passed in the hot, bright street, arguing over a loaded garment rack. The coffee, unmistakably, had been fresh ground that morning.

'Are you Harry?' Robert indicated the mug.

'Nope. Nor Frank either.'

The silence returned. There was a newspaper lying crooked on the desk, and Woolston started reading it, twisting his head.

'I'll tell you a funny thing,' he said absent-mindedly, still reading. 'I had a phone call this morning. Guy from Immigration, so he said. Checking all the hotels.'

Robert considered. This, then, was what Woolston had wanted to tell him. He leaned on the desk, drinking his coffee, feeling suddenly very tired. Worn out, past it. It didn't really matter how soon they came for him. The *Fimbulvetr* had been on its own from the moment he delivered the ultimatum. His job was done. But he'd wanted – he still wanted – to keep them at arm's length for just a little longer.

'Seems like they're looking for some English guy. Visa's run out or some such. Name of Graham.' He pronounced the word with a very American emphasis, with the *ham* as in sandwich.

Robert made an effort. 'Someone like that will never be using his real name,' he said, tactfully thickening the accent. 'Not if he has the Immigration Department on his trail.'

Woolston grinned. 'Description, too. Old guy with a beard.'

'Anyone you recognised?'

He shook his head. 'They said to call back if I did.'

'And will you?'

'What's the point? They ain't serious. Some old English guy ain't no Hispanic bum. They're serious, they send round the National Guard.'

Robert thought the other man deserved at least a part of the truth. 'They're serious,' he told him.

Woolston lifted his gaze from the newspaper. Their eyes met. 'Ah. Then I guess they're still only fishin'. New York's a big city.'

'And this Mr Graham,' he copied Woolston's pronunciation, 'may not even be in the city.'

Woolston spread his hands. 'In this lousy weather, Mr Goldsteen? He'd be crazy to be here.'

He was a man you could really love. And to offer a man like that thanks, let alone some kind of reward, would be insulting. Robert drained his cup and said: 'This is a very fine cup of coffee. If you're not careful, you may find yourself stuck with a regular breakfast date.'

'I'd really like that, Mr Goldsteen.'

Robert wondered why. But there were gifts you didn't question. He picked up the interface and went slowly upstairs. He felt better. The news might be ominous, his pursuers half a step nearer, but he still felt better.

Up in his room, he connected the machine up to his computer and loaded his daughter's message. Then he paused, not yet ready to hit the key that would display her words on the screen. Why *was* he still in New York? Being there made him easier to find, more at risk. The fact was, he seemed to need to know he was no more than a subway ride away from Georg and the UN. That knowledge made him believe their project was safer. If there was some emergency, some idiot misunderstanding, he felt he could reach Georg personally and straighten it out. It was foolish, of course; but he felt right staying here.

He hit the return key. Words filled the screen. Colly said that there was a Russian trawler with elaborate radio equipment just arrived in Hellnar. She was pretending she thought this was only a coincidence; Robert wondered who she thought she was fooling. She went on to say that Flynn had found an excellent mooring, and that their calculations had worked out perfectly. The bomb was in position, and the second seabed unit. Now, if the Icelandic authorities arrived, the cover story was in working order: they were busy analysing strata, measuring sound wave distortion between the two units.

She had little else to say. The six-hour watches were tiring, and Flynn's drinking might be getting worse. Neither item was exactly a surprise. They all sent their love. She signed off.

Robert stared at the screen, wryly fingering his freshly shaved chin. *Weather lovely. Wish you were here.* One terrorist to another. *Auntie Gladys has a touch of sunstroke . . .*

Suddenly, his eyes filled with tears. He mopped at them angrily, and laboured downstairs to post his letter to Lily King.

On board the *Fimbulvetr* that morning, a priority radio message was received shortly before eleven. Discreetly worded, and given no signature or place of origin, it stated that, in accordance with the New York agreement, two official scientific observers were on their way. Arrival should be expected around four, and arrangements for their safe reception were requested.

Flynn took the signal down to the wardroom, where Colly was alone, finishing her mid-morning coffee. Werner had the watch on deck; Kassim, who had been on duty until six, was sleeping. Colly read the signal. She whistled softly.

'So they've actually got Fard's ultimatum. I guess I never really believed they would . . . And now they're taking us up on our offer. That's a relief. Once they see for themselves that we can't be shifted, maybe they won't feel they have to try.'

Flynn scratched his beard. 'I wouldn't count on that, darlin'.' He took the signal back, stared at it. 'Any bets on who they'll send?'

'One of each, surely. That's why we made it two. Only one, and they'd never have been able to agree on which. And they'll choose pretty senior guys, I reckon. After all, they're going to have to let them in on the most sensitive stuff there is.'

'Myself, I'd expect serving officers in the military. They'll have the technical background, *and* they'll be used to holding their tongues.'

'A pair of uptight service types . . .' She grimaced. 'At least we'll know where we are with them. Flynn – they're sure to want to go down and have a look at the bomb. Can you help Werner get the Beatle ready? And I'll fetch up a couple of wet suits later, in case they'd rather swim.'

After Flynn had gone she lingered a while over the coffee, thinking. Day two, and their first real test – two opposition agents, loaded with cameras and bugs and dirty tricks and what-all, tramping all over the ship. She'd been wrong the night before. There was more to this thing than simply watching and waiting.

This thing . . . She smiled, stirring her coffee and remembering back to 'this thing's' tiny, almost childlike beginning, two years before. An Oxford afternoon. Another summer, sunshine, heavy green foliage, midges crowding the shadows under the trees.

And the standard, cliché situation, so standard and so clichéd it had to be true – this handsome American woman in her bright cotton dress, this handsome German man in his white shirt and slacks, in a punt on the river. It still did happen. She with her fingers trailing in the water and he leaning handsomely on the varnished pole, as they glided along the narrow winding stream in the University Parks and ducked beneath low branches to the drowsy sound of wood pigeons and the distant click of cricket ball on bat.

Until suddenly:

'Christ, Werner, doesn't all this make you want to puke?'

And he, his English still very careful, 'Of course. But that is not, I think, a reasonable reaction.'

'Not reasonable? When all this goes on while half the world starves and the other half builds bigger and better bombs and bubblegum dispensers? While we tell the Indians and the Chinese they mustn't have refrigerators, because it's bad for the ozone layer, but just because we industrialised first we just turn down the airconditioning by a degree and think we're saving the world?'

'That is true.' He nodded seriously. 'The world, you see, is a very untidy place. But to puke is not reasonable; that will simply make it more untidy.'

She ignored his heavy German joke (she assumed it *was* a joke). 'So what would you rather I did?'

He allowed a pause, heaving the pole up and bringing it forward, but leaving the muddy end trailing in the water. 'For us, Colly, for you and me, it is pointless simply to complain about the mess. We must either accept it, or – ' he thrust the pole down again ' – or we must do something big. *Big*. Somebody must. We can. Why not us?'

Something big. She remembered thinking how dumb he was. Dumb, but very sexy.

That night, in her bed, they'd made love for the first time. It was no big deal – something comfortably traditional. The traditional sequel to their traditional afternoon on the traditional river. And afterwards, in her narrow English bed, the light from the lamp outside in the street shining in an even narrower strip on the leprous plaster of her ceiling, they talked. Their talk was no less traditional, to begin with. But it did not continue so.

'What's needed,' she began, picking up on their conversation in the punt, 'is something *visible*. Something to make people wake up and see reason. But they're so fucking stuck in a rut it'll need something really obvious to shift them. Obvious and obnoxious. A war. Some catastrophe.'

'How big a catastrophe? If the floods in Bangladesh have not made them see reason, what will?'

A car hummed past in the street. Then silence. Werner often thought things out, carefully working out the English phrasing in his mind, before presenting his thoughts to her.

'No, Colly,' he said at last. 'I do not agree that a catastrophe will do the trick. We talk now of American and Russian nations, do we not? Other nations have bombs, of course, and other nations like to be rich. But it is America, and now the states of Russia, that keep the great big money machine running. Without them, nothing. So, then, it is their leaders who must be made to see reason.'

'That's stupid. *People* count, Werner. Even in Russia, they have elections now. And they're all turning into greedy little consumers, just like the West. How many individuals care about the global environment? It's the people who have to be frightened into action.'

'Not true. Even *glasnost* has its limits. I speak of what I know, OK? Wenceslas Square; the Baltic States. In the East, it is still the leaders who decide such things, weapons or consumer goods. The leaders decide how much power to let the people have. Too much, and they go down, and the army chooses some nice, well behaved leaders instead.'

She shook her head, unconvinced. 'And as for the US, what's needed is enough Congressmen worried about re-election. About what the people think. The voters. Then – '

'Listen, Colly. Congressmen worry about jobs. Employment. And every general tells them that no Star Wars means fewer employments.' She felt him tense with the need to convince her. 'Now, Colly, you know the generals lie, and so do I. That money would not disappear, it would be spent on something else. Hospitals. Food for the starving. Aid – *proper* aid, not just food but technology, irrigation systems. We know this, and we are not so very clever. But I will tell you something else. I have been to America and I know. I tell you that an American's greatest freedom is the freedom not to think intelligently about anything except making money. And that is not clever at all.'

Her thigh was going to sleep. She shifted it out from under his leg. 'They could cut taxes. Lower interest rates. Make it easier for the Third World to repay their debts. Hell,' she began to see the logic of the scenario, 'they could *write off* the Third World debts.' But there was a snag. 'What about the Russians? What is it *they* think intelligently about?'

He shifted on to one elbow. 'I do not have the usual tidy, unkind things to say about the Russians. Maybe they think mostly about not thinking. But I will tell you this – every Soviet leader knows that as long as there is an arms race, Russia will be poor.'

'So why don't they quit? It takes two to make a race.'

Werner reached for his cigarettes. 'Fear. Lack of trust. Remember they no longer have the Warsaw Pact. They still remember what happened fifty years ago. And they have never let us Germans forget that our country was responsible. And the Soviet Union is a young nation. It is filled with youthful pride and the need to stand tall in the world.'

'So's the USA a young nation.'

'Just as I say.' His lighter flared in the darkness. 'Both these nations are big, but young. They are both frightened, but proud. Generals know this, and use it. But it is still leaders who lead. East or west, through secret police or manipulating ordinary people's greed, the result is the same. Leaders lead and people follow. And so it is that I tell you it is the leaders who must be made to see reason. Then the people can follow down a new path.'

He blew out smoke, carefully away from her, in a thin stream. She didn't like him smoking, and in a few months he would have given it up.

She sensed him smiling. 'What's the joke?'

He laughed softly. 'Just two men. It should not be so difficult, waking up just two men.' He turned his face back towards her. 'Let's start tomorrow. A toddle, would you not say?'

'A *toddle*?'

'A toddle. I heard it this morning. It is English, is it not?'

'Maybe it is. So darned English I don't know what the hell it means.'

He turned his head away again, smoked in silence. He wasn't pleased. He'd liked his new word, *toddle*. He was so determined to make his English correct. Just as he was now determined to find a way of ending the division of the world into poor and rich. The resources devoted to the arms race and uncontrolled consumerism could solve that problem – many commentators had pointed that out. It was just a matter of finding a way to make those two leaders see sense.

He was determined in everything he did. That, and his foreign sexiness that turned women's heads in the street, was why Colly liked him. He was solemn, but he believed that he had things to accomplish. She too believed that she had things to accomplish. She didn't yet know what, but until she did she could coast along in Werner's wake.

It was her way. She wasn't proud of it, but time was, out in California, when she'd coasted along in her father's wake. High School physics, the same at college. Then she'd made the break, gone to England, switched to oceanography. Got out from under. Stints on research ships in the Red Sea and such places. Deep hot brine pools. Underwater volcanic activity. She kept busy.

But she still had this tendency to coast. While her father worked tirelessly for SANE, and on laser fusion, and notched up Nobel Prizes, she, with all her advantages – perhaps too many – was content to teach her students, do her routine research work, and wait for God to lean down and touch her.

And then, two weeks later, God forgave her her advantages.

Preparing a weekend seminar on underwater volcanism, she was reading back over the literature concerning the 1973 eruption on Heimaey, one of the Westman Islands off the coast of Iceland. Much of the material, although dramatic, was familiar. Iceland lay directly on the mid-Atlantic fault, where the sea floor was cracked and pushing apart from a spreading ridge, widening the Atlantic by a couple of centimetres every year. The island's turbulent geophysical nature – earthquakes, hot springs, active volcanoes – was basic knowledge for every student in earth sciences. But a marginal pencilled cross-reference in one of the journals, drawing attention to an issue of *The Times* in September of that year, took her off on a fresh tack; the *Times* piece, when she looked it up, turned out to be based on a well-reasoned paper by two acknowledged experts, Colgate from the New Mexico Institute of Mining and Technology, and Sigurgeirsson, from the University of Iceland. When she tracked down their original paper in *Nature*, none of the information was precisely new to her. The writers' conclusions, though, were fascinating.

She checked with her head of department. He agreed with Colgate and Sigurgeirsson – it was very fortunate, he concurred, that they had been on Heimaey to discourage the local emergency team from trying to control the lava flow in the harbour with high explosive, designed to mix water with the molten lava and cool it enough to make it solidify. He shook his head wryly. The results would almost certainly have been catastrophic. And, to be perfectly frank, he doubted if he himself would have foreseen the danger of a fuel/coolant interaction.

Colly left his office trembling with excitement. In the crumpled photocopy she carried was information that gave her the power to change the course of history.

Typically, she slept on it. She slept on it for an entire further week, while she ordered her thoughts, checked out the details. Then she told Werner what she had discovered. She chose to tell him in the churchyard of St Thomas the Martyr, a tiny oasis of green sandwiched between the GPO sorting office and the site of the car-breaker's yard. They often went there to eat their lunch, escaping the summer tourists.

The sun was shining. It seemed, in her memory, that the sun had shone every day that summer. Werner heard her out, the apple in his hand uneaten, his jaw very still. After she'd done he was thoughtful, staring past her. Then he polished the apple on his sleeve and bit into it.

He swallowed. 'This eruption you make happen – how big is it?'

His casualness disconcerted her. 'Huge. At least ten times Krakatau. Far bigger than Tambora. Maybe the biggest ever. Makes St Helens look like a firecracker – and that baby released a cool 17×10^{17} joules over a period of only nine hours. That's effectively twenty-seven thousand Hiroshima-sized bombs. And we're talking far bigger than that. It's an exponential reaction, you see – self-sustaining until the reservoir is fully depleted.'

He still seemed unimpressed. 'And dirty?'

'That depends.' She considered, brushing at the grass that tickled the backs of her bare legs. 'If a nuclear starter is used, then obviously there'll be *some* fallout. But it'll be massively diluted. I don't see any serious problem. Less pollution than Chernobyl.'

He chewed noisily. 'And you'd do it to Iceland. Poor little Iceland.'

She didn't understand his mood. He seemed to be wilfully missing the point. 'Poor northern hemisphere, you mean.'

'Ah yes. Of course. The dust cloud. No sunlight . . .' Sardonically, he studied the bite mark in his apple. 'You choose Iceland because any big eruption there will affect the whole northern hemisphere, especially the temperate and high latitudes. And you choose the northern hemisphere because you hate it so.'

'Judas Priest, Werner – what the hell's got into you? It has to be Iceland, because that's where the faults are accessible. It's just luck that the Rich North will be affected.'

He held up a calming hand. 'Very well. You do not *hate* the northern hemisphere. But you think it should be taught a lesson.'

'Its leaders need to be woken up, Werner.' She controlled herself. 'Russia and America. I thought we'd agreed on that. And we get Europe as a bonus.' Suddenly, she realised what was bugging him.

She'd thought of it first. He was the man, still chauvinistic in his slightly old-fashioned, East European way. But she, a mere woman, had picked up his ball and run off with it. This was his way of saving face; pointing out objections and making her spell it out to him.

He looked straight in her eyes. 'Do you have any real idea, liebling, exactly what this dust cloud will do? How long it will last? What will happen?'

'Certainly I do.' She met his gaze. 'The dust will have a high sulphuric acid content, spreading droplets through the stratosphere; it will effectively block sunlight at high latitudes for three years, minimum. On the North American continent, that will mean Canada under permafrost, no summer at all down as far as Boston. Complete social breakdown. And in Northern Europe the same thing. The death of the central grain-growing regions. Maybe ice in the Black Sea, even. Famine. Plague. Also the crippling of the industrial base. An energy crisis. Outright revolution.

'But the tropics won't be much affected at all. Some regions might even benefit. A slight cooling could stop the edges of deserts drying out; the monsoon might be enhanced. Peasants and people who live close to the land will manage fine.'

He shook his head. 'You can really do all this? You really *want* to do all this?'

'Please, Werner. Listen to me. A single explosion, correctly positioned on the seabed near a fault line, with the crust at the right thickness, will be quite enough.' He tried to interrupt, but she wouldn't let him. 'I thought you understood. It's the sudden mixing of water and molten lava in large quantities that does the trick. You know as well as I do how hot that magma is. Eleven hundred Celsius.'

He tried again, but she was in lecture mode, inexorable, the facts welling up from her brain.

'When that mixes with water, the water doesn't stand a chance. It gets blasted into steam, while the magma hardly cools at all. The water *explodes* into steam, making the crater bigger and scattering lava like a bomb; the hole gets bigger, so there's more mixing, more water explodes into steam, and so on until all the magma has gone. Which only takes a few seconds. Nothing can stop it, if the initial charge is located correctly. It doesn't even *have* to be nuclear, if you've got enough old-fashioned HE.'

'Please.' At last he succeeded in checking her. 'Please, Colly. I do not mean to question the possibility of such an eruption. I simply wondered if it was reasonable. To do such a terrible thing . . . to cause so much human misery . . . for whatever reason. Could you do it, Colly? Could you?'

'I don't know.' Her fervour had abated. She smiled, shrugged, stretched her legs out in the grass. 'Probably not. But here's the beauty of it, Werner. *It doesn't matter.* We don't have to do the terrible thing.' She paused, dusted cake crumbs from her lap, smiled at him again. '*We only have to be in a position to do it.* We only have to be able to threaten to do it. Convince just two men that we *might* do it.'

His eyes widened. She watched his expression change, open like a flower, become beatific.

'*Nun aber sprichst du die Wahrheit*,' he whispered. 'You speak the truth, Colly. Anything we want. Anything. We only have to threaten.'

He leaned back, amazed, his head against a gravestone. 'We only have to threaten.'

He looked up, cupped his hands around his mouth, and called through the yew tree branches at the blue summer sky. 'We only have to threaten . . . !'

Beyond the churchyard railings, unimpressed, the traffic ground on by. He began to laugh. He spread his arms, laughing until the worn stones of St Thomas's rang. At first nervously, then with more abandon, she joined in his laughter. Anything they wanted. Anything. They only had to threaten . . . Soon they were both helpless. And yet, in some part of her, she was curiously afraid.

He stopped laughing. Suddenly sombre, he looked across at her until she became serious also. He had her full attention. He was the man, and in his own mind at least he was in charge of the situation again.

'Two important considerations,' he said. 'First, this threat must be real. And second, it must be believed.'

And then she knew why she had become afraid of him. For the past week her scheme had been a toy for her to play with. Mind games. Such a mighty project, holding half the world to ransom, its absurd grandeur all just a game. But now the game was Werner's.

She'd given it to him, and in his hands the game would no longer be a game. He would make it happen.

And she would help him – as an equal partner.

She was no longer coasting . . .

An autumn of snail-like progress followed. Calculation and re-calculation. Seabed profiles, seismic charts. The geophysics was vital – it would have to convince the highest levels of government scientific advisers. And then the practicalities. A ship would be needed. A crew. A pretext to be in Icelandic waters. And a bomb . . .

And most important of all, after the bomb was in position, and after the advisers had been convinced, and through them the world leaders had been woken to reality, what then? What to demand? With half the world as their hostage, what demands were big enough?

They discussed the problem endlessly. Often the subject became absurd to her, the ultimate in *folies de grandeur*, but his Germanic seriousness never faltered. Obviously they wanted nothing for themselves. But how about trillions of dollars for the starving? Or total mutual disarmament? Why not both? She would giggle then, and he would frown.

Their basic difficulty was to devise concessions that would hold. Agreements made under duress could be reneged upon. Further-more, at least in the USA, agreements had to be voted on, funded, in some democratic manner ratified. For a while, it seemed that the only concessions that could realistically be exacted were maybe a few million dollars in cash, the release of a few political prisoners. And neither gain was equal to the occasion.

For a while, indeed, the project became to Colly just a game again, unreal, a harmless conversation piece for the long winter evenings. She felt safer. She taught her classes and waited for Werner to lose interest.

Christmas came. Disgusted as always by the seasonal festival of love and greed, Werner changed his approach. The demands could wait: he started to think seriously about funding. With proper funding the ship and her crew would be no problem. Even bomb components could be obtained, from abroad. Israel perhaps, if sufficient money were available. He began asking her heavy questions about her father's financial situation. She told him she didn't know, that she'd never really thought about it.

She could also have claimed, and truthfully, that she didn't really think about the project any more, either. But her subconscious stayed busy. So that, one morning in January, she woke very early and sat up instantly, straight up in bed, her eyes wide, her heart pounding. In her sleep, on the subject she believed she no longer thought about, she had received a revelation.

'The threat would be too terrible,' she said aloud. 'No leader would dare to make it public.'

She pictured the panic any announcement would cause: riots in the streets, millions in their cars, whole populations fleeing blindly south.

'Nobody could even talk about such a threat,' she whispered to herself. 'Certainly we couldn't – not if we wanted to gain anything from it. And no government leader could . . .' And even afterwards, for governments to make anything public would be to encourage the risk of similar action by some other group of – she used the word in her mind, for the first time in the context of the project – *terrorists*.

The room was bitterly cold, frost thick on the inside of the windowpanes. She shivered. Her flat wasn't bad, except that, being British, it lacked proper heating. She lay back on her pillow, pulled the quilt up under her chin.

What if the threat could be made in secret? Distantly, she heard whistling, and the clatter of bottles as the milkman came up the short garden path. *Secret negotiations.* A car passed. Somewhere a radio was playing Bach. *After all, any concessions gained in secret negotiations couldn't later be disclaimed.* She curled up, excitedly hugging her knees. *Ratification? No difficulty, assuming concessions that would be electorally popular in the first place.*

And then, in a second flash of revelation, she received the answer to the question of what those concessions must be.

Her doubts and fears disappeared. On that drab grey morning, in her drab grey room, she was fired with bright courage, with certainty, and with joyful determination. At last she had found her purpose, the end towards which her whole life had been directed. Just because many of the world's evils – conspicuous consumption, the tragedy of over-population – were beyond her, that didn't mean she was powerless. She knew now the great thing she must accomplish.

She was her father's child. She believed, like him, that the dangers of nuclear extinction had scarcely abated. She'd heard his arguments a thousand times, and had elaborated them herself: nuclear disarmament, unless total, was simply cosmetic, a technique for treacherously reassuring frightened peoples. The bombs and rockets continued to be built. Nothing changed. Half the world starved, while a fraction of the money needed to give them security was squandered on armaments. Sea levels rose, while resources that could have been used to build flood defences were wasted by the military.

And yet to hope for total, immediate superpower nuclear disarmament, a complete diversion of resources from the military to tackle the real environmental problems threatening humankind, was unrealistic. What about Israel? India? Maybe Pakistan and South Africa and God knew how many other countries. Neither Americans nor Soviets would feel safe with that. So what remained?

The answer, now, was obvious. *Partial*, balanced reductions in the arms budgets. Maybe by thirty per cent, on each side. A proportion of the savings – maybe half – publicly committed to the United Nations Environment Programme, putting it on a war footing, a war against environmental catastrophe. She remembered the disgust she'd felt, back in '89, when Margaret Thatcher had flamboyantly announced that Britain was doubling its contribution to UNEP – increasing it to a munificent three million pounds a year. At a time when Britain's economy was running a *surplus* of fifteen *billion* pounds a year. Admittedly that had been in 1989, and such surpluses were a thing of the past. But, at its new level, the same relative greed still operated.

What UNEP had achieved on peanuts was magnificent; what the organisation might achieve with real resources could scarcely be imagined. Meanwhile, the superpowers would still have enough weaponry for everyone to feel safe. And when the years passed and war failed to break out, the message might sink in. More reductions in wasteful arms expenditure would surely follow. The arms race would be put into reverse.

And how about some icing on the cake? Fard's pet dream: a complete ban on nuclear testing. The more subtle strategists in SANE had worked it all out years ago. In the short term it would halt the race to develop more sophisticated technological weaponry, releasing money for other uses. Nuclear proliferation would be checked. And in the long term, as stocks of weapons decayed and could not be replaced, a comprehensive test ban would reduce to zero the insane capacities for mutual overkill.

And all of it would be easy to agree – the test ban easiest of all. It would be popular. Simple to verify – a nuclear blast is a nuclear blast is a nuclear blast. No fiddling about calculating kilotonnage and quibbling about fine points of the agreement. In both super-power states, a test ban, vigorously supported by the president, would easily gain approval. It would halt Star Wars research, but that was more or less a dead duck anyway. The shift in emphasis from death to life ought to be equally appealing, since it wouldn't cost a penny. Half the savings from the military budgets could be used to bolster the home economies . . . everybody would gain, except the generals. So, tough on the generals.

They'd fight, of course. Try to convince the leaders that it wouldn't work. But when the alternative was the real and comprehensible threat of the long winter, the generals' arguments would never win out. The leaders would listen, and weigh the alternatives, and concede . . .

She and Werner were late that morning. Over breakfast, hunched round the open door of the lit gas oven in Werner's kitchen, she explained what they must ask for, and why. He listened, questioned her gently, accepted her answers. Both of them understood that the balance of authority between them had shifted, for the last time. The plan was hers, now.

And now, neither of them found this change important. After all, the price they would both pay – their lives – was equal and indivisible.

She remembered that morning as the first occasion when they spoke openly of dying for the sake of their dream. Not that there was ever in their minds any possibility that they might be driven to carry out their monstrous threat – its mechanisms must be set up genuinely, down to the smallest detail, but only in order to convince the opposition's experts. Only as a bluff that nobody would dare to call. And if, impossibly, the bluff failed, then the entire scheme failed, and any action after that would be mere vengeance, pointless and inexcusable.

But whether it failed or not, they both recognised the retribution that would be exacted. They would die. Men would hunt them down and kill them. Official murderers. Escape from the ship, from the immediate danger, might (just *might*) be possible. But where to? The world was small. Retribution was the only certainty.

It was not a certainty that they spoke of lightly, even on that first eager morning. They were not death-wished people. But she remembered that it gave their lives together a fresh intensity, a fresh seriousness and a fresh capacity for recklessness and laughter.

Their plans progressed. February passed, then March and April. A suitable ship was found, soon to come on the market. Locations in Icelandic waters were analysed. Eventually a cove with the ideal combination of underwater features was discovered, on the Thórsnes peninsula. Only the fissionable materials for the bomb, and the necessary funds, remained elusive. Oxford possessed plutonium, but probably not enough, and certainly not all in one place. Stealing it seemed out of the question.

And then, on May 24, Ruth Graham died.

Even now, fourteen months later, Colly still deeply regretted the evasions that had kept her in England during the few short months of her mother's dying. Admittedly her father, obeying Ruth, had played down the seriousness of her illness. But Colly had known it all the same, had heard it behind every transatlantic call, had read it between the lines in every letter. And still she'd chosen to stay away.

It had been her father, she realised, who had taught her to fear her emotions, as he feared his. But that was no excuse. She'd had eleven years away from him. And still she'd found reasons to stay in England, fired up with saving the world, rather than risk going to Maine to hold a dying woman's hand.

She'd gone there only when it was safe. After her mother was dead, for the memorial service. A white clapboard New England church against the wide, cloudless New England sky. And inside, a wheezy organ, and spring lilacs competing with the smell of dusty hassocks and hot, varnished woodwork. The minister's eulogy was simple, and short, and it allowed her to weep without shame. Many local people were there, far more than Colly had names for. But they'd known Ruth personally, and loved her, every one.

Afterwards, not expecting it, returning beside her father to the old grey house with the sea in all its windows, she found him close to death; without purpose, without identity, without hope. Her dear, troublesome old father; brilliant, egotistical, the tireless campaigner, brave and innocent, brought down by bereavement to emptiness and despair.

She'd gone to Maine with no thought of involving him in her plans. On his past record of peaceful protest, he'd have opposed them vehemently. But she found in him bitterness instead of peace, and a deadly inertia. In the days immediately following the memorial service he did little except sit on the porch at the front of the house, watching her keep busy; watching her prepare meals, serve them, take them away uneaten; watching her swim, and lie in the sun . . . watching her, and occasionally weeping. His silence was an appeal. It was as if he were begging her for a reason, not to *go on* living, but simply to *have* lived.

She imagined it must be a common enough plea. She didn't want to fail him as she had failed her mother. And she came slowly to realise that it was a plea to which she might be able to respond.

She talked to him. Aside from his bereavement, he grieved also for his work. Even that had been betrayed. Once upon a time it had been inconceivable that his pioneering research in laser technology could be put to warlike ends. Now that work was central to US armaments technology. The responsibility wore him down. It made laughable his work for SANE. He'd been pissing into a wind finally of his own devising.

She began with caution. Patiently, in the sun-filled parlour with its rag rugs, creaking wicker furniture, and the children playing on the sand beneath its open windows, she showed him a possible way through his hopelessness. They walked on the beach in the long summer evenings, sometimes quiet for hours on end, simply together, their footprints stretching for ever in the golden, un-marked sand.

A gale came up, and they sheltered in the house, feeling its wooden walls shudder, and watching fearfully as waves marched up the level shore towards them. Such summer gales had been unheard of until recently; with the rising sea level, the most obvious sign of the anthropogenic global warming, the years that lay ahead of the old house were surely few. This time the waves stopped short. But in the morning there was dry white salt on every windowpane, and sand behind the upstairs shutters. They read it as an omen.

Back in Oxford the long vacation was beginning. She sent for Werner. He came reluctantly, still busy with ship specifications and just disappointed in a will o' the wisp chase after a source of fissionable materials suggested to him by some shadowy organisation of east European exiles. But the Maine house delighted him. Its bare-boards brand of luxury beguiled his puritanical soul. He discovered that capitalist wealth could buy more than gold-plated Cadillacs, even in America. Also, the two men hit it off. Thirty-five years apart, and political strangers, they still made sense to each other. They were both scientists. It was Werner's combination of passion and practicality that finally convinced her father. That and – Colly felt certain – the children playing in the sand.

Once Robert was convinced, his lethargy disappeared. He threw himself totally into the project. He even re-established his consultancy with Bell Labs, for the facilities it brought him, the access to databases and library material. He hoped for (unofficial) access to plutonium transportation schedules, once he was back on the computer networks. He spoke, only half-flippantly, of organising a heist.

Inevitably, he'd soon taken the project over. Once this would have angered her. Now, like Werner, she found such matters unimportant. Robert had strengths neither of them could match. He knew his way around. She was amazed, also, in purely practical terms, by the amounts of money at his disposal. Telling his attorney he planned to go back to settle in England, he emptied his share portfolio, consolidated his life's savings, even raised mortgages on the Maine house and the New Jersey apartment. More than three-quarters of a million dollars – four hundred thousand of which were soon to go on the *Fimbulvetr* alone, then called the *William Wilson*, bought from Britain's Environmental Research Council.

The ultimatum, too, came to be his. Right at the beginning, she and Werner had asked him to describe, out of his unique knowledge and experience, the most effective, politically realistic step towards shifting resources from weaponry into environmental husbandry that he could imagine. Reassuringly, his answer had matched theirs: a total test ban.

Second, the threat: at the end of fourteen days, should the treaty not have been signed, and the diversion of resources to UNEP not have been made public, a small nuclear device already in position off the Icelandic coast would be detonated, bringing about an autocatalytic mixing of water and molten magma, a fuel/coolant interaction that would initiate a catastrophic volcanic eruption. The resultant cloud of dust and acid droplets, circling the Earth high in the stratosphere, would last for at least three years, blotting out the sun and freezing the high and temperate northern latitudes. The countries that would be devastated would be those that, by and large, had been responsible for the destruction of the global environment in the twentieth century through their greed and ill-considered industrialisation. At a stroke, the increasing global warming and attendant climatic disruption would be halted. As snow fell on the frozen land, ice would build up, engulfing Boston, Amsterdam, Berlin, the Black Sea ports. But further south, the poor countries of the Third World would be scarcely affected. There would be an opportunity for them to think again, to avoid following the mistaken path of over-development followed blindly in the North, and to develop their own economies, free from crippling debts to bankers that no longer existed, more soundly, more in tune with the global environment.

Third, the documentation: comprehensive scientific evidence of the threat's viability, included in the ultimatum with full technical details of the Icelandic end of the operation. Security measures there were described, and an invitation extended for two unarmed observers to visit the ship and satisfy themselves that all was as the ultimatum claimed. The nuclear device would have two triggers. One would operate automatically following any great shock or change in atmospheric pressure, the kind of change that would be caused by the detonation of explosives nearby, and there was a manual over-ride, both to de-activate the mechanism (for servicing, for example) and to trigger the bomb directly if the crew felt sufficiently threatened.

It was at this stage that Robert contributed the project's mythology. In a final section of the ultimatum, drawing on his knowledge of Norse legends, he introduced them for the first time to the mystical Ragnarok event: the end of the world in fire and ice, the long winter, and the world's eventual rebirth. Magically apt, it spoke to them with pain and passion of the timelessness of human imagination, and of human striving. Robert included it in the hope that it might speak similarly to the proud, fearful understandings of the two most powerful men on Earth . . .

Colly stirred her long-cold coffee. Soon, now, they would know if their hopes were vain. Twelve days, at the most, remained. Perhaps less. If the ship's elaborate security failed, or if the opposition attacked in spite of it, perhaps a lot less.

Fewer days to wait, also, if their hopes were rewarded and the men in Geneva came to quick agreement, acting on new instructions from Moscow and Washington. But Colly doubted that. Bureaucracies moved slowly. Face must be preserved. A fortnight was the period her father had thought reasonable; but he'd also expected the opposition to use every day of the time they were given. And twelve days still remained. It was going to be a long wait.

She got up slowly, left the wardroom, went forward to collect the wet suits for their afternoon visitors. She couldn't imagine what they would be like, but the prospect of their arrival, though threatening, was also welcome. One more hurdle surmounted. And a break in the already dull routine.

5

On the *Fimbulvetr*'s deck that Thursday afternoon, the second day of the countdown, Kassim Latif was also impatient. His timescale, though, was shorter than Colly's. He was spending his last day on the ship, and was anxiously awaiting the night, so that he could leave. He had arranged to take the watch from midnight to six, because he needed the darkness.

He would have preferred to leave sooner: yesterday's news of the Russian trawler worried him. If he could have gone last night, he would have. He had been ready. But all through the night watch, it seemed, one or other of his companions was restless, not adjusted to the new routine. He wanted them all to be soundly asleep when he left – not so soundly asleep that they couldn't be woken by the carefully planned noise of his departure, but sleepy enough to give him a vital head start.

In itself, the delay was unimportant. *Il Signore di Genova* understood that he had to choose his moment, and a day or two here or there didn't matter. It was the arrival of the Russian trawler that made the difference. He had to get away in the dark, unobserved, and he didn't want the beach crawling with Soviet agents. On the other hand, their presence might help to confuse his companions about his disappearance. On balance, Kassim would rather his exit was clear and they were left unconfused. But it was gone midday now, and so far no agents had shown themselves. He was tempted to believe that the trawler was in Hellnar for some other, quite innocent reason.

The weather that afternoon was good, a few feathers of cirrus in a high clear sky. The ship lay in the shadow of the black lava cliffs, its reflection flawless in the mirror-smooth water. A second windless night had stilled even the small rustling of waves outside the cove, so that the only sounds in the vast hemisphere of shore and sky were the cries of seabirds. A bucket dropped on *Fimbulvetr*'s deck raised a clatter that echoed startlingly round the shore.

For the moment, Kassim was alone on deck. With the sun now high overhead, the air in the cove was pleasantly warm. But Kassim's clothes were as careful as ever, clerical grey flannels and a crisp white shirt, his hair neatly braided beneath a turban that was, today, immaculate. His false identity irked him, but he kept it up attentively. He was an attentive young man. He was also highly intelligent. These were the qualities that Il Signore had noticed. Kassim had long been able to handle plastique, and at fifty metres could take out the driver of a car with armoured side panels, passing at 90 kph. Many men could do that, however, and Il Signore had noticed that Kassim had other qualities.

Raised a Christian, the spoiled son of a rich Bombay shipping agent, he had abruptly left the university after stabbing to death a policeman, armed only with his lathi, in a minor student riot. His father arranged passage for him on a German cargo ship bound for Southampton via the Suez Canal, making it clear that thereafter the young thug was on his own. Britain did not interest Kassim; he left the ship in Cairo. His first job in Egypt, with his excellent English and aversion to manual labour, was as a brothel tout; but he soon progressed to less orthodox, better paid work. His Moroccan mother was entirely his own invention: usually claimed to have been a cheap Tangier whore, she made him more acceptable in those coastal areas of the southern Mediterranean where he mostly found his work. The region was increasingly in turmoil, with many refugees from further south, where the rains no longer seemed to come at all. There was good work smuggling these new boat people across to the European shores of the Mediterranean (and even better work in taking their money and abandoning them, or worse, at sea; Kassim took particular delight in offering his expert help to families that included pubescent girls).

It had been while Kassim was on a trip to Sicily, running raw heroin as well as warm bodies (though they didn't know it, the only reason the bodies were still warm was that they provided excellent cover for the heroin operation), that he'd come to the attention of Il

Signore di Genova. Himself an intermediary with ill-defined allegiances, Il Signore staffed and ran an extensive European network of spies and hatchet men. It was said that his services were always available to the highest bidder, but this was not true. In fact Il Signore sanctioned major operations only against the enemies of a second, nameless man, known only as the Dreamer. The Dreamer had many enemies, and if his few friends were occasionally hit also, in a modest way, by Il Signore di Genova – well, it was good cover, and it helped keep Il Signore in funds.

For Kassim specialist training followed, at a camp in northern Greece run by two ex-KGB majors who liked the climate there, and the other advantages of capitalism. Ostensibly, the camp was for refugees, displaced by the upheavals to the south. Its more permanent occupants were, indeed, refugees; others, like Kassim, were just passing through.

Then, finally, Kassim's Indian educational qualifications were refurbished, references were forged, and a place was found for him at a college in Oxford. Not one of the colleges of the university, but a lesser institution specialising in technical qualifications. But still, Oxford was Oxford, and in addition to the value to the network of a degree in mining and engineering, should he stay long enough to obtain one, there was value to Il Signore's organisation in having him there, with his eyes and ears open, to identify people of interest to the long-term aims of the Dreamer. The identity established for him as a devout Hindu would give him contacts, especially within the British peace movement. Such contacts could be useful, and must not be squandered for any short-term gain.

And so it was that his path crossed with those of Colly and Werner. Word was passed on to Kassim from Italy, where Il Signore knew many things that were supposed to be secret, of a German mineralogist, a Dr Werner Dietrich, who appeared to be curiously interested in sources of high-grade plutonium. He attended a few of Dr Dietrich's lectures – nobody knew or cared whether he had a right to be there. And during one of the after-lecture discussions Kassim happened to mention that his father worked in India's atomic energy industry. Furthermore, that Latif senior did not approve of India developing a nuclear deterrent while so many of the people went hungry. While nuclear power for peaceful purposes was, of course, highly desirable, not least because such sources of energy made no contribution to the greenhouse effect, the world's biggest evil was the proliferation of nuclear weapons. Did not Dr Dietrich agree with him? And that India should show the world her moral leadership of the Third World by condemning such proliferation?

The German's interest was unmistakably caught. They met in a pub later that week, by chance it seemed to Werner, where they chatted at the bar, Kassim indulging only in tomato juice, both jostled by other drinkers, both slightly uneasy with this very British custom.

Eventually Dr Dietrich used concern about Kassim's future career as an excuse for pumping him about his mythical father. The Indian was innocently forthcoming; his father was indeed a man of education, and with great technical skills and experience. His department was Procurement and Disposal, and he ought to have been its head. But he had been passed over for promotion because he lacked the right connections. He was not a bitter man, but the corruption of Indian society was hard to accept. It would be the same, regrettably, for Kassim himself when he returned to India. Without good family connections . . . He shrugged. It was an unjust and corrupt society.

Dealing with Westerners was easy, like taking candy from children. An invitation to tea in Dr Dietrich's flat followed, where he met for the first time the American woman, Dr Graham. Over foul English fruit cake the conversation was general, but touched inevitably upon the climatic situation in India and around the world, and the arms race, about which he professed strong views. He mentioned his religion, and his desire to work for peace.

Too late, he sensed Dr Dietrich's withdrawal. The German was suspicious. Kassim had been over-confident, in too much of a hurry, trying too hard. He eased off.

Over the next few weeks he concentrated on the woman. He despised her. Like all women, sex clouded her judgement. She might pretend, for the German's sake, to be merely amused by this funny little brown student, but he often caught her eyeing the flatness of his belly, his well-muscled chest, the jeans tight across his thighs. He flattered her, therefore, continually asked her opinion, and allowed himself to be taken to concerts of unpleasant western music.

Dr Dietrich, meanwhile, was checking up on him. Kassim's contacts reported that inquiries had been made, through his college. He was unconcerned. A father had been established as part of his new identity, with an address in Lahore, where fortunately India's principal nuclear research facility was located. Closer investigation, at India House in London, for example, would draw an unsurprising blank. Staff lists of sensitive nuclear installations are not available to casual callers.

So far, of course, he had no idea what the two scientists were up to. But clearly they were planning something concerning fissionable materials, and therefore outside the law; so he continued to play the earnest, slightly comic young Asian, and let them take their time. Sooner or later they'd get round to it.

And when, finally, in mid-November, after several more weeks sizing him up, they did get round to it – purely hypothetically, omitting all specifics – it was better than his wildest dreams. Overwhelmed, he stalled frantically, claiming the understandable need to consult his father; not sure that even Il Signore could handle their requirements. Such things would not be cheap, he said. Dr Dietrich replied that he had not expected them to be.

That night he requested an urgent meeting with Il Signore. It took place in a Paris café two days later. Kassim described what was required, and went on to explain the picture he had established of himself and his imaginary father. Il Signore stated himself – or someone he acted for – as able to supply, but doubtful of the merits of the project. It was against the arms race. The Dreamer rather liked the arms race – for the first time, Il Signore openly acknowledged to Kassim the existence of the Dreamer. What was in it for him?

Kassim told him. Power. North Africa as Europe's new centre of wealth and influence. He'd given the question a great deal of thought. And wasn't anything that was good for North Africa good for the Dreamer? Who else was there? Mubarak? Surely not.

Il Signore was intrigued. A telephone call to an unlisted Libyan number confirmed matters. Provided that Kassim could guarantee his own presence on the crazy team, the ingredients for a small and relatively basic atomic device, readily assembled by anyone with technical expertise, could be made available. No problem, Kassim said lightly. The woman would welcome him on board. If the German objected, she'd talk him round.

Kassim and *Il Signore* discussed a suitable price. One hundred thousand pounds to compensate a disenchanted Indian for the corruption of a society which had failed to recognise his natural abilities seemed not unreasonable. It was high enough to show that Kassim's father was not to be bought cheap, but low enough (although sufficient to go a very long way in India) not to frighten off what Kassim suspected to be a financially limited Oxford team. And, a nice touch, the money had to be delivered in good time, to allow Kassim's 'father' to disappear before the ultimatum was presented, and the authorities got wind of Kassim's involvement.

He reported back to them. He was told they must consult a third partner. Less than a week later, over dinner at Brown's, he was introduced to a sharp-eyed old man, Dr Graham's father. Werner was not present. The restaurant was crowded, as always; deafeningly noisy, an ideal place for the business under discussion. It was to be Kassim's severest ordeal.

Professor Graham had chosen a table in a corner, under uncomfortably dangling ferns, but away from the loudest of the music. At first Kassim was uneasy, not sure whether to present himself as a hard-headed entrepreneur or as an idealistic peace-and-love freak. The old man solved the difficulty for him.

Once they had ordered, he sat back calmly and fixed Kassim with a cold, shrewd gaze. 'The money you ask for is no problem,' he said. 'Obviously the sum is extortionate, but that was to be expected. At least it gives us some idea of the kind of people we are dealing with.'

Kassim attempted a rearguard. 'We are men of honour, my father and I. No matter how small the amount had been, we − '

'Quite so. And now my daughter tells me you wish to join us in our dangerous enterprise.'

Adjusting rapidly, Kassim decided that some slight sanctimoniousness would be in character. 'The money is for my father, sir. This other thing, the joining, I tell you, is my own. I do it for the world.'

At that moment the wine arrived, obscuring Professor Graham's response. While the bottle was opened, tasted, and poured, Kassim sipped at a glass of mineral water. The wine waiter went away.

'Tell me, Mr Latif, how old are you?'

He was taken by surprise. For once he was not in control. 'I am twenty-six . . . But that is not, I would say, of great importance. I have useful laboratory skills, sir. I – '

'And now you are here in Oxford. How did you get here?'

'I do not understand you, sir.' He looked anxiously at the woman, but she was giving him no help. 'I am travelling British Airways. Always I – '

'I mean, Mr Latif, how can you *afford* to get here? You hardly make a habit of selling bombs, I imagine. Oxford is not cheap; it is a long way from India. Where does the money come from?'

Kassim took refuge in pride, mixed with bitterness. 'This *Oxford* you speak of is not my Oxford, Professor Graham. Has your daughter not told you? Fine Oxford colleges with their great traditions are not for poor Indian students. I study *in* Oxford, but at a lesser institution. And my family is not so poor that it cannot afford to pay for my simple needs.' He pointedly raised his glass of water and drank from it, emphasising the simplicity of his lifestyle. There was an opportunity here to excite shame, and shame would disarm suspicion.

'You smile at me, sir.' He glanced sideways at the woman. 'Your daughter, sir, does not smile at my poverty.'

Silence descended on the table. Not yet back in command, Kassim tried a different tack. 'You trust me to provide your bomb, sir. Because you have no alternative, you trust me to deliver what you need. It is an insult that you do not also trust me to go with you.'

The old man sighed. 'Would you be happy, Mr Latif, to join a group such as ours if it did not check its members very carefully? Like Groucho Marx, you should be wary of accepting membership of any club so incautious as to offer it to you.'

The allusion was lost on Kassim. He leaned forward. 'Check me, then. I have no secrets. I ask you, sir, to check me.'

Still the professor resisted. 'You know I cannot, Mr Latif. Beyond a certain point, you know I damn well cannot. It comes down to trust, young man. Most things do.' He paused, momentarily lost in thought. 'But I would rather have anyone who knows as much as you do about our plans with us, in plain sight, than left back here in England, perhaps having second thoughts.' He raised a hand to still

Kassim's protestations. 'One more question, though. We are a terrorist group. You must realise that we expect to die. We three have our reasons for accepting this. What are yours?'

Kassim hesitated, judging that to this old man more right-eousness would cloy. He risked innocence instead. 'What does a young man know of dying, sir? Perhaps he prefers to believe that afterwards he will escape.'

'You won't escape, Mr Latif.'

'But I am Hindu, Professor Graham. For me, dying is not so terrible. And besides, can you truly manage without me? Just the three of you? You will need more help. How many more people can you dare to trust with your secrets? So you really *must* let me be that help . . . And if I lose, of what consequence truly is my death in the eternal wheel of the living?'

The old man grunted. He reached for the wine bottle, poured. Kassim waited. He saw that the decision, one way or the other, had been made.

Professor Graham cleared his throat. 'Don't try to upstage me, young man,' he said gruffly. 'In the eternal wheel of living, of what consequence are any of our damn lives?'

He raised his glass in a silent toast. His daughter, meeting his eyes, did the same. Kassim had been accepted. As he had always known, dealing with Westerners – certainly Westerners as delightfully innocent as the Grahams – was easy.

And now, more than half a year of play-acting later, his final arrangements made, he was leaving the ship. His plan was complete, its details arranging themselves to perfection over the past day and a half, as the bomb was set and its trigger located. He had only one regret: Colly's death would be too quick, he would not be able to punish her adequately for the humiliations she had heaped upon him.

Their roles had been laid down right from the start – she the employer, he the servant. He was useful; indispensable even. He amused her, certainly he aroused desire in her, but she was white, and rich, and American, and he was only a poor Indian student. She'd open her legs for a communist German, but never for Kassim Latif.

And she'd never know. Even in the instant that she died, she'd never understand the fatal stupidity of her mistake. Every single day for ten long months he'd outwitted her. He'd outwitted them all. He was *absolutely* her superior. *And she'd never know.*

Alone on the bridge of the *Fimbulvetr*, nursing his resentment, Kassim still kept a careful watch. At this late stage he wanted no trouble. Most of all he wanted no Russians setting up observation posts on the shore.

Shortly before four he heard the expected helicopter approaching. Flynn was running the ship's generator, so that the sound of the helicopter didn't reach Kassim until it was almost in sight above the eastern headland. He had time only to call down to Colly before it seemed to rise, like a large, graceless insect, from the cliffs to starboard. She joined him on the bridge, wearing her usual jeans and a red checked shirt, her hair tied back in its elastic band. Her informality taunted him. The obviousness of her breasts. He moved away, down on to the deck.

The helicopter was a substantial twin-rotor amphibious military craft, well armed and equipped. Although clearly American, all traces of national insignia had been obliterated. It circled the cove, then put down on the calm water a kilometre or less from the ship. Its racket brought on deck both Flynn and the sleepy Werner, who were joined by Colly, coming down from the bridge.

Blearily scratching his head, Werner peered out across the water. 'The official inspection visit?'

Colly nodded. 'What else? The time's right. And I like the anonymous chopper. Bi-partisan, I think the word is.' She grinned. 'I wonder how many hot line calls it took to sort that one out?'

As soon as the helicopter's engines died a loud hailer crackled and whistled, then settled into a loud electronic hum. Two burly men in civilian suits appeared in the machine's open loading bay.

'Ahoy there; *Fimbulvetr*.' The accent wasn't American. To Kassim's experienced ear it was certainly Russian.

Flynn cupped his hands, winked at Colly. 'Ahoy there yourself, whoever you are.'

'My name is Ivan. My colleague is Joe. I think you are expecting us.'

'By those names or any other.' He turned to Colly. 'Shall we send the boat?'

She shook her head, pointed. Flynn looked back at the helicopter. 'Ivan' and his companion 'Joe' were already lowering an inflated dinghy into the water. The Russian spoke again.

'If just we two come to you, and you search us as we board, it will be better for you, I think. We do not want any misunderstandings.'

Flynn spat over the rail. 'Patronising bastard,' he muttered. But they were right. He lumbered up to the bridge and returned with the NATO-issue Swedish automatic rifle he'd bought, not cheaply, in a back-alley shop near the naval dockyards in Belfast. That and a small pistol, supplied by Kassim, were their only armaments.

In the helicopter's dark interior men in drab olive uniforms could be seen, again with no insignia of nationality, or of rank. One of these men threw out an anchor to hold the helicopter in position. Ivan and Joe climbed into the dinghy and motored across to the *Fimbulvetr*'s ladder, tying up alongside the ship's boat already moored there.

Kassim stationed himself at the head of the ladder with a hand-held metal detector. He called Flynn to help him. Werner stood by with the rifle.

Ivan and Joe came up the ladder. Flynn detained them while Kassim checked them over. Joe was carrying what seemed to be a pocket tape recorder. Kassim examined it, pressed a button and watched the tape whirling round. He handed it back. A little Asian quaintness was in order, he thought. 'If that is a bomb, sir, it will do you no good. You will see – we are very much protected against such devices.'

Joe took the recorder, grunted non-committally. He and Ivan were big men, authoritative, their movements suggesting that they were less accustomed to their well-cut civilian clothes than to high-ranking service uniforms. They both had short hair and square confident faces. But they were not indistinguishable. Ivan was the one with the smile. He was also the spokesman.

'I am told we have a nuclear device to inspect, and an automatic trigger mechanism. Also your charts of this cove's sea bed. The bomb is underwater – Joe will examine it, he's a diver. We recognise that he is a large man, but we have information that he is no larger than your Captain Flynn. We assume you may prefer him to use one of your own insulated wet suits. If not, we have one waiting for him back in the helicopter.'

Colly stepped forward. 'Flynn's suit'll do fine. We're glad to have you aboard. Dr Dietrich takes care of the underwater business. Werner, look after Joe, will you please? If he wants to go in the Beatle, take him. He may prefer for you to show him where the bomb is so that he can go down on his own.' She turned to the American. 'Don't take too many liberties with it, Joe. I'm sure you realise that it can be a bit temperamental if it isn't handled with care.'

Nobody smiled. Werner returned the rifle to Flynn. Colly spoke to Ivan. 'The automatic trigger is in the wet lab on the upper deck. Kassim will come with us. Flynn stays out here on watch. He is armed, as you see.' She surveyed their two visitors. 'The bomb trigger is delicate. Detonations close to it are not recommended. But out here they are perfectly safe, and Flynn will shoot if he has to. Should you or the helicopter crew try to take over this ship, I promise you the consequences would be terrible.'

She walked briskly away, having no need of an answer. Ivan followed her, and then Kassim. As he went he saw Werner nod to the American and move off aft. These two outsiders on the ship made him uneasy. The others were too trusting, he thought. Anything might happen.

Colly led on up the companionway to the upper deck, then round the deckhouse to the wet lab door on the far side. Behind her the Russian's gaze circled constantly, never still, noting every detail. Kassim could imagine the plan he would draw later, for assault troops to work to.

They entered the small rectangular laboratory. Colly crossed to the stainless steel-topped workbench and carefully opened the heavy drawer beneath it. Inside this Werner had installed the trigger. It was a small, neat apparatus: a perforated metal cylinder, a mercury switch, some complex electronic circuitry incorporating two transputer chips, and a pair of dry batteries, all mounted in a cushioned cradle that was attached to the sturdy sides and bottom of the drawer. The front of the drawer was drilled with large holes, exposing the apparatus inside to the air in the wet lab.

Ivan leaned forward and looked cautiously inside. 'That is a simple diaphragm switch.' He sounded disappointed.

Colly stood back out of his way. 'Sure. Nothing fancy – the KIS philosophy. Keep It Simple, and nothing can go wrong. But it responds only to major changes in atmospheric pressure. We're talking about gross pressures here – at least five atmospheres.'

'I understand. There is no chance of accident. Loud sounds won't do it. Nor a sudden wind. Certainly not the sort of pressure changes associated with the weather.'

'Lordy, no. Blast is needed. The sort produced by explosions. Quite small explosions, though.' She smiled disarmingly. 'Any loud bangs associated with an attack on this ship, in fact.'

'Ah.' The Russian produced a pencil and drawing pad. 'I may make pictures?'

'Of course. We want your chiefs to understand just how secure we are. There's a manual over-ride, naturally, either to de-activate or detonate.' She pointed. 'It's linked to others all round the ship. One of us is always on duty.' She let him work for a moment. 'We don't want to die, Ivan; but you must believe that we are prepared to if we have to. And if we do die, then I guess a helluva lot of innocent people are going to die with us.'

Ivan shifted his position. 'It is a bluff, of course.' He began a second sketch, speaking thoughtfully as he drew. 'But it is a good bluff. I am not in the political branch, you understand. I am a technical officer on a nuclear submarine. Yes, it is a good bluff; I know I would not like to be the man to call it.' He straightened his back, looked across at her. 'Whatever it is you want, Dr Graham, I think I would give it to you.'

Her eyes widened. 'They didn't tell you what we want?'

'It is not our business.' He closed his drawing pad, put it back in his pocket. 'And now, perhaps, you would please explain the – '

'I think it *is* your business.' She pushed stray strands of hair back from her forehead, watching him closely. 'We want nuclear disarmament. We want a test ban treaty at Geneva. And we want action to help the poor countries that suffer because of *our* thoughtless abuse of the environment.'

'I see.' The Russian spoke quite neutrally. He met her eyes, then looked away. 'And now, if you would please explain . . .'

Kassim was observing over Colly's shoulder from the corner of the lab by the twin stainless steel sinks, under the tool rack. He smiled secretly to himself. In spite of what he said, this Russian must know that their bluff wouldn't work. Colly didn't have the guts to carry out her threat: Kassim knew this. So, really, he would be doing her a favour.

Colly started to speak, then changed her mind. It was not this man, here, who needed convincing. She moved on. 'If the trigger is activated it transmits a coded series of sonic impulses, on the Asdic principle. This code fires the trigger that detonates the bomb. There is another code that goes out at certain intervals. *Unless* that code is heard, the bomb detonates anyway. Accidental detonation is impossible, but if you try to block our communications the bomb will go off. Or if you try to tamper with it – but that's Joe's department.'

The Russian nodded. 'Joe, yes. For the sake of convenience. He is navy, like me, but from a carrier. His speciality is warheads.'

'What a vile job.' She shuddered. 'And you trust him?'

'We have talked about that. Very frankly. And trust is not necessary. We simply have no reason to cheat each other. We both want our two governments to know the true situation here.'

'Yes. Good.' Colly tucked her shirt determinedly into her jeans. 'I'm glad to hear it. We want them to understand how crazy it would be to attack the ship.'

'Yes, Dr Graham. Very crazy.'

Again the Russian spoke neutrally. But behind his words Kassim heard the thought that such a craziness was just what his chiefs might opt for. Once again, therefore, why not forestall them?

Ivan turned back to the trigger in its drawer. 'I see batteries. The unit has its own power supply?'

'Quite separate from the ship, yes. The batteries should sound a warning tone when approaching full discharge, but to be certain we test them every night. I do the job myself.'

'And if an operative could get to the switch and disconnect its power supply?'

'There is a fail-safe. A warning buzzer would sound, then, after a certain time with no signals from the ship, the bomb would detonate. Always assuming your . . . operative . . . disconnected the power properly. The system has certain subtleties. A wrong move, and it will transmit the command to the trigger anyway. The operative would need skill, and time. And luck.' She paused, significantly. 'And he also has to get here.'

'Have you thought of nerve gas, Dr Graham?'

'Gas that would disable every single one of us? With no warning, and so quickly that not one of us would get to an over-ride?' She shook her head. 'No, Ivan. There's no way we're going to lose this one. No way at all.'

The Russian didn't argue. No doubt he could see, like Kassim, that she genuinely believed what she was saying. Kassim smiled again. No way, he thought. And no win, either.

They went into the plotting room and large general-purpose lab next door. Ivan was shown their blow-ups of the geological chart, with fault patterns superimposed. All of Helgavik lay in an area where the Earth's mantle was perilously thin, and a major fault-line crossed its inner, north-eastern corner. Colly began to explain the geophysical processes they were able to exploit, but the Russian stopped her.

'That is not why I am here. Other men, other experts, study already these questions.'

Colly took him, instead, on into the laboratory, to the empty lead-lined crate in which the device had been delivered to the ship. Kassim remembered the January night very well. A hundred kilometres off Marseilles, a swine of a sea in the Gulf of Lyons, a heavy overcast, half a gale blowing, no moon or stars, and Flynn making the rendezvous with the Greek tramp as if he was picking up a package from the post office on his way to work. Their shake-down cruise, he'd called it; at least the weather had convinced Colly that she must take on a proper crew for the passage up to Iceland.

Ivan opened the crate briefly, long enough to measure the residual radioactivity inside it with the meter Colly gave him. He wrote down the reading.

'You worked with the plutonium yourself?'

'Werner did. It was only a small job. We purchased a do-it-yourself package, you see. You'd be surprised how easy it was. With so many nuclear weapons around these days, is it any wonder some bits and pieces go astray?'

He grunted.

'We kept the exposure well within limits. The ship was lying in Southampton at the time. My father had set up a workshop in a lock-up garage down there. I can give you the address if you like; probably still some traces of radioactivity round there.'

The Russian shook his head. But his eyes were puzzled. 'Your father? He is a scientist also?'

'They really didn't tell you very much, did they?'

He stiffened. 'As I said, it is not our business. You claim certain things. Technical things. We check that your claims are true. More than that is not necessary.'

'My father is known even in Russia. He won the Nobel Prize. Twice. His name is Robert Graham.'

'I am impressed.'

'So now you know all about us. Does it make any difference?'

'To what?' He smiled crookedly. 'You think that I might join your group? But I am navy officer. That is my life. Even if I thought you could win, I would not join you.'

'I guess not. Sorry.' She reached out and touched his arm. 'You're not so bad, Ivan – for a naval officer.'

She walked out, on to the open deck: paused just outside the opening, and looked back. 'But we *will* win, you know. We're bound to. We're fighting on the side of the angels.'

Kassim was touched. Innocence often moved him. It was so western. This whole enterprise was innocent. And he was especially touched because in his experience fighting on the side of the angels was bad news; the angels seldom win.

They all went out on to the upper deck. Thorough as Ivan's inspection had been, Joe's was taking longer. Evidently he had chosen to be ferried out in the motorboat to the area where the bomb was set, and to dive from there. The boat was moored away across the water, empty, the two men presumably diving beneath it. Staring at the boat, Kassim suddenly realised that if the big American cared to attack Werner underwater, the smaller man would stand little chance.

Colly and the Russian were leaning on the winch block, discussing the minisub. Kassim wandered to the starboard rail and looked down into the water by the ship's ladder. If he had disposed of Werner, the American's next task would be to get back on board the *Fimbulvetr* unobserved; any other course of action, save returning pointlessly to the helicopter, would leave him a target for Flynn's rifle.

A few minutes later, two heads broke the distant surface of the cove beside the motorboat, and Werner and the American quickly hoisted themselves aboard her. Kassim relaxed. They returned to the ship, tied up, and climbed the ladder. Dumping their masks and oxygen cylinders, they picked up towels and joined the three on the upper deck.

Joe showed his colleague the meter strapped to his wrist.

'There's enough fucking radioactivity down there to melt Fort Knox. The exterior shape is consistent, and so's the mother's location.' He dried his hair vigorously, nodded in Werner's direction. 'And this guy knows what he's talking about. Offhand, I'd say we have a good bomb-making capability here.'

'You're speaking,' Ivan said mildly, 'of people who have the famous Professor Robert Graham on their side. Also some angels.'

Joe craned his head forward, blew his nose between his fingers. 'Graham I know. Fucking peacenik. Angels I can do without. And that water's cold enough to freeze your balls off.'

He walked away, paused. The cold seemed to have made him gabby. 'I tell you, Ivan, that thing's booby-trapped all to hell. There's even a detonator rigged to a pressure gauge. Lifting the bomb is out. So's towing it away. Vary the depth by more than a few feet up or down, and you're in deep shit.'

He hawked violently in his throat, spat over the side, then went on down the companionway, stripping the top of the suit from his torso as soon as he reached the bottom. Werner winked at Colly, then followed him. Kassim could see that his time with the American had been profitable, if hardly agreeable.

Flynn was up on the bridge now, the rifle still in his hand. The helicopter waited silently, swinging gently in the slight breeze that had sprung up. The other two men were a long time below; Colly and the Russian had run out of conversation. Kassim was amused. Non-eastern people never ceased to amaze him. Their reserve was a myth. In fact they showed each other far too much of themselves. None was truly watchful.

Which was why, he reflected, they were so easy to fool.

Eventually Joe returned, dressed again in his good American suit, and he and Ivan took their leave. In Joe's presence the

Russian became a similar, stiffly stereotyped figure. He declined Colly's proffered hand.

But he allowed his companion to go first down the ladder. And while Joe was climbing into the dinghy, Ivan, with his head just above the coaming, spoke softly to Colly.

'This bluff of yours is mad,' he said softly. 'But you, you are not mad. I do not believe, therefore, that you will ever carry it out.'

She took a step towards him, bent down. A loose lock of hair flopped forward in front of her eyes. 'Are you going to put that in your report?'

He stared up at her. 'No.'

'That's good.' Their eyes broke contact and she tossed her hair back angrily. 'And anyway, you're absolutely wrong, you know. Our one bomb will be kinder than all of yours. So I bluff you not.'

He shrugged and went on down the ladder. If he replied, Kassim didn't hear him.

The helicopter's rotors had already begun to turn. The two men were aboard it and airborne in an impressively short time. As the ungainly craft heeled overhead before taking them out across Faxaflói, back in the direction of the NATO base at Keflavik, the Russian waved from its still-open hatch.

Werner joined Colly and Kassim at the ship's rail. 'That bastard American poked into everything,' he said angrily. 'Searched the galley, the cabins, everything. That's why it took so long. And he kept dictating what he saw into that stupid tape recorder.'

Colly laughed. 'I'll grant he wasn't my favourite fellow-countryman. But that *is* what he came for. And we've nothing to hide.'

Kassim caught his breath. He had not thought that his cabin might be searched. Admittedly any danger was very small. But all the same . . . he excused himself, and went below. His belongings had been disturbed, but not seriously. And the cardboard Ajax container packed with plastique beside his washbasin had clearly not been touched.

He felt hungry. Along in the galley he prepared himself a salad, chopping the raw cabbage resentfully. He'd been obliged to eat vegetarian food for far too long. Tomorrow morning, in Reykjavik, he promised himself a breakfast of sausages and bacon. He leaned on the galley counter, salivating at the thought.

Werner came through with an electronic scanner, sweeping the place for bugs. He was laughing. He'd already found two, one left by the American in the wet suit locker and the other on the upper deck, under the plotting room table. Tiny self-adhesive buttons – it had clearly been ridiculously easy for their visitors to plant them.

So much for all that Russian charm, Kassim thought. He was unamused. He knew such bugs well, and one of their snags was that they had a very short transmitting range: within a kilometre at most, therefore, there had to be a receiver. If one was already in position on the shore somewhere, and he blundered into it in the night, then he'd have to kill the operator. And then there'd be questions asked, questions that might lead to a shutdown at the airport.

And then, too late to do anything about it, he'd be stuck on the island to die with the others.

At four o'clock that afternoon in New York, Robert Graham was sitting on a bench in Times Square. He'd spent a quiet day. After posting off to Lily King the diskette containing his first day's log, he'd sat with a new edition of Shakespeare's sonnets in the reading room of the great New York public library. Whenever he felt that his faith in humanity needed renewing he read Shakespeare's sonnets. And today, as always, they had not failed him.

Then he'd slept for a while. The day was fine, cooler than the day before, with a fresh clear sky; so later he'd walked in the city. He bought a bagel with cream cheese from a Puerto Rican's cart, found an empty bench in Times Square, and sat there eating it. After the bagel he just sat. Another old man came and sat beside him. The other old man showed Robert a live mouse he had in his pocket, and told him all about it. Robert listened, and nodded intelligently in all the right places, and on the second time around the story he dozed off again.

Then it was four o'clock, and nearly time for him to ring Georg at the UN again. He had no particular expectations of the call. The two superpowers would be stalling while they talked to their experts and waited for reports to come in from Iceland. But the call made a punctuation mark in his day.

The old man with the mouse had gone. Robert took a subway to 77th and Lexington. Tomorrow he'd commute out to Stanford or some such – there was no need to make the opposition's job easy for them. But for today, the city would do. He rang the UN from a booth close to the Lennox Hill Hospital.

Once he got the Secretary-General's extension, Georg took the call direct.

'Bob? Hey – it's good to hear your voice. How're you doing? I worry for you.'

It sounded unforced.

'I worry for me too, Georg. So far I'm doing fine. How are our great leaders?'

'Angry. What did you expect? They'll get you, Bob.'

'I don't matter.'

'They'll get the ship.'

'No. If they touch her, the long winter's what they'll get. Ragnarok.'

'I hope they believe that . . . You know Moscow's recalled their chief man at Geneva?'

'I saw that.'

'The President's been in touch with the US team there. He's instructed Kramer to offer test ban.'

'I'll believe that when I see it. They won't move until they've checked our defences.'

'Naturally.'

Robert became testy. 'No, Georg. Not *naturally*. In the *natural* order of things they'd jump at the chance. Halve their defence budgets. Without being pushed by me.'

'You might push them, Bob. But you'll never press that button. I know you too well. They asked me, and I had to tell them. You'll never do it.'

'I mightn't.' He glanced at the traffic passing in the street, then at his watch. 'But I don't have the button. Colly does. She's tougher than me; she believes that people get the governments they deserve.'

'So the people deserve this Ragnarok?' Robert didn't answer. 'Either way, Bob, I've got other things to worry about than your daughter. Your team out there – on the list you gave us, there's a guy called Latif. He – '

'Time's running out, Georg. Look – next time you talk to the high ups, point out the value of getting in first with the announcement. They're going to have to do it anyway, so why not get some credit?'

'Don't change the subject, Bob. Hell, did you really think you'd get away with that background on Latif? Dietrich and Flynn check out straight down the line. But Latif's story wouldn't fool anyone –'

'You're trying to keep me talking.' Robert spoke firmly, suppressing the doubt provoked by his old friend's words. 'I must go. You know as well as I do that Latif's dossier is genuine.'

'He's a phony, Bob. Phony from start to finish. No father in Lahore. He's a cheap crook. Drugs, gun running, human cargo across the Mediterranean – you name it, he's done it. Under about half a dozen different names. Dropped out of sight a couple of years ago, then he turns up with you, under yet another name. He's probably a Libyan agent by now.'

'No, Georg. That's nonsense. You –'

'C'mon, Bob. The European universities have been full of them since the sixties. The CIA knows Latif well. From years back. And the French want him. They say he's a killer.'

Robert leaned his head against the back of the booth. The traffic lights on the corner had changed, and taxicabs were streaming past the hospital opposite in a yellow blur, lurching in the potholes. He looked beyond them, months beyond them, back to a noisy Oxford restaurant, dangling ferns, an earnest young Asian in a neat clerical grey suit. Such a genuine young man, and with all the right answers . . . Colly had trusted him, and he was providing the bomb. Robert shook his head from side to side, anguished. Perhaps it had been the bomb, and not the genuineness, that had decided him.

Georg was still speaking. 'I'd like to believe you didn't know. But if he's your source of fissionables, and I'm afraid he must be, then the background's a joke. It had to be Libya, and you had to know it.'

Robert didn't bother to deny it. There was no point. He hadn't known. None of them had. But it made sense. And, anyway, did he really mind? If Ghadaffi had backed their great adventure, did he mind?

'Bob? Are you still there? Bob?'

He pulled himself together. Across the road the traffic had jammed solid again. 'We have a countdown, Georg. Remind them of that. We must have a treaty. Signatures, publicity. And there are just twelve days left.' He tried to concentrate. Latif ... the Libyans ... images circled in his head. 'I'll be calling again tomorrow. Same time, different place.' He was pleased with that. 'Same time, different place. Have something good for me, will you?'

He rang off. Kassim Latif, that totally genuine young man, was a *genuine* terrorist. That he could accept. But the Libyan connection was ridiculous. There was no reason on earth that the Arabs could possibly have for backing the project.

A police car whooped down 77th Street, turned right against the light. Robert watched it absently. It bounced to a halt by the kerb not ten feet away from him, blue lamp still flashing. Only then did Robert realise that it had come for him. Two officers leapt out, strode towards him, hands on their holstered guns. He had nowhere to go. He would claim to be Richard Goldstein. He carried no identification. Nothing to connect him with the hotel, even. He would claim he was Richard Goldstein.

The police officers, a man and a woman, strode straight past him, into the building at his back.

It should have been funny. It had all the ingredients of a joke. But Robert felt empty, blank, hollow, as if he had died. For a long time after the police had gone he dared not move. He leaned in the booth on legs that would scarcely support him. He wondered, vaguely, why he'd been so afraid. He was expecting to be caught, probably before the end of the first week.

Eventually he moved away. He found a bar. It was down steep steps from the sidewalk, and he only just made them. It had a flickering red Budweiser sign in the window. Robert ordered brandy. He didn't remember to sound central-European. An electric fan behind the bar blew stale warm air in his face. He drank the brandy and ordered another.

The bar was dark. He sat in a seedy booth, an old man in an ill-fitting double breasted suit, drinking brandy, and nobody bothered him. He was trying to figure out why Kassim's backers had supplied the bomb. They had something in mind.

Hand-in-hand with that problem went another. What message, if any, should he send to Colly? Georg said that Latif was a terrorist, and Robert believed him. Georg was his honest broker. But was

Kassim planning to take over the ship? Disable the others and issue his own ultimatum? What could he possibly want?

Then again, if Robert sent a message Kassim might be the first to receive it. There was a one in four chance that he'd be on watch and check in with the High Seas Operator when it arrived. The small dish antenna mounted on the *Fimbulvetr* put Colly directly into the world's telecommunications net, via the North Atlantic satellite; she could call the computer in the Abernatheys' house any time, but she had no reason to check the dead letter drop yet. But *she had to initiate the contact*; going the other way, getting a message out to a ship at sea, was harder. You *had* to go through the operator, leave a message. He could hardly drop off the *Paramount's* phone number with a message to call him back; might as well call Washington and give it to them direct. So the message had to say it all. One chance in four. Lousy odds, if the man was planning to kill Robert's daughter.

Indecision paralysed the old man. There were too many imponderables. And the brandy didn't help. Kassim spoke no German. Robert toyed with the idea of sending a message in that language, ostensibly for Werner. But what message? He had to figure out what Kassim had in mind, so that he could send the right warning. Kassim had been her protégé; Robert was very afraid that she might over-react.

In the end he did nothing. He'd sleep on it, decide in the morning. The ship was unlikely to be checking in with the High Seas Operator for any messages in the middle of the night, anyway. So he returned wearily to his hotel, and took refuge in his nightly log. There was always the possibility that ordering his thoughts on to the word processor might show him a solution.

As the long Icelandic summer evening drew in, Kassim used the fine clear weather as an excuse to stay on deck. The watch was Flynn's, and the two men companionably shared a picnic supper on the bridge. Flynn was the only member of the team whom Kassim genuinely got along with. He was a bit of a drunk, and he didn't bother to be well-educated and clever all the time. Kassim ate soup and bread, one eye always on the shoreline away to port.

He didn't grieve for the Irishman. He'd have taken Flynn with him if he could. That being impossible, he didn't give Flynn's death a thought.

On land nothing moved. Either the opposition were very good, or they were waiting till dark. Kassim, too, was waiting for the night.

A crackle took Flynn across to the radio. The coastguard operator was calling with a message from the TV reporter, Pétur Einarsson. As he had expected, public response to his interview with Dr Graham had been very good. He hoped that they had seen it and that they were pleased. If she had no objection, he and his cameraman planned to tape a follow-up early next week. They'd charter a helicopter this time – assuming the coastguards had no more plans to visit the ship.

Colly was called, and an answer composed. Icelandic TV were welcome any time. Kassim listened to the radio chit-chat. They might as well have saved their breath. By tomorrow evening Icelandic TV would no longer exist, and there'd be no ship for them to visit if they did.

Darkness fell around ten thirty. Kassim went down to his cabin and dozed until the vibration of the alarm watch on his wrist roused him at five to midnight. He felt totally alert, his senses razor sharp. He left the cabin and crept softly down the darkened central passageway, as if on his way to the head, pausing outside the doors to Colly's and Werner's cabins.

The woman's cabin was dark and silent, but a light showed under Werner's door and soft music could be heard – probably Beethoven, knowing Werner, but Kassim could scarcely tell one western composer from the next, and had no wish to. He decided to put off his visit to the wet suit locker until later, when Werner was safely asleep. He returned to his cabin, added a warm sweater to the clothes he had been dozing in, and then climbed up to the bridge to relieve Flynn. They talked together briefly, then the Irishman left him and went below. He had no worries about Flynn sleeping soundly – the captain had a knack, the result of a lifetime at sea, of dropping off immediately into a deep sleep, but rousing instantly as soon as he was called.

For a full hour Kassim stood almost motionless in the dark of the ship's upper deck. Once a fish splashed. Nothing else moved. The sky had clouded over now, the loom of the cliffs only barely visible against the lighter blackness above. Even through the night glasses, there was no sign of life. Kassim decided it was time to go.

When he went below again all the cabins were quiet, and in darkness. He fetched his insulated wet suit from the forward locker and changed into it, adding trousers and a duffel coat on top. If one of the others happened to wake, he could explain being found below, but not the rubber suit. He took one of the spares from the back of the locker and hung it on the front rack with the others. It looked fine. That it wasn't his was of no importance. Nobody would have any reason to check, in the few hours left to them.

Back in his cabin, he gently prised the top off the cardboard Ajax drum, glanced at his diver's waterproof watch, and set the timer that lay just inside the container, with its battery, detonator and the tightly-packed six ounces of plastique underneath. Then he replaced the metal top, tapping it down all round with the heel of his palm. He dumped the clothes he had been wearing in with those already packed, plus a large towel, in his seaman's bag, and carried it up on deck, together with the doctored Ajax drum.

Leaving the bag by the rail, he went on up to the wet lab and squatted in front of the two stainless steel sinks. In the cupboard under them, lined up on one side of the bottom shelf, were half a dozen or so other drums of Ajax. It had been Werner who had originally given him the idea of using one of them as a casing. Werner had teased Colly as he unpacked them from the carton and stowed them: a lifetime's supply, he'd said. A woman's typical priorities – cleanliness next to godliness. Or was it just that they'd been on special offer?

Now Kassim reached in and added his own canister, tucked safely in behind the others. There was absolutely no chance it would be discovered in the few hours that remained. The blast would be muffled back there, but quite sufficient.

Finally, he had to deal with the manual over-ride on the atmospheric pressure trigger. Relay switches from it were mounted in all the main areas of the ship. There was one in Colly's cabin, and she was such a phony that he knew she would be quite likely to use it to keep the trigger more or less permanently deactivated. In case of accidents, of course. In case she ever had to commit herself.

Kassim took a flashlight and a small insulated screwdriver down from the tool rack above the sinks, and eased open the drawer containing the trigger. Fixing the over-ride wasn't easy. There were fail-safes on every circuit, and any interruption simply brought one of them into play. But he'd had plenty of time to think about this, and anyway he knew the wiring like the streets around his Oxford college. He'd put together a simple induction loop that eliminated the over-ride without disturbing circuit integrity. He fished the tiny device out of his duffel coat pocket and bent low over the open drawer, frowning as he concentrated, the flashlight held awkwardly under his chin.

Somewhere on the ship a door banged. Kassim paused, listening. The *Fimbulvetr* was without motion, the water in the bay flat calm. He tilted his head. Somebody on the prowl? Or was the wind getting up? Nothing stirred. He returned to the trigger.

A minute, two minutes, later he was done. He shone the torch around, examining his handiwork. If anybody knew what to look for, it was fairly obvious. But nobody would know. He slid the drawer shut, replaced flashlight and screwdriver on the rack, and moved quickly to the door.

For a moment there he listened again, his eyes very wide as they adjusted to the dark. Very faintly he heard water lapping against the rocks of the shore line. Nothing else. The ship was still, and the silence boomed in his ears. He quit the wet lab, went down to the main deck, unfastened the painter to the ship's motorboat and climbed slowly down the ladder into it, lugging his seaman's bag with him.

Using a floorboard and paddling very quietly, he ferried his bag the short distance to the shore, topped it up with the clothes he was still wearing, and concealed it behind a boulder. He returned to the ship. The next few minutes were the only time when, wearing just his wet suit, he ran any serious risk of his plan being discovered.

After replacing the floorboard and tying up the motorboat in its old position, he went down the ladder again. He lowered himself briefly into the water. Then he climbed back up on to the deck and stood there for a moment, dripping. When a sizeable puddle had accumulated he walked slowly round to the port, landward side of the ship, leaving a clear trail of wet footprints. Once at the rail he stamped heavily about on the deck, gave several confused loud cries, and jumped noisily into the water, screaming as he fell. Once below the surface he swam quickly to the ship's stern and clung to the rudder there, well hidden by the bulk of the minisub hanging from the gantry overhead.

Almost immediately lights appeared on the deck above him. There were sounds of hurried movement, shouts, muddled footsteps. Voices called his name. Werner ran along the side of the deck, was joined by Flynn. The two of them searched and called. Up on the bridge the searchlight came on so quickly that Colly must have gone directly to it. She swept its narrow brilliant beam to and fro across the short strip of water between ship and shore. Kassim cursed. He'd hoped they wouldn't be so quick with the light. Colly and the two men were supposed to believe that Kassim's assailant had somehow escaped unseen, presumably taking Kassim with him, since no body would be found. Seeing no sign of movement so soon after, either on shore or in the water, made that scenario less likely. But still, one of them would be sure to think of the possibility of an assassin equipped with SCUBA gear; and it showed he had been right not to risk swimming immediately ashore himself.

In Icelandic waters, even in summer and wearing an insulated wet suit with padded gloves and feet, the human body has an endurance of about twenty minutes. This time was being used up unpleasantly quickly as Flynn, now in the motorboat, searched patiently across the dark water, and Colly quartered the narrow beach and cliffs with the searchlight.

After a while Werner, with a powerful flashlight, joined Flynn. Kassim, who had begun to shudder convulsively and was losing sensation in his hands, had hoisted himself on to the ship's rudder, taking advantage of the warmer air. Now, as the motorboat approached, he was obliged to drop back into the icy water. The muscles of his face felt stiff and dead.

He curled up, conserving heat and energy, and endured until the motorboat moved on. Eventually the searchlight was doused and the boat returned to the *Fimbulvetr*'s side. Muddled conversation up on deck, and then the ship fell silent. Kassim could wait no longer, whatever they were up to. He let himself drift slowly out from the stern's protection. Lights showed at the wardroom portholes. Conference time. They were great ones for conferences.

A tiny red disc flared and faded up on the bridge wing, suggesting that Flynn was back on watch, smoking one of his cigars.

Kassim drifted away with the current. When he was far enough not to be heard, he paddled clumsily for the shore with unfeeling limbs. He was bone tired, his extremities felt like lead, and he only just made it. He crouched for a long time, just clear of the shallows, gasping. Then he stumbled up the stony beach. It seemed an age, in the darkness, before he located the duffel bag he had stowed earlier. And he had to pause frequently, listening for the presence of strangers.

He struggled wearily out of his wet suit and into his clothes, rubbing vigorously at feet and hands with the towel. At last he began to feel warmer. He headed away across the stones, towards the base of the winding glacier bed that led up to the road. With the wet suit inside it the bag was heavy, but he dared not dump it. Experience told him that good hiding places found in the dark often turned out to be painfully obvious by daylight. Also, as an ordinary seaman flying out from Keflavik, he would need convincingly bulky baggage.

So far, so good. He considered his chances. If the opposition were already watching the airport, then his gamble would have failed. But he doubted this. They had no reason. They thought the crew of the *Fimbulvetr* were there to stay. Their problem was to flush them off the ship, not to stop them getting away.

And for the three he had left behind, the arrival of the Russian trawler in Hellnar gave useful extra credibility to his staged abduction. They had always accepted that they would be on their own once the countdown had begun. But now –

He froze. Something had moved. He strained his ears. Silence. The darkness was total. But a sixth sense, honed by training, had picked up warning signs. His skin prickling, he softly lowered his bag to the ground, stepped away from it, and crouched, ready.

Only then did the sounds penetrate his conscious hearing. A pebble rolled. Rubber heels scuffed softly. Clothing rubbed, arm against side, trouser leg against trouser leg. There was breathed laughter. Men were approaching down the track, made confident by the darkness, their quietness less than absolute, judged to the two-hundred-metre distance of the ship.

Kassim eased to one side of the narrow rocky shelf, dragging his bag after him; was still again, his back against the cliff, listening. Two men only, possibly – certainly – with weapons; he detected the slap of webbing on steel. Suddenly there was a lightening in the darkness up ahead. Rounding a corner, the slim beam of a flashlight probed the track, then died abruptly. The two men came closer. They were not very expert. Now Kassim could have taken them both – the flashlight must have destroyed their night vision. He smiled grimly. In the words of the poet, they'd never have known what hit them.

They were whispering together now, just below intelligibility level. Kassim caught a few words clearly, stiffened. They were talking in American. Up by road from the NATO base, then; not from the Soviet trawler at all.

They continued down the track towards him, sliding their feet, then stopped some ten paces off. Briefly the flashlight shone again, playing over a map. They murmured together, reached a decision, shared a match to light a cigarette each. Their faces, seen in the light from the match, were soft and plump. They carried automatic rifles over their shoulders, night binoculars round their necks, and knapsack radios with long whippy antennae. They parted. One of them was coming on. The other was striking up on a path at a higher level. Making sure of reception, Kassim thought. One at the top of the cliff, acting as a relay, the other near the bottom, keeping close listening watch on the ship. He wondered if any bugs had survived for them to listen in to.

He didn't move. Other than back down the track, there was nowhere for him to go. The shelf was perhaps two metres wide. Behind him the cliff rose sheer. Opposite him it fell away, presumably to the shore below. The American advanced cautiously, alone now and shining his light close in front of his feet.

Kassim waited. His clothes were dark, his skin was dark, only his eyes might betray him. He closed them. The other man wasn't expecting to see anyone, therefore he wouldn't. If he did, Kassim would have to kill him. With his bare hands, very quickly. Break his neck, and drop him over the edge. And then the other American also, before he decided to use his radio to call assistance.

He listened. The man was very close now, muttering peevishly under his breath. He clearly wasn't used to this sort of thing. Probably dragged from a cosy desk job at the base. Now he was close enough to touch. Kassim could feel his presence in the air, could smell his tobacco. The man stumbled, grabbed at the rock close by Kassim's head.

His eyes flashed open, but apart from that the Asian still didn't move. The other man steadied himself, cursing, and went on by. The waterproof cape on his radio pack actually brushed Kassim's face. He grinned, wolfishly, in the darkness. The young American's blindness had gained himself and his companion another day of life.

It was four o'clock when Kassim finally arrived on the road that ran along the spine of the Thórsnes peninsula, and already getting light. He paused to comb out the braids from his hair. No more bloody turbans for him. Then he turned right, eastwards. He looked wild now, but no wilder than many seamen. He carried no knives or firearms, no drugs or contraband of any kind. His British passport was genuine, even if the name on it was not. And his money, for the flight to Rome, was as good as anyone else's.

He had a further two hours' walk before he reached the next village, Arnarstapi; but he'd be there in plenty of time. The bus for the long ride down to Reykjavik did not leave until seven. He knew the bus timetable by heart: he'd obtained a copy during the *Fimbulvetr*'s short stopover in Akranes. He strode out, unhurriedly, into the Icelandic dawn.

6

Day Three   AUGUST 6. FRIDAY.

It was as if he had Colly in the room with him. Her words were so immediate, and so dramatic, that the machinery in between was forgotten. Robert could actually hear her voice in his head, could feel her unhappiness and fear, as the words rolled up the screen.

Dearest Fard.
Hi. It's me. Hell – that's dumb. Who else? I hope this lousy thing's working. It's four o'clock in the morning up here, Fard, and God knows when you'll read this, but I've got to talk to you. Frankly, I'm scared shitless. Couple of hours ago, everything was fine. We've had our US-Soviet inspection, and it went well. We scored A+ for sincerity and technical competence, I'd say. Werner's fine, so's Flynn. But Kass isn't.
    I know I shouldn't be burdening you with this; you can't do a damn thing about it. But we've just lost Kass, and I'm scared. I mean he's been taken. Gone. A couple of hours ago, just like that. Not a trace, just some guy's wet footprints on the deck. I tell you, it's creepy. And I've had to be this rah-rah team leader in front of Flynn and Werner ever since, so now I've got to tell you how bad I really feel. I mean, that's what Dads are for, *n'est-ce pas?*
    I mean, there's that Russian trawler along the coast, and they've come over the hill in the dark and taken him. Spirited him away. Or it might be the Marines from Keflavik. But what next? *Who* next? I don't mind dying, you know that. But I want it to be *for* something, not just in the night. Not just wasted.
    So what do we do, Fard? He was a weird little guy, but I guess I was fond of him. We all were. Now there's only three of us left, and God knows how many of them. If they can come and go and not leave a trace, what chance have we got?

The file ended, but the computer signalled that there was another file still to be read. Robert closed his eyes. His hands were shaking.

Colly's distress was so real. And he had no answer for her – except that, with what he now knew, he didn't believe in the abduction. He should have sent the information about Latif out to the computer up in Maine – but no, it wouldn't have done any good. Even if he'd got it together by eight, that would have been midnight, Icelandic time. And the only reason Colly had called up the Abernatheys' number in the middle of the night was because Kassim had already gone. It wasn't his fault – but now he had to do something to calm her fears.

He hit the return key.

It's me again. Look Fard, I'm sorry. I tried to scrub that last message, but I can't. We never set up this system to have second thoughts. Things aren't really so bad. No excuses, except that four a.m. is a lousy time to be worried. Hell, it's a lousy time, period.

Anyway, I've been talking to Flynn, and the panic's over. If they're going to try to pick us off, we've just got to be more careful. They'll only try at night, for sure, so there's no real problem with the watches. Werner can even do token trips in the Beatle, we reckon, if we want to keep up the masquerade for the benefit of the locals. Make like we're busy surveying. So – forget it.

I mentioned the inspection. Two guys – Ivan and Joe, they called themselves. Isn't that flaky? Still, Ivan wasn't a bad guy (guess where he came from!) and it went very well. They both left bugs. Funny, really. W's sure he's swept the place clean. But they sure got the message about the trigger. Maybe that's why the guys were sent in to take Kass. Well, we won't be caught again. Flynn's moving us out into the middle of the cove, for one thing. So don't – well, I won't say *don't worry*, because I know you will. But don't fear for the future. It's up here in Helgavik, and it's in great shape.

Just keep at Georg to keep at our leaders. And stay safe. We need you – I need you, if only as a shoulder to cry on. I don't reckon there's anything Kass knows that can help them, if he's still alive. Poor Kass. I'll call in later, Fard, after you've had time to talk to Georg. I'm fine; we all are. Won't it be just dandy when the two weeks are up?

This time, the screen told him that there were no more files to be read. But Robert sat on, at the uncomfortable dresser with nowhere for him to put his legs, and stared at the screen. Outside his window the morning heated up, and cats squabbled among the dustbins three storeys below. He scarcely heard them. He was terrified. His daughter had been scared, but was over it; now, he was terrified. He wasn't yet sure why. Some instinct told him to be. Some scientific intuition. There was a theory creeping up out of his subconscious, and it wasn't friendly. Already, before he had worked it out, it terrified him.

The abduction wasn't real. It came too soon. Operations like that, quick and clean, took longer to mount. And it would be too much of a coincidence if they had just happened to pick Kassim, the only rotten apple in the barrel.

No, Kassim had left the ship willingly, and probably alone, having taken care to leave the impression he had been abducted, or worse. *How* didn't matter. *Why* was vital.

And suddenly Robert knew why he was terrified. Everything came together. He'd wondered, the previous evening, why the Libyans should supply the Ragnarok team with the nuclear means to carry out their great bluff. He'd also wondered, long ago in Oxford, why a man like Latif should be so eager to be on the team. Now, the answer to both riddles was clear.

Latif had left because he wanted to be far away from the blast. And he had made his disappearance seem like abduction because he didn't want the remaining members of the team to suspect what he might have been up to before he left. What he might have been up to could only be – *sabotage.*

And sabotage aboard the *Fimbulvetr* meant only one thing. Triggering the bomb.

Which was why Libya had been happy to supply the fissionables. They *wanted* it detonated. So Latif had joined the shipboard team because his job was to detonate it. The advantages were clear. With the world north of the Mediterranean destitute and oil-thirsty under the long winter, not only would old enemies be hard hit, but the world south of the Mediterranean would be able to dictate its own terms. The very regions that had suffered drought and turmoil in the burgeoning greenhouse world would see the rains return. Desperate boat people would be migrating southward, not north, across the Mediterranean. Robert shivered at the thought of the reception they would receive.

Latif had left the Fimbulvetr, but only after hiding a timed explosive device somewhere near the trigger. Timed to give himself a chance to escape from Ragnarok. He would need at least twelve hours to get airborne and clear of the island. Colly had mentioned disturbances at about two a.m.; call it one a.m. when the timer was started, to be on the safe side, and the earliest the nuclear explosion could be expected would be around one this afternoon, Icelandic time.

Robert looked at his watch. The time was ten to nine. In Iceland, ten to one. Colly would not be checking in on the computer link until after he had spoken to Georg. Not for at least another eight hours.

His terror passed. More exactly, he had passed beyond it. Wryly, he observed that with the scientific method came scientific detachment. It really did. Obviously, in just ten minutes he could do nothing. He had to act on the hypothesis that Latif had been more cautious, had allowed himself longer for his getaway. If so, something might be done to avert disaster. He had to contact *Fimbulvetr*.

Contacting a ship at sea was straightforward, but took time. Only large ocean-going craft, cruise liners and the like, had floating telephone numbers that enabled them to be called direct over the satellite. For lesser craft, the High Seas Operator would take a message, but that still had to wait until the other party called in. In this case, he could go through the Icelandic coastguards. An urgent message could be phoned to them, and they would radio the ship on the local channel.

So the message had to be urgent. The real message would sound urgent enough, but he couldn't send the real message through such an insecure channel. If they believed him, it would cause panic; if they didn't, the message would never get through. Either way, it might screw up the negotiations that he hoped were now going on at the UN and in Geneva. He had to create a message that would sound urgent to the coastguards, convey the facts to *Fimbulvetr*, and yet say nothing suspicious or violent. And every second he took might be the second which made it too late to do any good.

He took just over 700 seconds. Nearly twelve minutes. This wasn't the sort of call he could make with a handful of small change. While he raided his suitcase for his telephone credit card he turned on the TV. Idiot faces twittered. Tax cut hopes were improving; bush fires raged in California; the Canadians anticipated another record harvest; the Mexicans were protesting about the latest tightening of US border controls. No news flashes reported a nuclear explosion in Iceland.

The credit card was genuine, Robert Graham's. He'd kept everything that didn't belong to Goldstein locked away in his case. But this was an emergency. He would probably be traced through the card, eventually, but that didn't matter. He'd have to phone away from the hotel in any case.

He turned off the TV and went downstairs. A slow old man, for all his hurrying. He was dizzy and gasping by the time he reached the foyer. At the desk Woolston was checking out a fat, dapper little man in parti-coloured shoes. Robert leaned in the staircase archway, obsessively snapping his telephone card with a thumbnail.

The guest took his receipted bill and left. Robert approached the desk.

Woolston smiled. 'You're late this morning, Mr Goldsteen. Oversleep? I saved the coffee.'

Robert scarcely heard him. 'I need a telephone. Not coins – a phone that'll take one of these.'

Woolston stared at the card. 'You'll do better if you have that coffee first, Mr Goldsteen.'

Robert's irritation flared. 'I might have to walk miles. It's urgent. Look, just tell me where there's a card phone.'

Woolston considered. 'That ain't so easy. I don't use them things myself. But if it's real urgent, you could try the Port Authority.'

'The bus station?'

Woolston nodded. 'That's it. The Port Authority. All kinds of phones there. Here, I'll draw you a map. It ain't so far.' Taking a hotel tariff card from his desk tidy, he laid out a grid on the back and began marking street numbers. Robert's anger abated.

'That's very kind of you. But why don't I just take a cab?'

'Quicker to walk, Mr Goldsteen. Just look here.' He gave Robert the card. 'Now then. This is us, right? And this is West Forty-second . . . you got to know West Forty-second, Mr Goldsteen.'

Robert peered at the grid. There was a singing in his ears. Woolston watched him. 'Look,' he said gently, 'why don't you just sit on that stool there. Use the phone on this desk. If you ask them, they'll tell us the damage after; we'll just put it on the tab.'

Robert sat down. Woolston was always very good to him. The time showing on the clock above the desk was seventeen minutes after nine. Seventeen minutes after one in Iceland.

'I'll leave you, then.' Woolston drifted away round the end of the desk, stood tactfully by the hotel door, looking out.

Robert's dizziness had passed. He made the call. Ascertaining the telephone number of Icelandic coastguard headquarters took a long time, but eventually, he got through. The girl on the switchboard was very efficient. She took down the message he dictated, read it back, promised it would be radioed through to the *Fimbulvetr* immediately.

He hung up. He'd done all he could. He rested, breathing deeply. The time was nine thirty-three. An impressive thought occurred to him. Maybe he'd just saved the world.

Perhaps it was time to take up Woolston's offer of coffee.

Half an hour earlier, on the third floor of the tall TV building in Reykjavik, Pétur Einarsson and his senior news editor, Björn Karlsen, were staring sourly at the monitor on Björn's desk. Backed by the national flag of Iceland, the Minister for the Interior stared straight back at them. The tape was of an interview with Pétur from that morning, and they were viewing it for the third time.

'. . . my dear Pétur,' the Minister was saying, 'of course I know what the team of British scientists is doing in Helgavik. How could I not? The Research Council vetted all their applications, and naturally the Council consulted with the ministry.'

'I've seen the applications too, Minister.' Pétur was off camera, an unseen voice-over. 'They claim they're prospecting for rare earth minerals. Does this satisfy you?'

'Satisfy me?' The Minister registered great surprise. 'The team leader comes from similar work in the Red Sea. The geological conditions, I gather, are very much the same. Why should this not satisfy me?'

'What exactly *are* rare earth minerals?'

The Minister eased himself comfortably back into his chair, clearly preferring this question. 'Now, Pétur, I'm not a scientist – you know that. But Professor Valdason of our university tells me the rare earth minerals are seventeen in number. They're not, in fact, all that rare; they were simply thought to be when the name was given out. They occur in many parts of the world, but principally in areas where molten rock – '

'I see you've done your homework, Minister. But perhaps I should rephrase my question. Could you tell our viewers what commercial value these minerals have?'

'Commercial value?' The Minister's eyes flicked briefly sideways as his blandness went into overdrive. 'Nothing very special, I understand, but useful in a small way. These days one or two of them are used in the red phosphors for colour television, so there's a steady market there – one which all our viewers will appreciate. But otherwise – '

'So they are not all that rare, and they are not all that valuable. Yet a British research ship comes all the way to Iceland to look for them. Has it occurred to your ministry that they might be being used as a cover for something else? Something *more* valuable?'

'I can't imagine why. After all, Iceland is closer to Britain than the Red Sea is. And I'm not sure that I approve of this line of questioning. The British effort is not aimed primarily at a commercial return. Dr Graham is a research scientist. As far as I know she has no business connections.'

'So she's here out of love for the Icelandic climate?'

The Minister frowned. 'Out of scientific curiosity, I should think. Now, this adversarial tone is quite uncalled-for. This isn't Europe, you know. There's no special award to be won for being offensive to government ministers.'

'I'm sorry, sir. I didn't mean to be offensive. My point was that the *Fimbulvetr*, humble as she is, represents a considerable investment. If she is engaged in pure research, as you say, I was wondering what return the investors are expecting to receive on their investment.'

For the third time, Pétur, watching the video, winced at the clumsy phrasing of that question. Thank God he could re-record his voice-over – *if* the interview ever looked likely to be screened.

'Then you should ask them.' The Minister became heavily jovial. 'And I did *not* say that the *Fimbulvetr* was engaged entirely upon pure research. You're trying to put words into my mouth, young man.' He leaned into the camera, conspiratorially. 'It won't do. We both know I'm much too old a hand for that.'

A pause followed. This time, Pétur did not apologise.

'One last question, Minister. Has Professor Valdason ever talked to you about the periodic tables?'

The minister smiled. 'Women's periodic tables, d'you mean?'

Pétur swore, reached forward, paused the tape. The Minister's face froze on the smile. It seemed more mendacious the longer it lingered.

'He knows,' Pétur exclaimed. 'I tell you, Björn, he's in it with them. And that's the giveaway. Anybody with even the most elementary schoolboy chemistry has heard of periodic tables.'

His companion grunted. 'I haven't.'

'Which only goes to prove what an ill-educated slob you are.' Pétur got up restlessly, went to the window, stared down at the bright clean roofs of the city. He turned back. 'I don't care how ignorant you are. Even I can understand it. The periodic tables arrange the elements with similar chemical properties in nice easy-to-read columns. The Minister knows that. He also knows that elements with similar properties tend to be found in similar geographical locations. I looked up rare earths, just out of curiosity. And there's one very interesting element that has similar properties to the rare earths and lies in the same column in the periodic tables. *Uranium.*'

Thoughtfully, Björn lit one of his untipped, king-size cigarettes. He was a cadaverously thin, joyless man, near to a retirement he had no wish for, a newspaper man originally who had only come to television late in his career, after twenty-six years on the international desk of Iceland's conservative daily. Ministers of the government were fair game – especially, being socialist, ministers of the present government.

He exhaled smoke slowly. 'So what you're telling me, Pétur, is that wherever you find rare earths you're likely to find uranium, and that if the Minister behaves as if he doesn't know that, he's hiding something.'

'As to the Minister, of course he's hiding something . . . As to the uranium, I'm afraid that's not quite so simple. It doesn't just lie there in lumps.' Pétur returned to the desk and picked up the book his researcher had borrowed from the geology department at the university, the latest edition of the massive American *Glossary of Geology*. 'It says here somewhere that uranium comes in many forms.' He flipped through the pages, found his marker, scanned the dense paragraphs. 'Ah, yes . . . *one of these, uraninite, may be found in hydrothermal veins* . . . Iceland's got plenty of those, all right. And it also says here that uraninite may contain one or more of the rare earths as impurities. So you see how closely related they are. And therefore – '

' – and therefore there's a great government conspiracy to conceal from the Icelandic people the real purpose of the British ship's researches.' Björn dragged on his cigarette, coughed lingeringly. 'I love government conspiracies. They give me a warm glow all over. You know that.' He coughed again. 'But they've got to have a reason.'

'Money. How about that?' Pétur closed the book, straightened his back. 'If uraninite is discovered there'll be contracts going out to tender, and a lot of them local. Drilling, extraction, transportation . . . And those in on the ground floor, ahead of the pack, have one hell of an advantage.'

'I agree the man's unconvincing. But it may just be that he's being cautious. Doesn't want to end up with egg on his face if he announces a great uranium exploration programme and all they come up with is rusty sardine tins.'

Pétur spread his hands. 'I'm not suggesting that we press for an indictment. Yet. Simply that Finnur and I go and have another chat with this Doctor Graham.'

'Please remind me. Do I remember that she is attractive?'

'I've seen worse.'

'Ah.' Björn flicked cigarette ash in the general direction of a dying rubber plant. 'So it will make you happy, proving she's a liar?'

'Not a liar. I'm sure they're looking for what she says they're looking for, But they may be looking for something else as well.'

'Didn't a little bird tell me that you've already been on the blower, arranging this trip?'

Pétur grinned. 'You have to admit she interviews well.'
Björn coughed again, flapped a hand at the monitor. 'For God's
sake switch off that grin. It's getting on my nerves.'
Pétur did so. 'So, what d'you think?'
His editor sighed. 'I think that if you're hoping to prove they're
digging up uranium ore out there, you'd better pack a geiger
counter in your kit.'

The message from Professor Graham was passed to the
Fimbulvetr by the coastguard radio at one forty-three, local time.
And for the moment all was well. Kassim Latif, more cautious
than the professor had feared, had in fact set the timer for one
fifty-five, allowing himself thirteen hours for his getaway, and
was even now congratulating himself on so doing. He had
planned to travel via Heathrow, but his bus to Reykjavik had
been late, and by the time he reached Keflavik the morning
Icelandair flight to London had left. The afternoon flight,
scheduled for five, was liable to be cancelled owing to unforeseen
circumstances, so he took the Oslo route instead. Stopover time
in Norway had been less than an hour, and now he was airborne
in a Boeing 727, on his way again.

He looked at his watch, still set to Icelandic time. Less than ten
minutes to go. He drummed his fingers on the armrest. He was
aware of how unsavoury he looked, and delighted in it after the long
months of being a neat and respectful Indian student. His long hair
was unkempt after hours of travelling, and his clothes were
crumpled from their stay in the duffel bag. But that was his
neighbour's problem, not his. Even airport security hadn't been
able to fault him, though not for want of trying.

He felt a slight lurch, presumably as the Boeing pilot made a
minor course adjustment. It had to be that. He reckoned they were
already over what used to be East Germany. Even if the detonation
were early, he wouldn't know anything about it. At such a distance
he'd hear nothing, and the most he might see, even at altitude,
would be a momentary lightening of the sky astern. He wondered
how quickly the news would reach the Alitalia pilot, and if it would
be passed on to the Boeing's passengers. He thought not. Probably
they would be kept in ignorance until after the Rome touchdown.

Airlines tended to feel that they had a responsibility not to distress their paying customers.

The 727 settled to its new course and flew calmly on. Kassim leaned his head back against the cushion and closed his eyes, savouring his momentous secret.

In Helgavik the nuclear device lay quietly on the seabed. In the wet lab on board the *Fimbulvetr* the atmospheric pressure trigger waited. Near to it, the timer in Kassim's modest explosive package moved silently towards its moment of self-destruction.

The package had given Kassim no problems, either practical or moral. He had built it for a purpose, and he expected it to fulfil that purpose. As to the bomb, the trigger, and its over-ride safety switch, however, there was serious confusion in Colly and Werner's thinking. From the beginning they had agreed between themselves that there could be no circumstances whatsoever that might justify them in actually exploding a nuclear bomb. The trigger must, of course, survive detailed examination; it had to be a real trigger. Similarly, the presence of enough radioactive material in the right configuration to be triggered into a nuclear explosion, located in the right place on the seabed, had to be capable of verification.

Logically speaking, however, there was no need to have a working bomb at all. Either the threat would be enough to gain the concessions demanded, or the ultimatum must be allowed to fail.

And yet the bomb, like the trigger, was real. Even while it was being put together, neither Colly nor Werner had thought to question or challenge what they were doing. At one level, both, in their own way being perfectionists, it had seemed only right that having gone to the trouble of obtaining the material to build a fission device they should put the pieces together properly. But also, on some subconscious level, it seemed that both conspirators were willing to justify what they strenuously claimed to be unjustifiable. Thanks to the devious workings of the human mind, not just a working trigger but a working bomb was built, while its makers continued to adhere to the belief that, no matter what, they would never consider using either.

The message from Colly's father came through to the *Fimbulvetr* shortly after a quarter to two. In Helgavik the latter part of the morning had been spent moving the ship out into the middle of the cove – Flynn having pointed out that if she hadn't been so close to the shore the previous night, the opposition would never have got away with Kassim so easily. Now Flynn was taking the afternoon watch on the upper deck and Colly and Werner were resting below. It had been a disturbed night, and of the three of them Flynn was most used to going without sleep. And when the radio receiver on the bridge suddenly came to life his seaman's ear instantly picked the faint voice out of the surrounding murmur of seabirds. He went up the companionway three steps at a time.

The coastguard operator delivered Professor Graham's text in excellent English. Flynn took it down without comment, thanked her for her trouble. She wished him well, and signed off. Flynn leaned on the chart table for a moment, staring at the words he had written on the message pad:

To: RRS Fimbulvetr, Helgavik Cove, Iceland.
Attention Dr C Graham.
The package you are worried about is safely with its
owners in Tripoli. The second, smaller package left
behind should be found soonest and despatched without
delay. Failure brings serious international
repercussions.
Signed, Professor R Graham, New York City, USA.

Flynn scratched his beard. He'd liked Kassim. You found his type anywhere in the Med from Marseilles to Casablanca – souls as black as sin, but they had a great enthusiasm for living. And now the old man was saying he had 'owners in Tripoli'. Tripoli meant Greater Libya, and Libya meant the little shit must have been an agent. He hadn't been bloody abducted, he'd simply folded his tent and stolen away. Mother Mary . . . But more than that, old man Graham seemed to be warning them that he'd left something behind.

It made no sense. But the professor wasn't a man given to talking through his elbow. 'International repercussions' . . .

Suddenly, Flynn leapt to his feet and hurried below. Colly and Werner were in the wardroom, Werner listening to his personal stereo, Colly dozing on one of the battered red leather benches.

Flynn put the message in front of Werner, who slipped off his headphones.

'Flap on,' Flynn said. 'I mean it. Wake the First Lady.'

Colly sat up. 'I *am* awake.'

Flynn was already at the door. 'You'll wish you weren't. Mustn't stay.' He went out, back on deck. Even if the flap was what he thought it was, they wouldn't thank him for neglecting his watch.

Colly got up stiffly, went to the table, read her father's message over Werner's shoulder. Abruptly her drowsiness fell away. 'My God. Kass? I don't believe it. Christ – the little shit.'

Werner looked up at her. Momentarily their eyes locked. Then, as realisation dawned, they both lunged for the over-ride relay on the after bulkhead of the wardroom. Werner reached it first. Colly collapsed against the bulkhead, on her knees, her heart pounding. She had never, in all her life, been so terrified.

She leaned her head on her arms. 'Thank God for Fard.'

'Thank God indeed.' Werner returned to the table, disentangling his lightweight earphones, ripped from their socket in his panic. 'One has to wonder,' he said, studiously calm again, 'where the professor got his information from.'

'Who fucking cares? It makes sense, doesn't it?'

Werner frowned. 'Tripoli, you mean? Yes, the plutonium *could* have come from there, from Libya. They've got the reactors.'

'And Ghadaffi's just the man to want to blow up half the world. He's never forgiven mad bad Sad for upstaging him. Besides, just imagine the power Arab oil will have in the nuclear winter . . .'

Werner shook his head. 'I'm not sure, We're talking about a man who's really willing to – '

'Lots of men. All the way down the line. And Kass at the sharp end of it, with his little package. Jesus wept. I trusted the little motherfucker.'

'We all did.'

'No. You wanted his bomb. I *trusted* him. And last night, when we thought he'd been taken . . . Godammit, I *grieved* for him.'

She thought about it. 'Christ, how pious we are. What's the difference, really, between him and us? We're giving them a choice, I know, but we believe we're so right we'll blow the whole caboodle if we have to. Won't we?' She appealed to him. 'Won't we, Werner?'

He stood up. 'We must get a message through to Maine.' He looked at his watch. 'It's nearly five to two. The professor will be worrying. We must tell him all is well.'

For a moment Colly was angry that he should treat her like that, like a child; change the subject, refuse to answer. Did he think she wouldn't notice?

Then she relaxed. Of course he knew she'd notice. He was moving her on. And rightly. All this breast-beating – she *was* behaving like a child. The effect of shock, no doubt. Which reminded her –

'Shouldn't we first try to find Kass's disgusting little going-away present? It won't be all that big, but it'll sure make a mess when it goes up, wherever it is.' She got awkwardly to her feet. 'Where would he have hidden it? Close to the trigger, of course, but where? He's a clever litle bastard.'

'Cleverer than us up to now, it seems.' Werner went thoughtfully towards the door. Suddenly he checked. 'And if he's so very clever, then maybe –'

He lunged forward, tore the door open, and was gone.

Colly followed him, caught him on the companionway to the upper deck and the wet lab. Neither of them wasted time or effort on talking. Like him, she'd worked out now that every moment might be their last. If Kassim was so clever, then he'd have managed to eliminate the over-ride. He'd have set his bomb to give him time to get right away from Iceland, twelve hours or so, and he'd gone last night at around one. And now it was nearly two. So they were living on borrowed time already. They and half the world.

At the top of the companionway Werner skidded on the corner, scrambled to his feet, flung himself along the deck and into the wet lab. He wrenched open the drawer, peered down wildly.

'I don't know, Colly. What am I looking for? I don't know, Colly. *I don't know . . .*'

She joined him. 'Slow down, now. Perhaps it's all right. It's probably all right. The over-ride's fine. I'm sure it is.'

'But I can't . . . I can't see, Colly. We never made an indicator. Why did we never make an indicator? How can I see if we never made an indicator?'

His hands were shaking. There was sweat on his forehead. Colly closed her eyes, breathed deeply, concentrated. There had to be an answer. An obvious answer. There always was, in all the *crises* of life, an obvious answer.

And there was.

'The fail-safe, Werner. Cut something, smash something – that's what the fail-safe's *for*. Fix it, Werner. For Christ's sake, fix it!'

He steadied, grabbed wirecutters from the tool rack, bent over the trigger.

Kassim's bomb exploded.

Seventy-five seconds late – the quartz movement he had used was a cheap, inexact affair – its timer detonated the explosive, vaporising the cardboard drum that had contained the device and releasing a non-directional pattern of blast that flung its companion canisters against the cupboard doors, bursting them from their hinges in less than a hundredth of a second. The canisters disintegrated. Colly was knocked off her feet by blast and flying debris. She slid along the floor, curling up tight, cowering pointlessly, pitifully, against the thunder to come.

The blast ended. There was a modest amount of heat radiation, no more than that, causing the woodwork in the immediate vicinity of the bomb to smoulder, and scorching the paint on the nearby steel wall of the lab. A thick white haze hung in the air.

Colly uncurled. She opened her eyes. In her joy to be alive a throwaway was expected. 'Werner? Werner honey, I guess you fixed it.'

Her voice sounded strange. She realised she was deaf. That was why she wasn't hearing the fail-safe's warning buzzer. Through the haze she saw Werner outside on the deck, against the rail, pulling himself painfully upright. He wouldn't have heard her. Closer to the blast, he had been blown straight out through the open door.

She fanned the air in front of her. The haze smelt strange, scented and at the same time acrid. It took her several moments to identify it as a perfume like that of cheap detergent. Cleaning powder, maybe. Ajax. Those goddamned cans of Ajax Werner had given her such a hard time over.

She began to laugh. It was good to be alive. Laughing hoarsely, she made her way on hands and knees out of the lab. There was a great deal of broken glass about, but with the luck of drunks and holy idiots she managed to avoid it. She joined Werner at the rail, pulling herself up him until she was in his arms. Suddenly she was weeping. It was so very good to be alive.

Neither of them had suffered more than minor bruising. Kassim had not intended his bomb as an anti-personnel device. There had been no need to include four-inch nails or other shrapnel, when he expected his victims to be at ground zero of a nuclear blast considerably more powerful than the Hiroshima bomb.

Colly leaned back in Werner's arms. Her eyes were very bright, and she wiped her tears away distractedly, with one finger, out across her cheekbones.

'Time was,' she said softly, 'when I nearly went to bed with Kass. Did you know that? I never did, mind, but that was luck rather than good judgement. Tells you something about me, doesn't it? I'd have gone to bed with a – '

'He fooled us all.' Werner, also on his feet now, put an arm round her shoulders. 'It is not helpful to reproach yourself.'

'Helpful?' She began to laugh, still in shock. 'What the hell *is* helpful? Look at us. He was our only pro – with him on our side we'd have stood some chance . . . Hell, but we did outsmart him, though. Wherever he is, he's going to be fucking pissed off, waiting for the big bang that doesn't come. Poor little feller – what'll he do now, d'you think?'

Flynn had arrived from the bridge. He saw that a calm hand was needed, and took Colly down to the wardroom, leaving Werner to silence the buzzer and use a small fire extinguisher on the smouldering woodwork. Werner also inspected the trigger. It was undamaged, still in full working order. But for the fail-safe, Helgavik would now be the centre of a raging, unstoppable volcanic inferno. They were playing with fire: fire beyond human comprehension. He wondered, not for the first time, if they had the right.

Down below, Flynn gave Colly the last of the Brennivin. He stayed until Werner joined them, then returned on deck, where he resorted liberally to his hip flask. A personal snort-time was badly overdue – he'd had the worst shock of his life when Kassim's parting shot went off.

Rationalising now, after the event, he realised that he should have known Colly or Werner would flip the over-ride the moment they learned of the danger. Presumably it was back on line now. But he shuddered at the thought of how he'd looked, stupidly, out to the spot where the bomb was located, as if he'd have time to see the water heave from the force of the explosion below. He wiped his mouth with the back of his hand, and drank again. He left the technical matters to the scientists. Old man Graham had really saved their bacon this time.

He eyed the shore. Nothing moved save the birds, settled again after the bang. High up on the cliffs something flashed that might have been sunlight on a binocular lens. Flynn waved jovially. He mightn't like the new mooring – any sort of northerly would bring a swell straight in across where they lay, making life on board uncomfortable – but the bottom holding was good, and their position had the advantage of being a good thousand yards (Flynn seldom thought metric) from the nearest land. So there was little chance of the opposition taking pot shots at him. He'd heard of shooting that good, but he didn't believe it.

He moved forward, checked the bow rope, looked up at the sky. Cloud was coming in, gradually obscuring the sun. The forecast was for rain, with perhaps some coastal fog. So much for the Icelandic summer. He thought of Kassim and wondered where the Indian – if he was an Indian – was now. The professor had said Tripoli – and one thing was certain, the murdering little bastard would be in trouble with his boss, now Bob Graham had somehow got on to him and the big bang hadn't happened . . .

Flynn took another nip, leaned on a davit. He sang softly to himself. 'Ta-ra-ra-*boom* dee-ay . . .' He stared down into the water. 'I'm sitting on a *tomb* today.' He grinned; Chekhov, wasn't it? The damfool drunken doctor in the Chekhov play. If it was a drunken doctor, then it had to be Chekhov. They went together. Love and marriage; horse and carriage. He sang again: 'You can't have one without the other . . .'

He straightened his back. He wasn't drunk. He walked on along the deck, totally alert. He was practically never drunk. Although a steady, day-long succession of snort-times might keep him feeling no great pain, he was practically never drunk.

Thirty-five years in the Merchant Marine, and not a hint of insobriety in his record.

Montague Valentine Flynn had been born of Nell and her docker husband Pat in a Liverpool back-to-back in 1932. For seven years a scrawny, cheerful slum kid, when the war broke out in 1939 he was evacuated to a farming family, the Slaters, up in the Yorkshire Dales. He behaved badly. He told his new family he was called Flynn, and would answer to nothing else, having already learned to despise the ambitious names his mother had unwisely given him. He didn't like the food given to him, and he wet his bed. He was missing his parents and the city.

The Slaters were generous people, but hardy. With the father and two older sons away in the services they all worked the farm, and they expected Flynn to do the same. Before going to school he fed the hens, after school he fed them again and collected the eggs, and at weekends he cleaned out the henhouse. It wasn't hard work, but he hated it. He hated country life. When it wasn't smelly it was boring, and he wrote home to his mother every week, saying so. Short letters, and mis-spelled, but sincere.

For a time his mother resisted them. A Lancashire girl, Nell Parks, up on a bank holiday spree to the city, had met Pat Flynn in a pub, and had married him four months later for the oldest, if not always the best, reason. Now, with Montague away in the country, Pat on a basic training course down in Aldershot, and herself with a job in a munitions factory, for the first time in seven years she was free, with money in her pocket. The war was a lot of fuss about nothing, she told herself; and Montague ought to think himself lucky, up in all that nice fresh air, living off the fat of the land.

But as 1940 passed, and France fell, and the Germans started bombing Liverpool, Nell Flynn began to change her mind. Her house felt empty in an air raid, and frightening. One ration card, too, all on its own, was hard to get by on. That autumn she went to the authorities and insisted they let Montague live with her again. She always thought and spoke of the boy as Montague. Nobody else on the street had a trisyllabic son.

He quickly settled back into city life. After school he stood in queues for her while she was still at work; he kept her company in the cupboard under the stairs during air raids; and soon he had the biggest collection of bits of bomber in the neighbourhood.

Pat Flynn spent his embarkation leave with his wife and son. The Flynns had a riotous seventy-two hours. Then Pat left for the war in North Africa, and three weeks later, on her way home from work, Nell was killed by a fragment of German bomber very similar to those in her son's collection.

Flynn went to live with his maternal grandmother.

It didn't last. Mrs Parks, now twice bereaved, her husband having been killed with the BEF in France, was drinking heavily and too often unaware of her grandson's presence. The authorities intervened again, and Flynn was listed on another evacuation roster when, unexpectedly, his Aunt Kathleen offered him a home with her in southern Ireland. His father's older sister was unmarried and childless, living in a decent red-brick villa in Dun Laoghaire on the south shore of Dublin Bay. Kathleen had inherited the house, and a modest income, from parents both dead in the Troubles. Her offer seemed the ideal solution.

In March 1942 Flynn – still not ten years old – was shipped across the Irish Sea. He toured every corner of the ship on the short voyage, and liked what he saw. There and then, he determined to be a sea captain when he grew up.

His Aunt Kathleen's motives for adopting Flynn were confused. They did not include an affectionate interest in little boys. Principally she was concerned that her nephew understand the full horror of the iniquities inflicted on the Irish by the murdering Brits – that he would not grow up 'over there' ignorant of his heritage. The people of Ireland had long memories, she would hint darkly, as she described to the boy the killers and torturers just across the water, by whose godless side his treacherous father had gone to war.

Flynn listened, and was puzzled. He had known many British people in his short life, including his 'treacherous' father, and remembered them as unpredictable, but mostly quite pleasant. He decided finally that truthfulness was not in general an adult virtue. This proved a stabilising conclusion: his father died in the Allied invasion of Sicily, and Flynn was obliged to spend the next seven years in his aunt's increasingly paranoid company.

In 1949, at seventeen years of age, Flynn joined the Merchant Navy. He prospered. Within ten years, although not yet a sea captain he had gained his First Mate's ticket. He took a job with an oil shipping line, Occidental Consolidated, and stayed with them. His routes, mostly to and from the Gulf, were boring, but added rapidly to his hours at sea. And if he wanted to be a captain then it was hours at sea, thousands of them, that he needed.

Also, he *liked* being at sea. If his life had a purpose, which he began for the first time to question, then it was simply that: to be at sea.

By his mid-thirties he had invented snort-time. As a life's purpose, being at sea now seemed hardly to be sufficient. But no other purpose presented itself, and snort-times became more frequent.

He married. When he was forty-three, in 1975, he was offered his own ship and took it. His marriage failed: he managed to keep going. Snort-times helped him to feel no great pain, and he was practically never drunk. But he felt no great joy either. He was ready for a change; more than ready, by the time change came.

Eight years later, the tanker he commanded was in collision with a large Dutch freighter in the English Channel. Neither ship was seriously damaged, there was no loss of life, and the resultant oil spillage was relatively small. At the court of inquiry that followed Flynn was completely exonerated. The Dutch captain and his officers were revealed as cocaine users who had believed just once too often that they could cover for each other.

But in Flynn the wreckage of their lives, and the manoeuvrings of the two shipping lines and their insurers, brought about just the change he needed.

He sat in the London courtroom and listened to the bland prevarications of the various counsel, their legal histrionics as soon as questions of liability were raised. The contrast with the day he had spent at the small bay where the remains of the oil slick from his ship had finally come ashore shocked him.

Until then he had never actually seen a seashore dying under thick brown slime. Devoted naturalists, with volunteer helpers, were trying to save both the birds and the beach. After the detergent sprays and floating booms had done their work, the affected area was in fact quite small. The numbers of dying birds and fish, like the gobbets of raw oil, were not large, and the stench that hung over the place, in spite of an offshore wind, was not outrageous. Occidental Consolidated was rich, just as the insurers and the Dutch shipping company were rich. Any of them could meet the cost of the clean-up without a qualm. Yet still the counsel in London passed compensation figures back and forth, and picked at them like vultures. All of them, Flynn realised as he sat in the stuffy courtroom, had gained their wealth through a long succession of similar buckpassing, penny-pinching exercises. It was called being successful in business.

The next morning, Flynn terminated his contract with Occidental. This act, from a man not given to such things, was one of symbolic protest. Not simply against his employers, nor simply in support of the naturalists he had seen up to their armpits in blood and slime and bird shit, conditions far worse than he had experienced cleaning out the henhouse as a boy. It was an act of protest against all the ways of the world: and most of all against his own part in those ways, a working life spent helping to make rich men richer and poor men poorer, while contributing more than his share to the irreparable damage being done to the Earth.

Occidental Consolidated threatened to sue him for breach of contract. He told them to please themselves. They decided not to. He was disappointed. He'd been looking forward to the case.

For more than a year he had no job. He joined environmental causes. He contributed money from his comfortable savings – a life at sea gave plenty of opportunity for saving. He stuffed envelopes, occasionally spoke at meetings, but not very well. He campaigned against seal-culling for profit, and against using animals to test cosmetics. He shipped as navigator (unpaid) on a vessel hoping (but failing) to obstruct the Japanese whaling fleet.

It was a wasted year. Entered into with the bitter conviction that mankind was no damn good, it was bound to be so. He needed miracles, and when no miracles appeared he took refuge in sour glee. He'd always suspected that mankind was no damn good, and now he'd proved it.

His drinking grew worse. Idleness, and the absence of miracles, was killing him. His alternatives seemed to be either suicide, for which he had no enthusiasm, or snort-times that ran together until he became incapable. Obstinately, he found a third possibility – he got himself a job.

In Britain the Natural Environment Research Council was looking for a captain for one of its small research vessels, the *William Wilson*. He applied, a tanker man with more years than he cared to mention, and was accepted. Possibly the interview board saw across the table a man who needed them more than they needed him, and were generous. Possibly they simply compared his sea-time with the money they were paying, and reckoned it was a good bargain.

The *William Wilson* didn't cure his drinking, but she helped him. The work was varied, and with people who often confounded his belief in humanity's no-damn-goodness. But penny-pinching continued, now at government level, and by the early 1990s the NERC was obliged to reduce its modest fleet. His ship and another were put up for sale. He was assured that his job was safe, although in what capacity was not explained, and he didn't believe a word of it. He'd seen the writing on the wall: it said the world was going to hell in a wheelbarrow, and there wasn't a damn thing he could do about it.

His ship was bought by a small private research foundation based in Oxford. She was lying in Southampton at the time, and her new owners, in town for the final transaction, asked him to have dinner with them in their hotel. During the negotiations he had avoided them and their buying agent; but now they wanted to discuss the possibility that he might stay with his ship. He accepted the dinner invitation.

But before the meeting, he carried out some research of his own. It led him to the city library's newspaper files, and to a recent issue of *New Scientist*. He took a photocopy of the piece away with him. It told him much that he needed to know.

GREEN LIGHT FOR GRAHAM

Robert Graham's efforts to buy the former British oceanographic survey ship *William Wilson* (*New Scientist*, 8 September) seem to have been successful. The Natural Environment Research Council (NERC) announced on Monday that it would accept the offer of the newly-established Graham Foundation for the ship, and that the vessel would continue a programme of oceanographic and sea floor surveying, although now in private hands.

Bob Graham, who heads the foundation which is purchasing the ship and has put up much of the estimated £500,000 cost of the project, is a man of many scientific parts. Born in England in 1920, he moved to the United States in the early 1950s and worked with Charles Townes at the Bell Laboratories. In 1966 he received the Nobel Physics Prize for his work on lasers, and more recently he has been a leading light in SANE (Scientists Against Nuclear Excess). His efforts to encourage nuclear disarmament led to the award of the Nobel Peace Prize, jointly with the Soviet dissident Yuri Tupolev, in 1979.

Why the sudden interest in oceanography? 'I was talked into it by my daughter,' says Graham.

Colly Graham, who works at Oxford University, is a geophysicist with a special interest in the production of minerals from volcanically active regions of the sea bed. She recently returned from an expedition studying the hot brine pools of the Red Sea, and will be running the scientific side of the Graham Foundation's work. 'Our aim,' she told New Scientist this week, 'is the peaceful exploitation of the mineral resources of the sea bed. The big studies of places like the Red Sea, carried out so far by the rich industrial nations like Britain, France and the United States, are a form of scientific colonialism. We intend to provide the scientific expertise for smaller countries to make their own studies of their own sea bed resources, so that they can develop these without being ripped off by the multinationals.'

David Turner, of the Department of Geodesy and Geophysics in Cambridge, commented: 'It is a sad reflection on the state of scientific research in Britain today when a private foundation has to pick up the pieces of one of our major research programmes.'

Flynn folded the photocopy away in his wallet.

Dinner, at Southampton's Royal George, was impressive. So, in their own way, were Flynn's hosts. The William Wilson's new owners, the Grahams, turned out to be a tall, white-bearded British scientist twice as old as God, and his sassy young daughter, very blonde and American. If they were Oxford University, Flynn decided, the place must be better than he'd thought.

They had with them his curriculum vitae and references from the NERC, which they told him were excellent. Also, the young woman remembered his face from a TV news item about the abortive attempt to stop the Japanese whalers. It seemed she approved of such activities. She described her recent work in the Red Sea and mentioned that she was hoping to take her own research team into Icelandic waters. Flynn told her frankly that he knew little of the North Atlantic, and what he did know he didn't like.

He had read smart articles about job interviews and their turning points. The turning point of this one occurred very early in the evening. Out in the cocktail lounge, still wary of each other, they were lightly discussing the week's international news. Suddenly Professor Graham had fixed him with a clear shrewd gaze.

'And what are your feelings about the arms race, Captain Flynn?'

A serious question deserved a serious answer. Even if Flynn hadn't known of the old man's background in the peace movement, he would still have answered the same. 'It's a terminal disease, sir.'

Graham smiled grimly. 'Then I take it you believe we still have an arms race, Captain?'

'What else? You mean, all this bloody posturing. Agreements to scrap missiles that are so old they won't work properly anyway.' His first gin of the evening, on top of the quick snort he'd had in his cabin before coming ashore, was taking effect. 'Would either of them big fellers put pen to paper if he didn't reckon he was getting the best of it? They've got a lot more cutting to do before the world's a safer place to live in. And I don't see any sign of the savings they're supposed to be making being spent on things the world really needs.'

The girl interjected. 'Such as?'

Flynn shrugged. 'You've seen me on the box, you say. It's no secret what we need. A cleaner environment. More concern for other creatures. And more for the poor human creatures who don't have all this' – he waved his arm to indicate the comfort of the Royal George – 'to enjoy.'

He saw the Grahams exchange glances. The old man gave a tiny nod, and Flynn knew the job was his if he wanted it. The rest of the interview was just coasting along – and enjoying a grand dinner on the way.

Around ten o'clock, over the brandy, Professor Graham offered him a six-month contract. He accepted the terms and the deal was settled. There was a gentleness and a radiance about the old man and his daughter that attracted him. Even in the stuck-up dining room at the Royal George they made the wheelbarrow ride to hell seem just a little less inevitable.

Now, months later, he couldn't remember exactly when he'd fully understood their intentions. Certainly, during the shakedown cruise to a mysterious rendezvous with a scruffy motorised caique off Marseilles, he hadn't been told what was in the container that was hoisted aboard and stowed so tenderly. Neither had he asked awkward questions, He trusted the Grahams. Obviously, they trusted him. They'd tell him what it was all about when they were ready. And by the time they did, and Colly was giving him a free choice between leaving his ship in Helgavik and staying on with her and Werner and Kassim to the end of the countdown, it was really no choice at all.

He said he understood the death she promised him, win or lose, and accepted it; but secretly he nurtured a spark of disbelief. CIA, KGB – they weren't God Almighty. There were still places he could retire to on this beautiful planet that were untainted by their evil presence.

Besides, Colly had bewitched him. Brains and beauty; she was the daughter he had never had.

Ambling in greasy trainers along the *Fimbulvetr*'s side deck, he found himself at the point where Kassim had staged his own abduction. Poor Colly. He walked on thoughtfully, crossed the after deck and paused, leaning over the stern rail.

Where was the little bugger now? Tripoli, the Professor said. Flynn doubted it. He hadn't seemed *that* crazy. But wherever he was, he was gone. But the great thing was, if the opposition hadn't taken him then they probably didn't even know he'd gone. Didn't know the *Fimbulvetr*'s crew was reduced to three. And long may they remain in ignorance, he thought, as he wandered slowly forward, reaching again for the flask in his hip pocket.

These days, he regarded his drinking with mild affection. Once he had needed it. Now he had the feeling it needed him. It must be terrible, he sometimes told himself, to be a snort-time nobody needed.

At eleven, New York time, Robert called the Abernatheys' number.

By then it seemed certain that the disaster had been averted, but it was still good to read the message Colly had left.

She told him that the trigger had been deactivated soon after receiving his warning. Kassim had hidden his bomb in a canister of scouring powder in the wet lab; they'd lobbed it overboard, into deep water. Everything was fine. Fog had drifted in. They were moored out in the middle of the cove now, and Werner was mounting lights round the ship to shine down on to the water and make the night watches easier. But how had he found out about Kass?

Robert cleared the screen. Perhaps he'd get around to telling her, but he doubted it. It could join the million other things there'd never be time for. He must pretend, too, that he believed her reassuringly tidy story about Latif's bomb. As if she or Werner would ever simply throw something like that overboard . . . obviously there'd been some kind of narrow escape she didn't want to worry him with.

The point was, they'd got away with it.

That afternoon Robert had called the UN from a booth out in Queens. What Georg told him sent him hurrying back to his TV set. CBS news at six, MacNeil Lehrer for the in-depth analysis, CNN for the non-stop overkill. So much talk of motives, and implications, and hidden meanings, that the good news itself nearly got obscured. The senior Soviet negotiator, back in Geneva from Moscow, had brought with him a new proposal. He was talking total ban. Not in so many words, but all the commentators agreed that was it. And Robert, who had been a negotiator himself, also agreed.

It was the first step. For Robert, who'd spent so long working for disarmament, it was the most important step. All the rest – Werner's dreams of a more equitable world, Colly's serious-minded, North-American concern about global pollution – that was just the icing on the cake. Deep down, Robert believed that humanity could solve the problems of its own devising, once the nuclear threat was removed. The symbolic importance of such a turning-aside from fifty years of megadeath brinkmanship would spill over into other areas. The nuclear sanction had never influenced smaller nations – witness the Iraqi conflict – but for the superpowers its abandonment must make them re-think all their global attitudes. With the Warsaw Pact dissolved and the Soviets crumbling from within, if their hard-liners made it to the top many analysts saw nuclear blackmail as their most likely option, one last-ditch attempt to unite their suffering people.

Robert knew the test ban alone wouldn't be enough to satisfy his younger conspirators, out there in Iceland. But *this* was the moment he'd been working towards, one way and another, for so many years.

His first reaction was uncritical delight. Not only was the Soviet government taking the ultimatum seriously, it was already preparing the way for public action. Whoever was pulling the strings – and for years now, that had been far from clear – it would be difficult for them to back out of that. Tears sprang into his eyes. The sensation amazed him. Mighty wheels had started to turn. Give them just a little more momentum, and they would never be stopped. And *he*, Robert Graham, the old man with a bee in his bonnet, had done it!

Except – He sobered. Except that there were snags, politically. The Soviets had got in first. Now the US was left lamely 'considering their response'. There were already White House suggestions that it was all simply a cunning Russian ploy designed to isolate the USA from an increasingly anti-nuclear Europe. The President would have to move quickly to stop that bandwagon, driven by public fears and insecurities.

He got up from the TV set and agitatedly paced the room. Could the President swing it? Surely. The voters loved him; he had a reputation for being tough on the international stage. It could still be done, though it would have been easier if his front men had been quicker off the mark.

Robert leaned against the window, mind reassured by the logic but with a twisting feeling still in his gut. The first step – but how many more steps still had to be made?

It was evening. The brick wall opposite, deep in shadow, gave him no inspiration. He switched on the overhead light, settled at his word processor, fed in a disk for the next instalment of his log. He had a lot of ground to cover. Friday, August 6: the day the world took a major step on the road to sanity.

7

Day Four. AUGUST 7. SATURDAY.

In Helgavik, thick fog obscured the sun. The *Fimbulvetr* lay in a hemisphere of shadowless light, giving a visibility of scarcely two hundred feet, and flattened so that the top of her foremast was lost to view. The air was cold, the seabirds hushed, and every exterior surface was damp to the touch.

Werner had the watch from six to noon. The fog seemed to make his job easy. From the bridge he could see the entire ship and a circle of water beyond it, while the silence made any surprise approach virtually impossible. He leaned his forehead on the glass above the wheel, watched it steam up with his breath. Nothing moved. He allowed his mind to wander.

He hadn't enjoyed showing the American observer the bomb in its yellow canister. He disliked diving with strangers, and particularly with a stranger so openly an enemy and of so overpowering a physical presence. But most of all he disliked the bomb itself. He disliked to see it, to be reminded of it. Even now the head-on thought of it brought him out in a cold sweat. So much power, and all of it for death.

The fusion bomb he had adapted to the five-foot length and ten-inch diameter of its container was relatively small and cheap. Small, because it weighed only around two hundred pounds, and in another sense small because it would release energy equivalent to the explosion of only half a million tons of TNT. Cheap, because its principal ingredient was uranium-238, in nuclear terms a commonplace element, used as a blanket around a much smaller quantity of plutonium, which was vastly more expensive and harder to obtain.

Brought to critical mass by a modest charge of conventional

explosive, slamming the two shaped chunks of radioactive material together, the fission of this plutonium would generate the enormous flash of energy and pressure needed to fuse the nuclei of a comparably modest amount of lithium deuteride and tritium in the heart of the bomb. The energy released by this fusion would send a flood of particles outward, splitting the nuclei of the surrounding blanket of uranium, and releasing yet more energy. The result, accomplished in less than a millionth of a second, would be a rapidly expanding cloud of vapourised matter, at this stage only a few yards in diameter but with a temperature of tens of millions of degrees. The fireball. And from that, inexorably, the familiar mushroom cloud.

So much power, and all of it for death.

He realised, now, that he lacked the objectivity of the true technician. The rare metals in their intricate shapes, the delicate kryton trigger mechanism, all these were technically beautiful, excellent in the purity and economy of their design. But they were also evil in its most refined essence, and as he worked with them he'd felt himself almost overwhelmed by their deep malignancy. Death, on an unimaginable scale.

It would be safer, psychologically, to think of the bomb simply as a kit of parts. The trigger was of American manufacture. The enriched plutonium had been obtained from a fast breeder reactor located somewhere east of Suez (although probably not, in the light of Kassim's departure, from India). Several of the electronic components were marked with cyrillic lettering, the Russian that was, to any educated East German, a second language. The uranium was commonplace, and could have come from any one of a dozen countries. And the bits and pieces that made it all work together were British, Japanese – anything that had been easily accessible in England. Viewed as a kit of parts, the bomb might be considered, like their little team, a fine example of international co-operation.

The joke was sick, but so was the situation. The US had the capacity to build four devices similar to theirs, but each a hundred times more powerful, every day of every week of every month. The Soviets had a similar capacity. Just how much of it was being used at present, who could say? But after all the smiles and handshakes, all the public signings of treaties, the superpowers could build new devices at a rate of eight a day, between them, to replace the worn out old systems they were so ostentatiously dismantling. Even sicker, the resources squandered in this way were desperately needed to ensure the health of the planet.

He had assembled their bomb so that it might never be used. It was the same tired paradox that had started the nuclear arms race. But their paradox rested on faith and hope, while the other rested on fear and greed. The difference was profound, and he was convinced by it. Their bomb would never be used.

But he still hadn't enjoyed showing that American the yellow canister.

Leaning now on the mahogany frame of the bridge window, he stared down at the *Fimbulvetr*'s foredeck. A few yards beyond her bow the fog rose in an opaquely shifting wall. The water of the cove, pewter coloured and oily smooth, slipped endlessly away beneath this wall, the seen and the unseen merging imperceptibly. Overhead, although it was nine o'clock and the sun well up, there was no change in the fog's dim translucency. The ship lay without movement, totally isolated beneath a grey, silent dome . . .

Suddenly, from the direction of the land astern, an engine roared. Werner shook his head to clear it, and moved quickly out on to the open bridge wing. The engine seemed to be a car's, in low gear, labouring downwards from a position high above the beach. Another engine joined the row. Werner closed his eyes, picturing the invisible shore. Two smallish motor vehicles were coming down the narrow, boulder-strewn glacier bed that led from the road.

He ducked inside the bridge, phoned down to the wardroom. Nobody answered. Colly would still be asleep in her cabin. Maybe Flynn had already heard the engines and was on his way up.

He arrived almost before the thought had formed. 'What have we here? Piccadilly Circus comes to Dunsinane?'

There were voices now above the engine noise: shouting and some laughter. The vehicles had checked and were moving very slowly.

'They've hit the fog,' Werner said. 'Perhaps they didn't expect it. It's probably clear and sunny up top.'

'They?'

Werner had been able to pick out some of the shouts. 'Russians. For sure.'

'That's what I thought.' Flynn cocked his head, listening. 'It's a language for poets.' He took the rifle down from its rack, checked that it was loaded.

Gradually the confusion on the hillside seemed to be getting sorted out. The vehicles stopped, men got out and went on ahead, directing them. Their directions were not always understood. There would be a sudden flurry of car horns and angry shouting, while engines revved hard.

Flynn commented: 'They're not exactly being secretive. What do we make of that?'

'That they're official. They have a cover, and the Icelandic government knows they're here.'

'So?'

'So nothing. I hope the bastards lose their way and fall off the cliff.'

'I'll drink to that.' He did.

The activity on the shore continued. Eventually, the vehicles reached the shore, where people disembarked and stores were unloaded, with much banging of doors. There was hammering, and the sound of heavy objects being dragged across the shingle, somewhere near where the rescue hut must be. A radio began to play, bringing in American pop music from the NATO base. As Flynn had said, the Russians were not discreet; it seemed they wanted to be heard.

Since this suggested no immediate threat, Werner delayed waking Colly. Time enough for that when they got an outboard going and started nosing around the bay. At eleven thirty, Flynn went below to prepare lunch. Werner made a circuit of the ship, confirming that there was no way a swimmer could get aboard without throwing a grapnel up first. Looking down at the motorboat alongside, he realised that it would make an ideal staging post for attackers. He frowned. They were such amateurs, he and Flynn and Colly. What else had they missed?

He listened to the cheerful sounds from the shore. The Russians there had every reason to be confident. The *Fimbulvetr* was crewed by dreamers: three innocents up in arms against the immense machines of war. They didn't stand a chance. Of course the Russians were confident.

But the boat could be moved. It could be hoisted on board. Hell, it could be sunk. They'd never need it again. Amateurs learned; innocents could have their eyes opened. The world could yet be saved.

At noon, the fog was as thick as ever. The new arrivals on shore had settled down; for the moment, only music from their radio drifted across the water. Perhaps they were eating. At the end of Werner's watch Flynn relieved him, and he went below to wake Colly. They carried up the food Flynn had prepared and the three of them ate together on the upper deck.

After lunch Colly and Werner winched the motorboat up on the port davits.

In the middle of the afternoon the fog began to clear. It thinned from the top down. First the sun became visible, a moon-like white disc. Then the black summits of the lava cliffs showed. Colly and Werner leaned together on the ship's stern rail, anxiously watching the layers of whiteness melt away from the hillside above the Russians' beach encampment. Peaks of bright blue tents poked up through the fog. Then, in a sudden movement of breeze across the water, the mist was gone.

Werner focused his binoculars. The Russians had arrived in two red, four-wheel-drive Mitsubishi LX2000s, vehicles easily hired in Reykjavik. Their camping equipment, too, was standard rental stuff: three lightweight four-man tents, a small toilet tent some distance away, and a substantial bottled gas cooker under its own awning. Firewood was too rare in Iceland for campers to rely on it for their cooking.

Bright orange sleeping bags hung over the tent guy ropes. Down on the beach a group of people in civilian hiking clothes were slowly picking their way along, stooping, picking up lumps of lava. Two men were fetching water in white plastic containers from the stream that ran beside their camp. The entire scene was studiedly non-military. Even the inflated rubber dinghy and outboard motor on the stones above the high tide mark could have been obtained in any large sporting goods store.

Werner counted ten people, sex uncertain on account of walking boots, heavy trousers and anoraks. They were young, jostling each other like kids on an outing. Binoculars hung from their necks, and cameras. They carried no visible weapons. Nothing distinguished them from any other party of tourists, outdoor enthusiasts camping for a few days on Helgavik beach. Their visas would describe them as such. Only there was nothing to attract tourists to Helgavik beach.

Someone on the beach looked up and spotted the *Fimbulvetr*. There were excited cries. People arranged themselves in a line at the water's edge, waving and shouting.

Colly waved back. 'Such nice, friendly people. I wonder where their guns are?'

Werner looked at her sideways. 'They *might* be tourists.'

'And Eleanor Roosevelt might be my auntie.' Colly waved again. 'Maybe they don't have guns. How could they smuggle them in?'

'If the trawler's still there, no problem.'

'I forgot. Well done, Werner. No point in looking on the bright side, is there?'

Flynn came aft, joining them beneath the stern gantry and the yellow minisub. As well as the rifle, he'd brought his own binoculars. 'Proper little Butlin's,' he grunted sourly, peering out across the water.

And over on the beach a holiday camp atmosphere did seem to prevail. Now that the *Fimbulvetr* had been seen there was a scramble to get to the dinghy and launch it. Colly wondered for whose benefit the pretence of surprise was being maintained. Who was watching the watchers?

Six people packed into the dinghy, and four remained behind. Werner was beginning to connect voices with heads, and to pick out beards and moustaches. There were seven men and three women. Two of the women were included in the dinghy party.

The motor started and the heavily laden craft ploughed out towards them. Colly turned to Werner. 'You're the one with the Russian. Tell them to piss off.'

'That I can do.' He smiled. 'But I'm sure it won't be needed. They'll all speak excellent English.'

He was right. When the dinghy was a hundred yards away it stopped, blunt nose wallowing as the helmsman throttled down.

'Good afternoon,' he called politely. 'Good afternoon, *Fimbulvetr*. My name is Alexei Karpovich. I hope we do not interrupt your work.'

His tone was affable, and the sarcasm might have been unintended. He smiled up at the three of them, leaning idly on the ship's rail.

Colly played the game. 'We were just taking a break,' she called back. 'I am Doctor Graham. What can I do for you?'

'For us, nothing. We are on holiday. A group . . . a club outing, I think you would say. The Tourist Agency tells us of your important work here. We understand well that we must not make a nuisance – although, of course, we are interested.'

'I'm glad to hear it,' Colly said evenly. 'How long are you planning to stay, Mr Karpovich?'

'That is not certain. A week . . . ten days . . .' He shrugged. 'As long as there are things here for us to do.'

Flynn turned his face away from the Russians. 'That's the first honest thing the bastard's said,' he muttered.

Colly raised her voice. 'Goodbye then, Mr Karpovich. I hope you all have a happy holiday.'

'That is very kind.' He lingered. 'We are Russian, you understand. Soon you will come and have a drink with us. We give you good Russian vodka. You know Russian vodka?'

'I'm afraid our work keeps us very busy. We don't go ashore much.'

'A pity.' Still he lingered. The dinghy rocked slowly in the swell, its passengers staring up intently, two of them taking photographs. 'I see you are about to launch your submarine. That will be a great treat for us.'

She shook her head. 'It is too late in the day, now. In fact we are about to do some work inside, in the lab.' Her voice was firm. 'So we must say goodbye for now, Mr Karpovich.'

'Goodbye for now, Doctor Graham.'

He slipped the motor back into gear. Under cover of its sound, he talked earnestly with his companions. Their smiles continued, and one of the women waved. But instead of going away the dinghy circled the ship, at a distance of about a hundred metres.

'Will you look at that now,' Flynn protested. 'Taking pictures of us from all angles. And you so charming – ' He hefted his rifle. 'Myself, I'd have put a bullet in their little rubber boat, and let them swim for it.'

'And face a complaint from the Icelandic Tourist Board?'

'Why not, for glory's sake? There's precious little the Icelanders can do now we're here.'

'They can ask us to move, Flynn.'

He glared at her, scratching his beard. 'They never would. Not with the Minister worried for his uranium.'

'Maybe. And maybe not. This whole thing has to stay secret, Flynn, or it won't work. Can't have the superpowers losing face. And there's nothing the opposition would like better than to have us distracted by an incident with the Ministry.' She patted his arm affectionately. 'Save the gun for later, Flynn. When we really need it.'

She walked off. Flynn returned to the bridge. Werner, watching closely, had seen tension behind her show of confidence. He hesitated, then went after her. The dinghy had completed one circuit and was starting another, cameras clicking furiously. If there *was* a way to board, they'd find it.

He caught up with Colly on the upper deck and followed her into the main lab. As he closed the door behind them she flung herself into a chair, leaned on the bench, hands pressed to her forehead. All at once, her face was old. Deep lines dragged at it.

He perched on the edge of the bench beside her, choosing his words carefully. She needed sympathy, not false comfort.

'The trouble is,' he said, 'they know they have plenty of time. They can play these games with us. We're the ones under pressure.'

Colly's eyes were closed. 'It's the phony grins that get to me . . . Or maybe they're not so phony. Maybe from where they're standing the whole thing really is one big hoot.'

'Could your father hurry the negotiations?'

'No way. You heard the radio. That's amazing progress.'

'The news *is* good, though.'

She opened her eyes, lowered her hands, sat up straight. 'Words. That's all it is, yet. Words. A proposal. Anyone can make a proposal. Don't you see, my dear Werner, while they figure out how to deal with us there'll be any number of proposals.'

'But they *can't* fix us. We've thought of everything.' He hunkered down beside her, hand on her shoulder. 'They *can't* fix us.' She looked at him keenly. 'You really believe that?' 'I do. I really do.' He stood up, took her hands and pulled her to her feet. 'It's going to work, Colly.' He hugged her. 'It's really going to work.'

She leaned stiffly away. 'You're not fooling me, Werner.'

'But it *is* going to work. What else can I say?'

For a long moment, she didn't move. Then suddenly, taking pity on him, she laughed. 'Of course it's going to work. Don't I know it better than you, Werner Dietrich? Wasn't it my idea in the first place?' She freed herself. By an effort of will her face was transformed, young again. She moved away, her energy uncontainable. 'We're fireproof, honey. We've pulled up the ladder. And the more guys they send to see for themselves, the safer we are. So you don't have to tell me it's going to work.'

She ended up by one of the big windows. He joined her. The wake of the Russians' dinghy lay in a straight furrow across the water as they returned to their camp. So they had made their first move. They would have to make others. He saw now that the *Fimbulvetr*'s great strength lay in her need to do very little. Always the opposition had to come to her, on her terms.

Colly's mood had been like a dark presence looming over her. Now it had gone away. Such moods came rarely. She leaned back against him, lightly affectionate.

Looking past her, after the Russians, he wondered what sort of people they were, what qualities they had been chosen for. He also wondered what their superior officers had told them. Not the truth, that was for sure. Less even than half the truth. How much would it be safe to tell them? Nothing. Simply to observe and report back. They were soldiers, surely. Soldiers didn't expect to be given explanations, only orders.

He breathed in the soft faint smell of Colly's hair, nuzzled into the back of her neck. She leaned against him harder. Flynn was on watch on the bridge. His left hand tugged at her sweater, freeing it from her jeans, while his right hand set to work on the buckle of her belt. Once, for a short time in Oxford, right at the beginning, they had been genuinely close. That special, gentle feeling between them had long since gone. But now, isolated on a boat in the middle of a bay in Iceland, waiting for the end of the world, they needed each other more than ever.

At three o'clock that Saturday afternoon, Kassim Latif was in Rome, waiting in St Peter's Square for the Vatican tour bus. The sky was cloudless, and since early morning the Mediterranean sun had slowly heated the square's ancient stucco walls and worn shadowless pavements, until by now the vast enclosed space was as hot and dry and airless and dazzlingly brilliant as a Colorado canyon. Kassim was acutely uncomfortable. His years in northern Europe, particularly in Britain, had thickened his blood, and he breathed shallowly, shading his eyes and moving no more than was strictly necessary. The bus, typically, was late.

The previous afternoon, at Rome airport, it hadn't taken him long to discover his humiliating failure. More than two years of his life, wasted. On touchdown a full hour had already passed since the moment when his device should have exploded, and thirty minutes after that, through customs and immigration, the sibilant calm of the airport building was still undisturbed. No news flashes appeared on the many TV screens. No hysterical Italians with transistor radios rushed around weeping.

In the airport cafeteria Kassim ordered a glass of unpleasant Italian tea and sat at a plastic table, not drinking it. Morosely, he drew smeared shapes with one finger on the table's surface. He was facing the bitter, incredible fact that somehow his bomb had been discovered and defused. The alternative, that it had simply failed to explode, he found even less believable. He'd been handling timers and plastique, with one hundred per cent success, for the last eight years. He drew an 8 on the table, then angrily rubbed it out.

Whatever had happened, he was now in a difficult situation. He couldn't return to the Ragnarok team – even if it were physically possible, his cover was blown. As far as Il Signore was concerned, at least a week remained before he had to report. The choice of day for the explosion had been left to Kassim, so that for the moment he could stay out of sight. But there was always the problem of assets.

After his air fare had been paid, these resided principally in his acquired skills, and in the information he possessed. Both were marketable. But should he try to market either before contacting his employer, and should his employer find out – which was likely, given Il Signore's comprehensive sources – then Kassim would be open to accusations of deceit, greed, and cowardice. Any of which was a killing matter.

He drew a dagger on the tabletop, and rubbed that out also. It reminded him that, now he was in Rome and done with security checks, he should obtain a weapon. As for his employer, the sooner he was contacted the better. Il Signore never welcomed news of failure – who did? But he welcomed evasion even less. And Kassim judged his own professional skills to be useful enough to overcome Il Signore's cruder impulses.

He fingered his wild black beard. Two years of his life, and more, just so much wasted labour. Sighing, he dug in his pocket, brought out his newly-acquired small change, and sorted from it enough hundred lire pieces for a local phone call. Never a man to delay unpleasant or dangerous tasks, he stood up abruptly, leaving his tea glass untouched, and went in search of a public phone booth from which to call Globewide Travel. The next man at his table, a harassed British tourist with two small children in tow, knocked the glass over with the corner of his tray. It broke on the terrazzo floor, forming a large, sticky puddle.

And now, in St Peter's Square, Kassim was keeping the appointment he had made from the airport, waiting for the tourist bus that would take him on the first stage of the three o'clock Vatican City conducted tour. The tour was well-chosen. For both him and the man he was to meet, Il Signore's representative, it was an ideal tail-shedding arrangement. For security reasons – supposedly – tickets for the tour had to be purchased the previous day, when passports or identification papers were examined. At the actual time of the tour, however, when the tickets were presented, nobody checked the identities of the people presenting them to see that they matched those of the purchasers. The precautions, therefore, were farcical. But they did have the advantage, for men like the one Kassim was to meet, of forbidding the tour to last-minute buyers. Any tail would be left stranded in the square.

So it was that any spy, murderer, terrorist or other wanted criminal entering the Vatican by means of the bus tour did so in a state of virtue, as it were, stripped of the world's encumbrances. As blessedly naked, in this one respect, as on the day he was born.

The bus arrived. The sweaty crowd outside the information office formed into an untidy queue and filed aboard. Kassim, who had stood some distance away, covertly watchful as he fed the ugly, insatiable pigeons with grain bought at an insulting price from an Arab vendor, tagged on at the end. He was satisfied, He'd been searching the crowd, hoping to identify his contact. Now, from one of the seats by a distant marble fountain, another man was drifting over at the last minute to join the queue. The man was European, immaculately dressed in a dove-grey suit, matching shirt and narrow, pale blue tie; but dark-skinned, almost swarthy, with crinkly black hair that failed to conceal a thin white scar running from his left temple, past his eye socket, almost to his left earlobe. A Sicilian, probably. But surveillance training, clearly, was the same the world over.

They stood together in silence, Kassim and his contact, at the rear of the queue. Once aboard, they squashed into seats in different parts of the bus. Kassim was wary. The moment was wrong, and he could be mistaken. The man carried a camera, as expected, but also a crocodile skin handbag. The rituals of mutual recognition had yet to be observed.

The tour official from the information office started counting heads. Their guide was a dark-haired, pretty, very tired-looking young Italian woman, whose lapel badge announced her name to be Maria Ricci. She leaned on the dashboard by the driver, unhurriedly finishing her cigarette. The bus wasn't air-conditioned, and quickly began to smell hot and sweaty. When the official had finished counting, comparing numbers with a list on a clipboard, he nodded to the girl, smiled mechanically, patted her bottom, and left the bus. Maria Ricci stubbed out her cigarette, stared woodenly down the crowded, airless seats, tapping the microphone in her hand. As the bus moved off she started to speak, first in English and then in German.

Kassim was instantly bored. The exotic Swiss Guards at the Vatican Gate didn't impress him, and neither did the overblown architecture. The historical details of popes and princes, artists famous and infamous, Borgias and banking systems, of wars and wars and more wars, passed him by. He knew such decadence had always existed, and he found it tedious. For the whole corrupt European mess, the long winter of destruction was centuries overdue.

At the Vatican Station they were allowed out of the bus to stretch their legs. This bombastic structure was now used just once a week, and then only for a few incoming wagons of duty-free goods – the Papacy obviously preferred whenever possible *not* to render unto Caesar what was Caesar's. Kassim waited for as long as he could before returning to the bus. He was expecting an approach from the elegant stranger, but none came.

Once they were all back in the bus, they learned that these days the Pope mostly travelled from the Vatican Airport, which turned out to be a small helicopter pad up at the top of the hill, past the masts of Vatican Radio, erected under the direction of Signor Marconi himself. The pad had been built, they were told, on the site of the one-time Papal tennis courts. It was particularly fortunate, therefore, their guide informed them with heavy humour, that the present Pope did not care for tennis.

Kassim fidgeted impatiently. He had found out in advance that the bus took them only to the top of the hill behind St Peter's. From there, beside the parapet high above the Viale Vaticano, they were expected to walk for a short distance, through the English Garden, until they were picked up outside the Academy of Sciences for the rest of their tour. And it was during this walk, he now realised, that he must expect his contact to make the necessary approach.

The place was ideal. The view out over the heat-hazed city was magnificent. And, with their guide launching into German, this chance for English-speaking visitors to take their photographs was irresistible.

'Excuse me, sir. Please forgive me for bothering you.'

Kassim looked sideways from his examination of the piled red roofs. 'Yes?'

The stranger was holding out his camera. 'Please – I wonder if you would kindly take a photograph of me with this? All you have to do is point, and press this button. The clever Japanese do all the rest.'

Kassim took the camera. It was a German Zeiss, not a Japanese model. Their eyes met over it. The stranger's were wide and dark, and peculiarly guileless. Kassim found it remarkable that any member of their profession should have so little to hide.

He smiled. 'It's no trouble at all. My wife has a camera just like this. They are clever, aren't they?'

Contact was made. For appearances' sake, the stranger moved away, posed in front of the view, and Kassim pointed the camera. He didn't press the button. Something about the other man worried him. Not the knife at his right calf, just visible through his fine cashmere trousers. That was to be expected. No, there was something else. Also, the camera seemed curiously heavy.

If the stranger knew that the button had not been pressed he made no comment. They rested companionably together on the shoulder-high parapet, looking down, discreetly isolated from their fellow tourists. There were seats at intervals, and taller sections of broken wall. A breeze, slight but blessedly cool, stirred the air.

The stranger pointed down, as if at a particular campanile. 'My name is Scotti. You are Latif. I have to tell you the Dreamer is not pleased.'

Kassim's gaze followed the direction of the pointing finger. 'I did not think he would be. I am not pleased myself. In fact this is a great humiliation to me. I'm sure the Dreamer will know that.'

He felt deep foreboding. The name invoked was that of the man behind Il Signore. It was a name with its own history, out of the Mediterranean underworld, not lightly used. The man with the final power. The Dreamer. Not the first to hold the title, but perhaps the most powerful of that name. *The Dreamer of Dreams and the Seer of Visions.*

Scotti turned his head. 'So?'

'So I am here. I offer no excuses.'

'That at least is good.'

They spoke in English, softly, the other man with an Italian accent as suave as his suit, Kassim plainly, with none of the Indian quaintness he assumed when dealing with the British. It might charm them, but it would do nothing for this ruthless Sicilian.

Scotti faced him. 'The Dreamer has made many preparations.

Abandoning them because of your failure will be very expensive. This distresses him.'

'He must not abandon them.' Kassim spoke urgently. 'Tell him he must not abandon them.' How much did the stranger know? Even in his urgency, Kassim was careful not to reveal too much. 'Even without my help, things will turn out as he has planned. Tell him . . . tell him, the American woman is very determined, and her demands will not be met. She will be forced to act.'

'I will tell him what you say.'

The tone was neutral. Kassim braced himself. 'Then there will be a place for me? I have many skills. There will still be work?'

'My dear Latif – of course there will.'

The reply and its accompanying smile were immediate. Innocent. Too immediate and innocent. The stranger's eyes, too, remained wide, meeting his in total frankness. So that then, at that precise moment, Kassim knew beyond any doubt that the stranger was lying. His purpose this afternoon was death.

Kassim felt a touch of scorn. The Dreamer should have sent one of his own. Europeans dissembled so badly. Scotti was lying, and therefore dangerous.

The tour guide had finished her German version of the panorama's points of interest and the others were moving off down the dusty path through the English Garden. Even so, Kassim and his companion were unremarkable as they continued to lean on the parapet. The view was a famous attraction; nobody expected the tour to run to a strict timetable.

Kassim eased a little closer to the other, and in his turn pointed down at the city. 'You tell me there will be work. That makes me very happy.'

He leaned on Scotti's shoulder, moved closer still. The other man stiffened, feeling the blunt, hard-edged pressure of steel in his back. Then he laughed.

'You will not shoot me,' he said calmly. 'Not here. There are too many people.'

Kassim narrowed his eyes. 'You will tell me exactly what Il Signore di Genova said.'

'This is a waste of time. You are a fool. If I do not kill you today, there are many tomorrows.'

'Is it Il Signore's wish that I die?'

Scotti laughed again. 'Of course. You have caused him great shame. It is a matter of honour, now. You have brought on him the scorn and anger of the Dreamer. Of course he wishes you dead.'

Kassim glanced sideways, to his left. The last pair of tourists was disappearing. To his right, perhaps eighty yards away, two priests stood in conversation. He shifted his stance. One more thing he needed to know. 'What is this shame that I have brought him? Tell me.'

'You believe he confides his secrets? To me? That Il Signore tells me, Scotti, all his plans?' The Italian worked his shoulders irritably. 'All this is foolishness. It is as I said. You will not shoot me.'

'That is true,' Kassim said softly. 'I will not shoot you.'

He had heard enough. Il Signore was keeping his own counsel, as expected. The truth about the long winter was still secret. Which meant it was still marketable.

He reversed the knife whose handle had been pressing hard against the stranger's back, and thrust the long, slender blade, fiercely and accurately, through the thick lumbar muscle, deep into Scotti's heart. The heart went into spasm. Through the short death shudder Kassim supported the man close against the wall. Then he removed the knife, wiped it on the back of the dove-grey jacket, replaced it in its underarm sheath, and turned the body, lowering it gently into the corner of a worn sandstone seat.

The two priests were still engrossed in their conversation. Kassim left the body there, propped against the wall, camera in its lap, eyes closed and head lolling back as if in sleep. It would be amusing if somebody stole the camera. He was sure it was a bomb and had been intended for him, set to explode when he pressed the shutter button.

He hurried away, down through the English garden – a curious name, he thought, for such a desiccated area of scrubby, unappealing trees – and caught up with his group as it boarded the bus again. The one danger was that the harassed guide might do a second head count. He doubted she would bother, and was proved correct. She hadn't last time they reboarded the bus, at the railway station, and she didn't now. It can't have seemed likely to her that she might lose a customer on the short walk down the hill.

Kassim endured the rest of the tour in a daze, alert only to the possibility of an outcry. None occurred. The dead man might sit up there in the sun for hours, perhaps until a gathering of flies, or carrion-eating birds, attracted the attention of some passerby.

The tour ended at the Sistine Chapel, where crowds of chattering tourists munched their sweets and sandwiches, scattering empty coke cans as they lounged on the floor and popped their flashbulbs at the ceiling. Kassim, who had been raised a Christian, was unsurprised. There was nothing these people held sacred; nothing they valued save their own crass pleasures.

He escaped, out into the city. He knew it well. There were friends who owed him favours, places he could hide. Safe corners where he could make new plans.

But time was limited. Favours ran out, and hiding places staled. He needed, soon, to get away. Asia beckoned him. India, his home. He needed a new life, very far away, where even Il Signore di Genova could not find him. And for that he needed a great deal of money.

That Saturday morning wasn't the first time Robert had seen himself on television. The networks were using a fairly old film clip: Professor Graham's acceptance speech at the Peace Prize ceremony in Stockholm. Voice-over gave the news of his mysterious disappearance, so there was none of the original sound track. Not much to identify him by, and the face not much like him now, even if he'd still had the beard. He stared at the screen, thinking that the Stockholm version of himself wouldn't recognise the current New York version of himself if they passed each other in the street. He wouldn't recognise the inside of his later version's mind, either.

A Peace Prize. He sighed. What had happened to the innocence, the scrupulous morality? Ground down, worn away . . . they hadn't been up to the job. Some people's were, but not his. Not strong enough. Now he had strength – armoured in the gross violence of his ultimatum, and its justifications.

Iceland. Even that country's instantaneous annihilation could be justified. His deceptions were merciless. He lied to her people with talk of underwater riches, and to her ministers with specific hopes of profitable uraninite deposits. And he told himself that Iceland had her NATO base, she joined in NATO policies, and therefore she must take her chance.

But what chance was that? She wouldn't even share in the eventual Soviet and US response to his ultimatum. And if she had not had that base, would he have taken his risk of annihilation elsewhere? While her coastal waters remained so ideal for their purpose? He doubted it.

He'd been to Reykjavik more than once. It was a fine city, with a fine university. The half million Icelanders were rare, brave people. And yet his involvement in Ragnarok implied that he was willing personally to destroy them all. Was his vision of a dying planet as the only alternative really so certain?

For his sanity's sake, he had to answer yes.

The networks gave him good screen time. He'd heard that August was, in news terms, the silly season. It had to be, for a missing scientist to come second only to a dog fallen down a well in West Virginia. But he didn't think it would help the opposition to find him. That probably wasn't even its purpose.

Right from the beginning, he and Colly had been concerned that the opposition would publicise his disappearance as a way of letting the media loose on her. A pretty girl . . . only next of kin . . . missing famous father . . . it was the perfect bait. In no time at all reporters would be swinging from the *Fimbulvetr*'s rigging. And he'd never come up with a satisfactory answer to the problem. Security would be shot to hell; half the 'reporters' would be CIA. She just had to find her own way to persuade the Icelandic government to keep them off her back.

He switched off the TV. His previous evening's euphoria had drained away. The USA was still considering its response to the Soviet proposal in Geneva. Both sides, in fact, were marking time while they probed for cracks in the Ragnarok team's armour.

The morning message from Helgavik told him they had fog. The food was tolerable. Colly was anxious that nobody should find out about Latif. Werner had just relieved her, and she was going to get some sleep. Robert erased the message from the screen. Nothing there worth preserving for posterity. He could imagine their lives: boredom and terror, in unequal, unpredictable quantities.

His own life was about the same. He went down the long flights of stairs to his breakfast cup of coffee with Woolston. One thing was new. He'd been picturing Woolston as the typical underprivileged ghetto black. Underprivileged maybe, but hardly typical – he *owned* the Paramount. Coming in last night after a greasy spoon supper, Robert had found the man still at his desk, asked how he came to work such long hours. He owned the place, was how. A dump, but he owned it. Which was why he worked every hour God gave, and why, he said, in a couple of years it wouldn't be a dump.

Woolston didn't have a TV set at reception, he seldom left his seat, yet he always knew what was new. That morning Professor Bob Graham was new. They discussed him. Woolston wondered if he was the same Graham as the Englishman Immigration had been asking about, and Robert said he almost certainly was. Robert told the truth to Woolston. It was the least he could do.

Woolston pounded the desk. 'A lot of no-good interfering bozos, if you ask me, Mr Goldsteen.'

'Who?'

'Them.' He pointed a curved black thumb. Its sideways direction, as if to the nearest toilet, was the one he always used to identify City Hall.

'Interfering?' Robert was cautious. Yesterday he'd been a harmless old man with an out-of-date visa. Today he was famous. The man who turned him in would get interviewed nationwide. 'Aren't they just doing their job?'

'Nossir. Something's fishy. Most days, if you got a missing person you got some other person missing him. Who's missing this Graham? If there's a complaint been laid, they sure ain't telling us. No tearful wife and kids on the TV.'

He had a point. 'So what d'you think?'

'I think they've got something against the guy.' He leaned forward, lowered his voice. 'Nothing they can get him for legally, but now he's took off they ain't smiling. So they spring this missing person gag.'

'And when they find him?'

Woolston looked at Robert with the peculiar knowingness of a man who has run out of ideas. He shifted his base.

'I tell you what I think, Mr Goldsteen. They won't find him. First thing, I bet he don't look much like the picture they put out. And second thing, most guys what take off, but don't do nothing that ain't legal, they got their reasons, and people ought to respect those reasons.' He paused. 'Even if they don't know what they are. Wouldn't you say so, Mr Goldsteen?'

Robert felt ashamed. Of course Woolston wasn't going to turn him in. He proceeded, like his thumb, sideways. But he got there in the end.

'Hi. I'm Reno Zebedee. This here's Harry Harker. The firm's NBC.' He held out a plastic ID. 'All right to come aboard?'

Colly eyed them warily. The flashy white launch had come into the cove noisily, at high speed, its pilot cutting the motors expertly so that it settled back into the water, overtaken by its own spreading wake as it drifted the last few metres and came to rest alongside the *Fimbulvetr*. Clearly, Reno Zebedee believed in the direct approach.

'Come aboard?' she asked. 'What for? This is a working ship. We don't – '

'Pardon me, Doctor Graham. Can it be that you haven't heard?' He broke off, offered her a cute, made for TV smile. 'It *is* Doctor Graham, isn't it?'

She nodded unenthusiastically. Zebedee was tall and big-jawed, tanned and affable, wearing chinos and a Nike sweatshirt. The man beside him with the TV camera, identified as Harker, was a skinny negro dressed in chic camouflaged combat fatigues. There were three other men in the launch with them, the helmsman and two gum-chewers in shorts and Hawaiian shirts. A scratch crew, probably raised by Zebedee at the NATO base. Or a highly professional and experienced team, but nothing to do with NBC.

He leaned easily on the cabin roof of the launch. 'Can it be that you haven't heard about your father?'

'My father?' Fear tightened her gut. 'What about my father?'

'I truly am sorry, Doctor Graham. I didn't expect to be the one to have to tell you. Fact is, uh, Colly, your father disappeared, oh, three, four days ago. Last Wednesday afternoon, I think they said.'

Disappeared. She breathed again. If the opposition were pulling the missing person story, they certainly hadn't found him. Disappeared was just what she wanted Fard to be. But she didn't want media, real or imitation, on board the *Fimbulvetr*.

'Ridiculous.' She made room for Werner at the rail beside her. The fake campers on shore had been quiet for the last hour or so. He'd been napping down in his cabin, but the noise of the launch must have woken him. 'How could my father disappear?'

Zebedee spread his hands. 'Search me, lady. News is he flew down from Portland to the Big Apple, called on some old friends at the UN, then just stepped off the edge of the world.' Zebedee just might be genuine, after all, she decided. That sounded like the story he'd have been fed. But the gum-chewers?

He was continuing. 'So if you'll just throw down a ladder, and give Captain Flynn up there the word we ain't going to eat you, then – '

'Hold on a minute, Mr Zebedee.' No, something about him wasn't quite right. He had everybody's names off just too pat. She glanced up at the bridge, happy to see Flynn, out on the open wing, his gun casually hefted. She turned back to the tall American, looking down on him from her vantage point on the deck, comfortably out of reach of anyone on the launch. 'You seem to know a lot about us.'

'Network likes us to do our homework.'

'And what exactly do you want from us?' She was delaying, gaining time to think. Fard's last message had been sent off the previous night, enthusiastic stuff about the moves at Geneva, not a word about a public manhunt. Of course the opposition didn't know they were in regular touch, so they wouldn't know she knew that. Fard's disappearance couldn't have been announced officially until this morning – and NBC had a team here already. It *might* be done, but it was cutting it fine.

'Colly, honey, look: if we could just come aboard, huh? My neck's getting an awful crick down here. Your father's a big man, one of America's finest, and the public want to know – '

'If you're so good on homework, Mr Zebedee, then you'll know how badly NBC treated my father last time he talked to them. Intercut him with a violent and irrelevant demo in Holland. Damning by association, I think it's called.'

He laughed easily. 'So now's the chance for you to set the record straight. Just lower the drawbridge, OK?'

She still wasn't happy. 'It was good of you to come all this way.

And I'm upset by your news. New York's a terrible place. But my father's his own man. He comes and goes as he pleases. Nothing I can do about it.'

'But you're his daughter. You know the old guy better than anyone. If he's sick, lost his memory maybe – you know where he might go. Friends. Whatever.'

'Then maybe I'd better discuss that with the FBI when they turn up here.'

'NBC will get you better exposure.' Unruffled, very patient. The complete professional. 'And I don't need to tell you that every young woman in America with a father will be rooting for you.'

'I guess I'd rather have the police rooting for me, Mr Zebedee.'

The smooth side of the ship offered the Americans no handholds, and their launch was drifting away on the tide. Her pilot gunned the engine, nudging her back into position. Zebedee looked up from the cockpit, thoughtfully observing the three of them.

'Don't you have another man on board? The guy from India? How well did he know your father? Maybe we could – '

With the mention of Kassim, Colly's doubts found a focus. She'd completely forgotten the pretence they'd agreed to maintain, that he was still on board. And now this American, believing that there were still four of them, wanted to have them all up on deck, where he could see them. Suddenly, she saw him and his thickset companions as very much a team.

But already Werner, that much quicker than her, was answering him. 'Kassim is on duty in the wet lab, Mr Zebedee. He can't be spared from his work there.' Werner paused, smiling mockingly as he leaned casually on the rail. 'I think you know why.'

Colly looked past him, down into the launch. Zebedee, if that was his name, grinned up at her. One hand was in the wide pocket across the stomach of the sweatshirt. He withdrew it slowly, bringing out a long-barrelled automatic which he pointed, casually, in their general direction.

'One bang and you're dead, Doctor Dietrich.'

'One bang and a whole lot more people die, Mr Zebedee.'

'So they tell me.'

He spun the weapon in the trigger guard, extended his arm full length to point it straight at Colly. His negro companion laughed, made an obscene gesture. Instantly there was a sharp report, setting up echoes between the surrounding lava cliffs, and a cloud of seabirds rose in noisy protest. Zebedee's gun was wrenched from his hand. It fell, turning as it did so, hit the launch's gunwale and disappeared overboard. The whine of a ricocheting bullet could be heard singing its way across the water.

There was an angry stirring down in the launch. The gum-chewers' jaws were stilled; their hands were deep in the folds of their voluminous shirts. Colly didn't need to look for the source of the shot. Flynn was on the bridge, with his rifle.

And it was Flynn who remembered their imaginary fourth crew member. 'Easy in there, Kass,' he called down. 'The gentleman here made a joke. It wasn't very funny. But no harm's done.'

Colly held her breath. It seemed such a schoolboy pretence. But Zebedee, nursing a wrenched and bruised right hand, seemed convinced.

'Flynn's very protective, you see, Mr Zebedee. Better if you don't try to come aboard.'

He corrected her politely. 'Colonel Zebedee, ma'am.'

And there it was. Out in the open.

'Killing us won't help you, *Colonel* Zebedee.' She raised her voice. 'Remember the old saying. *Last one to leave puts out the light.* You might kill us all, but the last one puts out that light – for half the world.'

There were tears in her eyes, and she leaned forward passionately. 'You won't shift us, nor will those Russians camped on the beach, nor all the ones they send after you. We've got right on our side, and we're fireproof. Go back and tell them that, *Colonel* Zebedee. We can't lose.'

'Can't lose?' At last his self control snapped. 'Crap! Lady, that's so dumb it's pathetic. Jesus Christ. I tell you, you can't *win*. You're like a kid peeing his pants, 'cos he doesn't know what his pisser's for. You don't stand a chance.'

He laughed again, harshly, then lowered his voice to a mocking, conspiratorial stage whisper. 'I'll tell you for why you don't stand a chance, lady high and mighty with right on your side. You're a bunch of fucking amateurs, that's why. Look at me. *Look* at me, lady. I motored in here, bold as brass, pointed a gun at you, and I'm still alive. You're chicken. Got no guts. Should've wasted the whole fucking launch as soon as we got in range. You talk about the big one, but you ain't got what it takes even for the little one. And *that's* what I'm going back to tell them.'

He grinned at her, cleared his throat ready to spit.

And Flynn shot him.

A single shot, as before, and as accurate. Through the left side of his head, at short range. The heavy bullet made a large, messy hole as it exited, blood and brains spewing out over a wide area.

Colly was appalled. Flynn was crazy. He'd cheated. Betrayed everything they stood for. This was murder.

Frozen, she watched the tableau in the launch below. Every man, including the pilot, was now poised, legs braced, gun extended: machine pistols for the two soldiers in Hawaiian shirts; an automatic for Harker, the negro; a revolver for the pilot. The launch lay motionless in the calm water, drifting slowly away, every weapon aboard her aimed and steady. The arsenal opposing the *Fimbulvetr* was formidable; one volley of shots and the charade would be over. All that saved them was the mythical presence of Kassim in the wet lab – where, a small voice at the back of Colly's brain reminded her, the trigger wasn't even armed.

Flynn spoke. Softly. 'Go back and tell them that. Tell them we *have* got what it takes. And the last one to leave *will* put out the lights.'

The tension eased marginally. Colly, suddenly weak, was clenching her jaw hard in order not to break out into hysterical laughter. They had been saved by a non-existent crew member guarding an inactive trigger. It was almost irresistibly funny.

The negro broke the stillness. He lowered his own gun, leaned sideways over the colonel's body and touched the pilot's arm. 'Let's go, OK?'

He turned to the other two men. 'All right, you guys. We got our orders. We're taking off. But we'll be back, and that's a promise.' He looked up again at Colly. 'It's a promise to you, too. We'll be back. Sure as hell we'll be back, and next time we'll have different orders.'

Once again, the motor roared as the launch surged into motion. The negro stood, watching the ship, until it was out of sight around the headland. Colly stared back, dragging out the moment, unwilling to go up to the bridge just yet. It was no longer funny. What could she say to Flynn? Blame would be hypocritical; praise would stick in her throat. And yet, he just might have saved the whole mission. She turned, and went below, without a word to Werner.

With the relaxing of tension, a griping in her belly took her to the nearest head. As she sat, huddled forward, sounds came through the open porthole behind her. She winced. The Russians were back. A woman's voice this time, heavily friendly. The game they were playing now was that Werner, up on deck, must field endless jocular, 'innocent' questions about the shooting.

Were they shooting birds? Didn't they know that seagull stew was disgusting? That guillemot soup made the palms of your hands grow hair? Wouldn't they rather come ashore for a good Russian meal, washed down with vodka?

Colly rested her forehead on her knees, and listened wretchedly to the banter. They were noisy, but at least they kept their distance. For now. One day they'd come closer. One night, more likely. Then there'd be assault troops, and ropes, and guns, and no more jokes. And only Flynn and his rifle to stop them. And until then, they wore you down with jokes.

On balance she thought she preferred the American approach. That way, people died, openly and messily, and everybody knew where they were. If it was the opposition that died, not your own people, you were winning. Simple.

She crouched lower, covering her ears to the Russians and their sinister camaraderie. Was her nerve going? Zebedee's cold-blooded murder hadn't helped. Somehow, she was going to have to live with Flynn, work with him, keep the team together. At least she knew him better now. She was willing to bet that if she never mentioned the killing, he never would either. But it was there, between them. She saw now that its possibility had been there, behind his eyes, behind his jokes, behind his ceaseless boozing, right from the beginning.

Robert's day was quiet. Around three o'clock he took a ride out of New York on the suburban line, forty minutes to Greenwich. He'd planned Stamford for the next call to Georg, but he knew Greenwich better. Ruth and he had lived there for a time, and the journey brought back happy memories. Cities tended to change, often out of all recognition. From trains, however, they tended to look reassuringly the same. The backs of factories, warehouses, brownstones, advertisement hoardings; the ride took him back thirty years.

Except that in his commuting days there'd been a club car full of expensively drunk TV executives. Now the club car was gone, and he'd heard the executives sniffed coke instead.

He didn't leave the station. It stood near the bottom of the hill, town on one side, Long Island Sound below it on the other. From it, looking down on the red shingled roofs, he could see all he wanted. Ruth had conceived Colly beneath one of them, close to the water; but he didn't care to make out which. The days of his innocence depressed him, even as they drew him back to places like this. Colly was in Iceland; Ruth was dead.

At four thirty, a stack of quarters on the box, he rang Georg from the station kiosk. He knew Georg would be working Saturday, and probably Sunday too. Liaising between the two superpowers was important: both sides were jumpy and mutually suspicious. Robert asked, for all the world as if this were a social call, about Georg's workload. He had a Press Club Lunch to address. And of course all his usual UN stuff. If his routine was disrupted too badly, people might start to wonder what was going on beneath the surface.

'Life goes on, Robert.' He paused. 'It's good to hear your voice, old friend.'

Georg sounded low. That made two of them. 'Bad news?'

'So-so. The signals conflict.'

'Don't tell me.' Robert tried to lighten the tone. 'The bad news is that the decision to use this missing person stuff comes straight from the President.'

'CIA.'

'Which is his agency.'

'He really wants to get you.'

Robert stayed determinedly bright. 'And the good news?'

'Also from the President. The Geneva team is to offer a unilateral six-month moratorium on all testing.'

'*That* old chestnut?' Robert was genuinely surprised. 'It's been done, Georg. Years ago – and by the Soviets, for chrissakes. Why now?'

'They've got some Pentagon whizz-kid saying they've completed all the tests they need – for the time being.'

'That's true enough. But "need" is a big word.'

'Of course it's true, Bob. But if they make sure the Soviets know that the reason for the offer is, ostensibly, that the nuclear program is complete, that way, they show they don't give a damn for Europe.'

Robert sighed. 'So it's nothing, after all. Just part of the "continuing dialogue".'

'They don't have enough time, Robert.' At last Georg was getting to the point. 'You've got to extend the deadline.'

'Absolutely not.' Three people, six hour watches – even the ten days that remained would stretch them to the limit. 'Even if I wanted to, there's no way to communicate with them. You've got to get the whole package approved and made public – it's the only way to stop them pressing that button.'

Georg was silent. Seconds ticked by. Robert wasn't worried: there was a train out in two minutes, long before the Greenwich police could get their act together.

At last, reluctantly, Georg spoke. 'I'm just the go-between, Bob. You don't have to take my advice. But wasn't it your theory that our leaders would only need a little persuasion to do what they wanted to do anyway? Seems to me, they're fighting you all the way. Certainly the President isn't exactly jumping at the chance you're giving him.'

Robert looked sadly down the platform, at the rails curving away, watery in the late afternoon heat. 'Evil men, Georg? Not just weak and foolish? Is that what you're saying? You're saying we elect evil men?'

He didn't answer directly. 'I only deal with the ambassadors. They have their instructions, but they are not evil. But they see no need to hurry. Reports are coming in from Iceland. I don't know what's in those reports, but neither of them believes the deal you demand will be needed.'

'Then they're wrong. We're going to win this, Georg. Tell them to get their act together. Make it good, and make it quick. We're going to win.'

He rang off. A faint singing in the rails heralded the approaching train. Robert regretted there was nothing in the democratic process that excluded evil men. On the contrary, no truly sane person, surely, would be willing to go through the electoral process. With current democratic processes, maybe *only* evil men could be elected to the highest office. If so, then the world was indeed in a sad state.

But they *were* going to win.

It was late Saturday afternoon, and Pétur Einarsson had just left the television offices on Langavegur. As far as he was concerned, the evening show had been put to bed. Finnur could fiddle with the tapes if he wanted to, but Pétur was going home.

He collected his Toyota and drove out through the sunny, tree-lined streets. He lived in a new suburb, Gradhaverfi, to the west of the city, close to the sea, where there were several apartment blocks. The ocean views were stupendous. By choosing an apartment at the rear, however, looking inland, he'd saved hundreds of kronur in rent.

He collected his mail from the box on his way up, glanced through it as he stood by the wide living room window, drinking his first beer of the evening. Bills, and a letter from a girl he was keeping on the back burner in London, in case a project he had in mind there came through. He tucked her letter, unopened, between two flowerpots on his windowsill – a philodendron and a rhoisissus rhomboideii, both of them running wild up the window frame and across the ceiling. The plants, he noticed, needed water. The letter he would leave for another day. Tonight there was a different girl in prospect, and he liked to keep his mind uncluttered.

He watered his plants with a big, black iron kettle he'd bought for the purpose in one of Reykjavik's street antique markets, then went to take a shower – his evening's plans stretched well on into Sunday. He was still in the shower when the telephone rang. He padded across the roughly-woven brown Swedish carpet to answer it.

A woman's voice asked him to wait. Reflexively, he glanced at his bare wrist, remembered his watch hanging on the toilet's flush lever, and craned his neck to check with the living room clock instead. Six twenty-five. No problem.

'Hello? Pétur?' A new voice, American. It instantly brought him an agreeable mental picture of Dr Colly Graham. He grunted.

'Oh, thank goodness. The coastguard operator's been so helpful. She tried your office, but you weren't there, so – '

'I hope nothing is wrong, Colly. How are you? You sound upset.'
'Upset? Not really.' She laughed nervously. 'It's just that I guess
I'm going to become a media event, and I'd like you . . . we'd all like
you to help us out.'

'Anything at all. You know that.' A media event? Wasn't her
expedition that already? 'As a matter of fact, I was planning to get in
touch with you. My producer thinks – '

'No, Pétur. It's something else. I've just had NBC here. You
know, American TV. They say my father's disappeared and there's
a big search on in the States.' She sounded close to tears. NBC?
How had they got to the *Fimbulvetr* without anyone bothering to
tell him? 'And Pétur, I just cannot, we cannot, deal with these
people. They wanted to come aboard, and ask all kinds of
questions. And there'll be more on the way. I – I just don't know – '

'Hold on there, Colly. Hold on.' He caught his reflection in the
hall mirror, automatically raising a hand to calm her. As always, his
naked image reassured. 'You say your father has disappeared? In
the States?'

'New York. I'm not worried about him, Pétur. I bet he's just
taken off somewhere for a vacation and not bothered to cancel the
newspapers, or something. But it's the reporters I can't stand. I'm
the only relative. They want anguished tears, like it was the
Lindbergh kidnapping, or something.'

'You can't blame them.' Pétur knew only too well how he would
react to such a story. 'Your father's famous; you're pretty.'

'Blaming them isn't the point. Nor have my looks got anything to
do with it.' A touch of anger seemed to have brought her more
under control. 'We've got work to do. We're a small team, on a tight
budget, with a tough schedule; and we don't want them cluttering
up the ship.'

'So what do you want me to do?'

Again the nervous laugh. 'You're a reporter. And, I mean, you got
to us first. So aren't we really *your* story, whatever happens to us?
Isn't there some sort of deal, you know, an exclusive deal, where
you could just tell everybody you're handling us? Syndication, or
something? We don't mind *you* coming back on board . . .'

'I hear what you're saying, Colly.' He thought fast, excited,
unaware of the water trickling coldly down the backs of his legs.

'The problem is, we can sign an exclusive contract with you, but we can't pay what NBC can offer.'

'We don't want money, Pétur. We want protection.'

He had to be firm with her. 'And in return Icelandic TV gets exclusive rights in your personal story and the expedition's?'

'Sure. Not that the rights are worth anything. Why not?'

He checked the clock again. Near enough six thirty. Damn. The missing father didn't amount to much. But if he was right about the Minister's uranium, this was a chance he couldn't miss. And *they* thought *he* was doing them a favour! But it was Saturday afternoon, and the contracts people would have taken off long ago. He had plenty of phoning to do; and a date to pick up at half past seven.

'You still there, Pétur?'

'Of course. Just thinking. Look, there'll be papers to sign. Why don't I come out to see you tomorrow, can't say when. Some time early.'

'Sure. We're not going anywhere. And you'll keep the others off our backs?'

'No problem.' He wasn't really sure, but he wasn't telling her that. 'Any inquiries, just refer them to my office. And good luck. Look, I must go now. Things to do. See you tomorrow.'

'Thanks, Pétur. You're a good friend. Bye.'

She hung up. A good friend? Just let him find some private deal between the *Fimbulvetr*'s team and the government for exploitation of uranium deposits, and she'd find out how good a friend he was. But meanwhile – well, she *was* pretty, even if she didn't like to admit it.

He dressed quickly, light suit and white shirt for a summer evening on the town. His Sunday morning might be shot to hell, but he still had Saturday night. The next half-hour he spent with the telephone. He was lucky. His news editor, Björn, he found at home. The programme controller was away visiting relatives for the weekend, and was finally located at a number in Eskifjördur, on the far eastern coast. The senior contract executive was unavailable, seeming to have fallen off the island leaving no trace, but her assistant, a keen member of the Association of Icelandic Anglers, could be found at the club's headquarters in Reykjavik. And Pétur's cameraman, Finnur, answered his phone immediately.

By seven fifteen Pétur was finished, ready to go. The contract would be ready in the morning, as would Finnur and his box of tricks. He ran a comb through his hair, inspected himself in the hall mirror, and opened his apartment door.

A large, thickset man in a dark business suit was outside, facing him, one finger raised to the bell push. Both men stepped back, laughed. The newcomer then took a pace forward again, held out his hand.

'Pétur Einarsson? Good evening. My name is Olaf Janssen. I – '

Pétur cut him short. 'I'm sorry; you've caught me at a bad moment.' Hastily, he shook the offered hand. 'Some other time, perhaps?'

'You have an important engagement. Yes. I can see that. A romantic engagement, I feel sure.'

Pétur tried to dodge round him, so that he could close the door and make his escape. He was unsuccessful. The big man filled the space.

'So what can I do for you? I'm sorry to sound rude, but if this is business then it really must wait. Call my office, on Monday.'

'Business?' Janssen smiled, moving forward heavily into the apartment. 'You could call it that, certainly. But I would prefer not to leave it until Monday. It has to do with a friend of yours, you see. A Doctor Colly Graham.'

8

Day Five. AUGUST 8. SUNDAY.

It was terribly English, David Lawrence decided wryly, to be drinking tea in Rome at eleven o'clock on a Sunday morning. Especially for an American like himself. He looked across at his guest – thirtyish, clean-shaven, olive skinned, with heavy, black-framed glasses. The name he had given, Majed Sayeed, was Arab, but he seemed to David dark enough to have come from further east. Perhaps Pakistan, or India. His accent too, in its well-educated British way, was more Indian than Arab.

In either case, David knew that the excellent if outrageously expensive tea served in Babington's was wasted on him. Arabs preferred their tea in tiny glasses, with sugar lumps; while the Indians of his experience had a distressing weakness for condensed milk, and additions such as cardamom or pepper.

This Sayeed, whatever his real identity might be, had called Associated Press at the International Press Building in Rome late the previous afternoon, and David had talked to him. On offer, David gathered, was exclusive information on some vast international terrorist plot. Sayeed had hyped it to the limit – unbelievable, catastrophic, world-shaking – but David was used to such excesses. *World-shaking* he toned down mentally to a largish car bomb, and *catastrophic* meant a few broken windows. Nevertheless, August was a slow month for news, in Rome as much as anywhere else. No AP man could afford to pass up even the remote chance of a workable story.

Rome's International Press Building went back to the days of Benito Mussolini. It was an impressive structure, built substantially of marble, and luxuriously appointed. Il Duce liked marble; he also liked to keep the press happy; and thirdly he liked to know what the press was thinking. Which was why almost every wall and pillar was fitted with hidden microphones, connected to the offices of his secret police.

The microphones were discovered during reconstruction work in the late 1940s. It was claimed that they had all been removed, and that any that remained were non-functional. This interesting self-contradiction caused many press men still to prefer to handle their more sensitive business elsewhere. Thus David Lawrence was content when his caller suggested they meet face-to-face before getting down to specifics. He'd flipped through his desk diary, discovered that a long-planned Sunday trip up into the mountains had fallen through, and suggested Babington's.

The English Tea Rooms lay across the square from the old Roman Catholic information centre – the Palazzo di Propaganda Fide which had, in a sceptical world, given the word *propaganda* to the English language. The Tea Rooms were one of David's favourite haunts. Their kitsch appealed to him: an entire Olde Englishe Tea Shoppe transported to Rome, complete with fake Elizabethan beams and fake Elizabethan waitresses, whose vocabulary derived much more from the Via di Venezia than from Stratford-on-Avon. Their clientele consisted mainly of German tourists (the British could not afford the prices), and smooth Italian businessmen in sharp suits, *molto chic*, carrying angular briefcases from the Gucci shop just around the corner, who were there to impress future mistresses, prospective clients, or simply each other. To which end the rooms were well lit, and the tables discreetly far apart.

David's guest was there before him, at a table well chosen both for observation and evasive action. Approaching him slowly, David was impressed. So far, the man's credentials as an informer were promising. Sayeed's barber and tailor, too, knew what they were doing. He was urbane, yet with the muscle and speed of a man able to take care of himself. Summing him up, David placed his guest as a small-time dealer, either armaments or drugs, who had recently got into trouble somewhere down the line and was putting on a good show while he tried desperately to recoup his losses. There was also, in the slight paleness of his jawline, the possibility of a beard recently removed, which suggested a new beginning.

Introductions were made, and the two men settled. A waitress came. David ordered Earl Grey and toasted teacakes. Sayeed inclined his head politely; he had acquired a great liking for teacakes while in Oxford.

They made small talk until their order was brought. The extra large number of tourists in Rome that year, and all of them seemingly German. The Master Race, Sayeed suggested, conquering Europe at last . . . David became more certain that Sayeed was Indian. There was a them-versus-us confidentiality that no Arab would have attempted.

The tea poured and the preliminaries over, David got down to business. 'You mentioned a deal, Mr Sayeed – '

'Please.' An elegant brown hand was raised. 'You must call me Majed. And I shall call you David.' He smiled deprecatingly. 'I looked you up in the Press Corps list, you see.'

'Fair enough. I'd have done the same with you, Majed, if men of your talents were in a directory.'

Sayeed flicked his eyes mockingly heavenward. 'God forbid.'

'Quite so.' David offered a token smile. 'As to any deal, I'm sure you understand that first of all I must know what it is that you are selling.'

'My dear David – naturally. That is, you must know enough to become tempted. But not, of course, so much that I am no longer necessary.'

'It's a familiar problem. How d'you propose to solve it?'

'Fortunately, in this case it is no problem at all.' He sipped his tea, eyes darting round the room while he gathered his thoughts. He was far less at ease than he wished to appear. 'No, the only problem we may have will be that of timing. This is a big story, worth a great deal of money. I understand that you need time to satisfy your superiors. But you must understand that time is short. Terrorists don't sit around waiting while accountants are doing their sums.'

David had heard such sales talk before. Time was always very short. 'How much money is "a great deal"?'

He didn't really expect an answer. He didn't get one.

Sayeed spread his hands. 'For a story so big? I tell you, David, we're talking about the end of civilisation as you and I know it.'

David was unimpressed. 'You said that yesterday. If it's so

goddam big, I'll just have to hand it over to the Italian police, or the CIA, or whoever.'

'The CIA knows. The KGB also. That is part of my story. Would you believe, David, that the Americans and the Soviets are working together in a cover-up? Would you believe that?'

'Frankly, no.'

'But it is true.'

In spite of himself, David was intrigued. 'Covering what up?'

'Such delicious teacakes . . .'

'Don't let's get too cute, Majed. You want money, I want a story. If the story stays vague, so does the money.'

'Very well.' Sayeed licked the last of the teacake's sugar crystals from his fingers. 'The story concerns the arms limitation talks in Geneva. Also the UN. The money is not negotiable. My fee is half a million dollars.'

David eyed him thoughtfully. These people were grotesque. The numbers they came up with were so much ritual. Half a million, a million – where did they think such sums could be found? And yet . . . possibilities were taking shape in his mind. This might not be a routine car bomb, after all. High level Geneva negotiators, a major terrorist attack – obvious hostage-taking situation – The idea made sense, looked at through their crazy eyes. Or maybe the lunatic Right, back in the US, afraid of an arms deal, planning to kill off a few delegates and blame the Arabs. That could involve a cover-up of some kind.

'That's a hell of a lot of money,' he said. 'You'll have to give me firm information before I can begin to talk numbers like that.'

'Ah. Firm information. My dear David, how far would Woodward and Bernstein have got if they'd waited for firm information?'

'They bought Watergate with their own sweat, Majed; not half a million of someone else's money.'

Sayeed's smile disappeared. His eyes were cold. 'Sweat all you like, Mr Lawrence, if it makes you feel better. You're not the only correspondent in Rome.'

David considered. The guy was right. It was upon such risk-taking that Pulitzer Prizes were built. There was also his responsibility to the Agency. It was possible that Sayeed was right and they already knew. But it was his duty to check. He must have a talk with

Frank. If necessary, the money *could* be arranged. For God's sake, he wasn't some cub reporter, fresh out from the Hicksville School of Journalism.

'You can hawk this around till Kingdom Come,' he said sharply. 'Without hard facts you'll get the same answer. Nobody, but *nobody*, hands out that sort of dough on what you've given me so far.'

They faced each other across the table. Around them the gentle murmur of voices rose and fell. It was Sayeed who yielded.

'I can give you one word,' he said. 'Pass it on immediately, this morning, to your people in Washington: I mean the CIA. And high up. Say this word to somebody who really matters. Do this, and his reaction will tell you all you want to know.'

David frowned. Did everyone in Rome know he was with the Agency? 'Just one word?'

Sayeed nodded. 'The word is *Ragnarok*.' He spelled it out. 'And if you want to publish, you must act quickly. Washington will try to silence you. You must come to me immediately. If you have the money, I will tell you everything. Everything about . . . Ragnarok.' He leaned forward urgently. 'But I warn you, David Lawrence. Until you have published your story we will both be in danger of our lives. I can take care of myself. I am protected. Three copies of the material I have for you lie with an acquaintance who I have reason to believe is trustworthy. If I do not contact him within three days, by Tuesday evening, he will despatch these copies to the three major news agencies other than yours. But you have no such protection. I can only urge you to take your danger seriously.'

David surveyed the possibilities. Either the guy was completely crazy, or this was really serious stuff. But a reporter who was being leaned on could drop out of sight, file his story, reappear later pleading public interest. He could get the story, fire it off over the nearest telephone through his portable Epson, and it would go into the office machine and out on the wire without being touched by human hands. He had the seniority, and the codes. The first anybody else would know would be the words on the international telex: GENEVA CONFERENCE HIJACK PLANNED . . . Jesus Christ.

Any senior reporter could do it. But problems arose when the reporter served two masters. Conflicts of interest. Fame and fortune versus Uncle Sam. The choice was painful. Painful, but in David's case not difficult. He was a reporter, but he was an American first.

'I'll need names,' he said. 'Names, places, dates. For half a million bucks, I'll need the terrorists' size in hats.'

'You'll get them, David.' Once again, Sayeed was all smiles. 'I was a founder member of the Ragnarok team, you know. There's nothing I can't tell you about them.' He raised his teacup. 'For the right money, in the right time-frame – which means tomorrow – there's nothing I don't know.'

David sat back, lit a cigarette. He'd made up his mind. 'OK. OK, Majed, you've got a deal. You give me the facts, I give you the money. And this is how we'll work it . . .'

Ten minutes later, the man David Lawrence knew as Majed Sayeed left the English Tea Rooms at the foot of the Spanish steps. He was clearly well-pleased. He left alone, as he had arrived, looking carefully round the square, high and low in every archway, before setting off briskly in the direction of the Via Garibaldi. He took no notice whatsoever of the harassed woman in the pale beige dress and shapeless straw hat, hung about with cameras and guide books, obviously a tourist, who stared at him quite openly as he went past. If he had one professional failing, it was that women over forty didn't register.

She was, in fact, amazed at her good fortune – for he registered with her immediately. Lise Schneider was one of several people looking for him that day, and the name she knew him by was Kassim Latif.

Il Signore di Genova had sharp ears. Less than eighteen hours after a pair of shabby rooms over a backstreet drycleaners' had acquired a new olive-skinned tenant, he heard of it. Less then seventeen hours after a fine handmade suit had been bought, but not paid for, he heard of that also. And less than sixteen hours after an optician and an expensive barber had been visited . . . but the list was endless. The outcome, however, was finite. By ten o'clock that morning, every Rome employee he could contact was looking for a clean-shaven, well-dressed young Indian in black-framed spectacles, known to Il Signore as Kassim Latif.

He had been reported in many places, with varying degrees of uncertainty, most recently (and implausibly) inside a Catholic parish church. This was the first definite sighting. Lise followed him. Her orders were simple – stay with him until she could reach a telephone. At this stage Il Signore simply wanted to know what the Indian was doing, and where. There was plenty of time. Latif had no money; he wasn't going anywhere.

In her hurry to keep up with Latif, the woman missed David Lawrence, leaving Babington's a discreet five minutes later. By such tiny margins are men's lives extended. For Il Signore was well aware, unsurprisingly, of the reporter's Agency connections. And his presence in the English Tea Rooms at the same time as Latif could be no coincidence. So that Il Signore would have been obliged to change his relaxed attitude to Latif's immediate future. As Frau Schneider would discover when she finally called Globewide Travel, CIA contacts were out. Right out.

Robert Graham lost consciousness that morning at ten thirty-seven.

He was on his way back to the Paramount Hotel from posting the latest floppy disk, his log covering Colly's most recent call. The arrival of the Russians, and Colonel Zebedee's death. She reported Flynn unrepentant; she herself was confused. Robert had worked hard to get the record straight; posterity must have the truth. But it was a shameful event, upsetting.

No letters would be collected from the mailbox that day. He was posting the disk simply to get it out of his possession. His days at liberty were numbered, and the existence of a separate, truthful account of their enterprise and its aims was important to him. Somebody, some day, would read it.

New York was hot, and Robert carried his jacket slung from one finger, over his shoulder. On a sudden impulse he dug in his pants pocket, brought out Lily King's postbox key. He had no idea why he'd kept it. Colly might live to pass hers on; he never would. He paused, about to cross the road, and stooped in the gutter between two parked cars, dropping the key through a drain grille. It disappeared unmomentously, and he set out again across the road.

As Robert emerged from the line of parked cars, the driver of an approaching truck blasted his horn. Robert dithered in the truck's path, received a precise vision of his death beneath its wheels, scrambled back out of its way, staggered, lost his footing, and fell. Striking his head on a parked car's bumper, he passed out. The truck missed his sprawled body by several feet.

When he came round he knew at once that he was on a stretcher, bumping through the open rear door of an ambulance. There was an oxygen mask over his face. He tried to sit up and was restrained by a bearded young man in a white coat. The stretcher rolled all the way into the ambulance. The door was shut, the siren whooped deafeningly, and the vehicle moved off, lurching in the potholes. Robert made noises through the mask, and it was removed.

'Hi, Richard, how're you doin'?'

Briefly, the name confused him. Then he remembered the wallet in his back pocket, and the business card: *Richard J Goldstein*, with a fictional address and phone number in Buffalo. Not much in this age of stacked-up credit cards and licences, but he'd wanted something to back up his new identity.

'I'm doing very well, thank you.' He spoke carefully, anxious not to give an impression of feebleness or injury. 'My head's a bit sore. I fell down.'

'You sure did, Richard. I'm Homer, by the way. I'm very pleased to meet you, Richard. And your head's got every right to be sore. Left a dent in that Chevy deep enough to hide in.' He was observing Robert keenly. 'But you struck lucky. Me and Bill was just around the corner with the rescue wagon, so we picked you up and now you'll be in Belle Vue in no time at all.'

'Belle Vue? The hospital?' Robert struggled again to sit up.

'Bear with us, will you, Richard?' A large hand was gently holding him down. 'We got you wired. And I got to say it looks like you're firing on all six.'

Robert discovered his shirt open, electrodes taped to his chest. 'My pulse rate is fine, young man. And my breathing, too. I just had a fall, that's all.'

'Hey Richard, I love that accent. Like on Masterpiece Theatre.' The ambulance leaned round a corner, whooping once again. 'You wouldn't be a Britisher, would you?'

The man was talking with less than half his mind, busy with dials and video displays. But it was too late for a change of nationality. Robert ignored the question.

'I don't have concussion. There's no singing in my ears and I don't have double vision. I can count backwards from one hundred if you like. And I can list for you the fourteen lanthanide elements.'

'You don't say. I'm impressed, Richard, I really am. But we're still taking you to Bellevue.'

Robert lay still. Ambulance men had a job to do. He had a head injury. He might have a fractured skull. If his vital signs remained good that became less likely. But they couldn't take chances. Apart from their medical pride, there was always the chance of a lawsuit for negligence from an angry widow.

But hospital worried him. They wouldn't like Richard Goldstein's lack of identity. Blue Cross, Blue Shield, Social Security, next of kin; a hundred questions, none of them with answers. And a Professor Robert Graham, of the same build and age and sex and race and nationality, on their missing persons list . . .

'These elements you mentioned, Richard. You some kind of scientist?'

You're so sharp, his mother used to say, one day you'll cut yourself.

'A . . . schoolteacher. Retired.' He fell back on the remains of his cover. 'I'm writing a book.'

The ambulance halted, increased its noise level, moved on again. The windows were obscured. Robert wondered how soon they'd be at Bellevue.

'A Britisher, writing a book – that's neat. We had all sorts in this wagon, Richard, Bill and me. But we never had a British author before.'

He'd been making notes. Now he leaned forward and removed the electrodes. Robert swung his feet to the floor, sat up, buttoned his shirt.

'But you're still taking me to hospital.'

The young man grinned. 'Delivery boys, that's us. Shovel 'em up and deliver 'em, still ticking if possible.'

Robert explored his head cautiously with his fingertips. 'I've got a lump, that's all. It's not even bleeding. And I've a son expecting me for Sunday brunch.'

'You can call your boy from the desk.' He fastened his notes to a clipboard. 'Have him come pick you up. I'd say you're in great shape, Richard. But they'll want to do a head scan, coupla X-rays. Maybe an hour, that's all.'

Robert gave up. If this was to be the day he got caught, so be it. For the first time he thought seriously beyond that moment. To be out of things would hurt. No more calls to Georg, no more contact with Iceland. And he hadn't been a waste of their time. The Latif episode had shown he could still be useful. He even liked to think Georg enjoyed talking to him. They went back a long way. And after he was caught –

The ambulance descended a ramp, halted. The driver got out and opened the rear door. A sign on the wall outside read EMER-GENCY. The young man, Homer, lifted Robert's feet and firmly pushed him back down on the stretcher.

'Sure, I'll bet you can walk fine, Richard. But you don't want us to lose our jobs?'

He was wheeled in through double doors, parked. The place was brilliantly lit, and as busy as an airline terminal. Nobody so much as glanced in his direction. Robert was about to get up quietly and leave when the bearded young man reappeared.

'I booked you in, Richard. Left your sheet. Sundays are busy. Great day for family disagreements. Hank here will look after you. Richard's a Britisher, Hank; see you treat him right. Hey, Richard, OK?'

He flipped a casual salute and left.

Hank was a morose, elderly negro who wordlessly pushed Robert's stretcher to the rear of the Emergency Room, past lines of curtained cubicles till he found one empty. He wheeled Robert in.

'You stay right here, Mr Goldstone,' he said, reading the name-tag on Robert's wrist. 'Doctor'll be with you soon as maybe.'

He shuffled off, closing the curtain behind him. Robert sat up. His wristwatch and the wallet from his pants pocket were beside him. He got off the stretcher. He didn't have long. His shoe laces had been loosened, and he lost time doing them up. Two men went past the cubicle, deep in earnest doctor talk. He slipped his watch on his wrist and pocketed his wallet. He listened. A stretcher trolley went by, fast. Ambulances whooped and doors banged. Somewhere nearby a woman was faintly groaning.

He peered round the curtain; froze. A nurse was coming towards him down the wide space between the cubicles. A stretcher dodged past her, going in the opposite direction, blood bottles lurching. She was carrying a man's blue suit jacket. It was his.

'Robert Graham?' she called. She was turning from side to side. 'Robert Graham? Robert Graham?'

She looked behind a curtain. 'Robert Graham?'

He hesitated. There was nowhere he could go. He was too old for running. The lump on his head hurt. He showed himself, looked at her enquiringly.

'Robert Graham?' She smiled up at him. She was tiny, and very young. 'Your coat got left in the rescue wagon, Mr Graham. The orderly left it at the desk.' She held it out. 'I had to come over this way, so I told them I'd bring it for you. It didn't have a wallet. We got your name from the credit phone card in the pocket.'

'My wallet's here.' He patted his rear pocket. He took the coat and put it on. 'Thank you.'

He'd never even needed the damn phone card. Made the radio call to the *Fimbulvetr* right from the hotel.

The girl touched his arm. 'Are you sure you should be on your feet, Mr Graham?'

'Probably not. But it doesn't matter.'

'Maybe you should go back in there and sit down.'

She wasn't a nurse. Her pink smock had fooled him.

'Maybe I should. Thank you. And thanks again for the jacket.'

A volunteer helper, perhaps. And the name *Robert Graham* meant nothing to her. She smiled, nodded and carried on in the same direction – away from the front desk and the doors.

He closed the curtain, waited until she had gone, then walked quickly and confidently away, past the admitting desk, towards the entrance. The automatic doors had opened when a loud, hard woman's voice stopped him.

'Hey. You – old man. Are you a patient?'

He turned, trying to hide the telltale label on his wrist.

'Nobody just walks out, old man. You got to go to the desk first.'

The security guard softened her gruffness. 'There's papers. You ought to know that.'

There were indeed papers. The desk didn't want him to go. But he insisted, and as Richard Goldstein he signed the waiver absolving them of all blame if he fell down dead in the street. They gave him the Head Sheet: instructions for patients with head injuries. It told him to watch out for forgetfulness, pains, or dizziness. Ideally he shouldn't be alone, and when he slept he should be woken every hour, in case he wasn't asleep at all, but unconscious. He thanked them for the sheet, and left. In the end, they had no way of keeping him.

The girl who had brought him his jacket was standing at the far end of the desk when he finished. Too far away, thank God, to greet him by name. She saw him, and waved. He waved back, before finally making it through the door and picking up a taxi outside.

He worried about the girl. If the opposition got to her, *when* the opposition got to her, if she heard his name on TV, she'd remember. But at least she couldn't tell them his address. New York was a big city. He took the cab to Grand Central again, just in case it was ever traced.

He had no headache. The lump on his head was tender, otherwise he felt fine. He'd been lucky. Unhurriedly, he tackled the walk back to his hotel room. The time wasn't yet noon. He began to sweat. Putting his hand in his jacket pocket for a handkerchief, he brought out his telephone credit card. And with it, the street map Woolston had drawn on the back of a Paramount Hotel tariff. The name *Paramount Hotel* seemed to be printed in very large letters.

She'd looked a bright girl. Robert was in no doubt at all that she'd remember.

That Sunday morning Pétur Einarsson met his cameraman at the Reykjavik airstrip, by the Flugstödin charter company's hangar, at eleven thirty. The day was cool but fine, with a light westerly wind and high broken cloud; the small Bell helicopter was waiting for them on the tarmac. As the pilot took off and heeled his craft low over the ancient buildings lining Tjörnin, the beautiful lake at the city's centre, Pétur handed his colleague two small, self-adhesive radiation discs. His researcher, pretending an interest in X-ray risks in local hospitals, had obtained them from the physics department at the university. Once processed after exposure, the film from each disc would show by its degree of fogging the amount of radioactivity it had been subjected to.

Björn had suggested geiger counters. The discs, though less accurate, were more discreet.

In his pocket Pétur also had the papers he'd picked up from the television centre on his way in from Gradhaverfi. All they needed was Colly Graham's signature.

Settling into his seat harness, Pétur nudged his friend, raising his voice above the noise of the machine. 'Had a visitor last night,' he yelled. 'Nearly made me late for Inge.'

Finnur eyed him dourly. If past experience was anything to go by, Inge would have waited. Pétur's women were a patient lot.

'But it's an interesting development,' he went on. 'The man said his name was Janssen. Sounded like a Dane, but he never said. And he was trying to rope us in on some industrial espionage. Came from an oil company – my guess is Dutch Shell. Seemed convinced the Graham lot are looking for oil.'

The helicopter lurched in a down-draught. They'd left the city behind and were climbing out across the bay. Already the peaks of Snaefellsjökull and the Thórsnes peninsula were dimly visible in the haze ahead.

'This guy wants us to help him get a man on board the *Fimbulvetr*. Actually wanted us to take a folding ladder with us; hang it over the stern while nobody was looking. Just like James Bond.' He laughed. 'You should have seen his face when I turned it down.'

Finnur grunted.

'In the end, he offered me about half the annual trade deficit to do the job. Got quite nasty when I still said no.'

'Offshore oil?' Finnur shook his head. 'I never heard of oil and volcanoes going together. Who does he think he's fooling?'

'I didn't bother to argue. It has to be a cover story. But he still wants to get on board that boat. When I said no to the ladder, he tried me out with a camera – a James Bond camera, got up like a cigarette lighter. I showed him the door.'

'What did he want photographed?'

'I didn't even ask. Inge was waiting.'

'He could be thinking the same as us.'

'Uranium. Yeah, the bribe was big enough.'

Finnur was thoughtful, gazing absently down at the sun-dappled water as it streamed past beneath them. 'Pity you didn't play along,' he said at last.

Pétur stared at him, then grinned. 'You just want to get your hands on the trick camera.'

Finnur, hunched defensively in his seat, muttered a reply lost in the noise of the engine.

Coming in over Helgavik, Pétur was surprised to see the camp on the beach by the rescue hut. Two red station wagons were parked to one side. A black inflated dinghy lay on the beach, near the end of a shingle promontory that enclosed a small bay, and a pile of diving equipment was neatly stacked behind it. As the helicopter approached, campers looked up and waved.

There was also an outpost, a curious hollow in the rocks some distance away and at a higher level, with two people in it, apparently sunning themselves. They had impressive binoculars, and looked like birdwatchers. Except that their hide looked straight out across the cove at the *Fimbulvetr*, rather than at the nesting places on the cliffs nearby.

As the helicopter touched down on the water, Colly and the German were already lowering the ship's motorboat: they came alongside very shortly. Colly's hair was loose on her shoulders. She looked marvellous. Pétur climbed down into the boat and Finnur followed with his gear. They shook hands formally, continental style.

Behind them, Flugstödin's charter pilot took off immediately for a sheltered landing spot up the valley behind the beach, where he could relax until he was needed.

Once on board the ship, the four of them went down to the wardroom. Pétur noticed that the Irish captain up on the bridge waved affably and shouted something down, but stayed where he was, as if on watch. If so, then it was a change from the informality of Pétur's first visit. He mentioned this to Colly, wondering if she'd got word of Janssen's interest. He hadn't yet decided if he would tell her about Janssen. A lot depended on how frank she was.

'Watches?' There was a simple bread and cheese lunch laid out on the table. She started adding to it for the new arrivals. 'Yes, we try to stand watches. There's a party of Russians on the beach – you must've seen them. They're friendly enough, but kind of inquisitive. And we've got some pretty fancy equipment. Can't afford to have it mucked about.'

'That's where Kassim is now,' Werner put in. Then he laughed, nervously. 'Not with the Russians, I mean. No – it's because of our watches he isn't here. He's sleeping. He was up most of the night.'

Pétur nodded. But he didn't believe in Colly's fears for her fancy equipment. If they were keeping watches round the clock, it was because they had something to hide.

'Russians?' he queried. 'How d'you know they're Russians?'

'They came out and introduced themselves.'

He remembered the birdwatchers. The thing was getting out of hand. First himself, then Janssen, and now a gang of Russians. It looked as if the Grahams' plans were the worst-kept secret of the decade.

'And how's your work going?'

'Fine. Absolutely great.' She held up a saucepan and tin opener. 'Who's for soup? We've got pea, oxtail – all the usual.'

Finnur was busy with his Nikon. He caught her slight glower. 'Please? You do not mind to be seen the cook? It is not a bad way, to be the leader and also to make the food.'

She checked herself. 'Of course.' She laughed. 'In fact, it's a very good way.'

Pétur had forgotten how young and easygoing she could be. Her hair was palest gold in a shaft of sunshine from a decklight. She was slim, her breasts pleasantly noticeable beneath the loose, red-checked shirt. Her bare arms were strong, but entirely feminine. He found himself comparing them with the arms of Inge. Very favourably. Going to bed with Inge had been like going to bed with a boa constrictor. His ribs still ached.

During lunch he produced the contract documents, got them signed and out of the way. 'I can't prevent other reporters from bothering you,' he explained. 'But now you have a legal excuse for turning them away. And when they find this out, they should stop trying.'

She grinned crookedly. 'I have to admit we haven't exactly been besieged, after all. But it's early days yet.'

He asked about her father, the pretext for his visit, and put together enough for a mood piece to hand round the agencies. She had no idea where the old man might be now, but she wasn't worried. He was in excellent health. He had no particular reason to report his movements, and no particular person to report them to. If he'd been mugged in New York, she imagined his body would have turned up by now. The whole thing was an unnecessary fuss. He was an independent old gentleman. If he'd disappeared, that was his privilege – why, he might even be flying out to Iceland to surprise them. They were very close; she loved him dearly, and had always supported his peace work. They'd always got on fine, but recently, since her mother's death, they'd been particularly close. He'd spent time in Europe with her, and they'd dreamed up this project together. He'd reappear when he felt like it – in Reykjavik, or New York, or wherever.

For the moment Pétur left it at that. Whenever the subject of their research came up she dropped into what he now recognised as a well-rehearsed spiel. By skirting round it he hoped to make it easier for her to tell him the truth later.

They went up on deck, leaving Finnur to chat with Werner and to film him clearing the galley. Pétur had known such times to produce good material: Finn's reticence often invited confidences.

They leaned on the stern rail, swapping memories, mostly of London, the one city they had in common. Six of the campers were playing a knockabout game of volleyball on the beach. Binoculars flashed in the sunlight from the direction of the hide. Pétur didn't comment on them, and neither did she. But he found it hard to believe she was unaware of the watchers.

Soon Werner relieved Flynn on the bridge. Finnur went up with him, then came aft with the massive Irishman to join them. Turning, Pétur was astonished to see beyond them yet another watcher, this time in uniform, squatting openly on a cliff ledge to starboard. Colly saw the direction of his gaze.

'You've spotted our friendly neighbourhood spy,' she said lightly. 'We've christened him Big Brother. There's two of them, actually. We think they're up from the NATO base.' She paused. 'It might be a training exercise. Or maybe they don't trust the Russians.' There was a longer pause. 'Or us.'

She met his eyes squarely. He didn't trust himself to answer. She was incredible. The whole set-up was incredible.

Pétur braced himself. Pretty face or not, there was a story here. She was a fool to think she'd get away with it.

'Well now,' Pétur said briskly, 'you mustn't let us interrupt you.'

'Interrupt us?' She stared at him. 'Interrupt our work, you mean?'

'What else?'

There was a blank pause.

Flynn was digging in the pocket of his dungarees. 'Wouldn't there be the sonar readings to check?' he suggested mildly, producing a small silver flask.

She picked up her cue. 'Trust Flynn to remember the boring jobs.' She tossed back her hair, suddenly animated. 'We're plotting the horizontal structure of the seabed, you see. Using a kind of horizontal sonar. The sound waves go out automatically from one pod and are picked up by the other one. It's all recorded on tape. Every other day, we take out the old cassette and fit a new one.'

Pétur frowned. People had tried to blind him with science before. 'Is that like oil surveys?'

She looked blank. He certainly didn't seem to have touched a guilty nerve. So much for Janssen's story. 'Oil? No – well, they do use seismic techniques. But much deeper; you need explosives for that.' She shivered, in spite of the afternoon warmth of the sun.

He tried another tack. 'Do you use the minisub?'

'When we change the tapes? No need. The units are only about ten metres down. It's a simple scuba job – down with the new tape, up with the old.'

He glanced at Finnur. 'That sounds like fun. I've done some diving. May I come?' He'd still have asked to go, even in the submarine. But he was glad that it wasn't needed.

She smiled regretfully. 'I don't think – '

'A drop for you?' Flynn waved the flask in her direction. 'No? Wise girl. But then, I'm not diving.' He took a drink. 'Why not let the feller go along? With Kass asleep, it makes sense to use the extra body. You can check everything out while me and Werner

look after the ship. After all, you mustn't dive alone. Might not get
another chance like this.'
    There was some interplay here that Pétur wasn't getting. But why
worry, if it was working to his advantage?
    'I'll do my best. If you've got a spare suit, that is.'
    'We got suits, boyo. Fit out your photographic friend, too, if he's
interested.'
    Finnur shook his head. 'Thank you, no. If God had wanted me to
dive, he'd have given me real fins, not just the name.'
    The Irishman laughed at the feeble and obviously well-worn joke.
'Excuses, excuses. If he'd wanted you to be a photographer, now,
he'd have given you a flashbulb socket in the middle of your
forehead.' He held out his flask. 'Here. Have a snort instead.'
    Pétur went below with Colly. While she was fitting him out, she
asked him about his diving, testing his claim of experience
underwater. She was a good team leader. Even under pressure, she
did her job.
    He took his suit away to a cabin and changed. He stuck one of his
radiation discs inside the facemask, to protect it from seawater. He
didn't expect radiation levels on the seabed to be high enough to
affect it, but what the hell, it was a chance. The ship's lab, where the
samples were handled, would be more revealing. He'd find an
excuse to take the other disc in there, later.
    Carrying his flippers, he rejoined Colly, who had also suited up.
Together they returned on deck. Flynn had readied the breathing
apparatus and lowered it into the boat. He was waiting at the top of
the ladder with the new GLORIA (Geological Long Range Inclined
Asdic) module in his hand: a small recording device in a watertight
box, maybe fifteen centimetres long and half as wide, about a
centimetre deep, the pins of a standard interface connection on one
end. He handed it over, together with a lighter-than-air
screwdriver.
    'Will you be motoring across, Colly?'
    She looked out over the water. 'It's nearer now that we've moved
the ship. I don't think I'll bother.' She turned to Pétur. 'Couple of
kilometres round trip; OK for you?'
    He shrugged. It sounded a long way; but he wasn't going to say
so.

They went down the ladder into the boat. It was indeed, Pétur
noted, a temporary ladder, which they could remove when the boat
was hoisted inboard. No chance of Janssen's friend creeping aboard
that way.

He eased on the aqualung harness, pulling the strap up between
his legs. He checked the air gauge and demand valve, and the diving
knife in its sheath at his waist. He sat on the edge of the boat and
slipped his feet into flippers. After blowing his nose over the side
between finger and thumb he fitted his nose clip. He felt Colly's eyes
on him, assessing his level of expertise.

He moistened the inside of his face mask with saliva, waited until
Colly reached the same stage of her own preparations, then leaned
over the side, careful not to wet the radiation disc (though it
probably wouldn't matter if he did) as he rinsed out the inside of the
mask.

When he straightened she was ready for him, module and
screwdriver clipped to her belt.

'I guess you just follow along,' she said. 'Your job is to buddy me
if anything goes wrong. We're looking for two bright yellow
cylinders. I have a bearing on one, and from there to the other. The
seabed's mostly compacted ash; it stirs up easily, so don't flap
around.'

He nodded. She fitted her mask and mouthpiece, gave a quick
thumbs-up, and disappeared backwards over the boat's side. Pétur
followed. The water was less cold than he'd expected. He located
Colly and struck out after her on the surface, driving strongly with
his feet. She set a reasonable pace: this wasn't going to be a
humiliate-the-male outing. Colly had nothing she needed to prove.

They were swimming diagonally across the cove, away from the
Russian campers, on a bearing Colly checked with a compass
strapped to her waist. After a while she slowed, lifting her head out
of the water and turning it from side to side to check landmarks.
Suddenly she waved to him and dived steeply, her flipper-clad feet
showing briefly above the surface. Pétur went down after her.

The sea sounds in his ears steadied. The water was crystal clear.
At three metres they hit a cold layer. The sun was still bright above,
and a few large, blue-sided fish swam unhurriedly to and fro,
watching them with bland, incurious eyes. The exhaled air from

Colly's breathing unit rose past him like a shimmering string of pearls, curving up towards the surface. Following her, he thrust on down.

At six metres the light was still bright, but the water ahead was dark, non-reflective, like the depths of space. Sparse strands of cord-weed swayed gently, shoals of tiny silver herring darting between them. Then Colly checked, pointing downwards and slightly to one side. The bottom was in sight; large lumps of red and black volcanic rock catching the distant sunlight, the hollows around them drifted over with a desert of grey pumice dust. Lying in the largest of these hollows was one of the yellow cylinders, as geometric as a piece of stovepipe, utterly alien in this muted, softly shifting world.

He swam closer. Colly was moving off: this must be the sender, not the receptor with its replaceable module. The yellow cylinder looked to him like nothing so much as a container for gigantic tennis balls. There seemed to be a lid at one end, screwed tight, and no other visible means of access. He checked that Colly was still in sight, looked down again at the cylinder and patted it, lightly. But when he looked again she wasn't waiting, and he hurried after her, towards the shore.

She slowed. Then, just as he caught up with her she stopped, gesturing urgently. The water ahead was disturbed, a bright haze of dust hanging in it, through which the dark shape of another diver could be seen, angled downwards, flippered feet stirring gently to maintain position. Close beneath him was a flash of yellow, suggesting the second cylinder. Colly touched Pétur's arm, showing him the knife in her hand, gesturing unmistakably. Reluctantly, he drew his own. Watchers above water, intruders below – this wasn't what he'd come for. They approached the other diver slowly, a couple of metres apart.

Pétur looked across at her. What did she expect him to do? The other was still unaware of their presence. She surely wasn't intending to attack. Undeniably, a piece of *Fimbulvetr*'s equipment was being tampered with. But –

A sudden weight bore down on him from behind. Something clashed, metal on metal, against one of his cylinders. He felt himself somersaulting, fought back desperately, struggling to maintain equilibrium, slashing out blindly behind himself with his knife. His feet touched bottom. An arm clawed over his shoulder, hand gripping for his air pipe. He beat it away, wrenched free, and turned.

Lava dust seethed whitely about his knees. He was aware of other furious activity behind him. The sounds in his ears were confused, meaningless; eddies tugged at his body. If Colly was in trouble he could do nothing for her. The man he faced was as tall as Pétur, and broader, the eyes behind his face mask wide and wild. He, too, was armed with a knife, and his movements were intent, coldly determined.

In slow motion they circled each other. Pétur was afraid. An afternoon's unambitious diving had become a nightmare. He'd been in fights before, but never with knives. And never underwater.

They were rising. The seabed was now invisible beneath its dust cloud. The other man lunged forward, misjudging his angle. Perhaps he too was an amateur. Pétur caught at his arm, felt it slip away out of his grasp. Again a hand came for his air pipe and again he tore it away. They closed ponderously, slashing and parrying. Dimly, ten metres overhead, Pétur was aware of sunlight glinting on the surface. Instinct told him he'd be safer there. Reason told him he could be killed as easily there as down here.

His opponent moved sharply forward. Pétur struck at him, made no contact, pitched sideways, momentarily helpless. At once the man was on him. The knife stabbed, slicing Pétur's air pipe at his shoulder, cutting into his insulated suit and the flesh beneath. He flailed desperately, water filling his mouth. If he didn't get free he would be held there until his lungs flooded and he drowned.

He heard a distant thumping in the water, looked up, and saw a dark hull, a screw turning slowly. The *Fimbulvetr*'s motorboat.

His captor released him, swimming rapidly away. He rose to the surface, trod water, gasping.

Werner was at the motorboat's controls, Finnur by the short diving ladder at the side. Werner cut the engine, allowing the boat to drift down on Pétur. Finn, forsaking his camera, leaned down and helped him up the ladder and into the open cockpit. Pétur dragged off his mask and noseclip and sprawled across a thwart, still retching and gasping. His fingers probed at the cut in his shoulder of his suit and came away showing blood.

'Where's Colly?' Werner shouted at him.

Pétur hawked and spat, shook his head. 'There are people down there. She went after one of them. A woman I think. Small, anyway.' He coughed painfully. 'Then I was attacked . . .'

'You left her?'

'I told you. I was attacked.'

'Where is she? Lieber Gott, what happened to her?'

'I don't know.' They were both shouting now. 'Some man cut my air pipe. I – '

'Get down there.' Their faces were scarcely a foot apart. Werner shook Pétur by the shoulders, oblivious of the blood. 'You've got a wet suit, get down there and find her.'

'My air pipe.' He gestured. The wound didn't hurt at all; must be the cold. 'I tell you, I – '

Finnur shouted something. They both turned. He was pointing. Some two hundred metres inshore of the motorboat a head had surfaced and an arm was waving. Werner swung back to the controls.

'A good thing for you she's OK,' he muttered.

Pétur was dazed. He sat, staring at his shaking hands, while they helped Colly inboard. She was fine. Laughing.

'That was some chase . . .' She squatted down in front of him. 'What happened to you? Where were you when I needed you?' she teased.

Gingerly, he rotated his shoulder. 'The old man of the sea jumped me.' She hadn't noticed the wound. 'Anyway, who were you chasing?'

'Some Russian girl. Olympic class, by the speed of her.'

'Russian? How d'you know? Was mine Russian?'

Colly's eyes glazed briefly. 'Just a guess.'

Werner leaned between them. 'Of course they were Russian. You should have seen their camp. That's why I came in the boat. When they saw you two set off, they started getting their dinghy into the water. And two guys were suiting up. Then they saw me and stopped.'

Colly laughed again. She was slightly hysterical, Pétur realised. Shock affected people in odd ways. 'They're a nosey lot, all right.'

Pétur frowned. It was hard to keep track of all this. His own brain seemed to have been slowed down by the incident. 'But what was she doing?'

'Oh, poking around the receptor. Guilty conscience, that's for sure – shot off like a rocket when she saw me.'

'The receptor?' Werner had gripped her shoulder. 'You're sure it wasn't – '

'No sweat, honey. Just a nosey tourist, that's all.'

There was a tension between them that even Pétur in his present condition couldn't miss. Questions. Answers. A range of communication just beyond his frequency. Only one thing was certain: this had nothing to do with nosey tourists. There was more to all this than simple curiosity.

Finnur had finished filming and was squatting behind Pétur, examining his damaged shoulder. 'I think,' he said quietly, 'it might be a good idea to get back to the ship, now.'

Colly followed his gaze, noticed the blood on Pétur's suit for the first time. The brightness faded from her manner. 'You're hurt?'

He nodded. Werner, taking his cue from Colly, attended to the boat, taking the four of them back to the *Fimbulvetr*, while Colly helped Pétur to remove the top of his wetsuit, examined the gash on his shoulder. After penetrating the thick foam of the suit, the knife had only been able to inflict a small gash on his body, out of all proportion to the amount of bloodstained water that smeared the suit. But she insisted that while Werner secured the boat and Finnur explained what had happened to Flynn, he follow her down to the ship's tiny surgery.

She left him there, reappeared changed quickly into shirt and jeans, then examined the knife wound more closely. It was clean and superficial. She disinfected it and tied a gauze pad over it. She was quick, but gentle.

When she'd finished she stopped and kissed his forehead. 'There now,' she told him. 'You'll survive.'

He looked up at her. For a time neither of them moved, their faces only inches apart. He tilted his head, eyes joined with hers, inviting a different sort of kiss. Her lips parted ready to comply, then she changed her mind and smiled instead, placing a warning finger on his lips.

He parted his own lips and kissed the finger. A powerful charge surged between them. She wavered, moving her hand down to touch the thick blond hair on his chest. Then she denied it, stepped back, clear away from him.

He relaxed. 'What are you going to do?' he asked.

'Do?' She turned away, busied herself with scissors and gauze and disinfectant bottle. 'Do? What about?'

'About the Russians. Hasn't that girl ruined your tests?'

'If she has I shall complain, officially. I shall also complain about the way you were attacked.'

'Good.' He pressed down the adhesive tape on his shoulder. 'Will it make any difference?'

'I'll get the Ministry to complain.'

He looked at her sadly. 'Poor Colly. You're not fooling me, you know.'

She paused in her tidying. 'What d'you mean?'

'Russians abroad are always so well-behaved. No ordinary Russian camper would interfere with a serious scientific experiment. And I don't believe for one minute any ordinary Russian tourist would attack me with a knife.' He shook his head. 'And most of all I don't believe in you taking all this so calmly. Official complaints? Why aren't you calling in the police? Honestly, Colly, I – '

'All these things you don't believe.' She flung the first aid equipment into a locker, slammed it shut. 'They're your problem, not mine. Aren't they?'

'What about our exclusive agreement, Colly? I thought you were going to tell me the truth.'

'First it's sexy kisses, now it's the truth. You don't want much, do you?'

'Don't joke with me, Colly.'

'Don't hassle me, then.' She swung round on him. 'Jesus Christ, you reporters are all the same. Let them get a toe in the door and they expect to be told your mother's dying words, and how your uncle diddled you as a kid.'

'Hey.' He grinned up at her. 'Did he really? Let me get my notebook. I didn't even know you had an uncle.'

'I don't.' She glared at him. 'Now who's making jokes?' She paused, thoughtful. 'Get a shirt on, will you? I need to concentrate on the lies I've got to tell you.'

He padded aft to the cabin where he'd left his clothes. By the time he'd dressed, he expected her to have escaped to the safer company of the others up on deck, but when he passed the surgery she was still there, waiting for him.

He leaned in the curtained doorway. 'I think you're in trouble,' he told her.

'No.' She shook her head vehemently. 'At least, not in any way you'd know about.'

'So?'

'So I wanted to tell you I really hate lying to you, Pétur. But I have responsibilities. I'm hoping you'll let me duck the questions I don't like, and leave it at that.'

'That's not the way they teach journalism in college.'

'I'm sorry.' She faced him squarely. 'It's the only deal on offer.'

'At least you're honest.'

He reached out in the tiny space and touched her cheek. She didn't flinch. His fingers traced the line of her jaw, strong yet delicately curved. He could sense her holding her breath. Her vulnerability, and his response to it, amazed him.

'OK,' he said gently, letting his hand drop to his side. 'OK. So you tell me what you can. What your . . . responsibilities allow.'

From the sharpness of her relief, from the flush on her cheeks and the tears blinked away from her eyes, he saw the importance of the concession he'd made. A great warmth of gratitude flowed from her. He took no advantage of it, which was unlike him. In the past, gratitude had been like a cheque, worthless until it was cashed.

He kept his distance. If his suspicions about the *Fimbulvetr*'s mission were anywhere near correct, he needed to be able to act with no betrayal involved. Would it make him happy, Björn had asked, to prove she was a liar? No. No, it wouldn't. But if necessary . . .

'But I have to warn you, Colly. I warn you of this so that you'll be prepared and won't think I'm deceiving you.' He picked up his face mask from the surgery table, peeled off the radiation disc inside it. 'Perhaps you know what this is.'

She nodded.

'OK, then you know what it'll tell me when it's developed. I have others; so has Finnur.'

He watched her face keenly, but it had told him all it was going to. 'So tomorrow, when these are developed, I'll have reports. You know what those reports will tell me, and the questions I'll want to ask.' He sighed. 'I can't promise that if you don't answer my questions, if your *responsibilities* don't let you, that I won't take them somewhere else.'

She nodded again. There was a long silence between them, broken only by the tiny creaking and ticking movements of the ship. Then –

'Me first?' Her words came out hoarsely, scarcely distinguishable. She cleared her throat. 'But you'll ask me first?'

He smiled. 'Scout's honour.' He made the sign. 'I'll ask you first.'

'Good.' She pushed past him briskly, on her way up to the deck. 'That's all right, then.'

And when he caught up with her, the conversation might never have taken place.

They radioed for the helicopter. Flynn, slightly concerned, reported that he'd seen neither of the Russian divers return. Pétur told him he wasn't surprised; how he'd noticed, flying in over the camp, the inlet angled to the beach, a shingle promontory masking its entrance. Werner objected. The chart showed no such thing. Pétur laughed. The chart was never up to date; shingle shifted from one year to the next. The Russians could enter and leave the water unseen any time they wanted. Flynn grunted.

The helicopter touched down nearby, and Colly ferried the two Icelanders over to it. She passed up Finnur's gear. Briefly, Pétur reached down and took her hand.

'I'll be back.'

'I know you will.' She looked up at him, tossed her hair back, laughed. 'Guys like you never give up.'

The boat drifted away from the float; the engine note of the helicopter increased as the rotor quickened, beating the water into ripples like hammered pewter, and they took off. The cove opened out beneath them: the shabby orange research vessel, the glacier-bed path up through the cliffs, the rescue hut on the beach with the Russian camp nearby, and even, now that Pétur knew where to look, the watcher, Big Brother, on his cliff ledge. Pétur stared down at the water, trying to place the two mysterious yellow seismic units.

He couldn't have said why he found them mysterious: Colly had
been quite open about them. She'd been open about a lot of other
things, too.

A sudden thought occurred to him. He shouted to Finnur, 'Did
you see any sign of that young Indian?'

Finnur shook his head.

'Could he have slept through all that drama?'

Finnur shook his head again.

'You're right. Where's he got to, then?'

Finnur shrugged. 'Hellnar?'

'Then why not say so?'

'Perhaps he's sick and they don't want to be quarantined. I tell
you another thing. Whoever keeps watch down there is armed. I
saw a rifle on the bridge. Not a sporting gun, some sort of
military – '

'Sick? Why didn't I think of that?' Pétur was excited. 'You
should have seen her face when I showed her one of our discs.
Somewhere on that ship is hot, and she knows it. Radiation
sickness – that's what the poor bastard's got, and they daren't let
on.'

'Would it show up so soon?'

'How the hell do I know?' It was Pétur's turn to shrug. 'It *must*
be. It fits.'

'Did you say you're going back?'

'Try to keep me away.'

By the time Robert reached the Paramount Hotel, his headache
was blinding. He had stopped once to vomit in the gutter. Since he
had had no breakfast, his heaving brought up only slime.

Woolston helped him, almost carried him, to his room. He
talked of calling a cab to take Robert to the hospital, but didn't
argue when Robert forbade it. They understood each other very
well. He made Robert lie down on the bed, removed his shoes,
then fetched a damp towel from the bathroom and laid it across
his forehead. Faintly, the bell sounded from his reception desk
three floors down. Woolston ignored it.

'You lie still now, Mr Goldsteen. I'm going for some aspirin.
Don't you run out on me while I'm away.'

Robert had lost the Head Sheet the hospital had given him, otherwise Woolston might have left him less readily. He lay in the darkened room, waiting for his pain to ease. It refused to oblige. He ought to be packing his suitcase. He must find a new hotel. If a routine report on his accident went to the police and they sent someone to the hospital to check, the trail would quickly lead them here. Or if the girl caught his name on a newscast . . . A foolish old man, that's all he was, in a panic over Latif, putting that telephone card in his pocket and forgetting it like that.

Things had to be done. He lifted his head, cringed as the pain danced in his skull, and looked through half-closed eyes round the room. His few clothes, in their curtained corner, he could deal with. The word processor, no bigger than a briefcase but weighty with its battery pack, defeated him even in imagination. He'd leave it behind. Colly's morning message had already been wiped from its memory: an uneventful night, clear skies, no visitors, the Russians out early in their dinghy, the Icelandic reporter expected any time with his contract. There was nothing there for the opposition.

The telephone interface could go with him. It didn't give much away. Even if he left it, they'd have every phone in the world to check. Without it, they didn't even have that much of a clue. And Colly knew the code to wipe the machine at the Abernatheys' clean when a long enough silence told her there'd be no more transmissions.

He was signing off. Without the portable he was deaf and dumb. Only the calls to Georg would remain. Was there any point? Yes. Anything was better than the isolation of capture, being dependent on the opposition for all his information. He closed his eyes, let the pain sing its cruel song. It still wasn't easing. In quick succession, he sweated, chilled, and felt sick again. He wasn't moving on just yet. For the moment, he wasn't doing anything. He slept.

When he woke it was as if in the same instant, the same silence, the same musty shadows, the same pain. But Woolston had come and gone, leaving Extra-Strength Tylenol and a glass of water on the chair beside Robert's bed, and a bunch of floppy daisies in a mug, and a get well card with a picture of smiling balloons. Robert took two Tylenol. He picked up the card. Woolston had written: *Don't worry about a thing*, and signed it *Florence Nightingale*.

Robert stood it carefully back on the chair. He knew he had to go and he didn't want to. This was his fifth day at the Paramount, and it seemed like all his life.

Woolston reappeared. 'Hey. You woke up.'

'I took the pills too, Florence.'

'And you read the card.' Woolston grinned. 'How're you doing?'

'Fine.' Robert sat up, wincing at the sharp assault in his skull. 'Thanks to you. But I have to check out. Now. Make up my check, will you? I'll be down in a minute.'

Woolston looked down at him. 'Something happened. I don't mean you getting sick. I mean something else happened, this morning.'

'I'll be paying cash.' Robert ignored him. 'And I'd appreciate a hand with my case on the stairs.'

'Just look at you, Mr Goldsteen. You ain't going nowhere.'

Robert had tried to rise, and was clinging desperately to the back of the chair. Woolston guided him down on the bed again.

'You're gonna kill yourself, keeping on like this.'

The way Robert felt, he could believe it. He sat, resting his head in his hands.

'I may have to go, no matter what. I may be called for.'

'Ah.' Woolston was thoughtful. 'If guys come, Mr Goldsteen, they won't get no great assistance from me.'

'No!' Robert mustered all the force he could project into the word; he could picture only too well the kind of men who would come for him. 'No. I mean it. If anyone comes, you do just what they say.' He reached for Woolston's hand and gripped it. 'Promise me? Anyone who comes, don't give them any hassle. Otherwise I can't stay.'

'It's a crazy thing when a friend ain't allowed to – '

'*Promise me.*' Woolston nodded. Robert released his grip on the other man's hand. 'And I do want to pay my check. Let's hope it won't be necessary. Let's hope nobody comes and we settle down again. But I want to get paid up.' He lay back against the pillow. 'If anyone comes, I may not have time to pay.'

Woolston asked him if he'd eaten, then went away and brought back the hotel account for four nights, and a chicken salad sandwich and a milkshake from the deli across the street. Some of Robert's money was in his suitcase under the bed. He insisted on having the case hauled out. He counted out dollar bills; then he ate and drank. He kept the food down, and felt better. Not good, but better than he had been.

As Woolston was reluctantly leaving to return to his desk, Robert asked him to take the telephone interface with him and dump it. Don't ask questions; just break it up and chuck it out with the garbage.

They came for Robert shortly after four. He'd dozed again, and was putting together the energy to go down to the foyer and ring Georg, and to hell with the tracer since it might be the last chance he'd get, when they burst in on him. A radio co-ordinated attack. Four men, two in from the fire escape and two through the kicked-open door. God alone knew what they expected to find – but discovering one sick old man alone on his bed didn't slow them down. They shouted orders at each other, pointed guns, seemed almost disappointed not to have guns pointed back at them. Robert stayed on the bed. The sandwich in his belly was having second thoughts about staying there.

They took control of him, stood him up, frisked him, let him sit on the chair. They were rough, but not unreasonably so. There was talking on hand-held radio transceivers. Then they grew calmer. Two more men brought in Woolston. Seeing him, Robert's spirits, such as they were, fell. Woolston hadn't kept his promise. The men didn't seem like sadists, yet two teeth were gone, and his nose, clearly, was broken.

Order was established. The men searched his room, beginning to emerge as individuals. Each looked and sounded American, strong, quick-witted, and answering to a vernacular American name. But six was overkill. Robert believed himself to be too rare a prize for either side to trust the other. Some of them had to be KGB. But all brothers under the skin. All agents.

Six was also too many for his small room. His headache returned in full force. The action, still over-emphatic, went on all around him. They found his reserve money, and the brown bag his sandwich had come in, treating each with the same serious respect. Robert thought the leader, who answered to Duke, was American; but he could well have been wrong.

'We're closing you down,' Duke told Woolston. 'Moving out
your fleabag guests. The hotel's unsanitary. It didn't pass inspection. And it infringes the fire laws. Health Department'll be round
with signs in the morning.'

Woolston touched his bloodied mouth gingerly. 'What do I tell
my folks? That I'm being arrested for a leaky crapper?'

'You don't tell nobody nothing. As of now, you don't exist.'

Robert knew nothing about Woolston's folks, had never thought
to ask. Too late, that made him ashamed.

The computer was still on the dresser. Duke considered it, then
held out one hand, snapping his fingers, and one of the men with
Woolston gave him the telephone interface. He matched the one to
the other. Momentarily Robert's eyes met Woolston's. He smiled
reassuringly. Even with it they had every phone in the world to
check. Even if they found the Abernatheys' place, it would tell them
nothing new.

'You've a telecommunications facility here,' Duke told Robert.
'So where's the other end?'

Robert stared at him.

'So where's the receiver?'

Robert coughed. 'I'm not going to tell you.'

A weight came down on Robert's shoulder, crushing him.

'Not now, Clancy.'

The pressure eased. Duke observed Robert thoughtfully, tossing
the interface from one hand to the other.

9

Day Six. AUGUST 9. MONDAY.

At two in the morning, Pétur was suddenly awake. The overhead light was on and a thickset man sat, quietly smiling, on the foot of his bed. The man from Dutch Shell. Olaf Janssen, with a silenced automatic in his hand.

After taking the radiation-sensitive discs to be processed, Pétur and Finnur had gone for a meal together and had stayed the evening, drinking and rehashing the day's visit to *Fimbulvetr*. No conclusions were reached, other than that there had to be a big story in it somewhere.

Janssen's armed intrusion seemed to confirm this.

'I told you you'd be sorry,' Janssen said cheerfully, pointing his gun at Pétur's belly, 'but you wouldn't believe me.'

His jocular tone suggested he wasn't going to shoot. But Pétur didn't bank on it.

'What do you want?'

'Me personally? Or us generally?'

'Either.' Pétur swallowed. 'Both. Is there a difference?'

'As a matter of fact, and fortunately for you, there is. We can't make up our minds about you. Either you're a member of the team or you're not. If you *are*, Washington wants you dead. And if you're not — '

'What team? And why Washington?' Pétur swung his legs out from under his duvet. The Danish accent still bothered him. He leaned his hands on his knees to stop them trembling. 'I guess there's no oil company?'

Janssen ignored him. 'And if you're not a member of the team, then they're leaving your disposal to my discretion.'

'You're CIA.'

'And *my* problem is, either you can keep a secret or you can't. Newsmen aren't exactly noted for discretion, though, are they?'

'You seem determined to think of me as your enemy.' Pétur shivered. 'Do we have to talk like this? Can't I at least get dressed?'

'My dear Einarsson, the whole world is the enemy of the CIA. *If* I am CIA. But put on clothes if you like.' He got up from the bed and moved away. 'If it'll make you feel more comfortable.'

Pétur dressed hastily. They went through to his sitting room. Looking to control the situation, he offered drinks. The perfect host. Janssen accepted Scotch. Neither sat. They stood awkwardly, by the wide uncurtained window.

'Convince me you're not a member of the team,' Janssen said at last.

'I want to help.' Pétur meant, *I want to live.* 'If I ask *what team?* it's because I want to help.'

'We're talking about the *Fimbulvetr*,' Janssen said patiently, as if Pétur might not have realised. 'You spend a lot of time aboard her.'

'She's news.' Pétur shrugged. 'I'm a reporter.'

'Nobody else gets on board that ship.' Janssen swung to face Pétur more directly, his voice hardening. 'You were in London with Doctor Graham. And yesterday you were involved in a diving accident. You helped her.'

'I've never been in London *with* her. We've both been in London, but not together. Your information is wrong.'

Janssen backed off, marginally. 'It sometimes is. And the diving?'

'A Russian jumped me. What the hell was I supposed to do?'

'But my dear Pétur, the Russians are our friends.'

He stared at Janssen, silenced, amazed. The man seemed to be in earnest.

It was a turning point. His obvious astonishment had proved something, but what he couldn't tell. He hoped it was good, feared it wasn't.

Janssen tossed back his drink. 'So I still have my problem. If you're not a member of their team, can I trust you with their story?'

'Trust me not to publish?' Pétur managed a sketchy version of his disarming grin. 'You'd never dare.'

'You could be useful to us. And the money's good.'

'You tried that one before. It didn't work.' He didn't even believe in the offer. Something else was afoot. 'But why do anything? You don't have to. Why not leave me to work things out for myself?'

'Why not tell me how much you've worked out already?' Janssen studied his empty glass.

And the loose ends joined. Now he knew what Janssen wanted. Janssen had come to kill him, but he needed first to know how much of the *Fimbulvetr*'s story was known, and how far it had gone. Whether Finnur knew – or his editor. Whether anything was committed to tape. But whatever story he told, the end, Pétur saw with bright clarity, would be the same.

'You don't have to worry about that.' He offered the whisky bottle; Janssen shook his head. 'About all I've been able to work out is . . .'

Delay was pointless. He swung the bottle with all his strength against the window. An unconsidered, inexplicable act, disconcerting his visitor with its violence. With a metallic ringing sound, the inner plate glass shattered, falling across the floor at their feet in brilliant daggers. Janssen's attention was diverted just enough for Pétur to launch himself forward, below the line of the momentarily uncertain gun. Its blast seared his shoulder. Then they were heaving together on the floor below the window, grunting as they struggled for control of the weapon still held in Janssen's outstretched hand.

Chairs scattered. Pétur was on top, but the CIA man was stronger. Breath rasping and muscles juddering, he tried to force his arm to extend. The gun went off again, burying its bullet in the ceiling. Janssen panted, his eyes wide, as he bent his arm closer towards Pétur. Unable to hold it back, Pétur pushed under Janssen's chin with the heel of his other hand, forcing his opponent's head back hard against the blades of broken glass beneath them. Janssen's head twisted suddenly, and he screamed. The gun fired again, uselessly. One ear was almost severed, and as he writhed against Pétur's grip the bright splinters, reddening rapidly, moved down his neck.

Janssen's arm weakened. Pétur shifted his grip, caught the wrist of Janssen's gun hand in both his own hands, and drove it back on to the floor with all his weight. Expecting a reaction from the other man, he found none. He became aware, appalled, of the blood pumping from Janssen's neck.

One of his own knees was bleeding, his trouser legs cut to shreds. Janssen's grip loosened on the gun. Pétur eased the automatic away, released the hand. Convulsively, Janssen pressed it to his gaping neck. His eyes rolled. Blood pulsed between his fingers.

Pétur stood up painfully, backed away. Shocked, stomach heaving, he watched Janssen die.

He leaned on the table, closed his eyes, shut out the nightmare. He understood nothing. He had intended nothing. Since waking to find Janssen at the foot of his bed he'd responded only to the moment. Acting without thought for the consequences. Consequences . . .

What was the punishment for bumping off a CIA hit man? He opened his eyes, walked stiffly into the hall, stared at the telephone. There was no way he could hide this mess. His hand was wet. Absently, he wiped it on his shirt, leaving long red stripes, before picking up the receiver. He'd been attacked, in his own home, by an armed intruder. Probably a burglar. He'd tackled the man; there'd been an accident. At worst, self-defence. At best, he might be a hero. Hand steady, he punched the emergency police number.

In the early hours of Monday morning Robert was driven quickly through New York in a black limousine, discreetly armoured, with a motorcycle escort. The car's windows were obscured: Robert had no idea where he was being taken, or why.

The opposition was treating him well. The question of the telephone interface was not pursued. Robert imagined he was being saved for some higher authority. The men's leader, Duke, had been away from the hotel for several hours, presumably making arrangements. During that time, Robert had been fed coffee and doughnuts, allowed to use the toilet, encouraged to rest. Woolston was taken away; no reasons were given. Robert protested, but vainly.

Robert still had moments of dizziness. His head hurt and he didn't always see clearly. But he kept these difficulties to himself; such stoicism helped, making him feel slightly heroic. Now he sat back in the red leather of the limousine, between Duke and Clancy. The seat was wide, sparing them physical contact. They were sealed from the driver, the doors had no knobs, and the interior lights, in tiny crystal shades, were permanently illuminated.

Now that they were on the move, neither of his companions spoke. Robert felt his isolation keenly.

'Is this going to be a long journey?'

He received no answer.

He offered a confidence. 'It's just that old men like me need to go to the toilet.'

It worked. 'You went before you left,' Duke reminded him. Then smiled: 'But in any case, no, Professor, this won't be a long journey. Not as journeys go.'

The *Professor* was reassuring, a sign of respect. Robert felt vaguely encouraged.

The car negotiated a right-hand corner, bouncing, and then another. Either a one-way system, or they were driving in circles.

'Are you KGB?'

Clancy stretched his legs. He was enormous. He said nothing.

Nobody spoke again until they reached their destination, an anonymous underground garage, then Duke advised him to behave himself. Robert had the impression that he'd been driven around unnecessarily, but he couldn't think why, and now all he knew for certain was that they were down by the river. As he was hurried from car to elevator a boat, not distant, sounded its siren.

They'd left him his watch. Four twenty. Not yet dawn.

The elevator, a normal passenger elevator, went up to the fiftieth floor. The foyer they entered was large and never-resting, bright copper-shaded lights shining vertically on to rubber plants, buttoned leather chairs, fine silver sand in the drum-sized ashtrays: a reception space for expensive people who would never notice it. Waste piled on top of conspicuous consumption. Surveillance cameras watched from tactful brackets, instantly bringing a crisply-laundered young executive from behind a beaten copper screen.

'Professor Graham. Good morning.' They shook hands. Duke and Clancy were ignored. 'We've been expecting you. This way, please.'

He set off fast, then slowed as Robert lagged behind. Robert's feet dragged. The carpet seemed too thick for them. He had to watch them carefully, head down, as he steered his course.

Following doggedly, he left the foyer. Two steps up, double doors, an anteroom, more double doors. A tap on the doors, and they opened to reveal a change of carpet from rust to olive.

'Professor Graham, sir.'

Robert found himself deserted. He looked up, saw that he was at the back of a small auditorium. Dull silver curtains backed the stage below him. There were pull-down chalkboards and slide screen, and a lectern with a shaded lamp. Full stage lights were on, leaving the raked seats in shadow, and behind the lectern Robert saw the UN Secretary-General.

'Professor Robert Graham?' Georg's voice, unamplified, reached him with perfect clarity.

He didn't know if he was supposed to answer. 'Here.'

'You are here, Professor Graham, at the request of two distinguished ambassadors to the United Nations Assembly: Ambassador Richardson of the host nation, the United States of America, and Ambassador Gronsky of the Union of Soviet Socialist Republics. They and their advisers wish to ask you some questions.'

Georg paused. His manner, though meticulously formal, carried traces of their long friendship.

He continued. 'Obviously you are under no obligation to answer. You may choose to help them or not, as you wish. But I have to tell you that they comprise no legally constituted body, and they have no control over your future conditions. Those are the responsibility of a two-nation Council, just established, whose people brought you here.'

Robert was at the top of a steeply-stepped aisle leading down to the stage. He began to descend it. The slope made him vertiginous. He held on to seat backs as he passed. At the bottom, still in shadow, he held on to a man's shoulder by mistake.

Georg advanced to the edge of the stage, leaned forward, and offered a hand. 'You're a sick man, Professor. You ought to be in hospital. You don't have to do this.'

Coming from his old friend, this *Professor* was ominously formal. He was advising Robert not to join in what was clearly a charade. This auditorium, the lights – they were an attempt either to intimidate him, or to lend the meeting's instigators weight and legitimacy. Neither ploy would work.

Robert took the hand, pulled himself up on to the stage. 'If important, busy people are willing to come out at this godforsaken hour to ask me questions, Mr Secretary-General, the least I can do is answer.'

He moved past Georg to the lectern. Rather than undermining his confidence, the lecture hall ambience restored him. Unlike many researchers, he'd enjoyed teaching. He turned, surveyed the banked seating. In the gloom on either side of the central aisle three darker masses bulked. He leaned on the lectern, a frail, angular figure in a shabby, ill-fitting suit.

'Gentlemen?' He peered closer. 'Ladies?' He remembered Ambassador Gronsky was a woman. The second group also included a woman. He smiled, trying for impish charm. 'I am pleased to see this evidence of international co-operation.'

Nobody moved. He was an impertinent old man, not at all a charmer.

Georg had seated himself in an upright chair to one side of the stage. He stared questioningly out into the auditorium.

'Ambassador Richardson?'

'Mr Secretary-General. Thank you.' Bodies shifted. Throats were cleared. The soft Southern accent continued. 'Professor Graham claims to be opposed to nuclear weapons. Would he not agree that it is only these that have kept the world from a major conflagration for the last half century?'

Robert almost laughed aloud. So this was supposed to be a formal debate – between the archetypal Mad Bomber and his intended victims? Besides, the question was footling. He hoped it was only a ranging shot. Richardson knew better than that.

'If true, Mr Ambassador, that's a sad comment on the leadership of two great nations. But I don't need to argue it. My point now is that even if not one single further nuclear weapon is tested or made, the superpowers will still be able to nuke each other into oblivion for the *next* half century.'

Somebody burst out, 'Rubbish. Typical ill-informed rubbish.'

Georg coughed. 'General Balenkov?'

The tone calmed a little, but the voice continued. 'That's rubbish because, in the event of such an agreement, future efforts will go into defence. Target diffusion. Silo hardening. With a known, and limited, attacking force, effective counter-measures could be taken. Wars could be won.'

'But we don't want the resources now being squandered on weapons to be diverted into hardening missile silos,' Robert gently reminded his audience. 'We want those resources diverted into helping the needy. Helping the planet. Removing the inequality that is the *cause* of wars. As recently as 1987, Mikhail Gorbachev told the Peace Forum in Moscow – '

'Gorbachev was wrong. The so-called Peace Forum was a mistake.' The flat, heavily accented tones, coming from someone Robert could not identify, sitting just in front of the General, brooked no argument.

There was a short silence, then an American voice was heard. 'I'll tell you what the real garbage is.' An army voice, for sure. 'The real garbage is us thinking we could ever get through to this guy's closed mind.'

Robert shrugged. He hadn't realised he was there to have his mind got through to.

'But it's humane to try, General Fitzgibbon. And our best hope, some might say, of coming out of this in one piece.'

A dry, quiet woman's voice. Robert knew it well. Aurelia Vargas, a presidential adviser from MIT. A brilliant woman. But he disliked her *humane*. By implication, it simply postponed its opposite till later. Which was only to be expected, but need not have been put quite so crudely.

'I'm afraid my mind *is* closed,' he said. 'Since the most recent Geneva talks began, four thousand *new* nuclear warheads have helped to close it. Maybe as many more Soviet ones. The Gorbachev/Reagan reductions have long since been made up. Cuts in conventional forces mean nothing. You and I know it, even if the public doesn't. Worn out, obsolete missiles have been scrapped publicly, while new missiles are installed without fuss.'

He was warming to his theme, headache forgotten. 'Depressed-trajectory missiles have helped to close my mind also. Sure, they reach their targets more quickly, with less chance of counter-measures. But that means shorter decision times, more reliance on computers, more room for panic and error. And I – '

'The professor has not been brought here to deliver a speech.' Ambassador Gronsky rose to her feet. 'I'd like to ask him this. My country and America are not the only nuclear powers. If we abandon our superiority, who will hold back France? South Africa? Israel, Pakistan, India, China . . . ? The Third World you want to help so desperately may not be there to help any more.'

She sat down. Robert spread his hands, opened his mouth to reply. Suddenly a pain struck blindingly behind his right eye. He waited, head bowed, for it to pass. But there was no opportunity to rest, to clear his mind. They hadn't come here to have their opinions changed, they'd come here to change his.

He looked up, eyes narrowed against the lights. 'Madam Ambassador,' he said, 'I think you are forgetting the power of economic aid. Israel, Pakistan, India, China – all these countries need the world's good opinion. Maybe even yours does too, a little. Nuclear conquest has never been proposed as a way of ending a nation's financial problems – it can only complicate them. France, self-willed though she is, knows that ultimately her interests lie within the European Community. And South Africa's future lies in trade also. She's only recently come out from under one set of sanctions – she'll never risk another.'

He leaned forward. 'Besides, the whole concept of nuclear superiority is a grotesque irrelevance. One thousandth part of the nuclear arsenals presently held by the superpowers would be enough to "hold back", as you put it, any maverick nation.'

Silence. Listening to himself, he knew how tired these arguments were. True maybe, but still tired – these people didn't need them. What were they really here for? What was *he* really here for?

Georg pointed into the darkness. 'Professor Grigoriev?'

The Soviet academician cleared his throat. 'To begin with, Mr Secretary-General, let me say that I believe Professor Graham to be a moral man, a just and honourable man.' There was laughter from the military on both sides. He rode over it. 'I also believe that the far-reaching effects he claims would result from his group's threatened action in Iceland are if anything understated. And I put it to him, therefore, that such effects, inflicted on largely innocent populations, are neither moral, just, nor honourable.'

Robert's vision had blurred. He closed one eye, saw better. 'I can only remind my dear friend Konstantin, who after all was one of the leading participants in the Peace Forum that we are supposed to pretend never happened, that the alternative would be worse. I refer him to the admittedly imperfect doctrine of the Lesser Evil.'

The MIT woman, Vargas, snorted. 'You're bluffing. You'd never pull the plug.'

'We don't have to. It's automatic.'

'Nothing's so automatic it can't be over-ridden.'

They were testing him. What was it they wanted to know?

'My people aren't suicidal. They'll be only too happy to over-ride the automatics. But only when the treaties are signed and made public. That's why you're wasting your time here. Whatever happens to me, Colly will only over-ride the system once you've gone public, and can't back down.'

'Your daughter, maybe.' It was General Fitzgibbon, his voice raised angrily again. 'She'll wait. But what about that crazy terrorist Latif? He might pull the plug any time, just for the hell of it.'

Anxiously Robert focused his thoughts. *They still didn't know Latif had gone.* Maybe this information could still be useful to him. He hedged: 'Kassim Latif is a man of principle.'

'He's a fucking terrorist.' Fitzgibbon was shouting now. 'And if you're with him, then you're a fucking terrorist too.' He checked. 'Begging your pardon, ma'am,' he mumbled to Vargas.

Richardson spoke. In contrast with the General, he was for once keeping his temper. 'I have daughters of my own, Professor Graham. Are you willing to sacrifice your own daughter?'

'Colly isn't afraid to die, Ambassador.'

'That wasn't my question.'

The pain struck again. 'I . . . I love my daughter.' He staggered, held fast to the lectern. *Colly wasn't afraid to die.* Did he really believe that?

Georg rose to help him. 'Professor Graham is sick. You mustn't ask him to – '

'Sick, nothing,' Fitzgibbon burst in. 'He's afraid to answer any more questions.'

Robert clung to the Secretary-General's arm. 'Not afraid, General – puzzled. You people have weapons far more dreadful than ours. You call them a deterrent, and when you say you'll use them under certain circumstances you expect to be believed. Even though your daughters and your sons may suffer. Yet you don't believe us when we say the same. Are you suggesting that we're more moral than you?'

'Naw – you're just more chicken.'

There was an uncomfortable silence. Robert wondered if the sentiment was shared, or was just being tried on for size.

Georg fetched his own metal chair from the side of the stage, put it in front of the lectern. Robert sat in it. He'd nearly broken, but he'd held them. They were all scared stiff of the crazy terrorist Kassim Latif. Latif was a weapon they themselves, by showing it to him, had placed in his hands. The weapon he'd lost. The weapon, mercifully and mysteriously, nobody else had yet found.

'Any more questions?' Georg asked curtly.

An anonymous aide, sitting to the right of Ambassador Richardson, raised a diffident finger.

'One point interests me. Your ultimatum, Professor Graham, makes no mention of a safe conduct for your team. Why is that?'

Robert leaned back in his chair. The dizziness had passed. 'Because we don't believe such promises would be honoured. Ergo, they aren't worth demanding.'

'You have a poor opinion of your elected government.'

'Not really. It's simply that morality has little to do with the business of elected government. Elected government's business is to serve the interests of its people. Our survival would not be perceived as in their interests.'

Ambassador Richardson, still patient, took up his aide's theme. 'Yet you believe that these treaties, once signed, will be adhered to?'

'Oh, yes. Safe conducts, secret promises, could easily be ignored by governments who could be seen to be acting in their countries' interests, hunting down a gang of ruthless terrorists. But publicly declared treaties, agreements made in open session of the United Nations General Assembly – you'd have to stick with them. For one thing, you'd be so popular. These are measures that the ordinary people of the world, everywhere, are longing for. Going back on them would be electoral suicide.'

Feet shifted out in the auditorium; there was a murmur of conversation. He was boring them. None of this was what he'd been brought here for. They knew it all – better, perhaps, even than he.

The US Ambassador left his seat and came up on to the stage.

'Help us,' he said gently. 'It's your only chance. Speak to your daughter.'

The gentleness was false. Why this appeal? His daughter – always they came back to his daughter. The weak link? Was that what they were looking for? And even if he was willing, did they really believe he still had some way of reaching her?

Richardson put a hand on Robert's shoulder. 'Speak to her, Bob. She doesn't want to die. Tell her to give us more time.'

Robert shook his head. 'Time I don't have. Weeks? Months? I've been working for this for thirty years. I'm an old man.'

The hand on his shoulder tightened. 'And old men get hurt, Bob. Sweet Jesus – don't you hear what I'm telling you? Old men get hurt. *They get hurt bad.*'

Robert knew it. It came with the package. He hurt already, but that was nothing to what they could do. His only comfort was that, like him, they too were running short of time.

'I hear what you say, Ambassador, but I can't help you.' He looked out into the dazzle of the lights. 'Better give me back to Duke and Clancy.'

That afternoon, in Rome, early for his meeting with Sayeed, David Lawrence was enjoying the special house aperitif served in a little pavement café/bar on the Piazza della Rotunda, opposite the Pantheon. Under the check-clothed table, he had between his legs the plastic Upim supermarket bag Sayeed had specified. Bag-snatching was a thriving local profession. He'd been stationed in Rome long enough to own shabby Italian clothes, and the bright plastic bag, carefully secured under the table, marked him further as a hard-up Roman. He and Sayeed would do their best to avoid the attention of the professionals.

In the bag, wrapped in a cheap cotton curtain, were bundles resembling five thousand US hundred-dollar bills. They'd stand the hurried inspection Lawrence had planned, in the half-dark, but nothing more. They wouldn't need to. With luck, they'd never be used at all.

He sipped his drink and watched the tourists queuing for the open horse-drawn carriages, plumes and rosettes bobbing jerkily on each tired nag's head. Beyond them pavement stalls offered small plastic Pantheons and battery-operated monkeys that clapped their hands. And beyond that stood ancient Rome.

David ordered a second glass. He too had a place in the corruption: both Sayeed and he thieves, and no honour between them. Sayeed's one word, *Ragnarok*, had produced all that the Indian could have hoped for. And more. Washington had rung back Monday morning. Four a.m. their time, and still they could come up with Grade III Directives. They wanted Sayeed, and they wanted him alive.

David told them this was out of his league: he picked up snippets, not men. But he wasn't surprised when they insisted. There was nobody else in Rome able to get close enough to Sayeed to take him.

Their meeting place had been a lucky choice. Suggested mainly for its quietness on a Monday afternoon, the Chiesa della Virgine turned out to offer useful possibilities. Transport from Rome Central was laid on to wait in the No Parking area outside the church. They'd promised it would blend in – nothing would be done to frighten Sayeed away.

David's second drink was brought. He shifted in his seat, easing his jacket over the unfamiliar holster beneath his left arm. He'd shot the required courses, naturally; but never enjoyed them. He was handicapped by a strong aversion to killing. Today, happily, his orders were quite specific on that point: disable if strictly necessary, but *do not terminate.*

David glanced at his watch, finished his drink, and rose. Dropping a handful of money on the table, he left the shaded café tables and stepped out into the August sunlight. He liked it here. His years spent with Associated Press in Frankfurt had been purgatory for a native Californian.

The cobbled alleyway leading from the Piazza to the Church of the Virgin was wide enough for two cars to pass. Its houses climbed to four or five storeys, flat-fronted, with balconies, and entryphones beside their vault-like doors. Both sides of it were lined with mopeds chained to ground floor window bars. Although a strict No Parking area, this afternoon David had counted seventeen cars parked in it. In one of them a couple was kissing passionately on the back seat. Another had its hatchback open and was being loaded with small bags of manure collected with brush and shovel from the horses out on the Piazza. The collector was a small, neat man in a shiny suit and disposable plastic gloves. Otherwise, the cars on the alleyway were empty. But beside the open door of one of them a woman was arguing fiercely with a policeman, pounding some papers she held in one hand.

David walked slowly down the alleyway to the church, keeping his eyes to the front. Sayeed might be watching. There was no need for David to identify his backup; enough that he himself be recognised from the Upim bag.

He paused on the worn steps outside the church, looked at his watch again, and up and down the street, then went inside. The scene was set. The time lacked two minutes to two thirty.

The church was large and cool and dark, seemingly a maze of aisles and side chapels. Centuries of incense pricked David's Protestant nostrils. Neon haloes quivered above saints in niches, and wax piled thick as bat droppings beneath banks of candles. The door closed loudly behind him. He wiped his feet on a big coir mat, listening. Echoes from the door clattered and faded. Then a footstep, very far away. And close at hand, a cough.

David looked for its source. There were pillars blocking him, a crimson baize door in a carved stone screen. The geography of Popish churches defeated him. It left him feeling horribly vulnerable. Blundering through into an aisle, he passed a woman on her knees at the end of a pew. In front of him, in a dusty beam of sunlight from high above, he spotted the sleek head of Sayeed. He walked towards him, clacking on the paved aisle like a diffident communicant, his right hand on the gun butt inside his faded denim jacket.

Sayeed too was dressed to match the Upim bag. He wore jeans and a Columbia University T-shirt, with flashy curved sunglasses pushed up on his forehead, and dirty white trainers. He moved along the pew, making room for David beside him. In front of them the anguished bleeding Christ figure was brightly spotlit.

'Change of plan,' Sayeed said curtly. A new, aggressive Sayeed. He didn't whisper. 'I refuse to do business with half of Rome Central outside.'

The echo broke his voice up into spiky jangles. He glowered. Gone was the smiling, deferential Sayeed. This young man was a routine thug.

'We can't talk here, Lawrence. I'm moving on. You follow. Alone. And bring the money.'

'No.' Reluctantly, David eased his gun out of its holster.

Sayeed's look of contempt suggested that he knew more about guns than David ever would; that he remained in control whoever held the weapon. 'And I say yes.'

'No, Sayeed. We do our business here.' David gestured with his head, back over his shoulder. 'If I have my friends, so do you. D'you think I'm blind?'

Sayeed turned to his right, stared at the woman kneeling near the rear of the church. 'Just some tourist. She's nothing to do with me.'

'I don't believe you. She's got a gun. I saw it under a map on the seat next to her.'

Sayeed, still contemptuous, stood up and leaned over the back of the pew to get a better view. The woman, still kneeling, shot him. The bullet entered his sneering, slightly open mouth neatly; it exited less neatly, taking most of the back of his head with it.

Before Sayeed fell, David had already ducked into cover. He took off his shoes and ran, silently, bent beneath the pew back, sideways to the nearest pillar. It was done instinctively. Christ, he thought, the training really does work.

The reverberations from the shot faded. He held his breath, waited, shoes in left hand, gun ready in right.

'Mr CIA? You can come out now.' The accent was German, with a smile in it. 'I won't hurt you, Mr CIA.'

David swore violently under his breath. Training be buggered. He'd approached this whole thing much too lightly. He stayed where he was, called out: 'What's the deal?'

'Deal? My God, you even talk like Mr CIA – '

A door slammed, cutting her short. Footsteps shuffled nearer. David peered round his pillar, saw the woman in her spotted dress standing at the end of her pew, gun levelled not at him but at the approaching footsteps.

'No need,' he hissed. Please God, no more killing. 'Just leave this to me.'

She shrugged. 'If you fail, I can always . . .' She moved the gun expressively.

David eased the slip-on shoes back on his feet, stood up, abandoning his pillar. As he put his automatic away an elderly priest appeared in an opening to one side. The dead man was on the tiled floor, invisible behind the pews; the bitter smell of cordite had already blended with the incense.

The priest glared suspiciously at the tall man examining the carvings on the altar screen, and at the woman, his wife or these days more probably his mistress, waiting impatiently for him by the door. The man wished him 'Good morning' in excellent foreigner's Italian.

The priest was unconvinced. 'What are you doing? I heard a sound. Very loud. Something falling or breaking.'

The tall young man gestured amicably. 'It was the door, Father. My wife left it open; the wind must have caught it. I apologise.'

'No.' The priest shook his head, muttered uncertainly as he looked around. 'Falling or breaking. Something falling or breaking.' But everything he could see was just as it should be.

The woman moved sharply sideways. The man gestured again. 'You have a very beautiful church, Father.'

'Pah. The church is hideous.' The old man, still glancing from side to side, groped in his vestments. 'I've been telling visitors that for thirty years. You people have no taste. It's the ugliest church in Rome.' By now, the sound was forgotten. He took a fierce pinch of snuff. 'And *that's* saying something!'

He turned away, sneezed, and departed. David listened to his shuffle, then to the sound of the distant door. He walked down the aisle to the woman.

'You owe me an explanation. Why did you shoot Sayeed?'

'Is that what you call him?' She tilted her head, keeping her own counsel. 'My name is Lise Schneider. How do you do.'

He avoided shaking hands. 'Sayeed was nobody, Frau Schneider. Just a messenger.'

She laughed. 'I know. He had information for you. That's why I shot him.'

A direct lady. 'KGB?'

'Sometimes. Not today.'

Laconic, too. 'We need to shift Sayeed's body. Otherwise that priest might identify us.'

She dismissed the priest with a wave of her hand. 'The man was a fool. Blind to everything. That's why I left him. He probably doesn't remember his own name.'

'All the same . . .' David, having failed to take Sayeed alive, felt compelled at least to take the body in, to show willing. 'I've got transport outside.'

'Of course. But few drunks with holes in their heads get carried out of churches into cars at two thirty in the afternoon. Even in Rome.'

He gave in. She was more of a professional in this business than he'd ever be. They went together to the body and Frau Schneider stood over him while he searched it. Sayeed carried no identification, and whatever information he'd planned to hand over wasn't on him in document form. Microfilm was a possibility, and harder to check for, but where would he have got the necessary equipment? *We can't talk here*, he'd said. The information was somewhere else, and he'd been going to collect it.

Which left David at a dead end. He picked up the Upim bag.

Frau Schneider stared at it. 'The paper?'

'Paper?'

'The rubbish you were paying him with,' she said impatiently. 'How much did he ask for? A million?'

'Half.'

She sniffed. 'Cheap. The stuff he was selling – what was it about?'

David saw a chance to regain ground. 'If you don't know, you surely can't imagine I'll tell you.'

She sniffed again. 'Which means you don't know either.'

Glumly carrying the Upim bag – Rome Central would want it back, there were genuine dollar bills at the end of each bundle – he walked with her from the church. They paused, shading their eyes in the sudden brilliance. David's backup team must still be here, indistinguishable amongst the routine of a Roman street. They might be puzzled by his reappearance with a woman alongside, but he knew they'd do nothing. The instructions were quite clear: he had to get Sayeed out into the street, alive and reasonably well, then leave the rest to the boys – and girls? – from Rome Central. No Sayeed, and they'd leave him in peace to report back on whatever had gone wrong. For all the backup knew, David realised, Sayeed had simply not turned up. Whatever. His job now was to find out everything he could and report.

He was still on edge. He'd never seen a man killed before. Poor, greedy Sayeed – he'd thought himself safe, taken every precaution.

Reminded, David turned to the woman. 'There's more to this,' he said. 'Sayeed took out insurance – copies of his stuff, left with a friend. To be published if he didn't come back for them by tomorrow night.'

'Can I believe you?'

'You can't afford not to. Would publication please you – or your employers?'

She thought about it. 'No.'

'Me neither. So maybe we could work together. Share information. We both need to find this friend.'

She thought again. 'If we find the friend, and the copies, you understand I take them? I take them *before* you see them?'

'Let's sort that out when the time comes.'

'No, Mr CIA, we sort it out now. You do not get to see the copies. I take them. That is what my employer wishes.'

He didn't argue. If she shared what she knew about Sayeed, he was ahead in the game. What he had to give her in return could be written on the head of a pin. Who took what could be sorted out later.

They set off down the alleyway towards the Piazza della Rotunda. Across the Piazza and on, through a few streets, lost in the crowds, until Frau Schneider pointed to a café.

'We will talk there. You will pay for the drinks.'

Again he didn't argue. They found a table, ordered.

She rummaged in her tourist's tote bag. 'On Saturday afternoon, this Sayeed killed a man in the Vatican City. If he put together the papers you describe, and deposited them, he did so between then and when I myself first saw him. That was yesterday morning, coming out of Babington's.' David tried to keep his face expressionless. 'You know Babington's?' He nodded. She continued. 'Since then, you see, I've been constantly on his tail.' There was a note of pride in her voice. Tailing Sayeed, clearly, had not been easy.

She produced a folder, and from it a neatly typed sheet of paper.

'A list of reported sightings during that time, between the Vatican and Babington's. Where I get this list is my business. No sighting is certain, and much time is unaccounted for. But it's all we have.'

David examined the list. Shops, bars, a bank, a church, a public library . . . unsurprising visits. Either the bank or the library could have provided photocopying facilities. Sayeed could have known someone at any of the places on the list, and left papers for safekeeping. If this was all Frau Schneider had to share, then they were wasting their time.

Except for one small oddity. And the more he thought about it, the odder it seemed. Angels, was it, who danced on the heads of pins?

He returned the list to Frau Schneider. He had to get rid of her.

'How d'you want to handle this? With so many places, if we check each of them together it could take until after his deadline.'

'That is always possible.' She nodded confidently. 'But you know something about this man that I do not. It makes you not certain, but very hopeful. So we will go first to this address that you have chosen.'

He looked up sharply, intending a denial. Her humourless gaze dared him to be so foolish. The arrival of their drinks saved him from any particular admission. He paid at once, adding a generous tip to the tray, and the waiter left. David raised his glass to Frau Schneider.

'It's a question of English teacakes,' he told her.

Her bewilderment was his morning's only success.

10

For the three on the *Fimbulvetr*, that Monday was hard. It began with a dawn visit from the Russians, chatter and loud 'Good mornings', waking the two who had the watch below. The dinghy came closer now, and its friendliness was openly mocking. Diving jokes were offered. Allusions to juicy yellow sausages.

Colly was frantic. The bomb was booby-trapped. They must know the bomb was booby-trapped. The previous day, as soon as the Icelandic TV men had left, she'd sent a message to her father, via the Abernathies', begging him to contact the opposition and emphasise the warnings in the ultimatum. So far there'd been no reply. Nothing could prevent Ragnarok if the Russians tried to move or defuse the bomb, regardless of the status of the over-ride on the wet lab trigger.

On the cliffs to starboard, the NATO watchers changed shifts. They were another itch upon her skin. Werner's binoculars had shown high-velocity rifles. The range was extreme, but not beyond luck and good marksmanship. Now the *Fimbulvetr*'s crew used only the port side of the deck in daylight. Common sense told them that piecemeal assassinations were a dead-end option; but nobody pretended to read the opposition's mind.

Pétur's return hung over her. She didn't know how much of the truth he'd need. Maybe she had exposed them needlessly – so far, the threatened incursion from the foreign media had been restricted to one phone call from an agency in New York. It had all been an opposition scam. And she hadn't mentioned his radiation discs to Flynn or Werner: she was simply waiting, frightened, to see what the future brought. If she couldn't enlist him to their side, the whole enterprise might be lost. If he went back and splashed the story, there would be no way left for the superpowers to save face – but the thought of getting rid of Pétur only entered her mind long enough to be dismissed.

Also, Pétur disturbed her. He disturbed her sexually. Werner had wanted so much – love, commitment – he'd scared her off, emotionally, although they still sought physical comfort with each other. It would be easier to satisfy that physical need, growing more pressing as the deadline approached, with Pétur. But it was impossible. The time and the place were wrong, and her enhanced awareness of sex shocked her. She felt lessened by this need in her body, chided herself with the thought that she'd be tearing the pants off Flynn, next.

But that was a double-edged private joke. Both her friends now gave her anxiety. Between Flynn and her there was coolness. She had made no great point of her anger and shame at Zebedee's death, but he knew. That, and the inactivity, were getting to him. He drank more, and oftener. And even Werner, who had been her rock, was faltering. He slept badly and ate little. Their amateurism bothered him, and he patrolled the ship obsessively, searching for weaknesses.

The Russian dinghy went away. Silence descended on the cove. Then the tapping began again. It had gone on half the night. They presumed it was Russian divers hammering on the *Fimbulvetr*'s hull, but it might have been anybody. It had begun the previous afternoon. Doing no conceivable harm, since the trigger was safe; but creating tension, irritation. Psychological warfare. Colly almost felt sympathy, after all these years, for the US generals embroiled in a losing war in Vietnam. Like her, they possessed the ultimate nuclear sanction; like her, their one unanswerable weapon could not be used on such a trivial disturbance.

Also, microphones had started to appear, stuck to the glass of the lower portholes. There *was* a danger here – that listeners might infer Kassim's absence. Werner made sweeps at irregular intervals, scraping them off. He even made sure that a turbaned head above a brown made-up face (his own) was sometimes briefly visible. Earlier, such charades might have amused, or embarrassed, them. Now they were grim and deadly.

The day was overcast. They were tired, but none of them dared sleep, and they had nothing to do. It was pointless to maintain the pretence of geological research. By the time the island's government began to wonder about their promised uranium, the countdown to Ragnarok would be over. And then they could wonder all they liked. One way or the other, the *Fimbulvetr*'s crew would be long gone.

At noon Colly tried the Abernatheys' again for a message from her father. There was still nothing. Twenty-four hours of silence. That was it. Looking up from the console, she caught Flynn's eye. He knew. They were on their own now: either Fard was sick, or he was taken. She checked her notes for the code to scrub the computer link clean, and sent it.

This cutting of the cord distressed her more than she could have imagined. Even across five thousand kilometres, and with a computer go-between, she'd relied on the contact. All her life she'd relied on the contact. Through the storms of leaving home, and growing up, and living, he'd always been there. He and her mother. Now she had neither.

She didn't dare think about what might be happening to him.

In the middle of the afternoon the Russian dinghy returned. Flynn was on watch; the truce between them following the American's death had lengthened until now it no longer signified. Events had moved on. Pragmatism ruled. She kept her principles, he kept his. And now Fard was gone.

Called by Flynn, she went on deck: a fine drizzle was falling. She saw the Russians coming, hurried below, shut herself in her cabin and covered her head with a pillow, waiting for them to go away.

In Reykjavik, Pétur had just got free of the city police. He'd been with them all day. They didn't like his story. He told them he'd met Janssen only once before, on Saturday night, when he'd visited Pétur's flat, obviously to case it, on the pretext of trying to sell him insurance. Then, in the early hours of Monday morning, Pétur had woken and surprised the man in his living room. Janssen pulled a gun, and the fight took place in which he died.

It wasn't a good story. It presented Janssen as a professional thief, a most unlikely man to carry a silenced automatic. It took no account, either, of the absence of fenceable items in Pétur's flat, which Janssen must have noticed on his earlier visit. But the truth would rob him of his scoop on the *Fimbulvetr*. And besides, he'd made Colly a promise, to hear her explanations first. It was just a coincidence that sticking to that promise meant protecting his story. In the late morning the police let him sleep for a few hours, while they checked around. Lacking anything positive to the contrary, since he'd washed up Janssen's whisky glass and replaced it among the others, he reckoned his story would stand. It did. If the police discovered anything curious in Janssen's background, or anything suggesting complications, perhaps a US connection, they didn't say so. They were hardly likely to. They accepted Pétur's statement, kept him at the central police station until the middle of the afternoon, then released him on bail pending further inquiries. The TV station paid: Björn wanted him back on the story. The chief inspector was an old friend, but even he would say no more than that Pétur should move his ass, and be grateful he had an honest face.

His wait in the cell had given Pétur time to think. Even assuming that the radiation discs showed up positive, he was almost convinced that the uranium was a side issue. The *Fimbulvetr* had stirred up too much aggressive international interest to be in the prospecting business: Colly Graham was involved in something far deeper. Lurid speculations crossed his mind. If the Indian was sick, perhaps he'd been involved in illegal experiments involving radioactive materials. It surely couldn't be drugs – or could it? Was the ship being prepared as a jail for unusual prisoners? He gave up. The possibilities were endless.

It struck him, more importantly here and now, that whatever was going on out there, if Janssen had been CIA then Pétur must expect other visitors, men more inclined to shoot first and talk later. He'd no answer to this – except to get out to Helgavik as soon as possible. After he'd talked to Colly he'd have a better idea of what came next.

As soon as he was released he did indeed move his ass – straight to the TV building on Langavegur. The film processing lab didn't have his discs: Finnur Sigvaldson had signed for them.

He found Finn in the cutting room. 'Well? What's the verdict?'

Finnur eyed him thoughtfully. 'You're here at last. Björn's shouting the place down for you.'

'He can wait. What does the lab say?'

Finn opened a drawer, produced the shiny processed discs, and laid them out in a row on the desk. Two clear, perhaps slightly fogged. One distinctly cloudy. One completely black, opaque.

Pétur pushed at them with one finger. 'So?'

Finn picked up the cloudy disc. 'This is one of mine. Slight radiation, possibly residual. From the upper deck – the bridge or one of the laboratories.'

'And the black one?'

'Yours. The colour speaks for itself. From your face mask.'

'So most of the ship's clean. But the stuff's strong on the seabed, and some of it's been taken up to one of the labs.'

'Or the other way round.'

'The other way round?' Pétur stared at him. Finn shrugged. It was just an idle comment.

'Björn's going to blow a gasket if you don't get to him soon. You've cost the company. Now he needs the inside guff on this killing.'

'Sure.' Pétur's thoughts were elsewhere. 'But I've got to get to Helgavik and back while it's still light.'

'Are you crazy? When did you last look at the weather?'

'The weather?' Pétur crossed to the window. He vaguely remembered rain, as he'd hurried from the police station, and maybe some wind. The sky over Reykjavik was down on the rooftops, hurrying by, and raindrops lashed the glass. He cursed. 'No flying?'

'Storm warnings out. And a small craft advisory. I kept the chopper on call till three. The Flugstödin called in. They're grounding their fleet. Icelandair's still leaving from Keflavik, but nothing else is moving.'

Another bloody summer storm. And the timing couldn't have been worse. If this was the greenhouse effect, Pétur wanted nothing of it. Give him snow and ice any day.

He cursed again. 'This could last for days.'

Finnur shook his head. 'Clear by morning, Met says.'

'I could always drive.'

'Wreck your car, end up on the cliffs in the dark, and swim the last kilometre in the tag end of a hurricane?'

Pétur shrugged, looked out of the window again, admitting defeat. 'Björn it is, then.'

Finnur bared his teeth. 'Making your own news, now. Our resident assassin.'

'It was self-defence, Finn. And it wasn't funny.' He checked himself, thinking back, and shuddered. 'Actually, it was bloody horrible.'

Finnur looked away. 'So I'm told. I gather the police photographer threw up.'

Pétur went quietly to the door. 'If I'm wanted, I'm with Björn. He can't use much before the inquest, but that's his problem.' He opened the door, leaned on the handle. 'And book the chopper for the morning. I'm going to Helgavik if I have to wind up the elastic myself.'

In the Paramount Hotel that afternoon time had stopped. All of its bedrooms, save one, stood empty. Undisturbed, curtains faintly stirring in the New York smog, they gathered dust and cockroaches. The desk in the foyer was in ruins: Woolston, who had chosen not to answer a few simple questions, was locked in a basement storeroom. On the upper floors taps dripped in bathrooms, and in one hastily vacated bedroom a TV set played silently at the foot of unmade twin beds.

In another bedroom, Robert's, a less tranquil silence reigned. The air there was heavy with the smoke of expensive cigars and the less expensive odour of burning hair and flesh. The cigars, Cuban and courtesy of the Soviet embassy, were Duke's; the hair and flesh were Robert's. He'd been wrong about Duke, but not about what came after the double doors and the rust-coloured carpet.

He regained consciousness. The doctor had been stooped over him with a stethoscope. Now he straightened his back and nodded, making a gesture with one hand, extending finger and thumb to suggest a narrow margin. Robert saw this. There were moments when he noticed more than the other three men in the room realised. He saw the table imported from the room next door, with the tape recorder on it. He saw the empty beer cans, and the takeaway pizza containers. He saw the sweat on Clancy's broad, unlined forehead, and the tightly closed window.

He lay on the bed naked, wrists and ankles tied to the iron frame. In the beginning he'd regretted this exposure of his body's sags and oldness, but he soon stopped caring. He'd come a long way from the white collar inquiries of the ambassadors, their military and scientific advisers. And yet he knew that in spirit those men and women were still with him. Even Richardson had cared, knowing what came next.

Duke was reading. That morning, in between interrogating Robert, he'd begun a paperback edition of Michener's *Texas*. A massive book. Clancy, who'd been listening to his Walkman, one foot tapping, took the nod from the doctor, pushed back his earphones, reached out and touched Duke's knee.

Duke put his book down on the table by the tape recorder. He started the machine. 'Professor Graham? We were talking about your telephone interface. You remember? There's a receiver somewhere, and we need to know where it is.'

Robert closed his eyes. Tears trickled from their corners. The receiver wasn't important. But his refusal to answer Duke's question was the most important thing in the world. A truth swelled inside him, like a seed pressing to grow and blossom. He could feel it. It pressed against the walls of his mind, beautiful and dangerous, promising peace for himself and comfort for his enemies. And if he ever told Duke about the receiver and who it had been used to communicate with then the walls would be down, and the truth would burst out into flower. There would be peace for himself and comfort for his enemies. He wept.

Cigar smoke blew across his face. 'Professor Graham? We need to know where that receiver is.'

'I'm sorry.' He really was.

'But we need to know.'

'I'm not going to tell you.'

He didn't brace himself or beg. He'd learned by now that it was better not to.

I I

Day Seven.   AUGUST 10. TUESDAY

In the early hours of the morning the depression centred in the North Atlantic deepened, as predicted. Such summer storms had become increasingly common in the 1990s, a feature of the climate shift. Mini-hurricanes, they swept northward up the Atlantic seaboard of the United States, veering sharply eastward and across the tip of Greenland, into Iceland and beyond, to dampen the Scandinavian summers, even while Europe south of the Baltic suffered repeated droughts. They never took long to cross the North Atlantic. But for a few hours, gale force winds swept Iceland. Massive seas thundered against the rocky coastline. In Helgavik, with the storm centre some two hundred kilometres away to the south-west, the waves had time and distance to gather weight and momentum until, already restricted by Faxaflói bay, they burst tumultuously in through the south-west facing mouth of the cove.

On her new mooring, the *Fimbulvetr* lay directly in their path. She rose drunkenly to each, in total darkness, rain lashing horizontally across her bow. As the rising tide shortened the effective length of her anchor chain the waves broke with increasing frequency against her stem, pounding her foredeck with tumbled cliffs of black water. Each impact was like an avalanche, its weight slamming down on the ship, pinning her for long moments beneath the surface.

Werner had the watch. Heavy bursts of spray were now mixed with the rain that lashed the wheelhouse windows. The *Fimbulvetr* shuddered convulsively as the jarring in her bow intensified. Werner was on the point of calling Flynn when the big Irishman appeared on the bridge beside him.

'I'm thinking we should give her some chain. Then she'll ride more easy.'

The lamps Werner had rigged round the ship were already lit: they showed a relentless succession of black gaping voids and sudden surging mountains. Flynn switched on the searchlight, directed it forward. In its beam the bow leapt into view, starkly outlined against a background of foam-flecked water, then disappeared as the next wave rose and broke.

Werner was appalled. 'Will she hold?'

'The chain will.' Flynn tilted his head judiciously. 'And the anchor *should*.' He reached for the engine controls. 'But it's the worst possible onshore wind, and we're in the worst possible position in the cove to deal with it. I'm starting the machinery. See to the chain, will you? I'm afraid it's going to mean a bit of a wetting.'

Werner scrambled into his oilskins. Beneath his feet the plates vibrated as the two big Maybach diesels were prodded into life, raced for a moment, then steadied to a regular pulsebeat. He took a deep breath, opened the stern-facing door and went out, down the outside ladder, clinging tightly to the slippery handrail. Torrential rain beat at him and a wave rose up over the ship's side, soaking him to his knees. *A bit of a wetting*, Flynn had said . . .

He reached the deck, turned, clung to the side as water surged round his legs, past and away down the scuppers. Ahead of him the bow lifted awkwardly on a wave, banged against the next with a noise like a gunshot. He braced himself, clipped on his lifeline, then started the journey forward, ten metres or so, to the electric anchor windlass.

There in the extreme bow, every vertical movement of the ship was exaggerated. He rode a rollercoaster, seeming to dash onwards through the water, from the heights to the depths, so fast that it was almost impossible to believe that the *Fimbulvetr* was in fact stationary. The throb of the diesels, felt through the deck plates, heightened the illusion.

The bow lifted and banged, lifted and banged. The next time, as it battered into an oncoming wave, he was knocked off his feet. He crawled, bruised, on hands and knees to the telephone station at the rear of the windlass. Wrenching the handset from its clip he waited, braced, staring back up at the bridge. The searchlight blinded him. Another wave struck, parted by the flare of the bows and flying outwards, twin rising black cascades on the edge of the searchlight beam.

Colly was up on the bridge now. She answered the phone. 'Flynn says six fathoms. Give her six fathoms.'

The wind howled in his ears. 'What?'

'The chain. Let out six more fathoms.'

He rubbed his smarting eyes. The storm seemed to have drained his capacity for thought. 'How do I know when – ?'

'The chain is marked.' She spoke slowly and clearly, calm and patient. 'A yellow band every fathom. Yellow, Werner. A yellow band.'

He remembered. He replaced the receiver. He'd been told all about the fathom marks. Stupid. Such a hopeless amateur.

He groped for the windlass switch. Where the chain emerged from the winch drum it ran with darkly shining water. Yellow bands. Would he be able to see them? The searchlight beam cast abrupt shadows, dazzling light and shade. As he watched the ship snubbed sharply and the chain tightened, scattering its moisture in a fine, violent spray. He pressed the waterproof switch. There were two positions, for lowering or raising the anchor. He chose the wrong one. Links of chain began to disappear into the drum. Fool. Amateur. He pressed again, urgently stabbing at the rubber switch, tearing a fingernail. The chain reversed and paid out steadily. The first yellow mark came up, clearly visible. Gradually the ship's pitching eased.

He counted the yellow bands. Momentarily, the *Fimbulvetr*'s bow swung to port, adding a corkscrew roll to her motion. He felt Flynn give a touch on the engines, bringing her stern round, straightening her to meet the oncoming waves. At the sixth yellow marker he stopped the windlass and crouched down, sheltered by the raised bow plates. Gasping, he brushed the salt water from his eyes. His pulse steadied.

Curiously, he found himself in no hurry to return to the bridge. His present isolation was a comfort. The small steel triangle of his world, although battered and drenched and bitterly cold, constituted a reality, and a degree of suffering, he could deal with. He might, he rationalised, be needed at the windlass again: therefore, he was useful here. Also, if he held on tightly he was safe. His problems were small, their solutions equally small. He was safe, and he was useful. It was, for a man tortured with the large, insoluble problems of others, a desirable situation.

This whole enterprise rested upon the foundation of Colly's serene confidence that the superpower leaders, given the excuse, would be eager to end humanity's nightmare race to the slaughter-house, to start moving down the road to equality and environmental harmony. Now it seemed this wasn't the case. The operations they'd mounted against the *Fimbulvetr*, the sudden silence from Professor Graham, suggested that if anything *was* to be achieved they'd have to be pushed to the very edge, to the last minute of the last hour of the last day of the countdown, to the brink of Ragnarok . . .

And there was Colly herself. By telling himself she'd never been his, he could bear knowing that he had lost her. But to bear her turning to the Icelandic reporter was harder. The game she seemed to be playing with Einarsson, the secrets that clearly already existed between them, might be putting the whole enterprise at risk. He could not believe this was merely for the sake of an infatuation. But still, he didn't know what was going on; she had secrets *from him*. This was the hardest of all to bear. Once, he'd been able to talk to her . . .

The bow beneath him rose, hesitated, descended like an express lift. The next wave caught it at its lowest point, broke over it. The bow climbed again, slowly. Werner was engulfed, head down, drowning; breathed again as the torrent streamed away around him. Such a small conflict. Such a blessedly small solution. *Hold on. Survive.*

Minutes passed. The *Fimbulvetr*'s motion was changing. Suddenly she swung sideways, rolled steeply, swung back, engines racing as the screw lifted briefly out of the water. Werner slithered on her streaming deck plates; found new handholds. The next wave broke over the starboard bow. Abruptly the beam of the searchlight was removed. It turned widely, pierced grey hurtling rain gusts that seethed like insect swarms, found only black cliffs of water beyond, and darkness. It settled again, shining aft. Very faintly, above the noise of the storm, Werner heard a cry. He could see nothing save the bridge's outline, a dim halo behind it from the searchlight beam. The other lights, his lights, had gone out – drenched, fused somewhere, perhaps swept away. The cry was repeated. A hail; his name, perhaps.

The ship rolled again, even more steeply. If they'd called him on the windlass phone he'd never have heard the buzzer. Reluctantly, he released his hold and staggered back across the foredeck, lunging his way from grip to grip. Above him the derrick on the forward mast banged self-destructively. He ignored it. Heaving open the door in the base of the bridge, he unclipped his lifeline and stumbled in over the high coaming. As the ship pitched down under the weight of the next wave, gravity helped him to slam the door shut once more. The sudden quiet, there in the lobby of the main plotting room, right under the bridgedeck, left him dazed, still gasping. Water that had entered with him swilled over the floor before draining away. He leaned against the wall, pressed water out of his eyes with hard, cold fingers.

'Werner.' Colly was there, shaking him. 'Werner – the stern rope's not holding. Flynn thinks we've lost the kedge anchor.'

He stared at her, angry to be burdened with new difficulties. 'So?'

'So we're swinging about all over the place. Can't you feel it?'

'So what do we do?'

'Find out what's happened. Run a sea anchor. It's not much, but it'll help. On a long enough line it'll help. For God's sake, what's the matter with you? Come on – '

She strode away, tightening the belt on her foul weather gear. He followed her.

On the after deck life was easier than forrard. The wind and rain were as fierce, but the motion was marginally gentler, and less seawater reached them. They went to the stern, under the gantry, lit by the searchlight, where the stern rope passed out through the hawsehole. Werner reached up above his head. At least the lashings on the minisub were holding.

Colly had begun to haul in on the stern rope. He helped her. It came so easily that it had clearly lost its anchor. Almost at once its end appeared. The mooring on the main bow anchor was a heavy chain. Here a steel hawser was used. Very recently someone had sawed this hawser more than half through. Not surprisingly, the rest of it had parted in the first real blow.

Werner stared, dumbfounded, at this evidence of insanity on the part of the opposition. They knew – surely Professor Graham had told them – that the bomb would detonate if at any time the transponder in its casing failed to get a reassuring echo back from its twin mounted in the ship's sonar bulge. If the ship had left the cove – or if it had run aground.

Perhaps they hadn't reckoned on a storm this bad; perhaps it was just supposed to be more psychological fun and games. If so, they might be getting more than they bargained for.

The ship lurched, throwing them back against the gantry supports. Beneath her stern the water fell away and they hung, briefly motionless, above a dark, hissing void. Then the next wave came, rising and rising till it swept in around their legs. Werner looked sideways at his companion, her face deeply shadowed in the white beam of the searchlight. They couldn't run out to sea; could they hold on here with only one anchor?

'Are we in trouble?'

'I don't know.' She managed a weak sort of smile. 'Let's ask Flynn.'

Captain Flynn was fully occupied at the wheel. In front of him was his unstoppered pocket flask, wedged between the gyro compass repeater and the glass of the bridge screen. He reached for it when he could. Most of the time he spun the wheel spokes, nudged the ship with her engines, spun the wheel back again. He didn't need Colly to tell him they'd lost their kedge. Neither did the reason interest him. He had more important things on his mind.

He sent Colly and Werner back aft to rig the drogue, something to check the stern's swinging, on as great a length of hawser as they had left. Werner lingered in the doorway.

'Are we in trouble?'

'Trouble?' Flynn laughed, reached again for his flask. 'Not so long as the bow anchor holds. And I'd say from here it looks bravely dug in.'

Werner went away. Flynn kicked the door shut behind him. They were both scared, Colly and the German, but it was Werner who asked the question. And got for his pains a less-than-honest answer.

He peered forward. Even through the spinning fresne he could see only black raindrops hurtling against the glass. *Were they in trouble?* For Christ's sake – a small, single-screw ship, moored like this in the teeth of a gale, on bow anchor only, in pitch dark and three hours to daylight, unable to move, in restricted waters . . . of course they were in trouble. If they swung too far they could roll scuppers under and maybe never come back. And if the anchor dragged they'd end up with the beach up their arse. Which was why he hoped the drogue would keep the others busy in the stern for a good long time. For the sake of morale, he hadn't mentioned the point; but if there were breakers to be heard, they'd be in the right place to hear them. Or maybe they'd pick out a white line of surf in the searchlight beam.

The ship twisted almost beam-on, up the slope of a giant roller. She was designed to ride high in the water, and the wind was shifting. It seemed to be veering almost at right-angles to the waves, pounding rain and spray against the port wheelhouse windows. Flynn wished to hell he could see something. He gunned the engines, crept up on his anchor, straightened the ship and slackened off. He needed to feel the tug of the chain: it was his one fixed point in a shifting universe. Beyond the anchor, less than a mile away, was the cove mouth – narrow, invisible, guarded by barren cliffs. His original mooring lay to starboard; deep water and well sheltered, but now unattainable. The *Fimbulvetr* was forty-five metres long, broad in the beam and very seaworthy, her gross tonnage a rugged four hundred and thirty. But in this wind, and these waves, she was as frail as a toy on a pond. Once blown against the cliffs, or even on to the beach, she'd break up in minutes.

So it was up to him. Keep her afloat. Survive the necessary seven more days. Give those bastards every chance to come through with a deal – even though Flynn was now more certain than ever, in his own mind, that the button would have to be pressed, in the end. He glanced down at Werner's little addition to the bridge controls. To the left of everything else, where it couldn't be triggered by accident. Concealed behind a little flap, so that it wouldn't be set off by somebody dropping a cup of coffee on it. Just as they'd told, and shown, their two official visitors – it now seemed like months, not days, ago – the ship was wired in several places.

It would be so easy, Flynn thought, to flip open the cover and press it now. End this bloody business at once, instead of worrying about being blown on to a lee shore. He reached out with his left hand, flipped open the cover, stared at the ridiculously large, red button. It had been installed back when the whole business was still some sort of a joke, at least in the eyes of his companions. Such buttons, they said, had to be big, and red. It had never been a joke to Flynn. Death, he knew, was inevitable. Staying alive was of no consequence. Dying was what counted – dying for the right reasons. And now seemed like as good a time as any.

But no. Colly wanted to see her deadline through. And in spite of her reaction to the Zebedee incident, he still cared about what Colly wanted. He flipped the cover shut once more. Seven more days . . .

At least the seabed units would be safe, astern and to port, between him and the beach. Certainly a storm like this could reach down the six fathoms they lay in. But the easterly headland protected them, and the unit containing the bomb was heavy, with its buoyancy tanks flooded. It might silt over slightly, which didn't signify, but it wouldn't shift.

He took another snort, fumbled for a cigar, thoughtfully lit it. He listened to his ship, anticipated her swings, checking them. The passage of the waves rushing by might give the impression that she had steerage way, but on the end of a chain it was minimal. Her responses were leaden. Heaving her bow round, back into the waves, required an effort more of will than of rudder. Suddenly he chuckled. He'd seen worse in his tanker days, *real* tropical storms, down where the hurricanes bred. The only difference was, today he lacked a little in the way of sea room.

He blew out cigar smoke, sang raucously above the pounding of the storm: 'Ta-ra-ra-*boom* dee-ay, I'm looking for some *room* today . . .'

He laughed again. If the ship were wrecked because of the Russians and that bloody hawser, it'd hardly be *his* fault if the bomb were triggered and the world got the clean-up it deserved. In his opinion, a chilly year or two would work wonders. Focus people's minds. But if that was the way God wanted it, with the Russians, not Flynn, to blame, then Flynn had a duty to do his best to keep the ship off that shore. His Auntie Kathleen, he was sure, would have understood the logic of his present situation.

A wave came in solidly over the port bow. He winced, spun the wheel, corrected with a touch of throttle. He stubbed out the cigar, reached for his flask, emptied it. But even as he prepared for an intensification of his battle with the sea, the motion of the ship changed, easing slightly and becoming more manageable. The drogue. They'd streamed it successfully, and it was biting. It wasn't much, but every little bit helped. He'd known they'd do it. Colly was the kind who got things done.

Colly and Werner returned to the bridge. They stripped off their outer clothing and stood over the electric radiator, streaming. Flynn tipped up his flask, shook it as if discovering that it was empty, and glanced across at them. Neither offered to go below and refill it for him. He hunched his shoulders resentfully. They both knew he dared not leave the wheel, even for a minute.

An hour later, the big bow anchor dragged. It was Colly who caught it, from the sudden change of depth on the echo sounder.

'Flynn,' she said softly, 'we're in less than eight fathoms.'

'Christ Almighty.'

He opened the throttles, creeping up on the anchor. Resignedly, Werner started climbing back into his oilskins.

'I'll go and winch in some chain.'

The ship staggered. Flynn braced himself against the wheel. 'You'll do no such thing, laddie. You'll let some more out.'

He saw disbelief on Werner's face, then panic.

'We're being blown astern, Flynn. Aren't we being blown astern?'

'We are that. And we haven't much time. So if you'll just get down there and — '

'But the bottom's shelving already.' The deck tilted steeply. Werner clung to a rail. 'If we go back further we'll be on the beach.'

'Right again, lad. So get on with it.'

'Have you gone crazy?'

Colly spoke sharply. 'Flynn's the boss, Werner.'

'Not if he's crazy.' Werner's teeth were bared, his eyes wide with fear. 'Or drunk, more likely. Not if he's drunk.'

Suddenly Flynn's patience snapped. He saw red. Abandoning the wheel, he extended a massive fist, caught Werner up by his collar, drove him back against the rear bulkhead and held him there, shaking him, his feet inches clear of the deck.

'So it's drunk, is it?' He banged Werner's head on the wooden panel. 'So shall I take time out from keeping you alive to tell you what's the matter then, you ignorant little gob-shite? Think you know better, do you? You're scared, Adolf. You know nothing about bloody anything, and you're scared shitless.'

The ship had rolled wildly to starboard, broadside on to the waves. She hung there. Colly was at the wheel now, clinging to it, checking its random motion. The engines raced as the screw bit only thin air; she closed the throttles, put the engines into neutral. Overhead the forward derrick had broken free of the mast and was swinging, crashing destructively. Somehow Flynn was still on his feet, oblivious, Werner still pressed against the bulkhead. The door to the starboard wing blew open; there was more crashing from aft. Rain burst in, and seawater, half a wave, and the gale itself, which shrieked round inside the bridge, setting charts and papers spinning.

'So I'm a drunken man in charge of my ship, am I? My God, Adolf, you'll regret you ever said that!'

He shook Werner furiously, his voice huge above the roar of wind and wave. The ship rolled back to port, water and detritus surging about their feet. Colly screamed. The derrick had fallen, a bright white bar that scythed down close in front of the wheelhouse windows, lodging under the ship's rail, its own weight making a cradle of broken metal there.

The thunderous impact of its falling stopped Flynn dead. As suddenly as it had flared, his anger died.

'Ah, what the hell . . .' He released the terrified German. 'Drunk or sober, Adolf my boy, I'm the only captain you've got.' He stepped back. 'So would you mind getting on down to the bow there, and giving this poor old ship another ten fathoms or so of cable? If that's not too much trouble?'

Kicking aside a sludge of sodden paper, broken glasses, sway-backed pilot manuals, he returned to the wheel, which Colly relinquished gratefully.

He got the ship's head round, into the seas again. He glanced at the compass, then out at the waves, spoke to Colly. 'Shut that bloody door, will you? My Auntie Kathleen always said standing in a draught was bad for me.' She did so. 'And tell Werner I'm sorry.'

Broken cables from the derrick lashed the wheelhouse windows. He'd no alternative but to let them, and hope the glass held. Out of the corner of his eye he saw Werner, ready in his oilskins. The German paused, hand on the companionway rail.

'I should not have said that, Flynn. It is I who must apologise. You are the captain. I know nothing. I'm sorry.'

Flynn was embarrassed. There was no time for kissing and making up. 'Just get on that windlass, will you? We're slipping back every minute.'

He didn't know that. But they could well be, and it would get Werner moving. Explanations could wait. The German left the wheelhouse. Colly swung the searchlight round, and a moment later Werner appeared on the foredeck. Thank God for that. Flynn saw a wave come up, high as a house above the starboard bow, turned into it, and the ship climbed steadily, steadily, steadily . . .

Explanations were common sense, really. An anchor that was pulled flat along the bottom had a better chance of catching than one being pulled upwards. The longer the anchor chain, the shallower the angle at the bottom – not just because of its length, but because of the extra weight of chain, shaping its curve. A simple enough equation, the main limitation of which was the amount of space available. In this case, very little.

As soon as Werner was installed by the windlass Flynn returned the searchlight beam astern. Colly was back at the echo sounder, calling out depths.

'Seven fathoms . . . seven . . . seven . . . six and a half fathoms . . . six fathoms . . .'

The stern of the *Fimbulvetr* drew fourteen feet. The swell might easily be running at that much again. At six fathoms, and on a still-rising tide, the anchor held. He called Werner back up into the relative comfort of the wheelhouse. But it would soon be high water, and after that . . . Flynn couldn't guess. The drogue was having little effect; it might be up on the beach astern for all he knew. He was somewhere in a small, storm-swept cove, the land too close for useful radar contact, the night totally dark. His only clue was the steady line of oncoming waves, from which he could deduce the direction of the open sea.

His hands shook. His whole body. More than anything, now he needed a drink. But his flask was empty and he would not, he *would not*, ask either of his companions to go below and fill it for him.

After half an hour or so the nightmare worsened. The anchor started to drag again. There was still nothing to be seen astern, and the depth held at five and a half fathoms, but he dared not risk it. He powered the ship up the length of her chain, had Werner winch it in. She leapt, virtually uncontrollably, as the anchor swung clear of the seabed. He increased speed, steaming blindly forward. There might be a mile of open water ahead; no more. There *might* be cliffs at two hundred metres. At less than five knots the *Fimbulvetr* was unmanageable, yet when she was at that speed she seemed to be going like a train. Werner screamed down the phone that he could see nothing. Her bow paid off to port. She could broach to at any moment. Flynn corrected, steered into the waves, and beyond them into the impenetrable wall of night.

Somewhere to starboard lay the sheltered waters of his first deep mooring. Repeatedly he sought the right moment to turn into them, the right slackening of the waves, the right combination of speed and wind for this dangerous manoeuvre. And repeatedly his mental image of the space available failed him. He might be wrong. If he was further away from the shore than he thought, then he'd be running directly on to the rocks inside the headland. If he was closer than he thought, the chart showed sudden shallows. His situation was impossible. The experiences of a lifetime at sea were useless. He wasn't at sea. He was caught in a trap.

Three days ago he'd agreed, for persuasive but unseamanlike reasons, to an exposed, insecure mooring. He'd taken a chance, his luck hadn't held, and now he was stuck with the consequences. His best hope was to keep head on to the waves, and go nowhere. To stay – in gale force winds, in currents he didn't know, and a tide he could only guess at – on a spot not only invisible but also of no known location, adjusting the ship's speed as best he could to balance the incoming waves and the press of the wind, while Colly played the searchlight forlornly around the ship in the desperate hope of spotting the shore before it was too late. Flynn, on a voyage to nowhere, softly whistled the tunes of his childhood, while Colly divided her time between the searchlight and the echo sounder, and Werner remained, for reasons best known to himself, at his lonely outpost in the bow.

It was the dawn that saved them.

Werner's fear had reduced him to no more than two icy hands that gripped the wave-drenched bow-rail and forestay, and two eyes that stared achingly into the impenetrable night. Fear, not of death but of its manner, of the whirling nothingness of wind and water that waited, fierce and eager, to engulf them all. The *Fimbulvetr* plunged, gigantic seas broke over him. He fought them, fought his fear, gripped and stared. Darkness was everywhere.

Dawn came, miraculously, between one instant and the next. Beyond the searchlight's beam the darkness changed. From the black of night it became, suddenly, in the space of one heartbeat, the black of cliffs. Close. So close he felt he could reach out and touch them. He lifted his gaze. High, high above him they ended. Black clouds seethed by, black on black. He cowered beneath them, appalled. The ship rushed nearer, climbing the waves at what seemed breakneck speed, falling till the cliffs leaned over, blotted out the sky.

Werner screamed. He pointed wildly. Spray beat back in his face from seas that burst against the towering walls of red-veined lava. He turned his head. Behind him the bridge outline showed now, faintly white. Then the dazzling beam of the probing searchlight caught him full on, blotting everything else from view. He cried out again, a futile, pitiful sound in the tumult. He spread his arms despairingly.

The next wave caught him, tumbled him back along the foredeck. Vainly he clung to a hatch cover, then to the base of the mast. He finished up, scarcely breathing, wrapped around a ventilator. He waited, eyes tightly closed, for the end.

It never came.

Slowly, incredulously, he relaxed. The ship's motion had changed. She was turning: Flynn had seen the danger. He lifted his head, glimpsed through a blur of rain the cliffs on the beam now, and slipping astern. The violent pitching of the deck beneath him became a long, seductive, seemingly irresistible roll. The ship, broadside on to the seas, leaned further, more steeply. Caught on a slick black slope, she slid inexorably sideways down it, engines racing as the screw clawed for a grip on the wave's broken summit. .

To Werner the deck had become a wall. He clung to the ventilator, legs swinging. And still the ship leaned further.

The wind, across the waves, rescued them. A blast of hurricane intensity funnelled down between the two headlands at the mouth of the cove, struck the *Fimbulvetr*'s ample topsides, stopped her roll dead in the water, and turned her, laying her stern-on to the waves that tumbled angrily past. Briefly, like a surfboard, she rode them, angling away before the gale and across the mouth of the cove. Then, inevitably, her stern dropped and the next wave fell before she could lift again. It hit her with a crash that jolted every plate. She wallowed, her stern still heavy and slow to rise. Another similar wave now, and she could not have recovered. But the cove mouth was past, and she was entering the lee of the opposite headland. The motion eased. They were in sheltered waters at last.

Werner clambered to his feet. He looked up, saw Flynn, laughing at the wheelhouse window, wave him cheerfully back to the winch. They steamed slowly on through the growing light of dawn. Soon they dropped anchor. Werner rested, leaning on the winch housing, looking back. Already the storm was abating. It was as if, having done its utmost to sink them and failed, it had abruptly lost heart. Even the rain, after eighteen solid hours, slackened to a weary drizzle.

He returned to the bridge. Colly brought up hot soup and bread, coffee, a brandy bottle on the tray. Flynn drank from it, without ostentation, neither making a comment nor inviting one. They discussed the storm, and the final wave that had ripped the minisub from its gantry and carried it away, without trace.

Flynn raised the coastguard and they reported the sub's loss. If it hadn't been smashed to pieces, if the ebbing tide had taken it out to sea, it could constitute a hazard to navigation.

Werner drank his soup. The quarrel with Flynn was over, but his shame persisted. He had mastered his panic, his uncomprehending fear, only through Flynn's strength. He was not only an incompetent amateur, but a coward as well. Even Colly had moved away from him, emotionally. What use was he to the team now? What had happened to all their hopes and ambitions? How could an incompetent, lonely coward justify his continued existence?

In New York it was still night, hot and airless. For Robert time moved in fits and starts. Now, while he slept, it shifted along. A new day had come, made it as far as four a.m. He rejoined it with great sadness, roused by an insistent twisting of the loose, mottled skin on the back of his right hand. He'd been deeply absent. Now, with equal intensity, he'd returned.

He saw his new day. He saw his room. He didn't need to open his eyes – it was there, tingling in the air around him. It crackled with the terrible electricity of human purpose. Reckless. Merciless. Nothing resisted. Chairs, dresser, bed, lamp, bamboo table from next door, curtains, walls, floor, ceiling – everything sang with a high thin joy. Robert heard the song. Everything was ready.

Earlier, his attention on more compelling matters, Robert had wet his bed. He needed, regrettably, to empty his bladder again. Presumably he soon would. He sweated also, naked, beneath the single, fly-spotted ceiling lamp, in the airless New York night. The salt stung his many small cigar burns. His headache, never far away, had returned. And he'd woken to a new discomfort: thirst.

'Robbie? Hey, you back with us? We were talking, Robbie, about your telephone interface. Remember?'

Had he? No. Duke and Clancy had talked about the interface. He hadn't. He was sure. But then why – he opened his eyes, said wonderingly, 'You let me sleep.'

'Hell, you're an old guy, Robbie.' This was Clancy. 'You needed it.'

Nobody had ever called him Robbie before, but he answered to it. 'And now I need water.'

'Ah.' Clancy's headphones were pushing his neat, preppy hair up into a surprised halo. 'Duke? What d'you think, Duke? Robbie here says he wants a drink.'

'Tell him to go to hell.' Duke's chair was tilted, his head propped against the wall, a monogrammed handkerchief over his face, hands clasped across his stomach. His feet were on the dresser. 'Tell Robbie to go to hell.'

Clancy patted Robert's arm. 'You hear that? Duke's the hard man, Robbie, I'm the nice guy. That's the way it always works in the movies. Me, you're supposed to like; him, you obey. It's no secret, especially to a guy like you, with a fistful of degrees. So, it's my turn now, Robbie. I get to tell you how much I genuinely sympathise with your reasoning. Guy down as low as you are now, he reckons there can't be no harm in *asking* for a drink. What's he got to lose, for Christ's sake?'

Robert turned his head away.

'What he's got to lose is nothing. That's what he's got to lose. Nothing. And a guy with nothing to lose is rich. Can afford to take chances. Who knows? Duke might've said yes, for Christ's sake. Who knows?'

Robert waited. The fun with his simple request was over. The man in the white coat had gone away. He waited for questions. For pain. None came. He turned his head back, swallowed dryly.

'Why did you wake me?'

'You'd slept enough. Also, you snore. It was driving Duke crazy.'

'So what happens now?'

'I told you; I'm the soft one. When it's my turn nothing happens. Nothing bad.' He started to place the headphones over his ears, stopped as if struck by a sudden thought. 'They say the weather's real bad, though, up in Iceland.'

Robert eased his wrists in their straps. 'We expected storms.'

'Sure . . . sure Robbie, you expected storms. Only sensible, up in those parts. It's no big deal. I just thought I'd tell you; thought you'd like to know.'

Robert stared at the ceiling. In a few hours his thirst would become serious. Then they'd start hurting him again. He knew what they were doing. Until then he'd be left to worry. About his thirst. About the storm. About being hurt. About being left to worry.

And about Kassim. The one thing they didn't know about, but the one that worried him most. If Kassim surfaced, anything might happen . . . and if there really was a storm, and it wasn't some fiction of Clancy's to worry him, then Flynn might have to move the ship . . . and the Russians might get a chance . . .

And then, worse than his worrying, his legs cramped up. First the left and then both. He juddered on the bed, ankle straps creaking. Calf muscles, and thigh, like iron rods, burnt and tore. He gasped, writhed, sounds strangled in his throat; he beat his head upon the mattress, pissed hotly, helplessly across one thigh.

The spasm passed. Clancy wiped Robert's forehead with a threadbare hotel towel.

'Don't do that, Robbie. Christ, don't ever do that.'

Duke seemed not to have moved.

'Don't you realise, Robbie? Don't you realise just how long we've got? Duke and me, we've got forever. This is for real, man – you're just gonna have to tell us. That interface. You can, you know. You can tell us. We've got forever, you see. You're just going to have to tell us.'

Could he? His headache kept time with his straining heartbeats. Could he tell them that? That and nothing else? *That* wouldn't matter, on its own. If he told them just that, and not the other thing, in return for a drink, just water, just *half* a glass of water?

Pétur was on his way to Helgavik. He liked to drive, and he did it well. That morning the cloud base in Reykjavik was virtually at ground level, but already he'd made it through the outskirts of the city and was safely on the coast road to Borgarnes. His present car was a black Toyota hatchback, sexy-looking if no great performer, but he liked to think he could handle anything with a wheel at each corner – car or truck, two-wheel drive or four, automatic or manual. The second-best thing about his occasional overseas trips for the company was the chance to drive a variety of interesting cars, and on good, fast roads. The first-best things were the friendly co-drivers.

He frowned, leaned forward, peered past the busy wipers. Here, now, there was more at stake. On waking, half an hour before, a quick phone call to Flugstödin had confirmed what the view from his now only single-glazed window suggested – that the previous night's weather forecast had been optimistic. Although the depression was indeed on its way out, the Flugstödin girl told him, winds remained high and visibility poor, and there was little hope of getting airborne before noon at the earliest. Even then, there was no

certainty that the conditions would allow a landing at the cove. And
Pétur couldn't wait. The exposed discs were burning a hole in his
pocket. He called the coastguard, asked them to get a message to
Dr Colly Graham on the *Fimbulvetr*, warning her to expect him.

Business *and* pleasure . . . and why not? Already there'd been
that electricity between them. And she wasn't an innocent; she
knew where he stood. His first responsibility was to get to the truth
of what she was involved with. After that, anything might happen.
There were too many unknown factors. He'd promised her nothing.
Only one thing was certain – he was on to one hell of a story.

And if he'd had any doubts about that, his little talk with Björn
yesterday evening, after his release from the police station, would
have dealt with them. He *was* on to one hell of a story.

He'd gone straight up from Finnur to the news editor's office,
exposed discs in his pocket. At first things went as might have been
expected. Björn had been kept waiting, and he wasn't pleased.

'Come in, Pétur, sit down.' A pause while Pétur sat. 'I gather
you've been at police headquarters.'

'That's right. I – '

'And you've come straight from there?'

'Right again. I'm sorry if – '

'Good. Glad to hear it.' Björn reached for a cigarette. 'I can think
of very few things that should be allowed to come between a
reporter and his editor.' He struck a match, broke it, struck another.
'So tell me about your burglar.'

Pétur told him. He offered the minimum, the story he'd given the
police. Björn eyed him, unimpressed, through a sour haze of smoke.

'Is that all?'

'More than enough, I thought.'

Björn conceded the point. 'Sounds nasty.'

'It *was* nasty.'

'How much can we use?'

Pétur shrugged. 'As much as you like. As much as it's worth.
Hedged around with the usual weasel words, of course – the *alleged*
crime, the *reported* victim . . .'

'You'd better do it then, hadn't you? And it's worth two minutes.'
He coughed extensively. 'I suppose you realise it makes no sense?'

Pétur's defences bristled. 'What d'you mean?'

'No need to lose your rag. Just take the hint, that's all.'

'The hint?'

'My dear Pétur, don't let's be naive. I've not seen your place, but since when has this company paid anybody enough for them to have things worth stealing? Petty burglary maybe. But not this sinister midnight visitor.'

'Two a.m.'

'Two bloody a.m., then. Even worse. Breaking and entering at two in the morning, armed and ready to shoot, and all for an old Pentax and some clapped-out hi-fi? I don't believe a word of it, and neither do you.'

'The police do.'

'The police know what's good for them.' He flipped ash in the general direction of the bin. 'I hope you do, too.'

'Meaning?'

'Meaning there are times when investigative journalism exacts too high a price.'

Pétur stared at him. 'You're not saying this, Björn. I don't believe it.'

'Meaning I'm sending you over to Braeddalshöfn first thing in the morning.'

'*Where?*'

'You heard. Word is, the Ashkenazeys are looking at a new summer home there.'

'You're kidding.'

'Where's the joke? Vladi's our favourite resident celebrity. He's news. Anything he does is news. Anything his wife does is news.'

'But Braeddalshöfn's way out beyond Vatnajökull. Right at the opposite end of the island.'

'Opposite?' Björn raised an eyebrow. 'Opposite to what?'

'You know damn well what. Opposite to Helgavik and the British research ship.' He pointed an accusing finger. 'You've been got at, Björn. You're trying to – '

'Of course I've been bloody got at.' Suddenly the older man had lost his temper. 'I've been got at, and now I'm getting at you. The Helgavik story's dead. D'you hear? *Dead.* It was never very much – a pretty face, some vague international connection – and now it's nothing at all. Dead. OK? What our viewers want,

Pétur, is *World-famous Pianist Plans Harbourside Retreat.*
That's what they want, and that's what you're going to give
them.'

'No.'

'Yes.'

Pétur dug in his pocket, flung the exposed radiation discs on
Björn's desk. 'Remember what we said about uranium?'

'You're not paying attention.' Björn swept the discs on to the
floor. 'Perhaps you don't care about your job. Well, Pétur, I sure as
hell care about mine. And it may not be fashionable, but I care
about national security too. So you're going to Braeddalshöfn, first
thing in the morning, and – '

'National security? Who's been feeding you that old crap?'
Incredulous, Pétur thumped the arm of his chair. 'The Minister?
Surely not the Minister? Since when did you listen to . . . ?' He
tailed off, momentarily speechless.

Björn sat back from his desk. Calmly, he stubbed out his cigarette
and reached for another. His eyes never left Pétur's. He lit the
cigarette, fanned away the smoke that rose between them. He said
nothing.

'So it *was* the Minister? You mean it's official?' Pétur couldn't
believe it. 'For God's sake, since when did we submit to official
censorship?'

Björn gave not the smallest sign. A shutter had come down
behind his eyes. Clearly he had said too much; was already
regretting it. But Pétur's mind was already working on the
connection with his visitor. '*The Americans*. CIA? But how? What
kind of pressure can they put on us? This isn't Britain, for Christ's
sake. What kind of lever have they – '

Björn had heard enough. He sat forward abruptly. 'Mrs Vladi is
already in Braeddalshöfn, Pétur. She's staying at the Hotel Bláfell. I
suggest you put a call through tonight, and – '

'I'm not going, Björn.'

'Of course you are.'

'No. You'll have to fire me.'

'Don't be melodramatic.'

'You're the one who said my job was on the line.'

'We're neither of us fools, man.' Björn blew out a thin stream of smoke. 'If I sacked you, the union would be down on me. There'd be tribunals, explanations.'

'So put me on suspension.'

'On what grounds? Don't make me laugh. Since when did a manager manage? In this great new socialist society of ours?' He checked, drew a deep breath. For a long moment he stared at the glowing tip of his cigarette. Then he relaxed. 'OK. You know it, and I know it. I can't *tell* you a bloody thing. All I can do is *ask* you, Pétur; ask you to drop the Helgavik business. If you come back with a story, and make enough fuss, I probably can't even keep you off the air. I can only ask – appeal to you, if you like.'

Pétur frowned. 'National security?'

'If you like.'

'But which nation?' There was no response. 'I don't like.' He hesitated, came to a decision. 'But I'll bear it in mind. When I get back from Helgavik, I'll bear it in mind. And I'll bring whatever I've got straight to you. OK?'

'I'd rather you didn't, but I suppose you'd better. And our resident celebrities?'

'Come on, Björn. You don't need me for that.'

Björn shrugged, actually laughed. A fit of coughing caught him. Eventually: 'All right. Officially, take a day off to get over that business with the burglar. Unofficially' – he opened a desk drawer, brought out a small, flat packet – 'if you happen to be going out to the ship, you might take this with you. Save a lot of bother. It's for Doctor Graham.'

Pétur took the packet. It was the size and weight of an audio cassette. 'Who's it from?'

'Shall we say, an American friend of mine. Someone interested in your wellbeing.'

'You bastard.' Grudgingly, Pétur smiled. 'He must have been pretty damn sure I'd be going.'

Björn nodded. 'He was. But he'd still like it better if I'd managed to stop you.'

'You did your best.' Pétur rose. 'I'll leave you a signed affidavit, if you like.'

'The door's over there.' Björn picked up a folder. 'See you close it behind you.'

He opened the folder, began to read. Pétur stooped, gathering up the scattered discs. Björn cleared his throat, but didn't look up.

'I hope you'll be careful,' he murmured. 'My friend isn't going to be pleased.'

Pétur straightened his back. 'I'd have thought he'd be delighted. Aren't I delivering his package for him?'

'Ah.' Björn turned a page. 'I hadn't thought of that.'

Pétur left the room. Important things were not being said. But at least he had clearance, of a sort, for his trip. He paused on the stairs, tossing the discs thoughtfully in one hand. Should he fill Finnur in about tomorrow? He decided not to. The fewer people involved in the Helgavik trip the better. He went straight on down to his car. The missing hours of sleep were beginning to catch up with him.

He slept well. The wind and rain wuthered around the building, but they didn't rouse him. And he'd bolted his outside door carefully, top and bottom. Not that he feared a visit from colleagues of the dead Janssen – not yet. The man had more or less admitted to being CIA, and now Pétur seemed to be acting as a messenger boy for the CIA. Presumably, he was safe from them at least until their packet was delivered. But if he was on the side of the CIA, that automatically meant he would have other enemies. The door wasn't sufficient to stop a determined intruder, but smashing a way in would involve a lot of noise, and give him plenty of warning.

What he'd do with such a warning he didn't know. He didn't have a gun, and didn't know how to use one if he had. Telephoning the police wouldn't be much help at that late stage; hiding in the wardrobe would make even less sense. But he slept well, all the same.

His radio alarm had woken him at seven. Now, shortly before eight, in a joyless mixture of mist and driving rain, he was on the road to Borgarnes, the packet for Colly on the passenger seat beside him. He'd thought about that packet a lot. If it came from the CIA, as seemed undeniable, then presumably Colly and the Americans were cooking something up between them. It gave a new twist to the story. Maybe her team on the *Fimbulvetr* was running tests on some experimental system – weapons, maybe communications. Maybe submarine detectors? If so, Pétur had stumbled into something way out of his depth; the talk of national security might be genuine, and he was lucky to be alive. He'd be better off taking Björn's advice to drop the story; but now, he needed to know, for himself as much as for the story. That was why he was a newsman. Newsmen did need to know things. He stabbed the brake, changed down for a murky corner, grinned. He enjoyed driving in difficult conditions; it gave him a chance to show off, even if only to himself.

Rain gusted across the road. He concentrated on his driving. It was over two hundred kilometres to Helgavik. In weather like this a break in Borgarnes would be sensible, so he'd need to move it along if he wanted to arrive in time for lunch. He settled into the state he called his automatic pilot, almost meditative, operating the car with neat economy, enjoying the feel of it, even enjoying the extra effort required to keep moving fast in the wet, blustery conditions. At least they scared most of the other traffic off the road. Since he'd left the city behind, there'd hardly been another car in sight. He straddled the line, belting straight down the middle.

The junction with route 36 arrived, the minor road leading off to the right, eastwards towards Thingvellir and the mountains and glaciers of the interior. As he followed the leftward curve of Highway 1, the main ring road round the island, the package for Colly Graham slid sideways on the seat. Unhurriedly, in one smooth motion, he found a lower gear, steadied the package, and changed up again as he accelerated into the climbing turn between the black bulk of Esja to his right, and the storm-tossed waters of Kollafjödur down to his left. The offshore islands were scarcely visible in the scudding rain. Pétur shivered, despite the efficient heater, and reached forward to punch a cassette into the player, smiling as the mellow nothings of the Beach Boys poured from the speakers mounted on the rear shelf. Iceland might lack the California sunshine, but at least he could have their sunshine music. He sang along with them, glanced at his watch. He was making good time. Coffee in Borgarnes, after the mountains, and then the long, straighter run across the marshes.

The road here was basically a long dog-leg round the Havalfjördur, which cut deeply into the western coastline of Iceland. Heading eastwards, along the southern side of the fjord, the road was squeezed between mountains and sea. The night's rain had brought torrents of water down off the hills to his right, often crossing the road surface before they formed waterfalls down into the sea below; it took all Pétur's skill to keep his speed up. With cloud pressing down from the mountains, it was dark enough to call for headlights; the occasional vehicle heading in the opposite direction announced itself several corners away as the beams flashed briefly like those of a lighthouse, and once or twice he caught a similar flash of light in his mirror from someone not too far behind – someone who must know the road nearly as well as himself, keeping about the same distance behind him all the time. As he noticed the lights for the third or fourth time, and speculated idly on the business that brought someone else out from Reykjavik to drive at his furious pace in this foul weather, Pétur smiled again at the memory of the old Reykjavik joke. It couldn't be a tourist behind him: tourists bought the guidebook, and the guidebook took them anticlockwise round the island on the coastal ring road, always heading out south and east from the capital, describing the scenery as it went. What tourist, natives asked, was bright enough to read a guidebook backwards?

Whatever the truth of that, Pétur passed only one car before rounding the head of Whale Fjord and running back west down the other side, through the small township of Midsandur and across the low-lying neck of the peninsula that led out to the industrial centre of Akranes. His follower was still in position. Suddenly it occurred to him to worry. But what could he do about it?

Swinging right again, he was soon climbing the side of Harnarfjall, with precipitous slopes down to an angry sea again on his left, before descending to the new bridge that would take him across the Borgafjördur and into Borgarnes. As he eased back on the accelerator he caught another flash of light in his mirror. But he was on the bridge now, and approaching the town. If something had been planned they were surely too late . . . just along here somewhere was the place he'd planned to stop. They did marvellous pastries. He glanced at the instrument panel. Just on a hundred and twenty kilometres, in comfortably under two hours. Not bad, on these roads and in this weather.

A hundred and twenty kilometres – it didn't sound much, though. He remembered covering nearly twice that distance in the same time, a couple of years back, travelling up from New York to Boston. But that had been in September sunshine on the Connecticut Turnpike, and in that agency girl's white Camaro – Paula, Laura, some such name – with her radar detector to warn them of speed traps. But here, he was doing well to maintain half that speed.

It was while he was crawling along, pulled in close to the side of the road and peering through his rain-blurred windscreen for the restaurant sign, that the glare of following headlights suddenly blossomed hugely in his mirror. He hardly had time for fear before the little Toyota was rocking in the slipstream of the other vehicle, a massive four-wheel-drive Chrysler, one of those wagons that had *Jeep* somewhere in its name but bore as much resemblance to a World War Two jeep as a Boeing 747 bore to a troop-carrying Dakota. Narrowly missing him, it hurtled on, obviously in one hell of a hurry, two men in the front, as far as he could see, scarcely noticing him. His own fault, he conceded as he watched the red tail lights disappear into the blowing rain. Shouldn't have been kerb-crawling in this sort of weather.

Presumably the Chrysler was the vehicle that had been behind him all the way from Reykjavik. With that kind of power and grip, they'd have had no difficulty keeping up. Nothing ominous, thank God. Just some macho pair of lads, probably amusing themselves by trying to catch up with his lights in front of them. He dismissed them from his mind as he spotted the sign he was looking for, and turned in to park. Sugar, starch, cholesterol . . . plus any number of harmful chemical additives. Wonderful. He was looking forward to his coffee break.

The Chrysler was waiting for him on the flat plain beyond the Langa river. Contentedly well fed, with the stereo blasting out more sunshine music – Bach this time, bright and joyful – he'd been remembering other visits to the river. Leaving the car by the roadside, walking with Greta the short distance to the waterfall with its salmon ladder. That was before Greta had gone to work for that architect in Denmark . . . He sighed. The salmon would be leaping now, it was the right time of year. But there would be no tourists, or lovers, to watch them leap today.

Then he saw the Chrysler, parked half on the verge, bonnet raised, its passenger anxiously waving him down. Instantly his mind focused sharply, narrowing to the one moment and the one decision. The set-up was too pat: he'd no doubt they were waiting for him and him alone. The place was well-chosen – fifty kilometres or more of uninhabited wilderness, on a road that few would travel in weather like this.

Even as he tried to tell himself that he was being paranoid, acting irrationally after Janssen's murderous visit, his reflexes were taking over. He flipped off the stereo. Instead of stopping to offer assistance to the forlorn figure by the roadside, instead of slowing, even, he changed down a gear and accelerated hard, swerving to avoid the man, lurching off the tarmac surface. His offside wheel spun helplessly, throwing up mud and grass, then momentum carried him round and clear, back on to the highway. Into top gear again, foot flat on the floor. If they *were* just a couple of innocent lads, stuck with a wet electrical system, then they would just have to –

The thought died as he saw in the mirror the man leap round the front of the Chrysler, frantically knocking the bonnet down as he passed. Already the vehicle was moving, headlights blazing, as the man out on the road struggled to climb in and close the door. It lurched wildly, skidded almost broadside-on, then settled in pursuit. Whoever they were, there was clearly nothing wrong with their machinery, and they seemed desperately keen to meet him. Björn's American friends? It seemed unlikely. Others, then. The Russians? The British? It didn't matter a fuck – they weren't trying to tell him he'd won the National Lottery, that much was certain.

They were a kilometre or so behind now, but gaining fast. They had weight, and the four-wheel power to keep it moving. When they caught him, they could simply bulldoze him off the road. He peered ahead. The rain was thinning. But to the limit of his visibility Highway 1 was hardly more than a narrow causeway through the boggy flatland, the underlying rock thrusting up here and there through a thin layer of swampy, badly-drained soil, forming outcrops on either side, almost at right-angles to the road. The landscape was corrugated, its ridges and troughs running from south-west to north-east, reflecting in miniature the geology of the whole island, split and stretched in the same way, by the same titanic forces that had created the Atlantic Ocean out of a crack between North America and Europe. Pétur had no interest in the geological background; but his mind searched desperately for some way to turn the peculiar geography to his advantage.

Off the road, though, his sexy hatchback would stand even less chance against the Chrysler than in a straight run along tarmac. He'd bog down in a few metres, while their four-wheel drive would cruise them through, laughing. His best hope was to get back into Borgarnes. No great distance – if he could only somehow reverse direction on this narrow road, and get past his pursuers. They were much closer, already. Two, maybe three, hundred metres. He looked to the side. If he could get off the road, on to a hard outcrop of rock, clip behind them and back on the highway, then he might, he just *might*, be able to stay ahead of them into town. And they'd already shown they didn't care to try anything much there.

The thought was hardly formed before he came to another long ridge of rock, swelling up through the bog on his right, only a few metres from the shaly verge. No time for hesitation. Down through the gears again, squelching off the road and gunning the engine desperately to keep the Toyota moving through the intervening mud and up on to the bare, slippery rock. Behind him, the Chrysler overshot, but came to a skidding halt and was reversing rapidly up the road before he could gain enough control even to think about turning round himself. Reversing, then edging towards him; they obviously thought they had him trapped. No rush, no panic; the occupants of the Chrysler seemed convinced that they had only to follow in their cross-country vehicle, and pick him out of the wreckage at their leisure.

Damn. He should have stayed on the road. Too late now. At least they were further behind, and not actually gaining at present. Pétur almost had time to plan logically – except that logic wasn't going to help him. His basalt island was small and narrow, and already he was near its end. Logic told him to stop. Desperation told him that ahead and to the right lay another outcrop – perhaps he could make it across to that one and begin to double back down the corrugations to the road.

There was rain-pocked water lying on the swampy surface of the intervening indentation, and more rocks concealed in the mud. One of them caught the plunging Toyota a savage blow, crumpling the bodywork and tearing at the nearside door as the car surged past, Pétur using all the momentum of his plunge off the last rocky island to carry him across to the next. He began to think this wasn't going to be too difficult – take a good run across the rock and she'll almost float the swampy bits. Then he saw the lights of the Chrysler turn to his right, still slightly behind him, and his optimism died.

They didn't have to follow him. All they had to do was get between him and the road. Now, if he turned towards the road they would cut across parallel to it and intercept him. If he headed away again, north-east, they would tuck in behind, wait till he did terminal damage to the car. And if he carried on parallel to the road himself, braving the corrugations, he'd simply smash the Toyota up that much sooner.

He tried turning the lights off, to make himself less visible, but quickly turned them on again. Even near noon, although the rain had eased, in this overcast he'd never see the details of the terrain without them.

Left again at the next outcrop. He'd no alternative, racing to put distance between himself and the Chrysler while it was still ploughing through the mud below the ridges, some few score metres back. He could choose a path that allowed him to stretch his lead, but only at the cost of being driven deeper off the road, away into the scrubby, sodden country. *It's more like bloody sailing than driving,* he thought, *tacking to and fro, with an occasional sprint downwind.* Furious with himself for getting into this situation, for not being careful, for not using his head, for not taking Björn's warning seriously enough; furious with Björn himself, with the CIA, with the weather, with whoever was chasing him now; and doubly furious with Colly and her friends for making the whole bloody mess come to the boil, Pétur tried desperately to make some sort of a plan. His thought processes were not helped by the need to control the erratic passage of his vehicle across the rocks. Out of the mud just now, more in a controlled slide than anything else, avoiding the worst of the cracks and ridges, until the end of the corrugation approached and he had to gather speed for the next plunge down and across the swamp below.

This outcrop had been bigger than the last, he suddenly realised, and fell away further at the end. He'd only make it across if he built up a good head of speed. And, once down, he'd be *out of sight of the Chrysler* for several seconds, until it came over the rise behind him.

No time to look for flaws in his new plan. Spinning the wheel, he changed the direction of the Toyota's course, heading out across the swamp – not towards the nearest high ground on the previous line he'd been taking, but to the left, diagonally across the swampy indentation, back to the tip of the ridge where he'd started this mad race.

If he made it, he'd be within a few hundred metres of the road. And – much more important – he'd be between the Chrysler and it.

Recklessly he cut the lights again, slamming down on the scarcely visible surface of the swamp and surging forward in a sheet of muddy spray that blackened the windscreen, the wiper blades only slowly making an impression as his speed fell and the wave subsided. To his delight, when the lights of the Chrysler showed behind him they were away to his right, and separating further, pointing out at right angles to the corrugations. He'd done it. The driver had lost him. All that remained now was to coax the Toyota along, just a couple of hundred metres or so, and he'd be back on the road, facing in the right direction, towards the town.

Logic cut in, telling him, *big deal*. He'd still never make it. Already, the lights behind were swinging round, back on his track. He'd gained time, but not enough, even if he made it back to the highway. The Chrysler was still far faster under present road conditions – probably under any conditions. He chose, once again, to ignore logic.

He'd been spotted, but he'd gained precious distance. And the Chrysler no longer seemed to be gaining. He puzzled over that, until a sudden impact on the Toyota's bonnet and the shattering of the nearside mirror provided the answer. The bastards were shooting at him, and had slowed to take better aim. Well, good luck to them. Pétur's fury had reached a state of glacial calm. Even as he coaxed and struggled with the controls of the car to force it onwards, he could look down, as if from above, on so much frantic and misguided activity. The pursuers were wrong. Stupid. In these conditions they had little chance of hitting the car even, let alone disabling it or him. The mirror had been a fluke. And every time they slowed to take aim, it gave him just that much more leeway.

Leeway. Christ, he was going to need it. The Toyota had lost momentum, and he fought through several permutations of power and gearing until he managed to start it inching forward. The glint of surface water to the left showed how close he'd been to disaster the first time he'd launched his car incautiously out across the swamp. If he'd chanced to hit the sort of semi-liquid region that lay beside him at present, at the low speed he was now reduced to he'd never have made it.

He had an idea.

As the mud thinned and the wheels began to grip, he kept in low gear, travelling more slowly than he need. His pursuers gained ground, still blasting off the occasional erratic shot. Their vehicle was almost up on the ridge itself, perhaps a hundred metres behind him, when Pétur tried his stunt.

A sudden burst of acceleration, then clutch in, handbrake on, wheel hard over. The lightly-laden car spun in a precarious hand-brake turn on the slippery surface of the rock. Choosing his moment perfectly, he released the handbrake, engaged the clutch and flattened the throttle to the floor again. After a brief burst of frantic wheelspin, the Toyota was heading straight back towards the Chrysler, its headlights blazing.

A split second before the collision, Pétur swung right again and out across the semi-liquid surface, picking the wettest region he could see, relying on his speed and the floating sensation he had felt before. Wheels churned. Again the wipers laboured beneath their weight of mud. The bow wave was like that of a small speedboat, subsiding as the car slowed. Then, just as all impetus seemed lost, it touched bottom, scrabbled for grip then surged up on to the rocky basalt of the next corrugation. Pétur stopped. Slumped over the wheel, he fought for breath as if he'd been running.

His adrenalin high was exhausted, and with it the calm omniscience of his logical mind. He was reduced once more to basic fears. He was on the run. If his trick hadn't worked, then he'd lost what little lead he'd ever had, and the run was over.

He lifted his head. As he'd hoped, the Chrysler hadn't imitated his headlong rush, what must have seemed his desperate bid for freedom. The driver took his time. He could see the Toyota stationary only a short distance away: perhaps he thought Pétur wounded. Whatever, he moved forward cautiously, not taking any chances. Where the Toyota could go, obviously the Chrysler could travel with ease.

Caution was the Chrysler driver's undoing. Four-wheel drive is invaluable over rough ground, even in thick mud; but in semi-liquid mud it's useless. As Pétur watched, the much heavier, slower-moving vehicle settled gently into the bog, up to its axles at first, then deeper as the wheels continued to spin. Christ, he thought, I really *was* floating. If I'd had enough sense to take it at a reasonable speed the first time, this little tin box would've sunk without trace.

The passenger door of the Chrysler opened, and the man who'd been by the roadside jumped out, sinking knee deep immediately. Clinging to the door for support, he raised a massive, blackly-gleaming handgun. Steadying himself, he rested the gun in the crook of his jacket's rain-soaked elbow. Pétur ducked instinctively, raced the engine, took off down the rocky outcrop, back towards the highway, as a bullet entered the Toyota through the rear window and exited neatly through the roof.

He drove on. The rain still fell, though thinly now. A scraping sound told him he'd have to stop soon and bend some twisted bit of metal away from his nearside front wheel. He grinned. The Chrysler was there to stay. The men in it had a long walk ahead of them. He wondered who they were. Maybe Colly'd be able to tell him. If the Toyota lasted that long, he'd be on the road above Helgavik in roughly an hour.

Duke was in charge again. The man in the doctor's white coat was also present. Electrical 'interrogation equipment' had been delivered, but he'd forbidden its use. Robert's age, and the present state of his health, gave the man serious cause for concern. The equipment, displacing the tape recorder on the bamboo table, rested meekly, its cables coiled, its crocodile clips waiting for younger, more resilient bodies.

Robert was grateful. Lucid now, and all his sad little worries past – the ship, the storm, Kassim, the Russians on the beach – his sharpest fear was of his own physical strength. He was ready to die, would welcome death as the alternative to his present wretched condition – and as the alternative to providing information to the opposition. But he felt himself immortal. His heartbeat, pounding in his ears, never faltered. His senses were acute, razor-edges of whimpering anticipation and response. His thirst was trivial, his swollen tongue no more than an inconvenient artifact. Every organ in his body seemed part of a wilfully indestructible machine. So the man in the white coat was wrong. The cables, the clips, could do their worst. Only Robert's spirit was in danger. The rest of him would never break.

Duke leaned closer. Robert writhed within his straps. The indomitable power of his own body appalled him. And all the while the walls of his silence trembled. He didn't look to see what lay inside them. He didn't dare. Peace for himself. Comfort for his enemies. He screamed, and gritted his teeth, and would not tell.

They were asking about the telephone interface. But he knew what they really wanted. They were asking about the seed, the seed that swelled, pressing against the boundaries of the possible. The boundaries he had set: the boundaries only he *could* set. This was possible; that was not. They were asking for the impossible. But the impossible could change. Could *be* changed so easily. Between one moment and the next.

A grubby hotel room, grey daylight through yellow curtains, stinking of stale cigar smoke, stale burnt flesh and hair, sweat, urine, blood, spilled beer, garlic and pizza. Robert wondered if it stank of pain also, and of his screaming. Duke no longer smoked. He had a knife, and he peeled back strips of skin where Robert could stare, and see the bright flesh beneath.

They were asking about the telephone interface. Time had moved along. City noises, the working day. Still they asked about the interface. He couldn't tell them. It wasn't yet possible.

In Rome that Tuesday morning David Lawrence had a rendezvous with Frau Schneider at nine on the steps outside the International Press Building. He didn't keep it. Neither, unsurprisingly, if for a different reason, did she.

His previous afternoon's enigmatic *question of teacakes* had referred to Majed Sayeed's religion. Examining Frau Schneider's mysteriously-acquired list of sightings, David had remembered the dead man mentioning that teacakes went with the Anglican Church, in which he'd been raised. He could have been lying, of course – but he'd only been showing off about his Oxford education at the time, so there seemed little point. In which case, if he had indeed been raised an Anglican, then his visit, halfway down Frau Schneider's list, to a suburban Roman Catholic parish church was curious, to say the least.

Frau Schneider had agreed. But Roman Catholic churches contained Roman Catholic priests, she pointed out, interrupting him. And it was remarkable, she said, what fine reputations such men had – even outside their own religious persuasion – for truthfulness, discretion, and reliability. She spread her hands. And in this wicked city, where else might a desperate man like Sayeed safely turn when he needed a friend?

David had let her spell all this out, just as he let her speak the Levantine name between tiny pauses like quotation marks, as if she secretly knew better but was humouring him. He reckoned she needed the Brownie points. He could rest a while yet on the laurels of his teacakes coup.

They had decided to pay a call immediately on the church in question. They travelled by rusting Fiat taxi, out to the flat, nondescript suburb some half-hour's drive from the city centre. It was early Monday evening now, and the shuttered houses baked beneath their wide flat eaves, drained of colour in the harsh sunlight. Streets lined with dusty lime trees crossed each other indistinguishably, their sidewalks sensibly deserted. The only living soul David saw was a postman, dozing in the cab of his three-wheeled *moto*. Things looked promising, he thought. The sole reason for Sayeed to come to a benighted area like this had to be a need for its anonymity. It was amazing, in fact, that someone with city contacts had spotted him on such a street.

David wondered again where Frau Schneider's list had come from, and who had compiled it. She sat beside him on the narrow back seat of the taxi, her knees together, her arms folded, silently discouraging all such questions. The taxi drew in to the side and stopped. Asking the driver to wait, David got out; Frau Schneider joined him.

The church was built out of unpleasant beige bricks, a modern structure with a swooping tent-like roof in some shiny blue substance, and a flat-faced tower stuck on the front, chastely decorated with an elongated shiny blue cross. Its interior was equally ecumenical: a centre altar, plenty of light oak pews and pale blue stained glass, but no mystery. And no people, either. David shouted, but no one came.

He and Frau Schneider went back out into the sunlight. They looked around uncertainly. The taxi driver shouted something, and pointed. Round the side of the church, at the end of a winding beige brick path, was the presbytery. Plastic Venetian blinds on the downstairs windows, electric coach-lamps by the door, a derisory entrance porch over it, supported by wrought ironwork with a Spanish motif. Frau Schneider's prolonged attack on the electric door chimes produced a thin, joyless woman blearily buttoning a purple flowered overall.

She told them she was Father Gennario's housekeeper. Father Gennario was out.

No, she couldn't say when he'd be back.

Today? Well, yes . . . But very late.

No. No visitors. Much too late. He'd be very tired. He needed his sleep.

Absolutely not. A visit to his beloved seminary, an address to the students, a dinner afterwards. The drive was long. He'd certainly go straight to bed. A man needed his sleep.

In the morning? In the morning, naturally, he said Mass. There might be confessions.

How soon? How soon could the lady and gentleman call? They required an exact hour?

Ah. Ten o'clock, then. Nine thirty, perhaps. But Father Gennario needed his breakfast. A man had to eat.

Yes. Yes, she'd tell him. But tomorrow was a busy day. All Father Gennario's days were busy. This wasn't some rich city parish, with assistant priests sitting around on their hands all day. This was a —

Yes; yes, she'd tell him. And now, if the lady and gentleman didn't mind . . .

What was that? Last Saturday, an Indian gentleman? Certainly. Very polite he'd been, too. But what business was it of theirs?

She hoiked at a shoulder strap, glowering. David thanked her ornately, left her final question tactfully unanswered, apologised for disturbing her rest. He returned with Frau Schneider to the waiting taxi, sweating but encouraged. Frau Schneider's informant had been correct. It had to have been Sayeed. The coincidence, otherwise, was too great.

They had driven back into the city, to the International Press Building. Frau Schneider insisted he pay for the taxi, just as she'd insisted he pay for the drinks. Americans, she told him, were rich. And besides, she was only a struggling freelance, while he was Mr CIA, with an expense account. He parted from her on the steps, having fixed to meet her there the following morning at nine. She hurried away, clutching her maps and other paraphernalia, every inch the harassed spinster tourist, in too-bright cotton summer dress and tired, unsuitable cardigan.

He had watched her out of sight. She could steal a march on him, he supposed: arrive out at Father Gennario's earlier than nine thirty and somehow force her way in. But he didn't think she'd bother. She was obviously confident she could handle him – get hold of Sayeed's papers and do what she liked with them. She was probably right. He sighed. She might be a freelance, but she was a damn sight more of a professional than he'd ever be.

And then he had a report to make on the morning's fiasco. And another on how he planned to cope with tomorrow, and after that there was his AP job. However divided his attention might be, he still had to go through the motions. He turned back into the building, went up to the office he shared with Frank.

Frank hadn't been there. A larger man, in immaculate yellow chinos, curly-haired and open-faced, sat in Frank's swivel chair, his expensive loafers up on Frank's crowded desk. He introduced himself, not rising, as Jake. He'd taken off his green madras jacket, in spite of the air conditioning, and slung it over the back of his chair. This exposed – indecently, in David's opinion, like some leather surgical appliance – his underarm gun holster. Certainly not accidental, it established their relationship. David had been on his own too long. Whatever Sayeed's 'Ragnarok' might be, it had brought the cavalry charging over the hill. Langley was taking a personal interest.

Jake was a friendly fellow. Explanations, particularly of Ragnarok, weren't in his line. But he took Sayeed's death surprisingly well, simply ringing an unexplained someone to check that the body hadn't created an international incident. A gang killing, he was told. No problem. As the man on the spot, David had done just the right thing, not involving Rome Central. And David's deductive powers, leading to the visit with Frau Schneider to Father Gennario's church, impressed Jake very much. But he laughed heartily at the idea that David, or anyone else, should bother trying to keep the appointment with Frau Schneider on Tuesday morning.

Whoever she'd been working for to begin with, if she hadn't been KGB then, she certainly would be by tomorrow. For one thing, they paid better than anybody else. It only took a phone call, and a mention of CIA interest. If a case were up their street – and this one clearly was – they also provided backup muscle that any freelance would welcome. And this Frau Schneider was clearly one sophisticated lady: she'd never expect to go on having someone as inexperienced as David to deal with, so she'd appreciate a minder.

David was grateful for that *inexperienced*. He could think of several less kind, but more accurate, adjectives.

At the same time, Jake observed, there was need for discretion. They were in a foreign country. Going in with guns blazing in the middle of the night was a thing of the past. These days, covert action was supposed to be just that: covert. And besides, nothing would be gained by being heavy handed. This priest was presumably a reasonable enough guy. He wasn't going to run away – he'd got no cause. If he had the papers, and was treated nicely, he'd surely part with them. Nicely, nicely. No corpses, please. It was the new way.

Privately, David was glad to hear it. Also, since Frau Schneider was clearly something of a corpse lady, it provided another reason for including her out. So what, he asked, did Jake suggest?

Jake had suggested private enterprise. No Frau Schneider; just David, Jake and a car from Rome Central. They'd arrive as early as they dared, at eight, well before the Father's breakfast, and hopefully before the opposition.

The road was quiet at eight, Father Gennario's flock having departed after Mass. The flat-pitched roofs of the surrounding small pink houses shadowed the empty sidewalks. As peaceful a scene as before – but now blessedly cool, with the heat of the August sun saving itself to assail the city later.

Jake was driving. As they drew in to the kerb he touched David's knee and pointed back over his shoulder with a thumb. 'So much for private enterprise.'

David peered out of the rear window. A second car, as anonymous as their own, had arrived unobtrusively behind them. The two vehicles halted simultaneously. Frau Schneider was in the other car. Like him, she was not alone; her companion, like his, was large and watchful.

Jake smiled. 'Let's go then, Dave, OK? Leave this to me. And remember – nicely, nicely.'

The two parties left their cars and met on the sidewalk in front of the church. David would have been happy to leave things to Jake, but Frau Schneider singled him out.

'Mr CIA.'

Two could play that game. He bowed ironically. 'Frau KGB.'

'That is so.' She was unamused. 'Yesterday, no. Today, yes. This is Comrade Colonel Kerensky.' She seemed irked by the title. She was temperamentally a freelance, a loner; she didn't welcome her companion. David, on the other hand, was delighted with his.

He introduced him. No hands were shaken. Kerensky said, 'This morning we work together, I think.'

Jake nodded. 'Those were my instructions.'

'Good. Then I go in first.'

'Great. That makes it easier for me to shoot you if you step out of line.'

David couldn't believe it. 'Don't you think it'll be better,' he said sharply, 'if we all go together and nobody shoots anyone?'

Frau Schneider told him, 'I think they joke.'

He didn't argue.

She went on, 'But we will go together, as you say. And you must understand, Mr CIA, that from yesterday nothing is changed. My orders are the same. You do not see the papers. The comrade colonel has agreed to this. I take them.'

She started off down the beige brick path beside the church. Jake raised his eyebrows, eased his jacket round his shoulder holster, turned questioningly. David stared at him. After all his talk about keeping this covert, was he really proposing a shoot-out? David shook his head. Shoot-outs weren't his thing. Given the choice he'd prefer to wait, see what happened if and when the papers were found. They hurried after Frau Schneider, and Kerensky warily brought up the rear.

At the third chime the housekeeper opened the door. Today the daisies on her overall were pink. She surveyed the group on the doorstep sourly: if she recognised two of them she gave no sign. But she interrupted before Frau Schneider had spoken two words, shaking her head.

Father Gennario wasn't available. Until nine o'clock he took his breakfast. The whole world knew this. If they wanted to see him they must come back at –

Kerensky pushed forward between the others and in past the housekeeper. He started looking into rooms off the long modern hallway. It was a graceless area: peeling orange vinyl tiles on the floor, soiled yellow-striped wallpaper, a chainstore print of the Holy Family in a plastic frame, and an old-fashioned mahogany umbrella stand containing a large black clerical umbrella.

Without hesitation, the housekeeper went to the telephone on the wall at the foot of the stairs, lifted the receiver, started to dial. Kerensky heard the click, turned, stooped and pulled the telephone flex out of the junction box on the wall. Jake, who had followed him in, snapped his fingers to attract the Russian's attention, kicked his left kneecap, and had two rigid fingers ready for his windpipe as his head came forwards. Kerensky sagged, Jake lowered him to the floor, and he lay there gasping. In charmingly schoolboy Italian, Jake apologised to the housekeeper for his friend. But he made no attempt to reconnect the telephone.

David and Frau Schneider crowded into the hallway, closing the door behind them. The housekeeper, terrified now, backed away until she came up against the stairs. Her lips moved but no sounds came. Her eyes were very wide.

At the extreme back of the hall a door opened, and a square-jawed, muscular young priest appeared, in formal black soutane, chewing, and dusting flakes of croissant from his chest. He took in his four visitors, leaned against the door-jamb, impressively unsurprised. His housekeeper found her voice. David occupied himself with Kerensky; although breathing again, the man wasn't happy.

Jake cut through the housekeeper's hysteria. 'Please excuse this intrusion, Father,' he said in his careful Italian. 'We are friends of Mr Sayeed.'

Father Gennario replied in rather better English. 'I'd expected Mafia.' He inclined his head. 'You don't *sound* like Mafia.'

'No, sir.' Jake hesitated, gave an embarrassed what-the-hell gesture. 'CIA, sir.' David half expected him to offer a business card.

The priest narrowed his eyes. 'And the others?'

'They're . . . with me, sir.'

David was impressed. With minimum effort a chain of command had been established. But for how long was uncertain. Kerensky was struggling to his feet, his face dark with anger.

'So many people.' Father Gennario shook his head disapprovingly. 'You're here for that poor man's papers, of course.'

'If that's at all possible, sir. I know it's not what Mr Sayeed instructed, but the circumstances are rather special.'

'Very special. Four of you, and one of me.'

So much, David thought, for nicely, nicely.

The priest moved forward, round him and Kerensky, and opened another door. 'We must talk about this. Perhaps you'd better come into my study.'

'No. No talk.' It was, in fact, Frau Schneider, not Kerensky, who ended Jake's rule. She produced her gun. 'No talk. No politeness. We want the Indian's papers.'

'I know you do.' He eyed her calmly. 'But I'm sure we can come to some agreement.'

The housekeeper was trying to sidle away up the stairs. David stopped her before the Russian could.

Frau Schneider said, 'I already have agreement.' She waved the gun. 'You give me the papers or I shoot your stupid servant.'

Father Gennario looked her over. David judged her dress to be even more touristy and shapeless than yesterday's.

The priest said carefully, 'I think you mean that.'

'I'm afraid she does,' David told him.

The atmosphere in the ugly little hallway changed. Jake was motionless, his eyes bright, his attention more on Kerensky than the woman. The Russian was recovered now, professionally cool, his right hand fingering the inside of his left lapel. Then the housekeeper began, very softly, to weep, and the tableau was broken. Father Gennario went to her, his robe swirling.

'Mr Sayeed's papers are in the safe in my study. Just take them and go. The safe is on the floor behind my desk; it is not locked.'

He had one arm round his housekeeper's shoulders, speaking to her softly in Italian. Kerensky had a few inaudible words with Frau Schneider, then went through into the study. Jake would have followed, but her gun discouraged him. David remembered how easily Sayeed had died. The priest looked straight at him, seeming to be aware that David was the least likely of the quartet to indulge in violence.

'Mr Sayeed's papers are not something I could let people die for.'

'Have you read them, Father?'

'Of course not: Mr Sayeed told me they were confidential. I was simply to hold them until he returned. And if he didn't return by this evening . . .'

A subtle shifting in the narrow hallway told him that Mr Sayeed would not be returning, neither this evening nor any other. He tucked his chin into his collar and was silent. Frau Schneider glanced at her watch. They waited.

David smelt coffee, the aroma drifting in from the room at the rear of the entrance hall. He looked at the priest and his housekeeper. What we do to people's lives, he thought. He was relieved that Jake hadn't got to use his smart leather holster. Jake was the boss, of course, but with one gun already in evidence, and that one Frau Schneider's, he prayed for things to stay uncomplicated. It might well be that the priest was wrong: that the information in Sayeed's papers *was* worth dying for. But dying *for*, and dying merely *because of*, were two different activities. Heroes performed one, fools the other, and the difficulty was to know in advance which was which.

Kerensky returned from the study, moving slowly. He had three identical cardboard folders in his hand, and he was reading from the contents of the top one. It seemed to be a single typed sheet. He finished it, closed the folder, looked up at Jake, smiled.

'It is what we both should have guessed. Obviously the Indian could have no real interest in Ragnarok. He had no wish to help the conspirators, but no motive to betray them except money. They were there, he was here. He simply needed money. That meant trusting the CIA, taking a chance. If the CIA betrayed him, this document would at least give him his revenge.'

Kerensky paused. David was bewildered. Ragnarok? Ever since Jake's arrival he'd hoped for explanations, but none had been given. Now, it seemed the KGB knew all about it – whatever it was – but that Sayeed's papers, which he'd expected to enlighten him, were about something else.

He took a step forward. 'I don't understand. Sayeed told me he had information. He said it was worth half a million dollars.'

Kerensky laughed, softly. 'He did have information. Believe me, if he knew the word Ragnarok, then he had information. Half a million dollars? It might have been worth a million, or more. But he's taken the information with him.'

'He told me he'd left it with a friend.'

'Of course he did. And you were stupid enough to believe him.' Kerensky raised a calming hand. 'And so was I . . . very stupid. What the Indian knew might have filled many books. But I should have known he'd never dare to put it down in writing.'

We can't talk here . . . David remembered Sayeed's words in the church, only seconds before he was killed. *Talk* – so, clearly, there'd never been anything written down. 'Then what's the point of that stuff you have there?'

'I told you – revenge. If he was killed before he got his money, he wanted revenge . . .' Kerensky tapped the folders thoughtfully. Then his face brightened. 'And I think he should have his revenge. Don't you?' Not waiting for an answer, he held Sayeed's material out to the priest. 'These are for you, Father. I'm sorry you've been disturbed on this beautiful morning.'

Father Gennario recoiled. 'Is this a joke?'

'A dead man's wishes, Father? Are they a joke?' He offered the papers again. 'You must send these to the news agencies. Mr Sayeed requests it: it is your sacred duty.'

'Not so.' Frau Schneider's voice was unnecessarily loud. 'Not so, Colonel. Give them to me. I must take them.'

Kerensky turned. His face was thunderous, all humour gone. 'It is not for you to give orders, Comrade Schneider. You forget who you are.'

'But it was agreed! I have . . . other commitments. You knew that. You knew that from the start.' Her tone was sharp. 'It was agreed that I should take the papers.'

'So now it is unagreed. I find, Comrade Schneider, that these papers are able to bring great embarrassment to the CIA. Therefore they must be published.'

'No! No, you cannot do that!' She was shouting now. 'Would you kill me? You know I have other commitments. Serious commitments. I don't care *what* you say is in the papers – my employer *must* receive them.'

'That is enough.' His bark silenced her. 'They will be published. That is my decision.' He stared at her, softened his tone. 'You have done well. Perhaps we could help you to leave the country. If your employer is who I think he is – a dreamer of dreams, perhaps? – then he is not a forgiving man.'

Suddenly Frau Schneider was still, her gun levelled, her voice quiet. 'We have worked together before. I do not want to kill you. Give me the papers. You say, leave the country. Where would I go? Nowhere is beyond his reach. So give me the papers. If they are as you say, I am sure he will return them.'

Her panic intrigued David. The corpse lady herself – so professional, able to run rings round his amateurism, yet she had an employer she feared even more than the KGB. Presumably he was the source of the mysterious list of Sayeed's movements. A dreamer of dreams? Incredible. It was like something out of T. E. Lawrence.

At that moment, when her entire attention was on the Russian, Jake saw his opportunity and took it. He kicked the gun out of her hand and drew his own. Kerensky, encumbered by the folders, was too slow in response. Frau Schneider fell back against the wall, cursing in German, nursing her damaged wrist. Father Gennario pulled his housekeeper protectively closer. David stepped round them, picked up Frau Schneider's gun from the floor by the foot of the stairs. He checked magazine and safety catch. Its action was cocked; it could have gone off when it hit the floor. Gently, he eased it to safe. Let Jake do the shooting, if there was to be any.

Kerensky looked calculatingly from Jake to him and back again, then shrugged and cracked an uneasy smile.

'So much fuss,' he murmured, attempting to recreate his former jocularity. 'As if a nice chap like me would seriously wish to embarrass my CIA friends.'

His effort went unrewarded. At a nod from Jake, David pocketed Frau Schneider's gun and took firm possession of the folders. He opened the first, looked through its contents. They stated, in faultless English, that the writer, Majed Sayeed, felt his life to be in great danger. At the time of writing he was engaged in delicate negotiations with an American, a representative of the CIA in Rome, for the sale of valuable but unspecified information. He was acting honourably, in good faith; but he had reason to believe that the CIA would try to kill him rather than pay. They had been known to do this, he believed, in other similar cases. Therefore he was leaving this account with a trusted friend. If he were to disappear, the authorities should look closely into the circumstances. And he suggested that they start their inquiries at the International Press Building, where the well-known CIA agent David Lawrence worked under cover . . .

David spread the folders. They were addressed to the three other major media agencies in Rome. If delivered, an embarrassment indeed.

He ripped the single typewritten page from each. Crumpling the three sheets into a ball, he turned to Jake and asked for a match. Frau Schneider started to protest, then fell silent. Preoccupied with Kerensky, Jake thrust a Bic lighter at David. Frau Schneider watched, as a mountaineer watches the fraying of his rope, while David burned the ball of paper in the metal tray of the umbrella stand. When it was gone she sighed deeply, then her normal resilience reasserted itself. She squared her shoulders.

'At least that is better than publication. It is possible that I may live. If the good Father here is asked, he can at least tell Il Signore that the papers have been destroyed. He wanted that, I think. He thought he knew what was in them. It was only because he did not trust me that I must take them to him. Perhaps he will be satisfied.'

'I hope so,' David said, realising suddenly that he meant it. As corpse ladies went, she wasn't such a bad old stick. 'Il Signore? Is he the dreamer of dreams?'

She smiled evasively, massaging her wrist. 'Before we go, remind me to tell you a secret.'

With the papers burnt, Jake had put away his gun. On every side, honour seemed to have been satisfied – except that Kerensky's masters would have to do without the CIA's humiliation. Father Gennario straightened, released his housekeeper, eased the cramped muscles of his neck.

'Ragnarok . . .' he said. 'That's an interesting word. I've heard it before somewhere. What does it mean?'

David, wondering the same thing, waited hopefully.

Kerensky stepped forward. 'That is a question one does not ask. You earn your living in your way, Father. We earn ours in ours.' He produced a wallet, took out a handful of ten thousand lire notes and gave them to the housekeeper. 'For the telephone,' he told her.

He opened the front door and went quietly down the path. Jake hurried after him and they talked together, briefly, on the sidewalk. David felt as if he'd been wrung through a mangle.

He said, 'We interrupted your breakfast, Father. I'm sorry.'

'You also took property that was not yours and destroyed it.'

'I did.' David offered Frau Schneider his arm. 'I hope it's what is known as keeping the world safe for democracy.'

They walked out, towards the waiting cars. Kerensky, already behind the wheel, sounded his horn. He lifted his wrist, showed his watch through the open window, tapped it impatiently.

Frau Schneider stopped, turned to David, disengaging her arm from his. 'You've still got my gun.'

'You've still got my secret.'

'Ah, yes.' She held out her hand and he put the gun in it. 'The man you call Sayeed,' she said. 'His real name was Kassim Latif. It might make a difference.'

She hurried away down the path. David couldn't see what difference it made. Latif or Sayeed, either way he was dead. But at least it gave him something to add to the report Jake would be filing.

13

Clancy was standing close up against the window, as if he needed physical distance between himself and Duke, and he'd turned up the volume on his Walkman. Robert could hear the tinny buzzing of the earphones. He himself was quiet now. He'd been quiet since the man in the white coat had intervened.

'I guess you've pushed your luck far enough for today, Colonel.'

'Crap. I've hardly started.' Duke was indignant. 'Be reasonable, can't you? The bastard hasn't given an inch.'

'Maybe he's not going to. They don't always, in my experience.'

'Forgive me for saying this, buster, but that could be a reflection on your style.'

The outburst elicited no more than a shrug. 'I'm telling you, his heart's not good. In fact it's very bad. Blood pressure too. If you push him any further, he'll die. He needs a rest.'

Robert watched them, his eyes stretched wide. He was amazed. They talked as if he couldn't hear them, as if he were deaf or halfwitted. He supposed it didn't matter. Either way, there wasn't much he could do. He'd tried wishing himself dead; it hadn't worked.

Was his heart so very bad? His pulse still pounded in his head. His heart didn't sound very bad. Apart from missing a beat now and then, it sounded fine. He wondered how long he'd been on the bed. They'd let him sleep, once, hadn't they? Now there was talk of giving him a rest. He couldn't imagine why. Rest or not, there was nothing he could tell them. Only that he wasn't going to die, not yet.

'A rest, you say. How long?'

The man in white shrugged again. 'A couple of days. A week. That and good food and – '

'For Christ's sake. *We don't have a week!*' Duke spoke as if to the village idiot. 'If we run this operation my way, we don't have two days. Two *hours*, may be. Give him another shot.'

'He's had enough. The heart's not just another muscle. If it goes into spasm the patient dies.'

'So we play the odds.'

'They're terrible.'

'You don't know how important this is.'

'For which I'm profoundly grateful.'

'So do your job. Give him a shot.'

'My job is to keep this body alive.'

'Maybe I should tell you what this body has been up to.'

Clancy swore. He got up, switched off his Walkman, flung it and its headphones on the dresser.

'You guys make me sick. Robbie here is OK. A little misguided maybe, but OK. Public spirited. He cares about people. Anyone with half an eye could see you're not treating him right.'

He crossed to the door, knocked. It was opened from outside. A hand. More than that Robert couldn't see. Clancy turned back into the room.

'A word in your ear, Duke. It won't take long. Our medical friend can keep an eye on the *patient*. See he doesn't run away.'

They went out together. The door was locked behind them. The man in the white coat stayed where he was, standing at the foot of the bed. He could see Robert's tongue move in his mouth, swollen like a parrot's. Robert decided not to ask him for a drink. He'd spelled out his responsibilities. Thirst at this level was hardly life-threatening.

Duke and Clancy were gone for what seemed a long time. Robert had been afraid of Clancy. He forgot his fear and dozed.

When Duke and Clancy returned they brought company. With a lot of shuffling, two other agents carried in something between them that Robert couldn't properly see. They they put it down and went away. The bedroom, already crowded, now had another chair in it.

It was a sturdy office chair, with arms. Woolston was tied in the chair. His ankles were tied to its legs, his waist was tied to its back, his wrists were tied to its arms. He was a tall young man, folded with difficulty into the chair's obscene embrace.

The other two agents locked the door behind them, leaving Duke and Clancy on either side of the black man. Woolston's face was a mess. It had been a mess for a long time. Nothing had been done to mend it. Cuts still gaped.

Clancy tousled Woolston's hair.

'Robbie? You awake, Robbie? Great. I thought you were. Now what you see here, Robbie, I don't want you to misinterpret. God knows, I'm no racist. I really mean that. Blacks in the Agency get my loyalty, just the same as white. Black, brown, yellow – it don't make no never mind. Same way, Robbie, when I got to hurt a guy, the colour of his skin don't signify. You take my meaning?'

Robert stared, sweated, shuddered. He took Clancy's meaning. He strove to die. His heart leapt and skittered, but wouldn't let him. Clancy had said enough. What came next was already abundantly clear. But Clancy was a man for spelling things out.

'So it's up to you, Robbie. Like always, it's about the telephone interface. Not much, is it? A little thing, Robbie, wouldn't you say? Sure, not so little for this guy here. A big thing for this man here. So you gotta make up your mind, Robbie, and whatever you decide, I'm sure your friend here will understand.'

Robert's heart danced mockingly in his chest. A little thing. Lower the walls a tiny bit; shift the boundaries of the possible. Not far. A little thing. Nothing else. He couldn't understand the fuss. What was there, walled up in his silence? He didn't remember. The telephone interface? Was that all they wanted? Such a little thing. Oh, *yes* . . .

Robert closed his eyes. Blood moved relentlessly behind their lids. Now? Enough? His hurt, Woolston's hurt, had there been enough? Was it time now?

Of course it was time. Of course it was.

He moved his tongue, worked his lips – *two, zero, seven* – but no sounds came. He wept, straining at the straps that held him down. *Area code two, zero, seven*. No sounds came.

He opened his eyes. Duke and Clancy hadn't noticed his effort to speak. Woolston's hands were tied down tightly against the chair arms. Clancy took one of the long, curved fingers and levered it upwards until it broke. The snap was sharp in the small, foetid room. Woolston's eyes widened. They bulged, the yellow whites brightly veined. Sweat ran down his face, and blood from his broad lower lip, where he'd bitten it. He didn't complain.

Still holding the broken finger, Clancy turned to Robert. 'That telephone interface, Robbie. Remember?'

Robert remembered very well. He nodded. It was time. He nodded and smiled and pleaded. 'The code,' he mouthed, 'the area code is two, zero – '

'You're going to have to do better than that, Robbie.' Clancy rotated the finger. Woolston gasped, as if in disbelief. 'You're making no sense. You're going to have to try harder.'

Robert tried. It wasn't Clancy's fault. He didn't blame Clancy. He knew he had to try harder. He swallowed, gagging.

'The area code is two, zero, seven.' And Clancy understood. 'You interface on eight, eight, three, zero, seven, five, six.' He'd never enunciated more clearly. Clancy seemed pleased. Robert was proud of himself; tears of gratitude welled up in his eyes.

But it was so little. They'd send Clancy back for more, once they found out. They'd never be satisfied with so little. 'The program's scrubbed,' he apologised. 'It's not your fault. But there's nothing there any more. Computer garbage. They'll ask for more.'

He frowned. More? He didn't remember. 'So tell them . . . tell them . . . it's not your fault. Just tell them . . .' He couldn't bear it if Clancy got into trouble. 'Georg guessed . . . he knew all along . . . other people might call it a character failing. I don't, but other people might. It's just the way she is. He knows the girl. And so do I. Dear God, so do I. Ask him. He'll tell you – please?'

There was a long silence. Woolston's head had lolled. He'd lost consciousness. Duke and Clancy were ignoring him. At the foot of the bed the man in the white coat hadn't moved. Somebody had started the tape recorder on the bamboo table. Its reels turned, ticking very faintly.

'Ask Georg what, Robbie?'

Robert was surprised. He'd already explained: people didn't listen. 'Georg knows the girl. He'll tell you. She's full of her mother. Full of love. It's not a character failing to be full of love.'

His heart had slowed. Suddenly he felt very tired.

'What girl is this, Robbie?'

'For Christ's sake, are you deaf?' He craned his head up at them, shrieking hoarsely, straining against the straps. 'My daughter, you stupid shit. She'll use the over-ride. All of them will. Ask Georg. The whole thing's a bluff – they'll use the over-ride.'

He fell back on the bed. A dark trickle of urine flowed. The man in the white coat moved quickly to his side, feeling for the pulse in Robert's neck.

Duke asked, 'Is he dead?'

'Did you get what you wanted?'

'I said, is he dead?'

'His heart's stopped. I could probably restart it.'

Clancy was removing the tape reels. 'Suit yourself.'

By the time he and Duke had knocked and been released from the room, the man in the white coat had injected a stimulant and was kneeling astride the bed, striking sharply with the heel of his hand on Robert's sternum. He listened, ear to the scarred chest. Then he joined his mouth to Robert's, breathing deep and long.

Robert turned his head away, sighed. The other man rested and looked up. Woolston had recovered consciousness. Their eyes met in shared loathing for what the doctor had become.

At noon, on watch on the *Fimbulvetr*'s bridge, Colly Graham tuned in to the BBC World Service. There were riots in South Africa, the Ford car factory at Port Elizabeth burnt. In America the Midwest was suffering a record heatwave. In Italy a terrorist attack at Milan airport had been prevented by quick police action. In the Middle East, Syrian troop movements were threatening Israeli borders again. At the disarmament talks in Geneva recent unexpected moves towards a treaty had stalled in mutual recriminations: unofficial sources reported intense behind-the-scenes activity, however, suggesting the possibility of a major breakthrough. In Britain, the Green Party had won a sensational by-election victory . . .

Colly switched the radio off, stared wearily out across the grey water. A major breakthrough. Did she believe in major breakthroughs any more? She supposed she must. What day was it? Tuesday? The halfway point. Exactly halfway into the countdown, and what had they achieved? Mutual bloody recriminations.

Her vision blurred. The Russian dinghy was out there somewhere: divers at work now that the sea was calmer. She screwed up
her eyes. Jesus, she was tired. She'd taken this watch to keep herself
awake, gather her thoughts. Pétur would be arriving soon. His
radiation discs would have been processed by now, and she'd no
doubt what they had told him. Her dilemma was acute. She'd
promised him the truth, but there were two truths.

The first truth was that she and Flynn and Werner were
threatening to vaporise much of Iceland, and bury the rest beneath
ash and molten lava. Pétur was an Icelander; he could only have one
reaction to such a threat. The second truth was that the threat was
just a bluff. Only two people in the world knew this, herself and
Werner. Dare she extend this number? Dare she trust Pétur?

She needed to know more about him. He'd come over as a nice
enough guy, not as macho as she'd thought at first, but one who
liked his arguments kept simple. If he didn't care about the state of
the world, then revealing the second truth wouldn't help. It would
simply give him knowledge that could destroy them all. On the
other hand, Iceland was hardly a superpower. An Icelander might
be expected to have sympathy with the plight of smaller nations –
and to care about what was happening to the planet. They lived
closer to nature, up here on the roof of the world, than the average
citizen of the European Community.

Maybe she was whistling in the dark. Just one thing was for sure –
things had gone horribly wrong. Those fucking discs put them at
Pétur's mercy. Once he was off the ship he could do what he liked.
Keeping him prisoner was out; so was killing him. Apart from
moral considerations, they'd get away with neither. The last
complication she needed now was the local police tramping all over
the ship.

She should have confided in Flynn, asked his advice. Poor Werner
was hopeless, now; caved in like an old man. But Flynn was still
Flynn. What could he tell her, though, that she didn't already
know?

The rain had stopped, patches of blue sky appearing. She moved
out on to the open bridge wing. From here she saw the Russian
dinghy, which had been hidden behind the high flare of the ship's
bow. Karpovich was organising a new game. He and his compan-

ions began tossing lumps of lava up on to the foredeck. The implication was crudely obvious – the rocks could just as easily be grenades.

She lifted her binoculars, looked for Big Brother on the cliff. He wasn't in his usual place – perhaps he'd been washed away by the storm. She searched for the antenna that often betrayed his presence. Crags of striated lava swung across her field of view. Ledges, trailing white screens of guano. Suddenly he loomed up in his olive drab uniform, so close that she felt she could reach out and touch him. He was kneeling, his NATO issue rifle to his shoulder. She looked straight down its barrel. His finger was on the trigger. He could have killed her, at any moment since she emerged on to the bridge wing.

She was reassured. He hadn't killed her. He had his orders. Somewhere, very high up, there were men who believed the threat contained in the ultimatum. The Russians too had orders; it was, after all, only a game they were playing with lumps of rock. The device . . . the detonator . . . any direct attack upon the ship or her crew . . . immediate activation. The pressure-sensitive trigger. They believed in it all, in the threat of Ragnarok. And why not? Sometimes, when she wasn't thinking straight, she believed in it herself. It was hard not to. Play a role long enough and it came to fit you. She shook her head. If they failed, they failed. Vengeance was for the gods.

She lowered her glasses, waved at Big Brother. It was well after twelve: lunch time. Time for her to be relieved of the watch. Time also for her to tell Flynn and Werner the full implications of Pétur's imminent visit.

The reporter arrived shortly before one thirty. Werner, on watch, saw him walking down the rough track up the side of the valley; obviously he'd left his car up on the road. Werner glanced sideways, confirmed the presence of the loaded rifle, leaning against the compass repeater. The big Icelander made an excellent target. But Werner preferred to wait until Colly had left the ship and gone to fetch Einarsson before killing him. He was counting on the confusion of echoes between the cliffs to fool her.

He'd seen the way she treated Flynn since Zebedee's death. And Einarsson was no ugly American hit-man: she'd take his death badly. So he wanted her to believe what everyone else would believe – that the shot had come from Big Brother, or from the Russians. They were the people with all the guns. The professional killers. The Icelandic police would know where to look. And so must she.

He called Colly on the phone, left Flynn sleeping, went down to lower the motorboat. Colly joined him at the *Fimbulvetr*'s rail, dressed in red woollen shirt and washed-out jeans. He was surprised: Einarsson was going to have to take her as he found her. Her hair had been brushed, but was tied back in its usual elastic band.

She touched his arm. 'We'll work something out, love,' she said. 'Don't worry.'

He nodded. If she treated him like a child, it was his own fault. For the last few days he'd behaved like a child.

She went down to the motorboat and cast off. He returned to the bridge. Sunlight was breaking through the overcast, a pale ray that sparkled briefly on the ruffled water. The ship rode easily at anchor, rising and falling on the gentle swell that still reached her from the larger waves at the cove mouth. Einarsson stood close under the cliffs at the end of the beach farthest from the Russians, waiting as the boat approached. Werner watched him through the binoculars. He didn't blame Colly for her interest. The Icelander's blond hair lifted in the breeze. He wore a tan leather jacket over tailored slacks. He was undeniably handsome.

The motorboat grounded. A moment later Colly was ashore, splashing up through knee-deep water. Werner saw them embrace, quickly, uncomplicatedly, like children. He frowned, exchanged binoculars for rifle, adjusted the sight, rested the stock on the solid rail of the bridge wing. He stood in shadow, hidden by the yellow column of the funnel.

Colly and Einarsson parted. He was laughing, telling her something, making steering gestures with his hands. She ran back to the motorboat, heaved herself in over the side. He followed. The boat swung on a wave, grinding in. Einarsson, still on the beach, steadied it. For a long moment he was quite motionless, straining against the bow, his head and shoulders in sharp relief against the grey shale of the beach behind. Werner chose the spot between his eyes, breathed deeply, took first pressure.

'Bloody davit. Once that thing rattles away beside your head, fat chance you've got of sleeping.'

The rifle jittered sideways. Where the shot went, Werner never knew. The frozen moment on the beach dissolved. Einarsson thrust the boat out on the next wave, flinging himself in over the bow as Colly reversed sharply away.

'Shooting the sparrows, is it?' Flynn leaned companionably on the rail beside Werner. 'You'll never hit them, Adolf. They'll run up the barrel and perch on your nose first.'

Werner pointed stiffly out to port. 'I was aiming at those big white birds.' He didn't know how much Flynn had seen. The big man was shirtless, fresh from his bunk, in his socks.

Flynn scratched his hairy chest, yawning. 'Beware the Jub-jub bird,' he said obscurely, 'and shun the frumious Bandersnatch.'

Werner turned away angrily. He didn't care what Flynn had seen. He had only to deny it, whatever the Irishman said.

Colly and Pétur were looking sideways over their shoulders, the motorboat throwing up a fine bow wave as it headed back at full throttle. The Russian dinghy, which must have set off from the camp on the other side of the cove as soon as they spotted Einarsson boarding the motorboat, was following a curving path, also flat out, bouncing from wave to wave on an interception course. But it was barely fast enough to make the interception. It was only as the motorboat approached the *Fimbulvetr* that the Russian dinghy came alongside, empty save for Karpovich.

'Excuse me. Doctor Graham, Mr Einarsson, excuse me.' Werner could hear every word. 'Last time you were here, Mr Einarsson, there was an unfortunate misunderstanding. I would like to apologise.'

'Apologise?' Colly laughed bitterly. 'What *is* this?'

'Under water, Mr Einarsson, men do not always think clearly.' How, Werner wondered, did they know his name? Were they ardent followers of the TV news, over there in the tents? 'One of our campers is very quick-tempered. I understand that he panicked and behaved very badly.'

'That's one way of putting it. I'd say he tried to kill me.'

'Yes. So I understand. And that is why I am here to apologise. We wish to be on the best of terms with our Icelandic hosts. We have no quarrel with *you*. Such bad things will not happen again.'

Werner wondered what was behind this. Were the Russians

concerned that Einarsson might complain to the tourist authority? It was hardly likely that he would, with what he knew already – let alone what he would learn in the next few minutes. Or were they under orders to leave visitors, as well as the crew, alone? Maybe Colly was right; the ultimatum really did carry some weight.

The rest of the exchange was lost in the clatter of coming alongside. The Russian dinghy sheered off, returned across the cove. Werner had a feeling that as long as Einarsson was on board there'd be no more tapping, no more porthole bugs, and no more lumps of lava heaved on deck. He almost felt that the visit might be worthwhile, after all. Leaving the rifle on the bridge with Flynn, he went down to greet the reporter. Werner wore his denim jacket loosely open, Kassim's revolver in its inside pocket. Colly could say what she liked. If it was necessary, for the sake of the countdown, he still intended to kill Einarsson. They could worry afterwards about what happened next.

Einarsson came up the ladder, laughing. He thanked Werner for the warning shot, which had attracted his attention to the Russian setting out in his dinghy. The last thing he wanted was more trouble with them. Two men on the road had already tried to kill him. He was ready for some explanations, but he'd like to use the toilet before they got down to business.

Werner wished the men on the road had succeeded, but said nothing. He showed Einarsson down to the head, left him to find his own way back.

They met again on the bridge. It was Werner's watch, and Colly wanted everyone to be present. Nobody mentioned the rifle shot again. Colly and Einarsson had thought it was a warning; whatever Flynn thought he kept to himself. He also kept the rifle close to his hand.

Einarsson was given the only chair, by the radio set. Werner hoisted himself watchfully on to the plotting table, still wearing Kassim's gun. Flynn had settled in the mariner's position, legs apart, elbows on the wheel spokes. Colly shifted restlessly, reluctant to begin.

The Icelander took over. He produced two radiation discs from the pocket of his jacket and laid them carefully on the radio shelf in

front of him. One was pale grey, the other nearly black. His bright
eyes looked from Flynn to Werner to Colly.

'I promised I'd come to you with them first.' He pointed. 'That's a
hell of a lot of radiation.'

Colly grimaced unhappily. She bent her head, pushed the band
around her pony tail more closely against her skull, cleared her
throat. 'I guess I'm going to have to tell you the whole long story.'

In fact she kept it short, but she told it fairly, omitting only to
mention that it was all a bluff. Werner listened, trying to remember
how things had been; but it was all so long ago, a story about
strangers. So young they'd been. So amateur. So innocent.

At one point the TV man suddenly looked around. 'Wait a bit.
You're not all here. Where's the Indian?'

Flynn dug his flask from his hip pocket. 'We used to have an
Indian. He left.'

Colly smiled nervously. 'That's another story. We'll get to it
later.'

She hurried on. Her father in New York; the cover story for the
Icelandic government. Flynn emptied his flask, watching Werner all
the while, daring him to comment.

Finally Colly was done. 'So there it is, Pétur. We really want that
treaty. An end to the waste of resources. Some effort diverted to
tackling the real problems of the world.' She shrugged self-
deprecatingly. 'We're like your actual crazy scientists in a movie.
The ones threatening to destroy the world if they don't get what
they want. Only, what we want is a second chance for all the people
who've been screwed by the superpowers for so long.'

There was a long silence. The ship leaned into the swell, a rope
slapping on the damaged foremast. All their eyes were on the
reporter. At the start, Einarsson had tried to make notes, but he'd
long given that up. He sat now, head down, slowly drawing circles
round squares in his notebook.

'Destroy the world?' he said at last, his head still bent. 'Is that
true? If you don't get what you want, will you do that?'

Werner tensed. Colly had opened her mouth to reply. He had the
certain premonition that she was going to tell Einarsson the truth.

He cut in. 'We said we would. We've proved we have the
capability. The Soviets and the Americans believe us. Don't you?'

Einarsson was considering his pencilled circles. 'That's not what I meant.' He looked up, his expression troubled. 'I don't understand how one bomb can do so much damage. I think someone should tell me exactly what happens when this bomb goes off.'

Colly frowned, undecided. She turned away, her eyes on the cove outside, sun-dappled now beneath broken cloud in a high blue sky. She answered Pétur softly, almost in a whisper, painfully. 'Everything within a six-kilometre radius of this place is obliterated, vaporised instantly and completely. The cliffs, the villages, the people, all life. Then seismic shocks and devastating tidal waves travel outwards. Maybe a hundred kilometres an hour. Borgarnes disappears. The entire western coastline is levelled. Earthquakes . . . volcanoes . . .' She faltered. 'Reykjavik can't survive. Thousands will die. Then the dust from the eruption begins to spread, blocking the sun. And after that – '

She stopped. She could go no further. She hadn't explained anything about the fuel/coolant interaction – but Werner could see that her obvious belief in what she was describing had done the job. Einarsson was convinced. He had covered his face with his hands.

Werner watched him sardonically. Now they'd find out. Colly had had such faith in this handsome TV person; such faith in the logic of their demands; such faith that any reasonable, well-informed person must support them. Now they'd see. Reasonable? Well informed? For all any of them knew, Einarsson might be a dedicated believer in the role of market forces, secure in the knowledge that he was a citizen of the rich world, with his hi-fi and his car and his over-rich diet, indifferent to the fate of the poor masses in Africa, South America, Asia. For all they knew, he was also paranoid about the Red Menace, an ardent supporter of the need for first-strike capability.

Finally the Icelander moved. He hunched his shoulders, peered out at them above a broad hand that rubbed across his lower face. 'I understand all that. I believe you can destroy my country. It is only a small island, after all. But that still isn't what I'm getting at.' He turned to Werner. 'It's this talk of destroying the world. Climate change, yes, surely I understand that. But climate has changed before. Even the sagas tell us of times when the climate was different.'

Colly swung round from the window. She looked down at Einarsson. 'I guess I was thinking of *your* world, when I said we'd destroy it.' She held up a hand, stilling his protest that there was more to his world than Iceland. 'Not just the island: your way of life. The world will survive. That's the whole point. People will survive. But the way of life that has grown out of control in the twentieth century, that corrupt, polluting, uncaring way of life, that world will be gone.'

He shook his head, sadly. 'So, many Icelanders must die. And in other countries, many more will die as the long winter comes. Your *Ragnarok*.' Was he mocking them? 'I'm taking you seriously, you see. My own father is a schoolmaster not thirty kilometres from here, in Hellissandur . . . but individuals, of course, are not important. And there are worse ways to die. Fire and ice we know very well. But when it comes to nuclear fallout – '

'There won't be any.' She crouched urgently beside him. 'Virtually none – our bomb is small, Pétur, and clean. What little fallout it produces will go very high, and be enormously diluted, diffused over a wide area. Radiation is not part of our threat.'

Werner looked at them. Their physical closeness hurt. But for all their apparent intimacy, Einarsson still seemed emotionally withdrawn. His expression was thoughtful. Calculating.

He narrowed his eyes. 'So what you're really threatening, you mad scientists, is the famous nuclear winter, without the usual nuclear side-effects?'

She took his hand. 'I told you, Pétur. Ragnarok. The long winter – I *told* you.' As she spoke, Werner saw tears in her eyes. 'And then the earth rises again, Pétur. It's *renewed*. You know the story, Pétur. We're offering both – the destruction of the old world *and* the creation of a new world. We can make it happen.'

Silence. Einarsson disengaged his hand. He sighed. 'Then what the hell are you waiting for?' He closed his notebook with a snap. 'Better your way than the other, isn't it? And you don't believe they're going to meet your terms, do you? Get in first, before the gung-ho generals.'

He looked around, as if surprised at the sudden hush that had fallen in the wheelhouse. He'd spoken quickly, yet clearly in earnest. He was tough, Werner thought angrily. Tougher than they were. More *professional*. He saw past all the woolly self-justification. Saw no need for bluff.

Flynn was the first to recover. He reached for one of his cigars. 'My own sentiments entirely, Pete. Why wait?' He struck a match. 'Stop the bastards dead in their tracks.'

Werner pulled himself together. Their justifications were not entirely woolly. 'We're waiting for the treaty.'

Einarsson eyed him bleakly. 'Maybe you're right. But a clean new beginning has its attractions.'

Colly tossed her head. 'Cynicism's too easy. People change. They can be helped to change. Persuaded.'

He reached out, touched her arm. 'I hope you're right.'

'But you think I'm wrong.' Disappointed, she moved back, away from him. 'You think we're all wrong. You think we're naive and silly.'

He shook his head. 'Not at all. I think you're – ' He broke off. Suddenly, his weariness seemed to fall away. He smiled, his blue eyes shone, his face was transformed. 'What I think doesn't matter a damn. In fact, I think you're all bloody marvellous. But you're here, prepared to die for what you believe in, and what I think doesn't matter a damn.'

He leapt impulsively to his feet. 'God, what a story!' Colly moved uneasily. 'No, I don't mean it like that – it's just the way I see things.' He sobered a little. 'Time was, I used to feel so bad about the mess people were making of the world that one day I tried to leave. But the pills didn't quite work; someone found me in time. Since then, I've simply looked the other way. Trips abroad, interesting job, nice apartment. There was nothing I could do, so I did nothing. Except pay my subscription to Greenpeace. But *you've* found something to do, and put me on the spot. If there's the slightest chance you're right, if people can be helped to change, I have to give you that opportunity. It's the greatest story of my life. But there's no way I can use it.'

Flynn, once again, was the first to respond. He coughed sceptically. 'Fine words, Pete. Left to yourself, though, you'd bang our bomb, and to hell with 'em.'

'Luckily for me, Captain, I don't have your bomb.'

Werner smiled, seeing how quickly the Icelander had won the other two over. 'We have the bomb, but you have power over us.'

'Power? What power? There's no way I can go public with this. Even if I don't agree with you, I can't be responsible for starting a panic, any more than the people you're negotiating with. And what the hell could I tell them, the people in New York, that they don't already know? I'm just a reporter. They've had experts checking out the ship.'

Briefly, Werner was at a loss. Then: 'You could tell them we've lost Kassim. If they knew there were only three of us left, they might – '

Colly intervened. 'But why *should* he tell them? He's on our side.'

'Of course he's on our side. He's not a fool. He wants to leave this ship alive, doesn't he?'

The moment froze. He glared round. He'd said it, brought their other option out into the open.

Einarsson had retreated, quietly watching them. Flynn whistled tunelessly for a while between his teeth, then stopped. 'From what I gather,' he murmured to no one in particular, 'it's on shore that the poor man's in the worst trouble.'

The Icelander broke the renewed silence. 'One thing.' He raised a finger. 'One thing I still don't understand. This bomb of yours – such things can be set off by timers, right? Or by remote control?'

They stared at him. Werner said shortly, 'Of course. It could all be done by radio. No problem.'

'And yet you're here.' Einarsson looked round, into each of their faces. 'You're all here. There's no need, it could all be done by radio, and yet you're here.' He folded his arms. 'Why?'

For a moment no one answered.

Colly shrugged. 'Hell,' she said, 'I wouldn't be anywhere else.'

'I'm like the bilge pumps,' Flynn said curtly. 'I come with the ship.'

Werner hesitated, turning his head away. The question sharpened his shame, his sense of his own failures, of his cowardice, his guilt. He remembered Einarsson's words: *a clean new beginning has its attractions.* No more woolly self-justifications. To detonate the bomb wouldn't be an act of vengeance: rather, a clean new beginning.

'Of course we're here,' he said awkwardly. 'It's where we belong.' To his surprise, he realised he meant it.

The blond Icelander relaxed. He'd proved something. He'd known what they would say. He spread his hands wide. 'You're crazy. But I hope I can help you. You'll make the world a better place.'

He paused, head on one side, then snapped the elastic round his notebook and put it away. He grinned. 'And now I hope all these kind words will buy me some food. I must've missed out on lunch somewhere: I'm bloody hungry.'

Flynn had left them, gone back to his bunk. He'd better things to do, he said, than watch the world's food reserves dwindle. Werner was on watch, up on the bridge. Halfway through an omelette, and hash browns from the freezer, Pétur remembered the packet for Colly, given to him by Björn and now in his jacket pocket. He stopped chewing, put the fork down on the table and moved his hand to the pocket, where he fingered the package thoughtfully.

If, as he'd decided, it was from the CIA, then – with what he now knew – she'd be unlikely to welcome it. It might even be a bomb. He sat very still, scarcely breathing. No – she'd said they were safe from bombs. Even a small one would activate the trigger, and the CIA knew it. He relaxed. Christ, it took some getting used to, this living on top of Krakatau. Wasn't that what she'd said, a hundred times the power of Krakatau?

Colly paused by the wardroom table, coffee pot poised. 'What's the matter? Weevils in the bread?'

He shook his head, resumed chewing, swallowed. 'I remembered something.' He took out the packet and handed it over. 'For you. It's not a present. My news editor asked me to bring it. He's got some curious friends; I reckon it might be from the CIA.'

Colly filled his mug, then put down the coffee pot. The packet was elaborately sealed with tape. She used a kitchen knife to open it. As Pétur had guessed, it contained an audio-cassette. She turned it over, puzzled, and read out the handwritten label.

'New York. Paramount Hotel. August 9. Afternoon and evening – ' She sat down abruptly, face like parchment. 'Oh, Christ.'

Gently, Pétur took the cassette from her. *Paramount Hotel . . .* he worked it out. That had to be where her father was staying. A tape from Professor Graham. But why should the CIA be sending her a tape from her father? And why should she be so upset?

'Look, Colly, you don't have to listen to this if you don't want to.'

'Yes. Yes, I do.' She held out her hand for it again. Her voice was dead. 'I'm afraid I have to.'

He gave it to her, stood up. 'Are you all right?'

'Fine.'

'If this is between you and your father, maybe I should – ' He gestured towards the door.

'Yes, Pétur. I think it would be better.'

As he left the wardroom she was fitting the cassette into the player mounted on the aft bulkhead. He closed the door behind himself and moved slowly away along the passage. Before he reached the companionway, the screaming brought him back.

Screaming. An ageless, sexless scream, from a tortured animal. Then groans and sobbing. Colly stood in front of the player, staring at it, her back to him, paralysed. He pushed past her, fumbled with the player's controls, stopped the tape. He felt sick. In his head the sobbing continued.

He ripped the tape from the machine and flung it across the room.

'You knew, didn't you?'

'I guessed.'

'And still you put it on?'

'I had to be sure.'

'Could it be faked?'

'Someone else? No. That's Fard. Besides, would it matter?'

His stomach heaved. 'What sort of people can they be?'

'Ordinary people.' She smiled at him. Her eyes were too bright. 'Ordinary people who vote and pay taxes.'

'No.' He took her shoulders and shook them. 'I don't believe it. No.'

Her head flopped to and fro, doll-like. 'The same ordinary people,' she said, 'who vote and pay their taxes into defence budgets full of nerve gas, defoliants, bacteriological weapons, space weapons, armaments aid for fascist dictators whose people are starving – '

'*No*, I said!' He clutched her to him. She didn't argue. She was quite limp now, beginning to shiver. The shivers grew to a wild, uncontrollable juddering. He held her tight. 'Hush, Colly. Hush, my dear. Hush.'

Eventually the spasm passed. He led her to one of the wardroom side benches, eased her down, sat beside her. For a time neither spoke. The ship rose gently, fell away, rose again. Seabirds cried from the cliffs across the sunlit water.

'He won't have survived much of that,' Colly said at last, matter-of-factly. 'He's an old man.'

Pétur nodded. She was looking for comfort. He didn't point out that it was a long tape, and he doubted they'd have sent it blank.

Instead, because she needed to talk, he asked, 'What did they hope to gain?'

'At this end? Sending it here?' She shrugged. 'I think it's called *alarm and despondency*. Bad for our morale. And at that end they expect to be told all those secret ways to disarm the bomb that don't exist.'

He waited.

She went on. 'We expected this sort of thing, of course. I shouldn't have let it get to me.'

Expected it? He didn't know what to say. He'd thought himself worldly-wise. Hard-boiled, even. And now this girl —

'I guess there's no need to mention this to the others, Pétur. OK?' Her hands were shaking again. She opened her eyes very wide. 'There's been enough alarm and despondency, wouldn't you say?'

'Shouldn't they know he's been taken?'

'They've known that for days. We had a link. He stopped using it.'

Her voice broke. It was the nearest she'd come, while he was there, to weeping. But she had no tears. She lifted her face up to his, put her arms around his neck, pulled him towards her, kissed him, long and hard. He was careful not to respond. She was still in shock. It was company she wanted, not sex.

She broke away. 'Thank you for being here, Pétur. And thank you for not telling the others.'

She got up, went to the table, poured herself some coffee. It must have been cold by now, but she drank it, watching him over the rim of the mug. Then, suddenly, without explanation, she set the mug down and left the wardroom. Pétur stayed where he was. When she returned she brought with her a slip of paper.

'You said this was the biggest story of your life.' She twisted the paper in her fingers. 'Well, maybe there's a way you can write about it. There's a post office in New York. On East Fifty-sixth. Just down from the subway. It's got a post office box in the name of Lily King. It's all written down here. You mustn't lose it. The box combination's there, too.'

She thrust the paper at him. He took it, uncomprehending. 'Why give it to me? I'm not going to New York.'

'You just go in, punch the combination, open the box. Nobody hassles you.'

'But why, Colly? What am I looking for?'

'The rest of the story. My father's end of it. It's all arranged. He's been sending discs there every day. Standard WordPerfect; any PC can read them.'

'I can't go to New York.'

'Well, I sure as hell can't, not now. Whatever happens.' Her tone was angry, red spots flushed on her cheeks against the pallor of her skin. 'You're the reporter, this is the story. Somebody's got to know the truth, to tell the world what really happened.' Her anger faded into a plea. 'Especially if the ship's attacked, we're all killed. Someone's got to — '

'But that can't happen. You told me.' She wasn't making sense. 'You're fireproof, you said; if the ship's attacked — '

Momentarily, her eyes glazed over. 'But that's what I mean.' She shook her head impatiently. 'We'll all be killed. If the ship's attacked, the bomb detonates and we'll all be killed. But not you.' She moved closer, touching his arm. 'You don't have to die, Pétur.'

Doubtfully, he folded the paper, tucked it into his wallet. 'If you're dead, then I'll be dead too.'

'No. You've got to promise me. Go to New York *now*, Pétur, while it's still safe. Just stay for a week. If nothing happens, you can come home again. But if not — somebody's got to know the full story. The truth. Get those disks. Please. And tell everybody. Promise me, Pétur. *Promise me!*'

He looked into her eyes. 'You don't believe you're going to get your treaty, do you?'

'No. Yes.' She waved her hands agitatedly. 'I don't know, I guess I'm like most people – hoping for the best.'

He tapped the pocket that contained his wallet. 'And preparing for the worst.'

'You'll promise?'

'I've got a job to do here in Iceland. I can't just go rushing off – '

'A job to do? Now that the opposition knows you've been back on this ship?' She laughed. 'They tried hard enough to stop you getting here. How long d'you think you'll last, just doing your job, before they catch up with you?'

He thought about it. Björn would probably be glad to see the back of him for a week. But . . . 'In that case, getting out won't be so easy.'

'Easier than staying. You'll try?'

'A small plane, maybe. I've got a good friend who – '

'Fly west, Pétur. Not just because that's the way to New York. If Ragnarok comes, the long night will black out Europe first. The prevailing winds are all westerly at high altitude. Go for Canada, Newfoundland if the plane won't make it to Canada. There'll be a hell of a lot of confusion, but you'll get through. Canada's got the longest undefended border in the world.'

He got up, walked to a porthole, looked out. 'You've really thought about this, haven't you?'

She stood close beside him. 'No. Honestly. Not until this moment.' Once again, she touched his arm. 'Promise me you'll go. Promise me you'll write the story. There'll be lies, excuses, so much nonsense. Promise me you'll write the truth.'

'And if none of this happens? If you get your treaty?'

'Then somebody in the world, just one person, will know the truth. Not to write about it, simply to *know.*' She pulled him round to face her. 'Promise me, Pétur.'

'But if you get your treaty you'll be able to go yourself.'

She frowned. 'We'd be mad to rely on it. Free pardons all round? After what happened to Fard?' They stood in silence for a moment. 'Hope for the best, Pétur, but prepare for the worst . . . and if the best happens, I'll meet you in New York. Won't that be a happy day?'

She needed his commitment. Whatever happened, he now saw as clearly as she did, they wouldn't be meeting in New York. With the tips of his fingers, he pushed back fine strands of hair from her wide, unlined forehead. 'I promise you, Colly Graham.' He put his arms gently around her shoulders, held her close. 'You're brave, and you're crazy, and what you're doing is terrible, and it's marvellous, and I love you, and one day we'll sit together on some sunny beach somewhere, and remember these desperate times, and be glad they happened, and be glad they're over. And I love you.'

And at last, after so long and so much, she wept.

He stayed on the ship until darkness fell. For much of the time they sat together in the wardroom. Colly slept, trusting him, hunched up in the corner of a leather settee. Pétur watched her. He watched her face, every curve, every bone, every line, every hollow. He learned her.

At six Flynn came through, on his way to relieve Werner. He checked when he saw her, and walked more softly. Colly scarcely moved. He collected the coffee pot from the table, renewed it, filled mugs, went up on to the bridge. Pétur followed him. The cove was mirror-smooth now, the black cliffs climbing above their immaculate reflections. A fine haze softened the sky. The Russian campers had lit a small fire of driftwood, and a grey strand of smoke hung vertically in the still air.

Werner reported a helicopter flying westwards along the coast some forty minutes earlier. It might have been the coastguards. It had hovered off the mouth of the cove for a couple of minutes, then continued on its way.

The three men didn't talk much. Their companionship was too recent, too soon to end, and uneasy. Werner went below as soon as he decently could. Flynn wasn't bothered by long silences between himself and Pétur. He occasionally drank from his flask.

As the sun was setting, Colly appeared at the top of the companionway. The round of conversation and food was resumed. Plans were made.

Darkness came. They waited another hour. Pétur's only means of return to the city was his car, parked up on the road. If that had been taken, he faced a long walk. And there was uncertainty about the opposition's plans – whether they'd let him return to Reykjavik, or whether the Russians might try to take him before he even reached the car.

The night was motionless, its stars obscured by the haze. The

motorboat was still in the water. Colly took Pétur silently down
into it. They cast off and paddled, unknowingly following Kassim's
example, drifting wherever possible, to the shore. The water was
silky, breaking in faint tiny ripples on the stones. Pétur stepped
quietly out before the boat grounded, and held it off.

'I must go now.'

Suddenly they were parting. She touched his hand on the bow,
gripped it fiercely. Her face was no more than a pale oval in the
darkness.

'Drive carefully.'

'And you.'

He lurched sideways, trying to keep his footing on the uneven
pebbles. The boat slid away on the next wave and the contact was
broken. Its black bulk disappeared into the night. He stood for a
moment, staring after it, the water lapping round his shins. Then he
turned away, waiting.

Ten minutes later a blaze of light showed on the *Fimbulvetr*. Her
engines started. There was activity on deck, a clatter of winches. She
seemed about to put to sea. Under cover of the noise Pétur began
laboriously to climb the cliff face, keeping well away from Big
Brother's ledge.

After half an hour or so the *Fimbulvetr* quietened. Her engines
died, and one by one the lights went out. The panic, whatever it had
been, seemed to be over.

By then Pétur was at the top of the cliff and making his way back
across the springy arctic grass to where the road must be. Although
helped by a faint glow from the rising moon, it was an arduous
journey. The cliff top was gullied and treacherous, but he dared not
stray too far from its edge, since that was all he had to steer by.

He'd left the cove behind. On his right the valley grew shallower.
He slowed, wary of blundering on to the track that led down to the
beach and the Russian camp. When he reached it, he waited, quite
motionless, for a full five minutes by his watch, listening for guards.
Nothing moved. No match flared, no foot grated, no cough was
suppressed. He went slowly on up the hill to the road.

A hundred metres from the Toyota he stopped again. If the
opposition was going to get him, this was where they had to be. He
could see the car, outlined against the sky. The road ran across

barren scree, no vegetation other than mosses and lichens. Nothing save the car broke the broad expanse of smooth hillside. He advanced slowly, eyes wide, straining for movement, for the unexplained shape, for the reflected glint in eyes like his. Still nothing. If the Toyota was under surveillance, he decided, it must be from a great distance. And there was only one way to find out.

He strode up the last few metres to the car, feet scrunching on the scree.

Suddenly the Toyota's interior light came on as the driver's door opened. Pétur ducked.

A man leaned out, featureless against the light. 'For heaven's sake, Pétur, stop playing games. I've been waiting hours. You took your time, getting here.'

Pétur knew the voice. He advanced, looked incredulously down into the car. Professor Valdason from Reykjavik University peered up at him over his bright little steel-rimmed spectacles. The physicist was smiling. He held in his right hand a small automatic pistol, aimed at Pétur's stomach.

14

Day Eight. AUGUST 11. WEDNESDAY.

In the administrative tower of the United Nations Building on New York's East River, lights always burned through the night. In some department or other of that vast organisation there were inevitably officials with briefs to study, computer programmers taking advantage of spare night-time capacity, delegates waiting for telephone calls, often from very different time zones. To those in the know, however, lights after eight or nine in the evening on the thirty-eighth floor suggested some manner of crisis. The Secretary-General had his offices there; and the Secretary-General worked enough of the daylight hours to feel justified, under normal conditions, in guarding his nights jealously.

A light burned in the Secretary-General's office now. The crisis he faced had changed its nature. For a week he'd survived it, managing on every evening but one – Sunday, an ugly time, best not spoken of – to be at home with his wife in their small Park Avenue apartment by midnight. The Secretary-General needed her strength and trust. But tonight he dared not face her. The crisis, acute as ever, had new knives. He wasn't yet ready.

On the otherwise empty desk top, Georg squared the edges of the transcript they'd brought him. They . . . nameless, nationless, powerful. He knew the transcript by heart. It was sanitised, obviously. Otherwise, why bother with a transcript, when they must have everything on tape? For his benefit they'd have tidied it up. They wouldn't hope, or even want, to fool him – rather, to spare him specific outrage. In consequence, the pictures that formed in his mind of Robert's interrogation were vague, their vileness undefined. He wasn't grateful for this. He wanted to know. He felt demeaned by not knowing. He owed his friend that much.

Ask Georg.

That was all that really mattered. Whatever had happened to Robert, he had told them that Colly would never press the button; and he was desperate that Georg should confirm this.

He got up. Leaving the transcript on the desk, he walked slowly to the uncurtained window. His single desk lamp was reflected in it, but the blackness of the rest of the huge single pane let through the midnight lights of the city. He stood looking down at the dark expanse of the river, the jewelled bridge that spanned it, the tower blocks high against the sky, the low bulk, on the far side, of factories bright with advertisement hoardings.

Ask Georg.

It was a burden he could have done without. They'd been very fair with him. They only wanted his opinion, nothing more. Just his personal thoughts. After all, he *did* know Colly Graham . . . not over the past few years, maybe, but as a girl, when such attitudes are formed. *She's full of her mother. Full of love.* Her mother, certainly, would never have been part of this madness. But then, he would never have imagined Robert to be part of it, either; and he knew Robert Graham better than anyone did, outside his family.

Would Professor Graham lie? If he wasn't lying now, then he'd been lying before, with his ultimatum. Was his word more to be trusted now, in statements given under duress? Or in a carefully prepared, long-planned statement, issued of his own free will?

They'd been very fair. All they wanted were his personal thoughts, as a friend of the family. And they didn't wish to exaggerate the importance of the question. There were many other factors being considered, many other pieces of the mosaic. But still, for completeness, they wanted his opinion.

As a friend of the family. It was an unfortunate choice of words.

But he'd told them. Because he was impartial, upright, a professional, and a friend of no family, other than the family of humankind, he'd told them the truth. His personal opinion was that Professor Graham had, for obvious reasons, lied in the ultimatum and during their subsequent telephone conversations. And that now, for equally obvious reasons, he was telling the truth. This meshed perfectly with Georg's personal knowledge of the Graham family, and of Colly Graham in particular. She was her mother's child; she'd never press the button.

Waiting until Pétur had gone round the car and climbed into the passenger seat, Professor Valdason turned the Toyota – awkwardly, the gun still in his hand – and drove off, back in the direction of Borgarnes and Reykjavik. With its rear window broken, the little car was draughty, and the wind whistled breathily past the bullet hole in the roof. For a while they drove without speaking. Pétur was reluctant to take his situation seriously. He'd known Willi Valdason slightly for years, as a tweedy, bespectacled little academic; now, he felt he was being made a fool of. He was damned if he'd humiliate himself still further by asking questions Valdason could choose not to answer.

Eventually Valdason put his gun in his pocket. Still in silence, he lit a cigarette. Pétur had never used the Toyota's lighter; he was surprised it worked.

Before Valdason had smoked enough for there to be any, he tapped ash into the tray. He was a mass of superfluous movements.

'I'm sorry about this morning, Pétur. It should have been so simple.'

'This morning?'

'Yesterday morning, by now. That cock-up over the car. Nothing unpleasant was intended. We only wanted to talk to you.'

'That's why they shot at me.'

'Wählin's good. If he'd shot *at* you, he'd have got you.' Valdason leaned forward, made sure for the third time that the choke knob wasn't still pulled out. 'He shot at the car. A lot of people give up when the other man shows he has a gun and will use it. You didn't.'

'Wählin may be good with a gun. His friend's a bloody useless driver.' Pétur, feeling a little better for having scored a point, watched the road rush by in the Toyota's headlights. 'Who's "we"? And where are you taking me?'

Two sheep loomed out of the darkness. Valdason avoided them. 'I hope I'm taking you back to your apartment.'

'I gather there's a condition.'

'You're a very favoured man, Pétur. Fate has placed you in a unique position. We – '

'I'm a reporter. I place *myself* in situations. And you still haven't told me who "we" is.'

Valdason tapped some genuine ash off his cigarette, tugged at his seat belt to make sure it was fastened securely, glanced in the mirror. 'Frankly, I'm surprised you ask. Obviously not the people who passed a certain packet on to you via Björn. Though we are supposed to be working together on this one. Who does that leave?'

Pétur smiled. '*You're* the KGB's man in Reykjavik?' Valdason didn't deny it. Pétur's smile died. He had to believe that the KGB knew their business. 'So you want to talk to me?'

'And here we are. Everything's turned out very well, in fact. This morning you might've had a harder time of it . . .' He pushed the sun visor up. It was already up. 'Look – can we save a lot of time, and assume you know why that ship's here, and why the whole area's crawling with special service people?'

'All right. But maybe I know more than you do. I'd like a code name first.'

'A code name?' Valdason frowned. 'Oh . . . that Voluspá thing. The twilight of the gods. *Ragnarok*. You've been reading too many spy novels.' He stubbed the cigarette vigorously in the ashtray. 'Anyway, knowing what you do, you're a lousy security risk. I've got colleagues who'd have had you dead days ago, long before you got this far.'

'I met somebody who had that idea.'

'Not one of mine.'

'You're saying I've got you to thank for a stay of execution?'

Valdason nodded. 'You won't like this. As head of station I told them not to worry. Told them you were a flashy performer, but lacked the stamina to follow through a serious story.'

'Not like it? If it saved my life, I love it. Somebody should have told Janssen.'

'He was Agency. Why should the Agency listen to me? But now the whole thing's academic. Your friends have got what they wanted. Well, they're about to.'

'You're joking. Last thing I heard, those bastards in Geneva were still shouting at each other.'

'They stopped a few hours ago. I have direct information that there's going to be a treaty.'

'I don't believe you.'

'Why should I lie?'

'To shut me up.'

'In which case you'd be rather foolish to tell me you don't believe me.'

They drove in silence while Pétur thought that one over. 'It was you who said I was the security risk. Why tell me anything?'

Valdason fiddled with the air vent, pressed the choke knob yet again. 'Which is why I'm going to all this bother. You've got more stamina than I thought. I'm going to be running a station here long after this little hoo-hah's blown over, and I don't want dead reporters muddying the water. The police hate it when local celebrities get killed.'

'I still don't get you.'

'Treaties take time. The itchy finger men don't like waiting.'

'Ah. So there isn't a treaty.'

'Certainly there is. It'll be signed tomorrow.'

'Treaties tomorrow. Never treaties today.'

Valdason took another cigarette from the packet in his breast pocket. 'Ask Björn Larssen. The Agency will have the same information.'

Pétur thought about it. He watched Valdason push up the sun visor again. 'You must've waited for hours. Why bother? Just to tell me the good news?'

Valdason shrugged. 'A demonstration. We don't like people like you thinking they can get away with things.' He looked sideways at Pétur. 'If you live, it's because we let you. Don't ever forget that.'

They drove on. Neither spoke.

Then Valdason slowed the car, peering. 'I'll be leaving you soon. Look for a Volvo estate.'

'I thought you said you were taking me home?'

'In this heap? Figure of speech. You can drive yourself.'

Pétur was relieved. Two hundred kilometres of Valdason would have been too much. 'So your lot are letting me live.' He tried to speak lightly. 'What about the Agency?'

'Fine, I expect. They gave you the tape to deliver, didn't they? Now it's all over, you'll be fine. As long as you keep quiet.'

Valdason flicked ash, glanced at his watch. 'By the way, what were you planning to do? If we hadn't met?'

'I'm not sure. Leave the country, maybe.'

'Oh, I wouldn't do that.' A parked car appeared ahead, a gleaming black Volvo estate, up on the verge. Valdason drew in behind it. 'Wouldn't look good, leaving the country. The itchy fingers wouldn't like it.'

'There's no need to, now.' Pétur turned to him, suddenly curious. 'Are you pleased? About the treaty?'

'Me? Makes no difference to me, old man. Still got my job to do.'

He opened the Toyota's door and got out. Pétur slid across into the driver's seat. 'See you.'

Valdason slammed the door, hesitated, then tapped on the window for Pétur to wind it down. 'You've talked to the Graham woman. You must know her pretty well by now. What d'you think she'd have done if her bluff had been called?'

Pétur craned to look up at him. 'What bluff?'

Valdason stood by the Toyota, thoughtfully slapping its roof with his palm. Then he walked away to the other car. The door was opened for him; he got in, and drove off. Pétur waited until the Volvo's rear lights had disappeared, then started slowly after them.

Robert had been released from the straps holding him down to the bed. Lanicane had been applied to the worst of his raw areas of flesh. He'd been washed a bit, helped into clothes, seated on a chair beside the old cast iron radiator, and handcuffed by one wrist to the radiator pipe. A man he hadn't seen before brought him a cheeseburger and a Pepsi. He'd have preferred water, but he drank the Pepsi. He didn't touch the cheeseburger. He didn't know he'd died. But he felt strangely disembodied.

Woolston, tied to his wooden office chair, was still in the room. He'd been given nothing to eat or drink, and his broken finger had been ignored. In the beginning, right after they were left alone together, he'd tried to talk to Robert. The old man had been unresponsive. Woolston seemed to want to console him. Robert had forgotten, did not know, why it was that he might need consoling.

He was remembering the house in Maine. Ruth on the porch, in

her Canadian rocker, Colly coming up the beach wearing the red
bikini with the silly little-girl frill. He knew that Ruth was dead, and
Colly far away, and that these were only memories; but they were
more real than the room in which he found himself. The brilliance
of sun on water dazzled his eyes. He could smell pine trees and hot
rotting seaweed. He could feel the worn wood-grain of the porch
handrail, the sand in its cracks. He heard Ruth's rocker creak, and
Colly singing Simon and Garfunkel as she ran, and the distant
waves hissing on the shore. The rocker creaked, Colly sang, the
waves hissed – it was a moment, perhaps, that had never been.

It was all their moments.

He wasn't mad. He understood that the handcuffs were real, and
the room, and why he was in it. He understood Woolston, and what
had been done to him. There was a ship, a bomb, an ultimatum.
There was Ragnarok. But Maine, too, was real.

He also understood that he'd been tortured. There, mercifully,
his understanding stopped. He had no curiosity. As he sat by the
radiator his eyes were closed for longer than they were open. He
didn't know he'd died, but his chest was bruised and painful, and he
thought he might be dying. The possibility didn't bother him.

It was dark outside the room. Another night. He liked the room,
now that it was quiet. He didn't remember when it hadn't been
quiet, but he knew he liked it better now. He'd been very happy in
this room, and hopeful. It wasn't much of a room, which maybe was
why it suited him. The feeling grew in him that he wasn't much of a
man.

People had loved him, though. His wife, his daughter – several
others, men as well as women. That had to mean something. Georg
had loved him. He smiled. He was thinking of himself in the past
tense. Maybe that was just as well.

The room's doorframe was splintered from having been kicked
open, but the wood had been roughly mended so that the door
could be locked again. Now it was unlocked from the outside, and
two men came quickly into the room. One of them Robert didn't
recognise. The other was the agent who'd brought him the
cheeseburger and the Pepsi. He went to Woolston, still tied in his
chair, and stood behind him. The first man moved Robert's chair
slightly away from the wall and stood behind him also. Robert

didn't identify the cold pressure on the back of his neck until he saw the gun against the back of Woolston's neck. His last thought was: at least they can't very well miss. He heard neither shot.

Colly stood the night watch. It began uneventfully: for some reason the Russians were giving them a rest. She almost wished they wouldn't. Their absence heightened the sense of expectancy, of agonised waiting for the next, inevitable crisis.

Whenever she dared obscure the surrounding silence, its unheard footsteps, its inaudible boarding parties, she listened to the BBC. The broadcasts gave her little comfort. In between the pop music and the sport there was a succession of news bulletins in which Geneva was mentioned last of all. A dismal succession of nil returns. A lull, like the Russians', and equally unpromising. It was Wednesday, now. They'd been in Helgavik for more than a week.

She paced the bridge, stared into the gloom, listened to the news. She decided to go down and check the trigger batteries. It was the routine she'd described to that other Russian, the man calling himself Ivan, on the tour of inspection so long ago. She never missed it. It made little sense, testing the batteries of a trigger that was inoperative, but she did it faithfully. It was part of the game she and Werner played. The actual bomb and the actual trigger. You had to play fair. Neglecting the batteries would be as much of a cheat as leaving the tritium out of the bomb.

She left the bridge, went out on to the moonlit upper deck, down the companionway to the wet lab door. The storm damage to Werner's lights hadn't been repaired, and the ship was in darkness save for a glimmer from the wheelhouse windows above her. She leaned on the rail, staring at the black bulk of the cliffs to starboard. Big Brother was up there somewhere, having another uncomfortable night. She wondered what he ever reported that could earn his keep.

She turned, went in to the wet lab, boldly switched on the light. In here, for as long as the opposition believed in the ultimatum, she was safe no matter what. She slid open the drawer under the aluminium bench top, depressed the test button on the battery casing. It buzzed at her vigorously, as it should. She released the button and was about to close the drawer again when her eye was caught by a tiny splash of red paint. Her heart missed a beat.

Since the panic over Kassim's bomb, they'd installed on the override a simple rocker arm, which showed a blob of green paint if the switch was on 'safe', and a blob of red if the trigger was active. They were still leaving it on 'safe' – the opposition wouldn't be any the wiser, and the risk of accidental detonation still seemed greater than the risk of being caught unprepared. Now, the red showed.

Impulsively, Colly reached down and pressed the relay. The indicator came up green. For a second she'd been horribly afraid. Now she relaxed. There'd been nothing to fear. Perhaps, at the worst, fear itself; but she'd long ago dealt with that.

So Werner had changed his mind. It had to be Werner who had reversed the relay – Flynn still assumed the trigger was always active; they'd never disabused him. Werner had done it without consulting her – yet he knew she checked the battery, so he knew she'd find out. He was telling her how he felt, but at the same time leaving the final responsibility to her.

She sighed. Their friendship had come to this. No more open discussion. Any communication between them, anything that mattered, now had to be at one remove, oblique, devious, a remote affair of implications and references. She wondered why he'd changed his mind.

Her first thought was to go straight down to his cabin and have things out with him. Her second was that if he'd wanted to explain himself he could have done so. Maybe she should respect his wishes. His reasons, anyway, weren't important. He was right – ultimately, the responsibility had to be hers.

She looked coolly down at the trigger, at its bright printed circuits and neatly organised components. It wasn't much. Maybe a hundred dollars' worth of metal and silicon, plastic and rubber.

She leaned on the edge of the drawer, resting. Let's face it, she told herself, everybody needs a framework of the permissible. Everybody needs to be told how far they can go. Otherwise all hell breaks loose. Once the checks had been supplied by the demands of elementary survival, then they'd been supplied by God. Now those two had run out of steam. So maybe it was all up to her. A salutary reminder. *Fimbulvetr.* The long winter. Time for humankind to rediscover its humanity, its relationship with the living planet. Time to cut out the cancer of western civilisation, eating away at Gaia.

Quickly, she flicked the relay back as Werner had wanted it, red blob showing. Sighing deeply, she closed the drawer on the active trigger. Fard, she thought, I hope you'd be proud of me. Did you ever guess that we were only bluffing? Well, now it's for real.

At six o'clock Werner relieved her. He didn't mention the trigger, and neither did she. No doubt he would creep down to check as soon as she was out of the way. They drank the coffee he'd brought, and watched the morning sky, cloudless, with the sun just clear of the headland to the east, cutting wide golden tunnels through the mist that lingered over the water. Then she went down to her cabin.

She had just undressed, and was washing before getting into her bunk, when Werner rang down to tell her that he'd had a radio message from the coastguards. They'd spotted the Beatle. The minisub was drifting, apparently undamaged, some fifteen kilometres out to the south-west; they'd bring it in to Helgavik once they'd got it on board, probably within the next two or three hours.

Colly was pleased. She didn't particularly want the Beatle back, but she welcomed the prospect of a visit from the coastguards. They smiled, and their lives were simple. Also, while they were around the Russians from the camp would behave themselves.

Pétur drove back to Reykjavik through the long dead hours of the night. He chose the most direct, obvious route, and he drove cautiously, inviting interference but ready to take evasive action. He reached his apartment without incident. So Valdason, it seemed, wielded all the clout he claimed.

It was scarcely dawn when Pétur got home, but he called Björn immediately. The bell rang for a long time. He waited.

The bell stopped. 'Hello?' Coughing intervened.

'Björn – it's Pétur. Listen, I'm sorry to wake you like this – '

'Pétur? Where the hell are you? D'you know what fucking time it is?'

'Björn, I'm sorry. It can't wait. Listen. I delivered your packet. I just got back from – '

'Fine. That's fine. I'm really glad you woke me with the news. I hope you've got something else for me.'

'Valdason gave me a lift. Professor Willi Valdason.'

'Ah.' There was a pause. More coughing. When Björn spoke again his anger had been replaced by something close to fear. 'I don't want to know, Pétur. If Valdason's showed himself, I don't want to know. You're in right over your head. Over mine, come to that.'

'Don't be like that. You have your American friends, now I've got my Russian ones.'

'That's not funny. I warned you to keep out of this. I tried to stop you. It was all very well, hassling the Minister. I didn't know what was going on. Still don't. *I don't want to know.*'

'I'm not going to tell you.'

'Thank God for that.'

'But I need a favour. A little favour, Björn. Ring your American friend. Ask him about Geneva.'

'Geneva? Are you crazy?'

'Just ask him, off the record, *Is there a treaty brewing?*'

'What fucking treaty? And what the hell has this got to do with —?'

'Just ask him, Björn. Call him now. Tell him I delivered his tape. No favour he can do me will ever make up for that.'

'Now? At this hour?'

'Just ask him. Tell him Valdason suggested it. And call me back.'

He rang off before Björn could give him any more flak. He undressed, got ready for bed while he was waiting. He wanted to be in the office when it opened at eight thirty, but the way he felt, he knew he'd be glad of even a couple of hours sleep.

Björn called back in a little more than ten minutes. His American friend had confirmed that a treaty was imminent. Björn hadn't asked what treaty, and he didn't want to know. He just wanted Pétur to remember that he was booked out with Finnur to Braeddalshöfn in the morning. A land agent would be there, expecting them.

Pétur thanked him, told him not to worry about Braeddalshöfn, wished him sweet dreams, hung up. He stood for a moment by the phone, grinning like an idiot. Valdason hadn't lied. The crazy, wonderful people on the *Fimbulvetr* had won.

He snatched up the handset again, eager to ring the coastguards, get a message to Colly. Then he checked himself. What could he say, through a third party? And the treaty hadn't yet been signed; nothing was public. Snags could develop. He'd be foolish to raise their hopes.

They had official lines of communication established; his bungling efforts to help would most probably confuse things. Valdason had promised a signing in the morning; that would be time enough to talk to Colly.

He went to bed, turned out the light, lay staring blindly at the ceiling. Somehow, he no longer felt sleepy. Where did all this leave him? He'd promised to go to New York. She'd wanted somebody, just one person in all the world, to know the truth. And he'd made his promise. Not to write the story, simply to know the truth.

He heaved himself over, lay on his side. He already knew the truth. All that way – it made no sense. Christ, what a romantic the woman was. All the way to New York just for some stuff in a mailbox that probably wasn't worth the disks it was printed on. And Icelandic TV had a New York representative, anyway. Couldn't he pick up the stuff, send it over in the bag?

Pétur tossed restlessly beneath his duvet. He felt sticky. He should've had a shower. What time was it?

He'd given his promise. But Valdason had advised him against leaving the country. *If you live, it's because we let you.* Balls. It was just melodramatic crap. But still, New York flights cost a fortune – and he'd already used up this year's vacation.

He remembered the tape, and his excuses shamed him. The old man, Colly's father, had suffered horribly. For Pétur now to grudge him even so inadequate a mark of respect was disgusting. An insult. He'd keep his promise. He and Colly would meet in New York. And what a day, he thought, that will be. He slept.

Finnur had been waiting for him at the office for twenty minutes, his gear ready. Pétur was late, but no later than his colleague was used to. His first impulse on waking had been to scrub the Ashkenazy assignment and let Björn do his worst. But discretion suggested that he might want to work again: he'd got used to eating. And besides, the Icelandair flight to New York didn't leave until six forty-five.

He let Finnur wait a little longer while he went upstairs to Björn. Björn's main worry turned out to be that Pétur should understand that his involvement with the Americans was very recent, and only very marginal. He wasn't a spy, he'd never been a spy, and he was never going to be a spy. He had his job to think of, he was hoping to have his retirement deferred, and he didn't want any fuss. If Pétur wanted leave of absence to fly to New York, that was fine by him. He supposed he should be grateful that there was time to fit the Ashkenazies in first. Mrs Vladi was expecting them.

Pétur left instructions with his secretary to book him on the New York flight, and went back down to Finnur. The gear was in the cameraman's venerable Saab station wagon. Settling back into the passenger seat, Pétur looked out through the window and noticed for the first time that it was a beautiful morning.

Finnur drove noisily. His car seemed to have lost synchromesh on most of its gears.

'So? How was it?'

'How was what?'

'You went to Helgavik, remember?' Finnur was heavily sarcastic. 'Showed that woman the discs.'

Pétur tried to recall how much Finnur already knew. This wasn't going to be easy.

'I'm sorry, Finn. The whole thing's out of my control. There's nothing I can tell you.'

Finn stiffened. 'That's not good enough.'

'It's pretty bloody, Finn, I know that. But what can I do?'

'You can stop playing silly buggers. I've been in on this from the start. It's our story. You can't – '

'But that's the point. There is no story.'

Finnur changed lanes, swore, slowed and waited to turn left. 'You mean the Minister's gagged you.'

'Piss off, Finn. You know me better than that.'

'What then? You rush off, full of this story Björn's going to be begging for crumbs of, and now there's nothing. *Somebody's* got to you.'

'Nobody's got to me.' Pétur ran his fingers distractedly through his hair. 'You're just going to have to trust me. If there was a story, you'd have it. You know that. The woman explained about the radiation. I believe her. End of story.'

'So what was the explanation? You must think I'm really dumb. I was there when that diver attacked you. And then you had that fight with your burglar. Come on, Pétur, what was the Graham woman's explanation?'

'All right, Finn.' Pétur gave up. 'So there is a story. We can't use it. I can't use it, you can't use it, nobody can use it. OK? So what use is a story nobody can use? So there isn't a bloody story. OK?'

Finn hunched his shoulders. 'Not by me it's not OK.'

Pétur lost his temper. 'It's all you're fucking going to get,' he shouted. 'So bloody well forget it!'

They drove the rest of the way to the airstrip in silence. They were late; the time was already nine thirty. It was a long flight to Braeddalshöfn, perhaps three hours. But Mrs Vladi was expecting them.

On his stool at the rear of the British survey vessel's bridge, Commodore Harry Harker was stoking up his ulcer. A US Navy career officer, on permanent secondment to his country's Delta anti-terrorist force, Harker was a wiry, tense-faced black man who seemed to live always on the edge of a nervous breakdown. He glanced at his watch. They were running late. There'd been intolerable delays transferring the minisub from the plane at Keflavik. They'd told the target ship two or three hours. They'd never make it.

The operation was his. Below him, among the small army of men in the *Roebuck*'s waist, were the two Marine sergeants and the petty officer helmsman who'd been with him the last time he'd sailed these waters. The *Roebuck* was in Faxaflói – the bay of Faxa – fifteen nautical miles to the south of Helgavik, and closing fast. Harker was keeping his promise, the promise he'd made to them, and to Captain Zebedee, his murdered friend. Like General MacArthur, he was returning. And this time, those crazy fucking peaceniks were going to pay.

He'd been in on Operation Sweet Talk all the way. And the waiting had burned him up. All those planners, those generals, those admirals, all with their teams of ass-licking advisors, and all of them scared shitless, every one of them had to put in his fucking two bits' worth. And after that it had still had to go across to the Russkies for the same fucking treatment. The miracle was they'd got the show on the road this side of Christmas.

He gripped the rail behind him, arms spread wide, and stared out ahead of the ship, willing it to move faster. He knew he wasn't really being fair. In fact, once the right intelligence had started coming in, they'd put the operation together faster than skinning a raccoon. Hell, the first real breakthrough had only come yesterday, just after the storm, when the communications guys struck gold with a report from the target ship's captain that his minisub had been carried away in the night. Sweet Talk needed a pretext; that gave it to them.

Then, only a couple of hours later, the news from Italy. They'd suspected for days that the Libyan plastique expert wasn't on the ship, but it wasn't a thing anybody cared to take a chance on. Local conditions were poor. Direct surveillance was too long range, the guys on the water could only do a limited job, and the bugs had all been discovered. The positive identification from Rome was a gem. The one member of the team definitely known to be a killer – apart from that bastard Irishman – the one person whose profile suggested he really might pull the plug, wasn't there to pull anything.

Up until then, the Kremlin guys in particular had dragged their feet. Harker had never taken the actual bomb all that seriously, but they did. Maybe he didn't altogether blame them – he reckoned they had most to lose. Not that either side really believed in the nuclear winter bit, which was a tired old bogeyman. But the Russkies knew fallout, and they knew prevailing winds, and the two together spelled bad news for the Soviet Union. But once they'd checked the Rome stuff, and the psychological profiles on the other three woolly liberals, then all the lights were turning green.

And now the latest information from New York was that Harker had been right all along. New York said it had independent confirmation that the *Fimbulvetr* crowd really were as soft as they looked. It was all a bluff. The only hard man on the ship had been the Libyan, and he was gone.

Harker wasn't surprised. He'd seen terrorists before, in Munich, and again in Jerusalem. Hard-faced bitches and sons of bitches, every one; the Graham girl was just too goddamned all-American. Spunky as all-get-out, but no way was she going to incinerate the folks back home. The German might have had it in him – a pale, fanatical look. You couldn't trust the Krauts, anyway. But everything about him said he'd leave the big decisions to others. The Irishman Harker didn't know about. He'd been up on the bridge, mostly out of sight, and he was the one who'd shot Captain Zee. He was the one Harker would go for first. All Irishmen were murdering mothers. But cowards, like the IRA baby killers.

But it made no never mind. He wasn't taking any chances. Whichever one he personally wanted first, all three of them on the target ship were due for the chop. Short and sharp. All at once, if the plan went right. Sweet talk them out on to the deck, then sweet talk them to death. Murdering bastards.

This morning, too, with any luck they'd be caught off guard. News should have reached them by now, from a guy they trusted, that a treaty was on the way. They'd want to believe him. After eight long days of constant psychological pressure they'd be wide open. Easy meat.

The *Roebuck* steamed northwards, making a steady twelve knots against the light head wind. The sky was clear, the time nudging eleven hundred. Harker glanced at the chart. They'd be in Helgavik within the hour.

He looked around at his companions. This was an incredible fucking operation. He'd never thought to see American, British and Russian naval officers together on the bridge of a ship heading for combat. Harker himself was top banana, but the ship was British, with a fair haired, rugger-playing British glamour boy, Lieutenant Dunbar, in command. Harker's number two was Captain Boris Grabov of the Soviet navy, a bulky Georgian with excellent English, a broad sense of humour, and a sharp eye for operational efficiency. The *Roebuck* was a coastal survey vessel of the deer class, brought up from the Irish Sea at twelve hours' notice, on account of her passing resemblance to an Icelandic coastguard patrol vessel. She was flying the British flag now, but would enter Helgavik under Iceland's red and white cross on a blue ground. Her name had been painted out, and *Thor* substituted – a name not in current Icelandic coastguard use, but plausible. A 57 mm gun, such as the Icelanders favoured, had been installed on her foredeck to complete the picture.

She was a sturdy craft, twenty metres longer than the target ship, and in place of her usual motorboat she carried a research minisub, identical to the Beatle, slung from her starboard davits. The submarine had been requisitioned from a Hebridean oil base, flown up to the NATO base at Keflavik; the yellow paint on it was still drying. The wreck of the *Fimbulvetr*'s own sub had been spotted by a helicopter patrol at the base of cliffs some five kilometres to the east of Helgavik.

The plan was simplicity itself, like shooting herrings in a barrel. Harker's one regret was that he had to leave the front stuff to someone else. Although, in uniform, he didn't look much like the indolent designer-chic negro photographer who'd gone in with Captain Zee, there was no way he'd take a chance on being recognised. Captain Grabov, in his ambiguous white shirt and dark trousers, would handle PR. His excellent, slightly-accented English made him an Icelandic coastguard captain to the life. Harker's place was by the radio, inside the wheelhouse, getting the act together.

It needed some getting together. On land was the American cliffside observation post: six marksmen, usually on four-hour watches, camped in a shallow treeless valley on the far side of the headland. Four of these, armed with their own choice of high-velocity weapon, were already in position, spaced out along the shore. If Harker knew his men at all, the two off-duty snipers were undoubtedly unofficially backing them up.

Afloat in the cove were the Russians, four armed men in the dinghy with grapnels and full boarding gear, and four swimmers with grenades.

And there were the men in the *Roebuck*. Twenty anti-terrorist specialists, in two teams, Russian and American. They'd been training since Day Two of the countdown, on an accurate mock-up of the target ship, lying in Canadian waters.

Harker's orders were simple, and clear. Go in nice as pie. Wait until Grabov sweet-talked all three members of the target ship's crew up on deck. Take no chances. It didn't matter what Harker believed, or what the New York source said. Take no chances, line them *all* up, ready to welcome their lost minisub. *Then* waste them.

Harker grinned. All this complicated fire power, when all it needed was one guy with an Armalite. But the evidence suggested that when there were visitors one of the *Fimbulvetr* crowd always stayed up on the bridge. And that posed some minor problems. The bridge was equipped with its own over-ride relay, and a guy standing beside it couldn't reliably be picked off in one. Just in case New York was wrong, therefore, sweet talk came first. Take no chances. If necessary, the orders insisted, leave the submarine and split. Time was on their side. But Harker had no intention of splitting. With this firepower, it wouldn't be necessary.

He stared past the helmsman, out over the *Roebuck*'s bow. Already the naked towering cliffs of the Thórsnes peninsula were in sight, and snow-capped peaks beyond them. Deliver the submarine and run? Not on your fucking life. He'd run last time. Then, he'd had no alternative. But he wouldn't run again.

In Helgavik the Russians seemed in an odd mood. There were only four of them in the dinghy, instead of the usual jolly crowd. They waved less, and kept their quilted jackets primly closed. Obviously they had guns: Werner wondered why they bothered to conceal them. Occasionally he saw a line of bubbles that might come from a diver. Well, that was nothing new. He kept careful watch, on edge for the arrival of a grapnel.

Colly was below decks, in her cabin. He hoped she was sleeping. The Russians circled the ship, talking loudly in English amongst themselves, commenting on the rusty condition of the *Fimbulvetr*'s hull, wondering whether she'd last the remaining six days of the countdown.

Werner hefted the rifle, his hands shaking slightly. He wasn't sure why he didn't shoot the four of them – bang-bang-bang-bang – and any divers he caught sight of. It mightn't help the *Fimbulvetr*'s image, but it would sure as hell give them a bit more peace for the rest of the week.

Flynn had kept him company for a time, but he was down in the engine room now. Routine maintenance, he said. As if there were any chance that this ship would ever be going anywhere again. Be better off shooting a few Russians while they could.

He'd checked the wet lab. Colly hadn't said anything, but the relay was as he'd left it. What was there to be said, after all? He remembered the words of the reporter: *a clean new beginning has its attractions*. All they needed now was the excuse. For Colly's sake, he'd wait for that. He glanced at the over-ride relay, close by his left hand. It was tempting, but for Colly's sake he would resist the temptation. No shooting of Russians, no activating of the trigger, as long as the opposition continued to play the game.

He realised how far he'd come. Since the days of his innocence, since the days of his youth, only a few months ago, to this. Old, so old. Innocent no more. *Almost* a professional. All he needed now was the excuse. A clean new beginning.

When the outside phone rang, Björn Larsen, feet up on his desk, was viewing some agency footage from South Africa through a decorative haze of cigarette smoke. His eyes still on the long untidy column of marching, fist-raised blacks, he lifted the receiver.

'Björn Larsen.'

At the sound of his caller's voice he leaned forward, punched the remote control, froze the picture. 'Minister. Good of you to call. What can I do for you?'

'You can tell me why you're sitting on the story of the research ship at Helgavik.'

Björn's feet came off the desk and hit the floor with a thump. 'Research ship? I'm sorry, Minister, I – '

'Don't mess me about, Larsen. A week ago it was the hottest thing you'd got. I'm not a fool – I know damn well there's something going on when you set your top tart on me.'

Björn relaxed. He looked at the hand holding his cigarette, saw it was trembling. He must tell his American friend he'd had enough. No more cloak and dagger. He wasn't up to it.

'Pétur Einarrson? I wouldn't say we set him on to you, Minister.'

'I would. Very adversarial . . . then he goes off and does his Dr Graham piece. Fine. Good, positive reporting. No complaints. And then what?'

'I'm not with you, Minister.' Björn drew on his cigarette. 'As far as I'm aware, we haven't mentioned the ship again.'

'Precisely. Yet your top tart has been out there again. It's a good story – pretty girl, prizewinning father, prospect of new resources. Yet you sit on it. Why?'

'It's a nice little story, Minister, but only worth so much time. In my professional opinion – '

'Balls. You people can spin out a story ad nauseam if you want.'

'I can only repeat, Minister; I viewed the footage Pétur brought back, and in my professional opinion – '

'Would it help, perhaps, if I dropped a tiny leak in your ear?'

If there was one thing Björn feared, it was a leak on this subject. *He didn't want to know.* As far as he was concerned, everything about that ship was bad news. But what choice did he have?

'Leaks always help. You know that.'

The Minister lowered his voice. 'Top tart was quite right.'

He paused. He needed connivance. Björn searched for another cigarette, mumbled as he lit it from the stub of the old one. 'He usually is.'

'Yes. The search for rare earths *is* a front. What Dr Graham's really expecting is uranium.'

'So why the front?'

'You know how it is. People get so excited. We planned to wait until she had something definite.'

'So why the leak?'

'Ah. Strictly off the record, then. The recent developments in Europe. The new central banking arrangements are putting heavy pressure on the krona. The Treasury feels that a rumour of valuable mineral deposits would give us a breathing space.'

After so frank and dangerous an admission, Björn felt a warm glow. He was prepared to help the Minister out. Yet he'd been warned that the entire *Fimbulvetr* operation was too hot to handle. Though what his American friend might know that the Minister didn't, he couldn't imagine.

He cleared his throat. 'There was that flurry about Dr Graham's father going missing. We could run an update on that, drop the word *uranium* in somewhere. Would that help?'

'Fine. Marvellous. There was never any intention to deceive, you understand. No dark conspiracy. Simple caution – that's all.'

'Of course, Minister. Simple caution.'

They laughed together. Then the Minister made his excuses, rang off. On the monitor in front of Björn, marching black men stood frozen, fists raised. He sat forward, killed the video, reached for a pad and pencil. He'd got a lot to do. The Minister would get his uranium mention. But if the currency weakened, there'd be a story in that, too. The trade relationship with Europe was always a thorn in the side of the administration. And of course the environmentalists deserved their say, once plans for extensive mining on the Thórsnes peninsula came to light.

He coughed, and began to make notes. Politicians thought the media such fools. He called his secretary, asked for a summary of what they had on the Professor Graham disappearance. Human interest. A peg on which to hang the story. And maybe the Minister.

15

In the engine room of the *Fimbulvetr*, Flynn straightened his aching back, wiped his hands on a bundle of oily waste. Reaching for a thin cigar from the top pocket of his dungarees, he bent it straight, lit it, and collapsed gratefully on to the bench below the main switchboard. The Maybach was a fine engine, but whoever had installed these two hadn't given much thought to the poor bloody engineer. You spent most of the time upside down, bent double, working in the dark with your elbow in your arse. And there was still the oil in the bloody reduction box to check. He mopped his brow, inhaled smoke deeply.

He remembered thinking, in the run up to all this, that he wouldn't have enough to do. That was a laugh. Not only the ship to mother, but the bloody crew as well. Green-eyed Adolf popping off at the Icelander. Colly weak at the knees. He'd seen it all, played dumb, kept things on an even keel. And when Einarsson finally went, oh the weeping and wailing . . . Would he make it to New York? Would he make it as far as his car even? And none of it what the trouble was really about.

The old man. Professor Graham. Her father. Her God. Christ, the opposition had a lot to answer for. She didn't want to tell him, didn't want to talk about it. In fact, it was the only thing she *did* want to talk about. But she couldn't. Ah, the poor girl. Wasn't love a terrible thing when it could hurt you so?

Adolf had a father too. Cold, his dark looks were, and easy to see why. His guilt years old, that's why. Walking out like that on father, mother, sister, home. No word of what might have happened to them in the troubles during the Gorbachev spring. And such demons men were for blaming themselves. And only yesterday, shit-scared in the storm, crying out to be made a man of. Ah, Flynn, Flynn, what a father you'd have made. The broadest shoulder to weep on in all the North Atlantic.

Six more days. If the opposition didn't pull something, six more days to coax them through, Adolf and Colly. He'd do it fine. The Prussian father to one, the guru father to the other. Just two kids. And he'd made a discovery – he loved them both. Six more days. Then, up with the wheelbarrow handles, a quick sprint down the slope, and blow the lot to buggery.

His cigar was burning his fingers. The bloody things didn't last these days. Another two puffs, then back to the reduction box. And while there he'd better check the shaft. During the storm, arse out of the water, she'd raced too often. And then, banging back down, stressed to all hell . . . He sniffed, wondering why he bothered. Another six days, and they'd all be blown to buggery.

He finished his cigar, stubbed it out carefully on the deck plates, rose from the bench, and made his way aft. The *Fimbulvetr* was a good ship. That was why he bothered.

Skirting the vast, snowcovered heights of Vatnajökull, the Flugstödin helicopter lifted in sudden up-draughts from the black basalt hills below. Pétur felt his stomach reluctantly catch up with the rest of him, looked down at the valleys swirling past, crevices growing like roots in the barren rock, up from the sea. The coastal plain was widening, and the shallow glacial lakes that once spilled icebergs into the sea were left behind. This was geologically the oldest part of the island, and the most stable. Lava beds had been laid down long enough to gather accretions of fertile soil. The glaciers had retreated, long-established fishing communities clung to the northern sides of the fjords, seeking the sun, and small red-roofed farmhouses dotted the treeless slopes inland.

But this was only a veneer on the rugged land beneath. From this vantage point, it was easy to see the whole island in the way that American astronomer had described it in the '80s. 'Scar tissue.' Solidified lava, scabbing over and healing a deep wound in the Earth's crust, a wound from which it had oozed like blood. A wound caused, according to that briefly fashionable theory, by the impact of a giant meteorite from space – an impact with such devastating repercussions for the globe that the last of the dinosaurs had died, sixty-five million years ago, under the shrouding layer of dust it had blown into the atmosphere. Pétur had covered the story. But he hadn't followed it up, and didn't know whether scientists still gave it credence. He would ask Colly. Icelanders, though, rather liked the idea that their home had been brought into being by the catastrophe that ended the reign of the dinosaurs – for, after all, it was the death of the dinosaurs that had opened the way for the rise of humankind. And some of the toughest specimens of humankind now lived on that geological scar tissue.

A tenacious people. Pétur loved them. He was one of them. And he knew, like them, that the area's equilibrium, whatever its origins, was precarious, tightly stretched. Although stable in human terms – four centuries with no significant volcanic activity – as the land masses of east and west moved apart, the thin layer of the Earth's crust that formed the scar tissue beneath him was continually tugged by tectonic forces. One day, that crust would tear. The catastrophe of Heimaey, on the same web of fault lines, was evidence enough of that.

A tenacious people indeed. He smiled, then felt ashamed. But he knew, thank God, that he could never really write them off, never write any living soul off, as lightly as, in a cynical moment, he'd pretended to Colly.

But that was in a different world, a different life. She'd staked everything on a dream, and the dream was coming true. Valdason had direct information; so had Björn. Why should they lie? He glanced across the helicopter's tiny cabin at Finnur. The two of them still weren't talking. Finn was bitterly resentful; understandably so. Pétur sighed. Once the treaty was public knowledge, and the *Fimbulvetr* team had gone home, perhaps then he could tell poor Finn the truth. For the moment they'd just have to work together as best they could. At least this Ashkenazy piece wouldn't strain their resources.

The pilot shouted something above the engine's racket and pointed down. Pétur narrowed his eyes, recognised the deep winding fjord of Djúpivogur. They were nearly there.

Harry Harker sat on his stool at the rear of the *Roebuck*'s bridge, agonising as Lieutenant Dunbar conned her in through the narrow entrance to Helgavik. *Leff*tenant, he called himself, in the stuck-up British manner – but he knew how to handle his ship. No crap with half a dozen different engine settings and as many course corrections. Just line her up and bang, straight in.

Harker relaxed. As the cove opened out beyond the twin headlands, the *Fimbulvetr* came into view. She was waiting for them, sharply outlined against the red-veined cliffs to port, just as Harker had pictured her. A thousand times, and more, he'd lived this moment; its stillness, its brilliance. In his imagination the sky was always as pale and clear as it had been then, the first time, and as it was now. The sky, the cove, the target ship. Everything perfect. He'd come back.

The *Roebuck* slowed, her bow settling, the Icelandic flag rippling on its staff. Her loudhailer came alive, hummed. Captain Grabov moved out on to the bridge wing, microphone in hand.

'Ahoy there, *Fimbulvetr*, Lieutenant Arason speaking. We have something that belongs to you, I think.'

The amplified words echoed between the cliffs. Seabirds rose in swirling clouds. On board the target ship nothing moved.

'Research ship *Fimbulvetr*. Ahoy.'

The *Roebuck* idled on, turning to close with the research vessel. Seamen in coastguard uniform were busy at the port davits, swinging out the minisub. Dunbar's intention was to come up on the stern of the *Fimbulvetr*, leaving her to starboard, the field of fire between them uncluttered. His was the larger ship, standing higher in the water. The men crouched in her waist and on her upper deck could stay out of sight until needed.

'We have salvage forms for you to sign. Permission to come aboard?'

Harker was on his feet now, still well hidden at the back of the bridge, talking urgently into his radio handset. The men on the cliffs behind the target ship had come in loud and clear. Now he was calling the Russians. He could see their dinghy, standing off some five cables on the target ship's bow. Karpovich was highly visible, his jacket zipped to the neck. The earpiece wasn't visible, but he'd need to be careful answering, even with a throat mike. Nothing must make the target ship's people suspicious. Everything depended on total surprise.

A man could be seen on the *Fimbulvetr*'s bridge. No beard, so it must be the German. Now a woman appeared on the after deck. Long blonde hair – even at five hundred metres, and if she hadn't been the only woman on board, Harker recognised her instantly. Dr fucking Graham; her *The last one to leave puts out the light* still stuck in his craw. Bluff or not, he didn't give a shit. He was putting out *their* light, the self-righteous mothers.

Dunbar slowed his ship, went gently astern. They needed to keep their distance. Two of the *Fimbulvetr*'s crew were in sight now. Harker just needed one more. He needed all three of them to be exposed; certain targets.

'Ahoy there, *Fimbulvetr*. Your little lost sheep has come home.' Sweet talk. Just the ticket. 'Permission to come alongside?'

A faint cry came back from the target ship's stern. Harker, who had just raised Karpovich on the radio, missed it. The Russian reported his divers in position, with grapnels. They could be on the *Fimbulvetr*'s deck in forty seconds.

'Great,' Harker told him, anxiously scanning the target ship for the third crew member. 'Well done, Colonel. Stay tuned.'

And thought, what a waste of fucking time. If it got down to using fucking Russki frogmen, the operation would be shitsville anyway.

He peered across the narrow strip of water. No sign of the Mick. They'd have to stall.

He leaned towards Dunbar. 'What did the bitch say?'

The Englishman grinned, tipped back his cap. 'I don't think she trusts my seamanship. She suggested we send the papers over in a boat while we're ditching the sub.'

'Judas fucking Priest. You think she's suspicious?'

'No reason. I'd do the same in her place. That old tub's not got so much paint she can afford to lose any.'

Harker frowned. It didn't fucking matter. The lines of fire from here were just about perfect. But where the hell was the murderous fucking Irishman? Deliver the submarine and run? Like hell he would.

Hanging head-down through an inspection hatch in the *Fimbulvetr*'s engine-room floor, torque wrench in hand, Flynn was straining to tighten a bearing ring. His toes scrabbled for a hold on

the deck plates and sweat ran out of his beard, down into his eyes.
He swore, softly and steadily.

Well beneath the ship's waterline, he'd heard the approaching
engines. He'd heard little ticks and scrapes on the hull also, nothing
unusual, just signs that the Russian divers were still in business. And
he'd heard, much more faintly and indecipherably, the other ship's
loudhailer. He rested, panting. He wasn't needed up on deck. The
coastguard ship could drop off the minisub, throw them a line, leave
it at that. They couldn't take her on board yet – they hadn't repaired
the gantry downhaul, the blocks lost in the storm. So she'd have to
wait, no matter what.

The other ship's engines had died to a rumbling idle. Two decks
above him Colly was shouting something about salvage forms.
Christ, she wasn't refusing to take the sub, was she? He couldn't see
the Icelanders taking kindly to that after all their trouble. He sat up,
listening. Beneath him, water sloshed in the bilge as the *Fimbulvetr*
rocked gently in the last of the other ship's wake. No, she was
asking for the Lloyds form to be brought over. A job for the
insurers. A bit academic, mind, when in six days they'd all be blown
to buggery.

He sighed, inserted himself back into the inspection hatch. The
wrench was at the end of its leverage. He shifted to the next, and
final, nut.

At Braeddalshöfn, the little Flugstödin helicopter was sidling in to
land. The town lay on a wide inlet, its level pastures shielded from
the sea by a curved sand spit. It was a prosperous settlement, one of
the prettiest along the coast, with good agricultural land and an
airstrip accessible in almost all weathers. Above it stood the little
ice-tipped peak of Prándarjökull, trailing a plume of cloud even on
this radiant day.

The airstrip, well kept, with decent modern buildings, was at the
north end of the valley, surrounded by hay fields. Several light
aircraft were drawn up outside the hangars, and on the taxiway a
twin-engined Britten-Norman Islander, one of Flugstödin's nine-
seater workhorses, stood with one of its propellers turning. Pétur
saw the other kick in as the helicopter settled on to the pad. Beyond
it the road into town led through meadows between the mountain

foothills. The town itself was visible, but further away than was comfortable. The time was already three minutes after twelve. He opened the helicopter's door, jumped down, waited for Finnur to hand out his boxes of tricks. A man in a neat grey suit, perhaps the airport manager, was approaching across the grass.

Pétur turned, looked back into the helicopter. Finnur was ostentatiously not hurrying. Pétur did a little dance on the tarmac, but said not a word. The late afternoon flight to New York wouldn't wait. Time was getting short. But if Finnur were hustled, he would take longer than ever.

The *Roebuck* had stopped. She lay astern of the target vessel, half a cable away on the port quarter, swinging on the tide. Harker waited, hidden at the back of the bridge. Soon, if Dunbar didn't fucking straighten her up, she'd foul the target ship's stern mooring. Meanwhile the men on the davits lowering the minisub took as long as they dared. Captain Grabov had left the bridge and was going through the motions of making ready to put off in the *Roebuck*'s tender. Around him, as he gave his orders, the bulwarks were lined with crouching marksmen, the top man in each of the two divisions equipped with an earpiece, like Karpovich and the snipers on the cliffs, listening in on Harker's net. One word from him, and the whole operation would spring to life.

On the target ship, the German had left the bridge and joined the Graham woman on the afterdeck. They stood at the rail, totally exposed, watching the *Roebuck*'s preparations. Harker pounded his fist against the bulkhead. Two shots, that was all it needed. Just two shots, and another for the Irishman. Where the hell was he? Come out, Mick. For fuck's sake, *come out.*

Captain Grabov cupped his hands to his face. The two ships were now less than a hundred metres apart.

'I will need a ladder,' he yelled. 'Please ask your captain to lower his ship's ladder.'

Harker tensed. Grabov was using his head. He watched the woman laugh, gesture apologetically, and turn away. *She was going to call the Irishman.* He gripped the handset.

'Wait . . . wait . . . he's coming, you mothers. Wait for the word. Cliff team take him if he makes the bridge. You've got the visibility.

Hang in there. He's coming. He's *got* to be. Wait for the word.'

But the woman had gone to the ladder winch herself. Now the German was helping her. They masked each other; a ventilator got in the way. There wasn't a hope of wasting them cleanly. The fucking Mick could present himself in full view on the bridge wing and take a round of applause, for all the good it would do now –

'*Wait*. Wait, you mothers. Wait for the word.'

And still the *Roebuck* was swinging. If the tide took her round any further the sight lines would mean his men would be shooting each other's heads off. Dunbar knew that. Why the hell didn't he do something?

On the target ship the ladder rattled down. At last Dunbar acted. He nudged the engine controls, and the *Roebuck*'s stern swung round a shade as the ship edged closer to the *Fimbulvetr*. The range was down to sixty metres. The Graham woman and her companion had returned to the stern rail, between the twin gantries. Dead ducks, both of them. Harker could see their faces clearly. The woman was puzzled, but not yet suspicious. It could well be the Icelandic flag alone that was keeping her sweet. For how much longer, he wouldn't like to guess.

'Wait, fuck it. Wait now . . . wait for the word.'

Flynn had got to thinking. Salvage formalities could be a bastard. Poor Colly wouldn't have a clue. It needed the professional touch. It needed him. He sighed. Hearing the *Fimbulvetr*'s ladder go down, he heaved himself out of the hatch in the engine-room floor and made his way up to the bridge. Surprised to find it deserted, he went looking for everyone. He noticed the rifle, still leaning against the radio table. He didn't take it with him. He'd no reason.

Out on the upper deck the sun was very bright. He squinted, saw Colly and Werner, their backs to him, silhouetted against the grey bulk of the other ship.

Harker was sweating. The Irishman paused in the doorway at the rear of the target ship's bridge on the starboard side, shading his eyes. Now he came forward to the top of the companionway leading down to the side deck. He paused again, staring across at the disguised *Roebuck*. Had the bastard spotted something? He was a big man. Standing there he looked eight foot tall, and just about as wide. Take no chances.

Harker gripped the radio handset till it creaked. 'Waste them,' he hissed into it. 'Waste the mothers. *Waste them.*'

Colly had turned, hearing the bridge door open and sensing Flynn's friendly presence behind her. She'd been worried by the curious silence on the other ship. Seeing Flynn reassured her. It was a beautiful day, and Flynn would sort things out. She smiled, touched Werner's arm, and he turned also. Still hopeful, the sun on her face, still believing they would succeed, she never understood the flail of steel that cut through her. It tossed her back from the rail, clear of the deck plates for seven feet or more, blood and brain and guts spraying.

Like her father, she had been prepared for death, if not its suddenness. The dead were dead. Suffering, and grief, were for the living. Her body struck a ventilator and slithered down, virtually every major bone in it broken. Werner's body lay close beside it, similarly destroyed.

To Flynn, on the upper deck, jolted, hit from shoulder to calf, it was as if he'd been massively struck by a shower of stones. He staggered, fell headlong down the ladder at his feet. He was struck again as he fell.

He could hear an alarming noise; a continuous ripping, tearing sound. By the side of his face the *Fimbulvetr*'s steel bulwarks bulged and rattled. He opened his eyes. Bullets? Jesus Christ – enough bullets to keep the IRA going to the end of the next century. And planned to be far enough from the wet lab not to disturb the trigger. So this was the opposition's grand affair. Well planned and smoothly executed. He grinned. It might've worked – the other two hadn't stood a chance, poor sods. He'd grieve for them later. Except that the opposition hadn't reckoned on Flynn, and there wouldn't be a later. An obstinate old bastard, Flynn was.

He started moving as the ripping sound stopped. The steel plates beside him were solid, the side deck was narrow, and the end of the deckhouse hid him from the other ship, lying astern and to port. He was safe. Fireproof. And he could see the door to the wet lab in front of him, only a few metres away. He'd pull the switch on them after all.

His movement wasn't exactly a crawl. He'd have needed the use of his legs for that. It wasn't an up-on-your-elbow-and-drag sort of progression either. He'd only got one elbow worth a damn. He wasn't in any pain; it was just that bits of him weren't working. But he moved nonetheless. Chin and left arm, mostly, with a bit of help from the local gods.

The bullets had stopped. Close above his head he heard a scraping clang. He looked up, saw one tine of a grapnel, precariously hooked over the bulwark, quivering as the man on the end of its rope tested it. He reached up his good left arm, lay sideways on the dead flesh of his right shoulder, and pushed against the rounded head of the grapnel. And pushed. It took more effort than he had expected, but he dislodged it. There was a satisfying splash from below as the climber fell back into the sea. He lowered his arm and resumed his forward movement.

The next grapnel to come in range he was able to dislodge before any great weight was put on it. Just as well. He was weakening. He found a need to rest. But at least that would have annoyed the bastards down in the water.

The deck plates beneath him were slippery. Blood stank sharply in his nostrils, and his body seemed to be lying in a puddle of the stuff. The door to the wet lab, secured open, was just an arm's length away. He started moving again.

He heard shouts. A diver's sleek head showed over the side of the ship. At the same time a grenade arrived. More shouts. The head, surprised, was quickly lowered. The grenade bounced on the deck, rolled, came to rest a few inches from Flynn, close in front of his eyes. He peered at it, and at the wet lab door just beyond. The grenade lay very still. He had lots of time. He had time to rub his tongue along his blood-wet lips. He had time to close his eyes, and rest. He had time to think, in precise words: *There's a big mistake, now.* And, foolishly, *Some poor bloody idiot's going to be in trouble for that.* And then time ran out.

At six minutes past noon on that summer's day, Wednesday, August 11, the Russian-made stun grenade exploded. The resulting blast activated the pressure trigger, which instantly sent its coded impulse to the detonator of the small, single-megatonne nuclear device lying in Helgavik, on the seabed little more than a kilometre away. From that moment on, significant units of time in the vicinity of the bomb came to be measured in millionths of a second.

In the first millionth of a second, eight evenly-spaced segments of plutonium, each the size of a baby's fist, were brought together by the chemical explosive in which they were embedded, releasing a blast of pure energy as they reached critical mass and the very nuclei themselves split apart. The heat generated by the fissioning plutonium nuclei produced a fireball with an immediate temperature of one hundred million degrees. Neutrons from this fireball streamed through the small mass of deuterium and tritium that made up the main fusion warhead, fusing them into nuclei of helium and releasing vastly more energy.

Then, still within this first millionth of a second, the outer mantle of uranium-238 was activated. Thus the creation of a one megatonne fireball, the explosive energy of one million tonnes of TNT, released but as yet contained within a volume measuring a metre or two across, was essentially complete. From then on, in the millionths of a second that followed, all that happened was that the fireball expanded.

Half its energy was directed upwards and outwards, through the water in which it lay. This it vaporised instantly, exposing the seabed to a distance of some three kilometres, and melting down to their component atoms all features within that radius, including the two ships and the cliffs themselves. Its upward progress released energy also in the form of light, a brilliance as intense as that of a thousand suns.

At the same time, because of the bomb's carefully chosen location, the rest of the fireball's blast was digging a crater through the thin crust of the ocean floor, expanding downwards to expose the glowing, bubbling magma, the fluid rock close beneath this most fragile area of the Earth's surface.

Already, in this second millionth of a second, Helgavik, everything upon it and everything within a three kilometre radius of the bomb, had ceased to exist.

As a broad, seething pillar of vapour began to rise above the site of the initial explosion, time resumed its more orderly, but no less inexorably horrific, progress. Out in the bay the walls of water, no longer held back by the force of the blast, fell inwards, covering the exposed seabed. But where there had once been cold rock there was now a bubbling pit of magma, a great wound in the Earth's crust, into which the waves poured.

Where the two met, the water cascading into the crater was engulfed by lava and turned to steam. Trapped in the superhot liquid rock, at pressures hundreds of times greater than normal surface pressure, this explosively expanding steam could only escape by blasting the lava apart. Which activity let in more water, creating a chain reaction, fed by the Earth's internal furnaces and ending only when the local reservoirs of magma were expended. By which time over two hundred cubic kilometres of molten rock, converted into a fine grey dust, and laced with minute droplets of sulphuric acid, would have risen on powerful convection currents to heights of eighty kilometres and more, creating a sunlight-excluding pall that would spread eastwards and southwards until it shrouded the entire northern hemisphere.

But for the moment the skies above the Thórsnes peninsula were relatively clear, dominated by a mushrooming pillar of dust and steam. Beneath it the mountains to the north, their foundations ripped away, slid majestically into the pit, pushing water before them in a growing wave that quickly spread beyond the visible horizon.

Within five minutes of the grenade landing on the *Fimbulvetr*'s deck, a vast crater, filled with sulphurous fumes and storming waters, split the peninsula virtually in two. And at its centre a new island grew, smoking and tossing out fire and white-hot boulders beneath impenetrable clouds that rained hissing fragments of rock, lava dust and a fine haze of acid droplets, so that the waters boiled again. And still the island grew, and burned, and poured forth its infernal bounty.

In Braeddalshöfn, his face to the distant explosion, Pétur caught its brilliance as a fan of pulsing, starkly-white light that climbed the sky in eerie stillness, reflecting haloes of blinding intensity off the icy peaks of Vatnajökull that lay between. He turned his gaze instinctively away, saw airport buildings colourless in the glare, long shadows black as night behind them.

The light passed, leaving time suspended, the countryside hushed, the birds silent. The twin engines of the Islander still roared, yet seemed somehow muted. A startled gasp from Finnur as he scrambled down out of the helicopter, a cry from the airport manager. They turned, stood motionless, staring.

The silence stretched. Pétur waited, sick at heart, filled with a deathly foreboding. A white cloud rose in the sky to the north-west. Muttering, Finnur bent his head, stooped to rummage in his camera bag. The movement seemed to free the other man, who broke away, in his neat grey suit, and ran back towards the airport buildings, stumbling and shouting unintelligibly as he went.

Then the sound hit them. It beat and thundered at them. It rolled back and forth between the mountains. Endlessly renewed, it tore down the valley, a force almost visible in its relentless power. Pétur bent double before it, huddled, covering his head. The ground shook. If a doubt had existed in his mind, none now remained. The *Fimbulvetr*'s bomb had exploded. Ragnarok was upon them. The end of the world.

The sound ebbed. It did not cease, but rumbled on like a distant summer storm, angry, bursting out and dying down, rattling its giant dustbins, unwilling to be still. Time moved on.

Finnur pointed, shaking Pétur's arm. He'd been shouting; now he could be heard.

'You see where that is? You see where that is? And you still say there's no bloody story?'

Pétur tried to break free. 'No story we could use.'

The cameraman held him fast. 'You're going to tell me, you bastard. We're going up there. And you're going to tell me.'

'Too late, Finn. We can't go up there. It's too late. We – '

A splitting roar sounded closer at hand, sharp, like a cannon. The helicopter pad was at the northerly end of the airstrip, close in under the hills. The tarmac shivered violently, and a black plume of smoke rose behind the high ground to the north-east.

'We're getting out, Finn.'

'Of course we are. I told you.'

Finnur released him, leaned in at the helicopter's door, shouted to the pilot.

Pétur retreated, called, 'I'm getting out of here. There's nothing you can do. Come with me.'

The roaring came again, continued, and the sun was blotted out by darkly rolling clouds. Pétur scanned the valley. It seemed to judder. The smoke to the north-east showed flashes at its base. Hot winds gusted. On the taxiway the Britten-Norman Islander was already rolling. Somebody else around here, at least, had the right idea. Get out.

'Come with me, Finny.'

Finnur turned. '*What?*'

Pétur cupped his hands. 'Come with me.'

'You must be crazy! This guy's going to take me over the glacier. It's the chance of a lifetime.'

'Don't do it, Finn. He's the one who's crazy. Tell him. That bloody clockwork toy will never make it. *Tell him!*'

Pétur began to run. He had to intercept the Islander. He reached the main runway, turned to look behind him. Finnur wasn't following.

The juddering of the ground had increased. He waved his arms wildly, backing out into the centre of the runway, keeping his eyes on the plane. He was almost at the turnaround, right in the Islander's path. The pilot held it on its brakes, gesticulating furiously, revving its engines until it danced on the nose wheel.

Pétur refused to be intimidated. He approached the plane, looking back over his shoulder all the time. To his right, one of the airport buildings sagged and collapsed. The air was thick with hot black cinders. Finnur was handing his equipment back up into the helicopter.

As Pétur reached the Islander's door a crack opened silently in the grass beside the runway. It spread in a jagged dark line, fast as a snake. The roaring had changed to a deeper rumble, and Pétur felt pressure build against his eardrums. The plane was rolling again even as he scrambled through the door. On the hillside behind the plane, telegraph poles lay at crazy angles. He wrenched the door shut.

'Wait,' he shouted. 'Wait . . .' He stumbled forward. The plane was empty except for the pilot. 'Two men in the chopper. Wait for them.'

It was too late. 'Fuck them,' said the pilot shortly. 'And fuck you, too.'

They were accelerating down the runway. As they passed the helicopter Pétur saw its rotor begin to turn. In front of the ruined airport building people were running aimlessly. The crack in the grass beside the tarmac was neither the only one, nor the biggest. The runway itself had sagged. Pétur saw the wing flex as the plane dipped into and out of the hollow. It was as if the whole valley were splitting in two.

And even above the din of the Islander's twin Lycoming engines the rumbling continued, growing louder and sharper. Closer.

The plane was gathering speed. Pétur crouched in a seat by one of its windows, gazing back. Smoke issued from the ground behind them. Thin lines of fire. The helicopter, still on the pad, leaned drunkenly. He couldn't see why. Its rotor spun in a fast blur, beating down waves of smoke and dust. Then a blade touched the tarmac, caught up the fragile craft and sent it cartwheeling away to explode in a ball of orange fire.

Desperately, the Islander's pilot flung his plane into the air. It staggered, caught in savage turbulence. Then it was clear, and climbing steeply away. Pétur stared bleakly at the burning wreckage of Finn's helicopter. Then he eased himself forward, into the co-pilot's seat.

'Where are we going?'

'I don't know.' The pilot was trembling, his face bright with sweat. 'Anywhere. Reykjavik. Anywhere. Christ. I don't know.'

Canada or Newfoundland, Colly had said. Pétur looked for fuel gauges, couldn't identify them among the banks of dials.

'What's our range?'

The man mopped his forehead. 'Extended wing version; fully tanked; two thousand kilometres.'

'We're all those things?'

The pilot nodded.

'Thank God for that. We'll go west then. First take a look at Reykjavik.'

The pilot didn't argue. He'd used up his decisiveness getting out of Braeddalshöfn. He settled on a westerly course. The coastline beneath them was clearly visible. It looked touchingly peaceful. But ahead of them, and to the north, an immense seething white tower rose into the sky, already unimaginably tall, higher than the highest clouds, still spreading and growing, and leaning, ever leaning, as winds of the high atmosphere pushed it eastwards. Not scar tissue, Pétur thought; just a scab over a wound that never healed. Now we've picked the scab off, unleashing the forces that finished the dinosaurs of humankind.

In Reykjavik the people were calm. There'd been volcanic eruptions before. Every Icelander lived with the possibility – geothermal heat warmed their capital city and provided the energy for the big diatomite plant near Myvatn. Admittedly this present eruption was larger than most, and closer to the city, but a reassuring official government statement had been broadcast over the radio and TV: the emergency services were standing by, low-lying areas were being evacuated in case of a tidal wave. Mostly, the eruption was a lunch-time event, an occasion for office workers to crowd into north-facing windows and watch the awe-inspiring display taking place two hundred kilometres away across the bay.

Björn Larsen, although no scientist, knew enough to take the situation more seriously. He had contacts in government, and the phone in his third-floor office on Langavegur had been busy ever since the flash of the first catastrophic explosion and the shock wave that followed it, rattling the city's windows. Reports were streaming in. Björn was trying to correlate the information, and had been in touch with the physics department at the University. The picture wasn't good. The scale of the communication blackout suggested that the entire Thórsnes peninsula and much of the adjoining mainland had suffered major devastation. Air reconnaissance described the area as covered by a low-lying ash cloud so thick as to disable any aircraft venturing into it. Very little, frankly, was known for certain. International sources were reporting a seismic event of major – some said record – proportions.

If Björn gave a thought to the research vessel *Fimbulvetr*, it was simply as one casualty among many. Similarly, Pétur and Finn only entered his mind as two members of his team whom he wished he had available for local work. He knew there'd been associated seismic activity around Braeddalshöfn, but even if they brought back film it would be tame stuff compared with what was going on just up the coast.

The NATO base at Keflavik was in turmoil. Every plane seemed to be taking off, every ship putting to sea, and nobody would tell him why. His American friend had completely disappeared.

At around one thirty, some ninety minutes after the first explosion, reports began to come in from coastal towns and villages on Faxaflói, outside the main devastation area. Björn didn't believe them. They introduced a new word, *tsunami*, tidal wave. They spoke of a tsunami thirty metres high. How could you measure a wave like that? It would be twice as high as his office window. The stories must, understandably, be exaggerated.

At two fourteen, one hundred and twenty-eight minutes after its convulsive birth in a volcanic crater two hundred kilometres to the north, the wave struck Reykjavik. Its height was, in fact, greater than advance reports had suggested, increased by the shelving of the seabed at the southern end of Faxaflói. It passed effortlessly over the islands of Engey and Videy, engulfed Sundahöfn and the houses and parkland north of the city, swept on undiminished. Simultaneously Orfirisey disappeared, and the harbour. Boats rode its crest now, sliding over rooftops.

It broke massively against blocks of city shops and office towers, surged between them, bringing many down and leaving the rest leaning and ruined. The ground before it shuddered. Björn, drawn at last from his desk to the window by the darkness and thunder of the wave's approach, looked into its foaming, cavernous face and knew he was a dead man.

Out of a population in Reykjavik that day of more than a hundred and fifty thousand, fewer than ninety thousand survived the tsunami's immediate passage. Many of these were to die in the aftermath – of injury, disease, and the grudging relief aid sent by a northern Europe struggling to adjust to new conditions. The power base was shifting. Ghadaffi, prompted by his friends, was fortifying his coastline against the first desperate waves of refugees.

Pétur Einarsson and his pilot arrived over Reykjavik a quarter of an hour after the wave had passed. The pilot made no attempt to land, either there or at Keflavik. Both airfields were covered with debris; landing would have been impossible. Unprepared by confused radio reports received during the flight from Braeddalshöfn, what the two of them saw convinced them both that – given the Islander's fuel capacity – Greenland, seven hundred kilometres away to the west, was their only possible destination.

They didn't speak. The pilot flew low over the harbour area, where houses had been wiped clean from the surface of the Earth, and there was no sign of life. Pétur looked down on the ruined city, his city, and wept. He wept for Reykjavik, and for its dead, and for his father, inevitably lost in the total devastation that must surround Helgavik.

The pilot, in shock, his eyes dry and unnaturally bright, flew the two of them safely across the Denmark Strait and landed at Angmagssalik. That same night he committed suicide, cutting his wrists in a concrete toilet block on the airport grounds.

Pétur found the pilot's body. He also found his passport. It listed the pilot's next of kin as his wife; there was an address, somewhere down in the new development on the far side of the harbour from Reykjavik city centre. In his wallet was a picture of a pretty young woman with a child, perhaps two years old.

The passport was useless without doctoring, but Pétur pocketed it anyway, together with the keys and documentation for the aircraft. He flew out for Nanortalik and then Newfoundland the following day. He lacked his own passport, and credit cards drawn on Icelandic banks were now meaningless. But many Greenlanders, especially those with access to official information about the scale of the events to the east, wanted out; possession of the Islander made him a popular man. He claimed to be a schoolteacher, Asgeir Sigurdsson, found an eager pilot, and bartered seats on the plane for fuel, and money, and an official blind eye. The Islander left Angmagssalik early in the morning, with three policemen and their families on board, and a senior customs officer. Pétur never knew how lucky he had been; another two days into the emergency and the plane would simply have been taken from him.

Newfoundland immigration authorities at Gander would have liked to send Asgeir Sigurdsson back to his homeland. He was a man without documents, a refugee. But all air transport was reserved for relief services, so they released him into the care of the Norwegian consul. Half an hour later he slipped out of the consul's office for a packet of cigarettes and never returned. It was a busy time. No very serious inquiries were pursued. He made it across the island and took ship for Halifax, Nova Scotia. He wasn't the only person moving south that August with inadequate papers.

EPILOGUE

It was August 11 again. Pétur woke early, before dawn. For weeks he'd been dreading this anniversary. Memorial services, gun salutes – and then parades. Americans were great ones for parades. The prospect made him shudder. It was too soon; he wasn't ready.

He got up. Treading softly between the still-occupied mattresses surrounding his spot on the floor, he left the hotel room and padded down the ten flights of stairs to street level. He used the men's room in the adjoining foyer; sometimes it had hot water, but not today. He stripped off his quilted anorak and shirt – he'd slept fully clothed – and washed in cold. He stared at himself in the flattering, amber-tinted mirror. Today was his beard's anniversary also. From Angmagssalik on he'd carried no razor. He didn't want to be reminded about the pilot.

He went looking for coffee. He was an American now – his day started with coffee or it didn't start at all. The machine in the foyer had been mended. Cockroaches scattered around it – Miami was dangerously overcrowded, and for every extra guy count five hundred extra roaches. The machine supplied a plastic cup of something wet, hot and brown. He took it out past the bored night security man, through the dented steel hotel doors, and sat with it on the low parapet bordering a clump of palm trees and sea grape. The palm trees were tired, and the sea grape didn't look too good either. He scuffed the littered sidewalk. He was an American now.

He looked out across the empty eight-lane boulevard. Beyond it lay the beach and the sea, invisible in the darkness. By now dawn had probably broken, but it wouldn't get itself noticed for a while yet. An armoured patrol car cruised by. He watched it indifferently. He wasn't, in fact, legally an American, but he'd long since given up holding his breath every time a policeman looked at him. He taught school, just down the street. The city needed him. With so many kids down from the north it needed all the teachers it could get. Since they were paying him only half the going rate, they must know he was an illegal; but since they didn't turn him in, he knew he was indispensable. It was a worthwhile bargain.

Peter Anderson, schoolteacher. He'd moved fast, believing all that Colly had told him.

Others hadn't moved so fast. For a while – two or three weeks – the Canadian government had been able to hold its people. Look at the terrible things happening in Europe. Don't make the same mistake. Wait and see. The scientists could be wrong.

And other scientists could always be found to say they *were* wrong. Just as there were scientists willing to declare the Helgavik eruption an entirely natural event. Some might study their readings and think otherwise, but the 'natural event' theory was the official line. And who was he, Peter Anderson, schoolteacher, to argue?

Pétur finished his coffee, crumpled the cup, and tossed it to join the rest of the crap in the gutter. He'd landed in Augusta, the state capital of Maine, broke and hungry, just as the early winter set in. He'd barely survived. Augusta had been on the move southward; all of Maine was on the move. Most of Canada was on the move, too; the Act of Union formally acknowledged the inevitable as the barriers, such as they were, came down. But what seemed inevitable in New England still looked like someone else's problem if you lived further south.

News reports told of troubles down in Georgia and Mississippi, sky-high prices and local hostility; but nobody took much notice. He'd worked in a Wendy's hamburger bar for the warmth. Times were hard. He was making for New York, for Professor Graham's disks, but he needed money first, and warm clothing. The opposition never found him. Maybe they never looked. Maybe his beard fooled them. Maybe they thought him dead, with Finnur, at Braeddalshöfn. Maybe they'd just got better things to do.

Then he took sick. The city was nearly empty, the job gone. There was a veterans' hospital still hanging on, and they took him in. He had no insurance, no Blue Cross, but they looked after him well. Familiar with the look in the eyes of veterans, maybe they recognised another veteran.

He was there, in the Togus veterans' hospital, when for a few weeks America came near to civil war. The South talked of secession. All over the North armed vigilantes took to the streets. National Guardsmen, called out to deal with them, mutinied. The Washington administration floundered. Violence spread. It had been an ugly time.

Pétur got up and crossed the broad, deserted, unlit highway. He listened to the silence, the faint rustle of ripples on the sand. By the time he'd been fit enough to leave the hospital, sanity had triumphed. In Washington a new administration, and in the South a new sense of community, and a new name – the Good Neighbor States. The example of a disunited, strife-torn Europe was salutary, even if the United States were lucky enough not to have the problem of fanatical Islamic neighbours. Expectations changed. People remembered the pioneering tradition. Now, six months later, the US had suffered the greatest social and demographic upheaval in history, had adapted, and had, for the moment, survived.

He went down the frost-cracked concrete steps to the beach. Above the tideline hundreds were sleeping out, huddled in blankets and sleeping bags. These guys were lucky to be here – even as close as North Carolina, the temperature had scarcely been above freezing all summer. Here it topped sixty on a good day.

Pétur stepped carefully among them. The tide was low now, and he made his way down across the beach's pale, unmarked surface to the distant water's edge. The sea was calm, casting up curved lines of tiny ripples under the lightless, overcast sky.

He stood, looking out, hands deep in his anorak pockets. Against his right hand rested Professor Graham's disks. He'd been carrying them round now for nearly three months, ever since he'd made it to New York. For two of those three months he'd had no means of reading them. Now, thanks to a wordprocessor at the school where he worked, he'd seen their contents. They covered the first five days, brought together the threads, filled in the background. And after that –

There were many reasons why he'd dreaded today's anniversary. His grief, certainly. And a sensible reluctance to open old wounds.

But mainly because he'd set today as his own deadline for beginning to write down Colly's story.

He turned, letting the water creep up round his battered white sneakers, and gazed back at the once-fabled shore. Even unlit, its hotels still loomed, tower upon tower, pale and massive against the sky. Daylight would reveal many to be fire-scorched, some pocked by bullets and larger missiles, the gardens around them dying for want of sun and warmth. But their sheer extravagance was still impressive. He looked to left and right – hotels, apartment blocks, condominiums, forty and fifty storeys high, as far as he could see. They glowed now, reflecting the first hazy light from the dawn behind him.

Dawn, twelve months ago. He'd not long left Helgavik. He'd said goodbye to Colly. They'd both known it was goodbye. He closed his eyes, remembering.

The water lapped round his feet. He let it. It was warm, warmer than the air. He was remembering the *Fimbulvetr*, her crew, their courage, much that he'd tried to forget. Today, he'd promised himself, he would begin to write, to tell Colly's story. To tell her dream – that when Fimbulvetr passed the Earth would rise again, green and fertile, and humankind would remember the past only as an evil dream. This his countrymen, in their ancient tale of Ragnarok, had believed. He wanted to tell the world that it was going to happen, to give them hope.

The tide was rising. Daylight grew. The brief pink tint of dawn faded as the sun rose above the grey line of scudding clouds. A few cars moved on the vast boulevards, and people, many on bicycles. The city woke early too, these days. Wet up to his ankles. Pétur roused himself, walked out of the water, turned again to look out to sea. Colly was dead. This afternoon, while his friends were at the parade, he'd sit down at a desk and begin to tell her story . . .

Thoughtfully, with one foot, he drew curving lines in the fine white Florida sand. But what good would the story do? He had his promise. But she was dead. He could write the story for Colly, but she would never read it. Was it really a story to inspire hope in the future? A story of courage, certainly; but also one of betrayal, of torture and violent death, of two governments locked in a ruthless determination to pursue manifestly evil policies. A bitter, accusatory story – for the sake of a promise to a dead woman?

He sighed. Maybe people were better off believing the 'natural event' explanation. What good could such a story do? He'd loved her; he loved her still. But some stories were best left untold.

And surely he hadn't, after all, promised to *tell* the story. Just to *know*. Just so that one person in the whole world knew the truth. He had read the disks, and now he knew. The promise had been kept.

His anxieties cleared. The decision, the real cause of his months of dread, had been waiting for him, so obvious it must already subconsciously have been made. He loved Colly, he knew the scale of her sacrifice, and that was enough. Her father, Flynn, Werner, she herself – their courage needed no bookshelf memorial. Today was their celebration, and the future was their memorial.

He took the five wordprocessor disks in their square, dark blue plastic cases from his pocket. He smiled. Lightly, he flicked them away, one by one, spinning them out to sea. No wind caught them. They bounced on the gentle swell, skipping from wave top to wave top like stones skimmed by a schoolboy, far out across the water, into the silvery haze of dawn. Like a schoolboy, Pétur turned and ran up the beach, kicking his heels. There was a parade today; he wasn't going to miss it.

As he ran, the snow softly began to fall.